Books by Kristie Cook

— SOUL SAVERS SERIES —
WWW.SOULSAVERSSERIES.COM

Promise
Purpose
Devotion
Power
Genesis: A Soul Savers Novella
Soul Savers Book 5 (June 2013)

— THE BOOK OF PHOENIX SERIES —
WWW.THEBOOKOFPHOENIX.COM

The Space Between

Find the author at www.KristieCook.com

WHEN LIFE FALLS TO
PIECES, ANSWERS LIE IN

THE
SPACE
BETWEEN

PART ONE IN THE BOOK OF PHOENIX

BESTSELLING AUTHOR
OF THE *SOUL SAVERS* SERIES
KRISTIE COOK

For Shawn Cook

Acknowledgements

First and foremost, I thank The Maker and His Son. My life, my writing career and this book are all blessings from above.

Second, I must thank my husband Shawn who woke up one morning in 2011 while we were on a motorcycle road trip and said, "I had an awesome dream!" He didn't understand everything going on, but I took the few things he remembered and his dream became The Space Between. Without that dream and his memorable exclamation the next morning, this book (and the rest in the series) would have never been.

Next I thank our fabulous sons, Zakary, Austin and Nathan, who often seem to test how far they can push me while I'm writing, but show their support in many ways. Like putting up with leftovers and carryout and Mom not being able to hang out because she's under deadline. And giving me great insight into the minds of young males that has given me great fodder for Jeric and other characters. Thank you most of all, my wonderful boys, for being you. I'm so proud of you all.

Chrissi, my business partner and publisher, who is nearly as much my "other half" as Shawn is. Thank you for your never-ending support, for your kicks in the butt, ear to whine in, shoulder to cry on, and for not being afraid to challenge me. I say it often, but not enough: I couldn't have done this without you.

Thank you to my brilliant Kristie's Crew: Claire, Julie, Marissa, Jessie, Mindy, Inga, Kate, Debbie, Stacey, Heather, Rebecca, and Christina. Claire, thank you for the fabulous UK fan site you created and thank you, Julie, for helping her admin it and for managing our UK distribution. Jessie (and Dave), thank you for sharing your beautiful phoenix. Marissa, thank you for helping with the release tour, and Claire, Julie, Kate, Debbie and Stacey for coordinating the UK signing tour. Thank you all for beta reading and for your continuous support, shout-outs and for all you do on the streets. You go above and beyond and I am so blessed to know all of you.

Thank you to author Heather McCorkle and Jessica Cook for critiquing The Space Between for me. Thank you to Jen Trammell for proofreading. And thank you to Regina at Mae I Design and Photography for my gorgeous cover. Brenda Pandos, thank you for being my Best Author Friend Forever.

Thank you to Cami and Reading Addiction Book Tours for organizing the cover reveal and release tour, and a special thank you to all of the bloggers who participated.

Last but most definitely not least, thank you, reader! I sincerely appreciate your giving up your precious time to read this story. I hope I've made it worth your while. (And if I have, thanks for the fantastic review I know you'll leave. *grin*) I appreciate my readers and fans more than you will ever know. Please don't ever hesitate to connect with me. I love to hear from you!

THE BOOK OF PHOENIX
Part One

THE
SPACE
BETWEEN

KRISTIE COOK

✴ NOW ✴
2012

CHAPTER 1

 If I could take the form of a bird and fly high above the roofs of the village and soar over the fields, it would feel like this. With me balanced on his hands, Alberto spun across the stage, my arms and legs spread like a bird's wings. After he gave me a push up into the air, I tucked my limbs in and twisted in a perfect spiral. My stomach dropped and my body followed as I slid down him and became a graceful heap at his feet just as the music came to its tragic end.

The audience exploded into applause, followed by a standing ovation. The thunderous noise reverberated into my bones, and my chest swelled as I took a bow for the very last time. When the audience showered me with white roses and Alberto and the troupe brought me a bottle of vino, I gave a heartfelt grin that hopefully hid the sadness battling within me. *A dream come true . . . but I'll never dance on stage again.* My heart knew this truth. Tomorrow I would fly home, and this would all be nothing more than a memory.

But tonight was still mine.

I hadn't been the real star of the show, not by far, but everyone made me feel like I'd been tonight. After the curtain fell, backstage became as loud as the audience as we all congratulated each other on a great show. I glided on air as everyone gave me farewell hugs and shouts of "Bravo!" and "Eccelenté!" Tomorrow, the dance company would move on to the next town, and the professional dancer who I'd been filling in for would join them. I, on the other hand, would be headed back to reality.

"Move on, move on! Take it to Alonzo's," the stage manager finally ordered in Italian. The lights over the stage went dark to emphasize his point. The theater owner was ready to shut down for the night. We all scurried to our dressing rooms.

I pulled out my cell phone right away and texted a message to Uncle Theo as I had every night after a show. I frowned at the phone when he didn't immediately reply. Since he'd lost nearly all his hearing, I'd taught him how to text and email before I left so we could communicate while I was gone. He'd been a trooper at using the "silly gadgets" up until recently. He hadn't responded to either my texts or my emails in three days now. A day or two was normal—sometimes he simply forgot. But three days? *There are many possible reasons. Maybe the battery died and he forgot to charge it. Maybe he knows you're coming home soon and is done with the "damn buttons." Maybe he's just too busy with Mira.* This last one was more like my Uncle Theo.

"Beautiful as always, *cara mia*," Alberto said to me in strong English heavy with an Italian accent as he stood in the doorway to my dressing room, distracting me from my phone. He'd already changed out of his costume into street clothes. With dark curls hanging to his shoulders, eyes like onyx sparkling with life and a perfect dancer's physique, he was a sight to behold, even in jeans and a tight white T-shirt. He knew it, too.

"*Grazie*," I said with a wide grin. "You were amazing, too, as always."

"Of course I was. You come to Alonzo's to celebrate, no?" he asked.

"Wouldn't miss it. I need a little more time than you to look beautiful, though," I said as I wiped a trickle of sweat off the back of my neck. "And I still need to change."

"Bah! You should wear that," he said, flipping a hand at my skimpy costume. "So *sexy*."

I laughed as I pushed him out the door. Alberto was nothing but a tease. After all, he truly had eyes for only one person—Bruno, the sound technician.

Alone in my tiny dressing room with the sounds beyond the door quieting as everyone headed out, I pulled off my golden leotard and the scrap of shimmery material that passed for a skirt. I left my tights on and slipped into a white lacey smock and faded red cowboy boots. My chest tightened and my eyes burned as I folded my costume with deliberation and tucked it into my duffle bag. I'd never again wear it. I'd never again be in a dressing room like this, overhead lights flashing as the theater owner gave a final warning he was about to lock up. I'd only used this particular room a couple of times, but it represented all of those in the last month as I'd made my way across Italy with this dance company. Not exactly what my dream had been, but pretty damn close. As close as I'd ever get.

This is it, I thought as I slipped on my collection of bracelets and rings. My final farewell to any hopes of a dance career.

My eyes followed my hand as it caressed the old, abused vanity before looking up into the lighted mirror. With a sigh, I pulled off the band keeping my wild curls in a tight bun. They sprang from my head in every which way, celebrating their freedom. I smoothed my hands over the light brown spirals, trying to control them, but as always, they refused to cooperate. The best I could do was what looked like a curly lion's mane. I dabbed at smudged mascara under my green eyes, rubbed some of the excess make-up off my cheeks and decided I was as good as I'd get.

The overhead lights fell dark for the last time when I opened the dressing room door. The rear exit stood open at the end of the hall, and the streetlamp spilled dim light down the corridor, the scuffed wooden floor dully reflecting its glow. I inhaled slowly, cherishing the musty smell of an old theater mixed with the rancid odor of dancers' sweat and the sweet fragrance of roses. I silently said my goodbyes as my feet carried me outside.

"Thank you, Uncle Theo," I whispered as I left the theater for the last time. Only because of him did I even have this opportunity. I couldn't wait to tell him all about it.

A large, muscular body flew at me, swept me into his arms and twirled me around as though we were still on stage. Laughter bubbled out of my chest.

"You ready to celebrate, *cara mia?*" Alberto asked as he set me down.

"Celebrate that you're finally getting rid of me?" I teased.

He clapped his hand over his heart, and his face fell into an exaggerated expression of pain. "Oh, Leni, you do not know how I will miss you and your mane."

He swatted playfully at the bottom of my curls. He had no idea how I would miss the way he said my name, drawing out both syllables, "laaaay-neee," like only an Italian could do.

"But you won't miss my heels on your toes or my arm in your face?" I said in mock disbelief.

He took my hand and danced me down the cobbled street toward the plaza at the center of town. "You are a stunning dancer, *cara mia.* Don't let anyone tell you otherwise." He spun me under his arm, my duffle bag smacking against my butt the whole time. "Of course, you have become much better since becoming my partner. But everyone does."

He winked at me before dropping me into a dip. My bag slid off my shoulder and a hand darted beneath me to catch it. Alberto swung me up and around, bringing me face-to-face with the most unbelievably stunning vision I'd seen my whole time in Italy. Which was saying a lot. His eyes—blue, I thought, though the light from the corner post wasn't enough to be sure—enraptured me. He held my bag out with a small smile that hinted at dimples.

"*Grazie,*" I said breathlessly as I wrapped my hand around the strap of my bag. He gave me a nod almost deep enough to be a bow, his shaggy blond hair falling in his face. Then, without a word, he turned and walked away. My mouth fell open. "How rude."

"Must be American," Alberto said. I punched him in the arm.

"Who goes out of their way to catch a falling object and then can't even say 'you're welcome'?" I asked absent-mindedly as I stared after the retreating body that rivaled Alberto's. No, scratch that. It totally beat out Alberto's even on his best day.

"What an ass," Alberto muttered.

"Rude, yes, but I don't know if I'd go that far."

"No, I mean what an *ass* that man has." He let out a low whistle.

I laughed and admired the view as well. "I *can* agree with that."

"He's going to Alonzo's. Lucky us."

Alberto held out his arm, I looped mine into it, and we sauntered toward the club, the heels of my boots clacking on the cobblestones. Discotheque music pounded from inside, drowning out the noise of my steps and even the fountain as we crossed the center of the plaza. Bruno waited for us outside. He flicked his cigarette to the ground and took my other arm. We made a scene as the three of us squeezed through the door, and then the party swallowed us whole.

We drank and danced and drank some more. Since I couldn't take it on the plane tomorrow, I opened the bottle of wine my fellow dancers had given me, took a swig and passed it around. It never found its way back to me. Almost all of the fifteen dancers and five crewmembers had come, including Bruno and Alberto, who was also the director.

I found this funny, in a drunken kind of way. Up until tonight, Alberto and Bruno had pretty much been the only ones to provide any kind of friendship. The rest of the dance company had grown from hating me to barely tolerating me to finally accepting me, on a temporary basis, anyway. I was American, I didn't speak Italian well enough, I was too short, too round, too pretty but not pretty enough, and definitely didn't dance at their level. In other words, I wasn't one of them. Tonight, however, they acted as though they might actually miss me.

Dancing with them at the disco was much different than our dances on stage. Maybe this difference was what had finally brought them all around to me in the last week. Throughout the tour, we'd traveled every night, crossing the countryside to get to the next town in the wee hours of morning, grabbed some sleep, performed, then boarded the train again. But for this leg, this village had been our home base, centrally located between the six towns we'd visited this week. We'd taken bus trips to the dance theaters for our performances, returning each night early enough to let loose for a little while at Alonzo's. And that meant dancing how we wanted to, and I was much better at modern freestyle than the structured ballroom numbers Alberto had us doing on stage. The other dancers finally saw how I could *move*.

"Our little Dirty Dancer," Alberto teased me as he moved around me and another girl on the dance floor. I twisted and swayed, my hips writhing to the beat, and I became lost in the music and the way it slid over me like a silken gown. Alberto pressed against my back and ground his pelvis against my butt.

"Like you should talk," I murmured without pulling away.

"Just making you look sexy and desirable, *cara mia.*"

I looked over my shoulder at him for meaning. His eyes glanced to our right, to a table by the window. The man from the plaza sat by himself, and his gaze was locked on us. His eyes shifted away as soon as he caught me catching him.

"Me or you?" I asked.

"Trust me—he's not my type. And I'm definitely not his. He's straighter than a nun's ruler and can't take his eyes off you."

On its own volition, my gaze returned to the guy who could have anyone in this bar, but sat alone. He stared out the window now. Alberto had to be mistaken. He was too pretty to be straight. And even if, by the smallest chance, he was into girls, it didn't matter. The intriguing thought of a one-night-stand on my last night here made my stomach do an excited little flip, but I shut the thought down immediately. Thinking like that would get me in trouble, as it always did.

Throughout the night, however, he proved Alberto right. Every now and then I'd feel the burn of someone watching me, and when I turned, his eyes would flit away. The one time they didn't, I began to make my way to his table to ask him to join us, but he gave a slight shake of his head and turned to gaze out the window. I hadn't caught his eye again the rest of the night. Probably for the better. The way my body reacted to him meant not only trouble, but Trouble with a capital T.

"I believe the sun rises soon," Alberto said some time later when the bar had essentially cleared out. We sat in a booth, his arms spread out on the seatback across from me, over Bruno's shoulders. Bruno's head lolled a little to the side as he obviously fought the desire to pass out. "You finally succeeded in closing the bar down, Leni."

"You worked my ass off, Alberto. I deserved one night to party."

"You forget about Rieti and Pizzoli?" he asked, referring to the couple of Saturday nights we partied in our hotel. "And last week, right here at Alonzo's?"

I giggled. "Okay, okay. But still. My last night here, and I don't want it to end."

"Ah, *cara mia*, it'll always be here," he pointed to my forehead, "and here." He pointed to my heart.

"Thank you, Alberto," I said solemnly, "for taking the chance with me."

"No, thank *you*, Leni. You did me a favor."

I rolled my eyes, knowing this wasn't exactly true. He could have found a much more qualified replacement if he hadn't been pressured into taking me. I picked up my martini glass and raised it in a sloppy toast—half my drink sloshed over my hand.

"To you, Alberto, for making my dream come true. And to Uncle Theo."

"Who?" he asked as he clinked his glass against mine, more sticky liquid spilling over my hand.

"Uncle Theo, of course. The one who made you bring me on."

Alberto's brow wrinkled, as if he'd never heard of the man.

"My great-uncle. Your father's best friend from way back. He talked you in to giving me this chance, remember? Probably even paid you to do it." I tried to remind him of how he couldn't stop talking about Theo when I'd first arrived, how much he admired him and would do anything for the man, but Alberto shook his head. I laughed as I stood on unsteady legs. "Okay. I think you've had too much to drink."

"And you have a train to catch in a few hours." He stood and pulled Bruno out of the booth. With one arm holding Bruno up, he gathered me into a hug. "Take care, Leni. It has been a true pleasure."

"You, too, Alberto. And I mean it. Thank you for everything. I'll tell Uncle Theo you were an outstanding host and a terrific boss."

He gave me a squeeze and then let me go to rub his jaw. "And don't forget sexy. Is this Uncle Theo guy single?"

I fought a shudder. I didn't want to think that way about eighty-three-year-old Uncle Theo. How could Alberto even say such a thing?

"Go," I said, shoving on his shoulder and making him stumble. For a moment, I thought he and Bruno were both going down, but they caught themselves. We all cracked up with inebriated laughter. "You need to get to bed before you forget me or even Bruno."

I watched as they left with more tears stinging my eyes.

"Ah, finally, I can close up," Alonzo said from behind the bar as I grabbed my duffle bag.

I hadn't realized everyone else had left. My eyes automatically glanced over at the table by the window. Of course, the guy was gone. But sitting on his table was my wine bottle with a single white rose in it, like the ones the audience had tossed at me earlier. I said goodbye to Alonzo and grabbed the bottle on my way out.

Back in my room at the little inn, I couldn't sleep. Every time I closed my eyes, the stunning face with the enrapturing blue eyes wavered behind my eyelids. After updating Facebook with tonight's pictures and seeing if Mira had put up a rare status update—no, she hadn't—I sat in my bed and stared at the rose in the bottle perched on the windowsill. Of the whole time I'd been in Italy, even the whole week I'd been in this village, why did he show up on my last night? Why not sooner, when we might have had a chance to meet, to get to know each other? He'd been the only person to truly catch my eye and I his.

Well, I thought maybe I'd caught his attention. It was hard to know for sure, the way he kept looking away. Maybe I reminded him of someone, maybe even his wife. I wouldn't be surprised if he were married, which would explain his strange behavior. *You're being ridiculous.* I shook my head. It didn't matter if he was married or not, or if the interest was mutual. I would never see him again and that was that.

So why couldn't I get him out of my head?

✻ ✻ ✻

My heart grew heavier than the humongous suitcase I lugged behind me as I boarded the train and took a seat by the window. I should have known better than to expect anyone to see me off, even Alberto who probably still snored away his multiple martinis. Although I hadn't made any real friends besides him, I'd still miss all the people I'd met while here. I'd also miss the beautiful countryside and the quaint little villages with their cobblestone streets and old stone buildings. I leaned my head against the window and pressed my palm to the pane. The train car jolted as the engine began its pull. *Goodbye, Italy. I'll be back.*

The train had barely begun to move when I saw Alberto rush out to the platform. His eyes scanned the train, and I swore they stopped at my window. I wiggled my fingers in a wave. His brow furrowed and he cocked his head, looking befuddled, like he had last night when I'd mentioned Uncle Theo. Was he still drunk? But he'd come out here to see me off, right? Perhaps he didn't actually see me through the window. Then Bruno and the rest of the company gathered around him, and I realized their train would be coming soon. Maybe he hadn't come to say goodbye, after all. I waved anyway. Nobody waved back.

But a blond-headed man rushed to one of the cars of my train. Was it *him*? The guy from last night? I pressed my head harder against the window, as if trying to push through it to see if he made it aboard, but I couldn't see that far down. The train picked up speed, and I sat back in my seat with a snort. I was probably imagining things.

I pulled my phone out of my skirt pocket, hoping to find a reply from Uncle Theo. Still nothing. My mouth pulled down in a frown as worry again niggled its way into my mind. This wasn't like Uncle Theo. He'd at least take the time to wish me safe travels, knowing I was on my way home. International phone calls were expensive, so I'd been avoiding calling Mira unless it was an emergency. This was close enough.

I dialed her number but her voicemail picked up. I didn't know if she ever listened to it—she was sixty-seven, quite a bit younger than Uncle Theo, but still not a big fan of technology. So I called Uncle Theo's house phone, thinking she was probably there anyway. Dread began to weigh my heart down as the phone rang and rang. What if he'd been hurt? He wasn't as steady on his feet as he used to be. *Oh, God, what if he's de—* No, I wouldn't finish that thought.

Dude, relax. Mira's probably at the store and Uncle Theo can't hear the phone. After all, if something was wrong and Mira couldn't reach me, surely she would have called my parents, and they would have called me. This thought, along with knowing I'd see him soon, calmed me. *Everything's okay. No news is good news.* I told myself I was tired after being awake for over twenty-four hours, letting my imagination get to me. But I suddenly couldn't wait to get home.

The rhythm of the wheels on the tracks eventually lulled me to sleep. The two-hour ride was long enough to leave me feeling even groggier than before. I was surprised I found my way through the maze of transfers to get from the train to the airport.

After checking my bags and receiving my boarding pass, I went straight to the airport coffee shop, grabbed a cup of cappuccino and then headed for my gate, only to find I had a three-hour delay. The waiting area was already full, so I made my way down the corridor, looking for a seat. As I passed a bar and considered taking a seat inside, a blond head turned toward me, and this time I wasn't imagining things.

Our eyes locked, and I halted in my tracks as my breaths stuttered in my lungs. He was even more gorgeous in the light of day . . . but also more dangerous. I could feel that even across the many yards of space between us. The tattoos on his arms didn't tell me this. Something in the way he held himself, the cock of his head, the gleam in those eyes that were pulling me in.

A movement next to him broke my trance. A dark-haired beauty sat in the chair beside him, although she may as well have been sitting in his lap, her body was welded so tightly against his as she looked over his shoulder at the phone on the table. She was nearly as beautiful as he was—definitely model material. She looked up at me with sharp eyes as a well-manicured, bright red fingernail traced his collar.

I withdrew my stare that by now had to be bordering on rude and ridiculous and hastened my pace along the corridor as the search for a seat resumed. The bar was definitely not an option.

A pounding of feet sounded behind me, followed by someone yelling in Italian. I stepped to the side to move out of the way and turned toward the commotion. Gorgeous guy was running toward me, and the bartender ran after him. I stepped farther out of the way until my back pressed against the wall, but he stopped in front of me. I stared at him, my mouth gaping.

The bartender yelled something about paying his tab, and my eyes widened as I looked over his shoulder. Did he really so blatantly ditch his bill? The guy turned to follow my gaze, then rolled his eyes as he dropped his phone into his t-shirt pocket. His hands moved in front of him—the ASL sign for "sorry" then "hold on." I only knew this because Uncle Theo and I had learned sign language together when he began to lose his hearing. Was gorgeous guy deaf?

He turned to me as he reached into his back pocket, probably for his wallet. I hoped for his wallet and not something crazy, like a knife or a gun. Yep. Wallet. But he hadn't been fast enough. The bartender's hand landed on his shoulder and forced him to turn. Gorgeous guy's fist went up as though to throw a punch.

"Whoa!" I squeaked, dropping my coffee cup to reach up and grab the tight muscles of his forearm.

My stomach dropped five stories.

I seriously felt as though I'd fallen off the side of a tall building, plummeting in a free fall. My heart took off in a gallop, while my lungs ceased working at all. I looked up and fell into the pools of those deep blue eyes, plunging further and further under. The word "*dyad*" echoed from deep within me, as if my soul itself had whispered it. I didn't even know what the word meant.

But I did know one thing for certain.

Before last night, I'd never seen this guy in my life—how could I ever forget *that* face?—but in some inexplicable way, I knew him. My *soul* knew him.

CHAPTER 2

Jeric
2012
What the fuck does *dyad* mean? The word bounced around my skull as if I should know, but I had no clue. Of course, I couldn't think straight about anything as those silvery-green eyes entrapped me in their snare, making my head buzz and whirl. I don't know how long we stood there staring at each other, but my stomach finally stopped its plummet, though my heart still beat harder than if I were actually banging the girl. I knew she was different, but this was way beyond anything I'd expected.

Something poked me in the chest. The girl blinked, then let go of my arm. The rest of the world stopped spinning and came into focus. The bartender jabbed his finger into me as his mouth moved angrily and a piece of paper waved about in his other hand. I fished some euros out of the wallet that was somehow in my hand—I didn't remember pulling it out of my pocket. Apparently, this gesture didn't satisfy the bartender. The vibrations of his voice beat against my cheeks —he must have been yelling loudly and quickly and in Italian, because I couldn't read his lips, but I certainly felt his anger—and it was all I could do to keep from punching his face. I was paying the dude, for shit's sake! But green-eyes had stopped me once already, and I didn't want to put her in that situation again.

The bartender's mouth finally stopped moving, his breath stopped assaulting me, and his eyes went to her face. She spoke to him, then turned to me. Her fingers fluttered in front of her, and I had to force my gaze from her face to her hands. How did she get through security with all those bracelets dangling on her wrists? It took me a moment to realize she was signing.

"Do you know ASL?" she asked with her fingers, every one of them banded with a ring, though none looked like a wedding or engagement ring, I couldn't help but notice. She tilted her head in expectation. Still in a bit of shock, I simply nodded. "He says he should call security. Did you really run out?"

My brow furrowed momentarily. Hearing girls tended to think deaf meant stupid, although it didn't stop them from hanging all over me, wanting me to do sign language on their bodies. But this girl—she *was* different. And I didn't want to make myself look any more of a jackass in front of her than I already had.

"Didn't mean to," I signed. "I was trying to catch you before you got out of sight."

Her dark honey-colored skin blushed a bright pink. Something inside me—deeper than any other girl had ever reached—stirred. I read her delicious, plump lips as she spoke to the bartender, changing my words from catching her specifically to catching someone who'd walked by. I held up enough euros to cover my bill as well as all the tables surrounding me to show I hadn't meant any harm. I did a lot of stupid things, but running out on my bill wasn't one of them. Not in recent years, anyway. The bartender glared at me for a long moment, then snatched the money out of my hand, spun on his heel and marched back to the bar.

"Thank you," I signed to the Beautiful Girl. Her eyes narrowed as they traveled over my face, then down my arms, taking in all the ink. I couldn't tell if she was impressed or appalled. For a moment, I was glad I'd had to take out my piercings for security, then I berated myself for caring so much what she might have thought. She was one girl of thousands. We were in an airport, each of us headed to other cities. I'd never see her again, so why *did* I care what she thought?

Her fingers moved as she used Signed English, not ASL. Which was good, because I never did catch on to ASL and its grammar any better than I'd been able to learn Spanish in junior high school.

"You're welcome, but I only did it because you obviously had the money to pay up," she said with a saccharine-sweet smile. "And because I was raised well, I'll forgive you for using me."

"How did I use you?" I asked, honestly perplexed. I'd already thanked her for translating.

"You were trying to catch me?" she asked with another tilt of her head.

I nodded. "And?"

Her smile wavered, and she blinked. "Why?"

I didn't answer at first. I really didn't know why. I'd seen her, remembered her from last night, and my body had pretty much reacted on its own.

"I recognized you," I signed, feeling like a lame-ass. But it was better to be lame than to tell her the truth—that I hadn't stopped thinking about her since last night. The look she gave me told me she was about to leave. I'd become very good at reading faces and body language since the accident. My hands moved quickly. "Don't go. Let me buy you a drink. Please."

She looked down at the coffee cup and the brown liquid pooled at her feet, then up at me, then over my shoulder. She rolled her eyes.

"I doubt your girlfriend would like that," she signed.

My girlfriend? I glanced over my shoulder to see what she was talking about, and there was the dark-haired model I'd been about to hit up in the club room before goldie-locks here sauntered by. Okay, so there were a few minutes I'd stopped thinking about this green-eyed babe in front of me, but now I'd already forgotten about the model who glared at us with fire in her eyes.

"I don't know her," I said. "Just met her. Definitely not my girlfriend."

Green eyes looked over my shoulder then back at me right as my phone vibrated in my pocket. I pulled it out and looked down at the text from the model behind me: "Club room in 5 mins. right?" Goldie-locks glanced at the screen, then gathered her bags and walked off.

Her body mesmerized me as she seemed to glide across the floor. Her long, hippy-like skirt and loose pink top hid what I'd seen last night at the show. She didn't have a traditional dancer's body—her arms weren't long and spindly, and her legs were thick with muscle, but shorter than most dancers'. And, although softer than it should probably be, her body curved in all the right places. I knew from my time spent with wannabe professionals that big tits got in the way when dancing and narrow hips made better lines, whatever that meant. They could have their boy bodies. I'd take the curves on this one any day.

I shook myself out of it—again—ran to grab my carry-on and, ignoring the model, sprinted after the girl who'd really captured my interest. And much more, if I dared to admit it.

After several steps of matching her pace, I finally got her to stop and talk to me. As soon as those green eyes were on me again, I faltered, once more losing my mind. I forced my brain to focus.

"Please let me replace your coffee," I insisted. "You don't have to sit with me if you don't want to, but let me do this."

She hesitated as her gaze swept all points around us as if avoiding my face, then finally it returned to me. She nodded and followed me to the café down the terminal. I bought her a cannoli to go along with her cappuccino—last chance for a true Italian one, I told her. After paying for our order, I found a small table with two spindly chairs and barely enough room for our carry-on bags. I was admittedly surprised when she sat down with me.

"So what do I call you? I've been thinking goldie-locks in my head, but those curls are really caramel colored."

She blushed again, and I could literally feel the heat from her skin. The girl would drive me insane.

"L-E-N-I," she signed.

"As in L-E-N-N-Y K-R-A-V-I-T-Z or as in—" I made the sign for *lay* and pointed at my knee.

Her mouth opened in a broad smile and by the way her body

shook slightly, I knew she was laughing. She told me it was the latter.

"I'm J-E-R-I-C," I shared before we both dug into the creamy goodness in front of us.

The cannoli might have been a mistake. I had one hour with her, only sixty minutes, but it was impossible to sign with ricotta-covered fingers. Watching her suck the sweet cheese off, though, made it worth it, although it also made me hard.

"How do you know the difference in sounds?" she asked when she was finished. She must have seen the confusion in my eyes. "Like how to say my name."

Ah. She was perceptive.

"I haven't always been deaf," I replied. "I was in an accident eight years ago. I was fourteen, so plenty old enough to remember sounds."

Her face darkened. "I'm sorry. That loss must have been difficult."

I didn't tell her what else I had lost—so much more than my hearing. We had an hour, and I wasn't about to make it a mopey hour of depression.

So I shrugged and made light of it. "I gained some superpowers, so it's all good."

She laughed again. "And what would those be?"

I tapped my temple with a finger. "I can read minds."

"Oh, I see. And you did such a good job with the bartender a few minutes ago."

I smiled, trying to think fast. "I hear thoughts, but can't speak my own."

She tilted her head again in that way she does, a gleam in her eyes. "So what am I thinking right now?"

I lifted an eyebrow. "Do you really want me to say?"

Her skin flushed even deeper. As if to distract herself—or me—she picked up her coffee cup and tilted her head back to finish the last drops. What *was* she thinking?

"You're thinking you'd like more cappuccino," I signed.

She laughed. I wished I could hear it. "Nice guess, but I'm good. I'm hoping to sleep on the plane, not bounce around it on a caffeine high."

Another reminder she was leaving. We both were. Life was a bitch. This girl fascinated me. Not only did she affect me like no other female had in my extensive foray with them, but she was literally the girl of my dreams. I'd been sketching her for years, and here she was in the flesh. I licked my lips. I couldn't help but wonder what that flesh tasted like.

Her hands moved again, returning me to reality.

"Why Italy?" she asked.

Heh. Good question. I studied her face as I debated how much to tell her about my screwed-up life. She stared back, waiting for my answer with genuine curiosity.

"I'd planned to see family," I hedged, and added, "but didn't find what I was looking for."

"In Sulmona?"

Of course this question would come up. The coincidence was too . . . coincidental.

"I ended up in Sulmona yesterday after spending a few days on the eastern coast. It was a place to stay on my way to Rome."

She nodded, but a shadow flickered across her eyes, and I could tell she wanted to know more, but she didn't ask. Which was good because I wouldn't tell her, but I didn't want to come off as a douchebag. Not when I might have finally won her over. Even if it was for only a few more minutes.

"So where to now?" she asked, changing the subject for me.

"I'm on standby for a flight to Paris. There I hope to catch a flight to Miami."

"Is that where you're from?"

"Yes," I said. The real answer wasn't so simple, but no need to get into details. I wanted to know more about her, but here we were talking about me. I needed to change that. "What about you?"

"Atlanta. Home's just outside of there." And now I imagined her words with a sweet Southern accent. "For now anyway. My dad's company moves him a lot, so I've lived all over."

So much for the accent.

"And what were you doing here?" I asked.

Her eyes drifted away for a moment, taking on a distant look.

"Chasing a dream," she said as her gaze returned to me. "I'd always wanted to be a dancer, since I was a kid. Life didn't turn out as I'd hoped, though. You know how it is."

I grimaced. I certainly knew how it was. I'd had my own dream once, but the accident had killed it. I wasn't cut out to be another Beethoven.

"My great-uncle arranged for me to spend a month over here to dance with the company of a friend's son," she continued. "I take care of him, so he said this was the least he could do for me in return." Her eyes glinted again, and she smiled mischievously. "Truth, though? I think he just wanted to spend some time with his lady friend."

"Can't blame a guy."

She wrinkled her nose and laughed. "He's eighty-three years old!"

"All the more reason. When you only have a limited time, a guy has to make the most of it."

She locked her eyes on mine, and once again, they trapped me. Her head tilted, as though asking if I spoke of myself as much as her uncle.

"How do you know how to sign?" I asked.

"My uncle. We learned together. He said he was too old to learn a whole new language like ASL, so we learned Signed English. I was pretty relieved to see you using it. You'd have to go slow for me to follow ASL."

I nodded with understanding, but I didn't get a chance to say anything else, because my phone vibrated on the table, startling the hell out of both of us.

The airline had a seat for me on the flight to Paris.

Was it bad I enjoyed the look of disappointment in Leni's eyes when she saw the text?

We both stood and gathered our things. My gate was on the way to her own, so she walked with me. I eyed the line of passengers waiting to board, and the thought of getting on that plane—of leaving the Beautiful Girl of my dreams—nearly threw me into a panic. Damn. I *needed* to get on the plane. Not only to get back to the States but if I didn't break this . . . whatever it was . . . with Leni, I thought I'd be jacked up for life. She was *that* kind of girl, but I was not that kind of guy. She put her stuff down to sign, then looked up at me with wide, green eyes and a small smile. Ah, shit. I was already jacked up for life. How would I ever be able to forget her?

"It was nice to meet you," she signed. Then she held out her hand. I didn't want a handshake. I wanted to yank her into my arms, press her body against mine, hold her, grab a fistful of those caramel curls, kiss her like she's never been kissed before, taste her mouth and her skin . . . I cleared my desert-like throat and took her hand.

That feeling of the floor dropping from my under my feet hit me again, though not as strong as before. The word "*dyad*" returned in my mind and the feeling I knew this girl, much more than was possible, exploded again from somewhere deep within me.

Leni licked those full lips of hers. "They're calling your flight for the last time," she mouthed since my hand still held hers. As though she might have forgotten, she slipped her hand from mine and signed the same thing. "Don't want to miss your flight, do you?"

Yes. I wanted to tell her.

I gave her a smile and signed instead, "I can read lips."

She returned my grin with a sexy smile of her own.

"Take care, Jeric," she mouthed before turning and gliding down the corridor. My heart faltered a few beats at the thought of how my name sounded rolling off those lips . . . that tongue . . . . If I only knew what her voice sounded like.

Once the plane was in the air, I reached for my backpack stuffed under the seat in front of me and pulled out my tablet and the used-and-abused, leather-bound notebook inside. I thought I'd look her up on Facebook, but realized I didn't catch her last name, so I went straight to the notebook. I kept notes of my search in it, but also used it for communication when texting on my phone didn't work and even had a few sketches in it. I was far from a great artist—my true talent was music. Or, at least, it had been before the accident. Now my talent lies in things much more sinister.

I flipped to the picture I'd drawn a couple of weeks ago after waking from a dream, one I'd been having for years. As I had previously, I'd felt the need to sketch the girl who had me waking with a painful boner. Now that I'd met her in real life, I couldn't deny the girl in my sketches depicted Leni—curly hair, exotic green eyes, full lips and breasts, dark-honey skin . . . As if the absolute best features of African and European heritage had been blended together to create my Beautiful Girl. The Leni I'd just met would probably never wear the leather bra, miniskirt, and knee-high boots I'd drawn her in, but damn if she wouldn't look hot in them. The vision came to me clearly. Too clearly. I had to place the book over my lap to hide the full-blown stiffy pressing against my jeans.

Damn. I needed a distraction. I needed to get her out of my head. Several airline bottles of rum dumped into my Coke weren't enough to blur the image of Leni's face in my mind. When the smoking hot flight attendant ran her finger over my arm then dropped a napkin with a message on my tray ("Meet me upstairs?"), I couldn't resist. I snuck up the spiral staircase to the empty upper level and found her in the bathroom wearing nothing but heels and thigh-high stockings, tendrils of bottle-bleached hair barely hiding her fake tits. Flight attendants like this had made me a lifetime member of the mile-high club—they wanted nothing more than something to make the long flight more interesting. My perfect kind of girl.

Unfortunately, my eyes only saw Leni's body under my hands.

The French babe who helped me through the Paris airport didn't distract me either. I had a little easier time communicating—I could read her lips as she spoke French—because I'd spent enough time in France for work for a couple of years. I thought she might actually recognize me, the way she flirted in a more subtle way than most chicks. When she told me the flight to Miami had been cancelled due to weather and the next available flight to the U.S. left in three hours for Atlanta, I forgot what she even looked like. Atlanta. What were the odds?

Not that I could really expect to see Leni again. Atlanta was a big city.

I took the flight, making new plans as we crossed the Atlantic. My search for a piece of my past had become an epic fail. Except for a few clues I'd been given along the way, I'd been going completely on instinct, following my gut even all the way to Italy. My gut was usually pretty accurate, but not this time. The one person who'd cared enough to tell me what she knew lived right outside of Atlanta. I didn't particularly want to see her because it also meant seeing her asshole husband, but maybe she knew more than she'd told me and a face-to-face was the only way to get any more info out of her. Of course, I'd changed a lot over the years—I didn't exactly look like the kid she'd seen last—but hopefully she'd see beyond the larger build and the tats.

Or would she slam the door in my face once again?

My jaw clenched and my leg bounced with agitation at the thought of what I had to do next. I *had* to—I was out of options. The guy in the next seat shifted, his eyes darting at me apprehensively with all the tension I threw off. Tatted up, muscular dude suddenly angry for no apparent reason must have freaked him out, especially on an airplane. I inhaled a deep breath, closed my eyes, and rubbed at my wrist, vaguely wondering why it had started to tingle.

Leni's face filled the backs of my eyelids, and I immediately calmed down. For one last time I allowed my imagination to run wild, promising myself I'd let her go before the plane landed. Once in Atlanta, I'd need to focus my energy elsewhere.

When I saw the caramel-colored curls bobbing in the customs line at Atlanta Hartsfield, though, how could I let go? Maybe life wasn't such an unfair bitch after all.

CHAPTER 3

As soon as Jeric left, I felt a strange sense of being lost. And lonely. In fact, I'd never felt more alone in this foreign land than I did now. My heart had been aching over this departure—I would miss the quaint villages, sidewalk cafés, and colorful buildings with their rows of windows hidden behind brightly colored awnings and flowers that made the façades look like beautiful tiered cakes. The theaters, too, some of them centuries old, where classic operas had once been performed in times when wigged men had played the roles of women.

And my soul—it had never felt so free. Although I hadn't made any lifelong friends while in Italy, I'd still been able to be *me*. The real me. Maybe because everybody's expectations of me were so low anyway or maybe because I knew I'd never see them again, but I didn't care what anyone thought here. I didn't feel the need to pretend to be someone I wasn't.

Uncle Theo had given me the best gift ever, and I certainly hadn't deserved it. But it was time to go and with Jeric's departure, I suddenly couldn't wait to leave, too, to get home to Uncle Theo, to my comfortable bed, to my familiar surroundings filled with people I knew.

Well, not so much that last part. Most of the people I'd known had left. My parents had moved to Alaska, and all of my friends had gone off to college or to New York City to pursue their dreams, and I'd become someone they'd once known in high school. It was mostly just Uncle Theo and me, and sometimes Mira. But at least the neighbors were friendly and the people at the coffee shop and stores were familiar. By the time I boarded my connecting flight in London, I was as excited to arrive home as I'd been to embark on this journey five weeks ago, especially to see my uncle. As weird as it sounded, he had pretty much become my best friend since I'd graduated high school. I missed his company terribly.

I tried to sleep on the trans-Atlantic flight, but rest eluded me. My mind wouldn't let go of Jeric's face and kept replaying our entire conversation, focusing on the way his hands moved, his muscular forearms, the beautiful images inked on his skin. My own forearm burned as though it imagined what all those tats felt like, and I instinctively slipped my finger under my bracelets to rub at it. The woman next to me made a noise of annoyance at the jangle of my bracelets. I fought the urge to give her a dirty look. She'd kept her overhead light on for the entire flight as she flipped through magazine after magazine, not helping my sleep pursuit at all.

I glanced over at her and became intrigued with the look on her face, then another cluck of her tongue. Maybe she wasn't annoyed at me. I stole a glance at what had her panties in a bunch, and my jaw dropped. I bolted upright in my seat and snatched the magazine right out of her hands.

"Excusé moi?" the woman snapped, but I ignored her.

My full attention had been captured by the magazine ad depicting a perfectly sculpted masculine body clad only in underwear—the defined pecs, the washboard abs, the thick legs, the only part covered .... But even all this didn't captivate me like the face did. Because I knew that face. I'd spent an hour at the airport looking into those same blue eyes. The tats were gone, probably airbrushed out, but I had no doubt. I burst into a fit of giggles. Jeric was a model. And not just any model. An *underwear* model. I'd had coffee with a freakin' international male model!

A few people around me made grunts of irritation as they shifted in their seats, annoyed my laughter awoke them. My conscience twanged with the old feeling of caring what other people thought, and the only reason I didn't apologize was because I didn't want to disturb them any further. The closer I came to home, the more Mama's lessons were returning.

I sat back and held the magazine toward the lady next to me, who'd been staring at me this whole time.

"No, no. You keep," she said, looking at me as though afraid I might be a little off my rocker, as Mira would say. She probably thought me to be some kind of perv the way I had stared at the nearly naked man on the page. With a huff, she pulled another magazine out of the pocket on the seat in front of me. Apparently she'd already been through the ones in her own pocket. At least now she stopped glaring at me.

I studied the picture of Jeric in his underwear and now that the initial shock had worn off, embarrassment overcame me. A male model. On the pages of a French fashion magazine. And most of our conversation had centered on his deafness, his disability. I was such an idiot.

And now glad I would never see him again.

❋ ❋ ❋

I should have known something was off with Uncle Theo's house the moment the cab drove up, but I was too focused on paying the driver and unloading my bags. The two-story, white house was nothing special, but it was home, for the most part. I paid little attention to the overgrown flowerbeds and too-tall grass, much worse than I'd expected. I'd have to deal with them soon enough. Right now, I wanted to see Uncle Theo and then my bed.

I went around to the side door that entered into the mudroom and then the kitchen, dug my keys out of my bag and selected the one for the house.

The key refused to enter the lock.

Feeling disoriented, I held the key up to eye level and stared at it for a long moment, then studied the lock. The key would never fit, and being the only brass key on my ring, I knew I'd selected the right one. What used to be the right one, anyway. *What the hell? Did Uncle Theo change the locks on me?* The thought was ridiculous. Why would he do such a thing?

I tapped my knuckles against the glass pane of the door, hoping Mira was there, because Uncle Theo would never hear me. When she didn't come, I knocked harder, now on the wooden part of the door. I pressed my face against the glass to see if Mira's gray-haired, plump body was making its way to the back door.

What I saw was all wrong.

The mudroom appeared to be completely cleared out—no brooms and mops in the corner, no cleaning bottles, soaps and detergents on the shelves by the washing machine. In fact, no washing machine or dryer at all. The maroon area rug no longer lay on the floor. I tilted my head to get a better view of the kitchen. All you could normally see would be the wooden table and chairs close to the mudroom doorway, but those were gone, too.

Weird, I thought as I pounded on the door harder.

"Uncle Theo! Mira!" I yelled, but no answer came.

I ran to the front of the house, up the steps and across the deep porch to the door, where I tried the key again. Nothing. My finger jabbed at the doorbell that would also flash the lights for Uncle Theo while my other fist banged on the wooden door.

"Uncle Theo! Mira! It's me, Leni," I called. "Open the door!"

With still no answer, I moved to the front window that looked in on the living room. Well, what had once been a living room. Now, it was only an empty space. Uncle Theo's big, brown recliner, the hunter green sofa, the large, wooden coffee table and matching end tables, the bookcases overflowing with books . . . all gone. No pictures or paintings on the walls. Hot panic rose from the pit of my stomach, threatening to take over my lungs, but I forced myself to swallow it down. To try to stay calm.

Still, my heart raced as I moved to the window on the other side of the door, the one for Uncle Theo's bedroom, but I already knew it'd be empty. My brain tried to process it all to come up with an explanation while my feet carried me around the house so I could peer into other windows. Most were too high off the ground for me to see into. I glanced up to the second floor, where my bedroom was, and my heart sank. No curtains, no pillows in the window seat, and, I was sure, nothing else, either.

I returned to the side door and sunk down to the step. Where was Uncle Theo? All his stuff? A glance around the overgrown yard made me think no one had been here for weeks. At least my old beater truck still sat at the end of the driveway. The only thing grounding me, confirming I was at the right house. Had Uncle Theo moved? But why? Maybe he'd moved in with Mira, though I found that highly unlikely. He may have liked spending time with her, but my uncle wouldn't like the constant presence. He didn't even like me around twenty-four seven. Besides, that didn't explain why they'd take my stuff yet leave my truck.

I dropped my head into my hands. This was all too much for my tired mind to take. It was nearly six in the evening in Italy, which meant I'd been awake for fifty hours with only a few moments here and there of sleep. My body probably needed food nearly as much as sleep, although I felt no appetite now. Only confusion and loss. And a little fear as horrible scenarios tried to pop their ugly selves into my thoughts. I pushed them away. Someone would have called me if something was wrong with my uncle.

He has to be at Mira's. The only answer I could come up with at the moment. That's where I needed to go. I needed to make sure he was okay, which he *had* to be. He and Mira probably had a sound explanation for everything, although I could think of none now.

I rubbed my temples with my fingers, trying to motivate my body to move. *Stand up. Pick up your bags. Put them in the truck. Drive to Mira's. Check on Uncle Theo.* That's all I had to do, and then I could sleep, but my body refused to move. I could have curled up on the concrete step and fallen asleep right there and then, if concern for my uncle didn't needle my brain and heart and soul. *He* has *to be okay.*

"Can I help ya?" a man's voice with a southern twang called from the driveway.

My heart jumped with the surprise, pumping adrenaline that shot my body into action. I sprang to my feet, shocked to find a stout man, about forty years old, with a thick mustache and a mop of brown hair on his head, standing right next to a silver, late model car. I hadn't heard the car pull up or the door as the man got out and shut it.

"Excuse me?" I asked, tilting my head with confusion at this stranger's offer of help.

"The neighbors called and said someone was bangin' on my house, tryin' to get in," he said.

"*Your* house?"

"For now anyway. Bought it several weeks ago on the courthouse steps. It's up for sale, though. Thought you might be interested. That's why you're here, ain't it?"

What was he talking about? Exhaustion had obliterated any understanding of his words. I suppressed a burst of giggles at how silly they had sounded to me. The guy's brows pressed together with concern. For what, I didn't know.

"I'm sorry," I managed to say. "I'm sleep deprived, so it sounded like you said this is your house. That you thought I'd want to buy it."

"I did say that. Guess I'm wrong, though."

"Uh, *yeah*, you are. Good joke, though. Did Uncle Theo put you up to this?" *That's it!* Uncle Theo up to his practical jokes, like the time when he ate all the cream out of the cookies and put the halves back together and into the box, or the time when I was still in high school and he set all the clocks two hours behind, making me think I had left school and come home early. He'd even acted mad at me for skipping class. A little extreme, this one, but he definitely had me.

"Who?" the guy asked.

I snorted. "You can give it up now. Great joke, but I really just want to see Uncle Theo, then go to bed."

"I'm sorry, ma'am, but I really don't know who you're talkin' about." He narrowed his eyes as he studied me more closely. His expression turned grave. "I think you need to leave now. I don't want to have to call the cops."

My eyebrows lifted at his empty threat. I straightened my back and held up my chin. "Look, sir, I don't have the energy for this. Please tell me where I can find Theo, and you can be on your way."

He shook his head, then pulled a cell phone out of his pocket. I watched as he pretended to call the police and tell them a trespasser was on his property. He snapped his flip-phone shut when he was done and glared at me with hard brown eyes.

"The poh-leece are on their way. If you don't leave, I'll tell them you were tryin' to break and enter, too."

"Whatever," I muttered to myself, knowing he'd really called Uncle Theo. My excitement to see him had disappeared with my patience, and my body trembled with exhaustion. I sank back to the concrete step and dropped my head into my hands while we both waited for Mira's car to arrive with Uncle Theo in it.

Instead, two county sheriff cars arrived, lights flashing and sirens blaring.

What the hell?

"You really called the cops?" I asked in disbelief. My body shook harder, anger combining with the fatigue. He wouldn't really have me arrested, would he? The curtains over the kitchen window next door parted a hair, and Mrs. Gingham's face peeked out at all the noise. When our eyes met, hers flitted away.

"Who did ya think I called?" the guy asked. "Yeah, I called the cops. I want ya off my property now!"

"But . . . but—" Surely Uncle Theo wouldn't go this far. "You really don't know Theodore Drago?"

Something flickered on the man's face. Aha! I knew it! He did know Uncle Theo.

"We got a problem here?" one of the officers asked, sauntering up to us the way cops do, his thumbs in his pockets. Big, dark glasses hid his eyes, but I felt them on me and not in a protector-of-the-peace-appropriate way. The other policeman stayed by his car on the street, watching us closely.

"Hold on," the guy said, lifting his hand out to the cop. "You said Drago? Are you Jacquelena Drago?"

I wanted to roll my eyes at my full given name, but relief the guy finally admitted his recognition flooded over me. "Leni, please, but yes. I'm Theo's niece. You going to tell these nice officers they can go now?"

The guy shook his head. "I still don't know no Theo or Theodore, but that ugly damn truck there is registered in your name. I was goin' to have it towed tomorrow. You can take it and get both you and the truck off my property."

That was it. I didn't think even my stoic, always proper mama could restrain herself a minute longer.

I threw my hands up in exasperation, then turned to the policeman and tried not to spit my words out. "Sir, please tell this man he is mistaken. This house belongs to my uncle, Theodore Drago, and I live here with him. I've been out of the country for over a month, been traveling for two days, and I'm too tired to deal with this nonsense. If this guy doesn't drop the charade, I'd like you to arrest *him* for trespassing."

"You're the one talkin' nonsense," the guy barked.

The deputy stepped forward, spreading his arms out to hold his hands up to both of us. "Whoa, now. This is easy enough to clear up. First, I need to see some I.D. for both of you."

With a measured breath, still barely able to keep my cool, I dug my driver's license out of my wallet and handed it to the policeman.

"Wait here a moment," he said as he took the dude's I.D. and walked toward the other policeman while talking into the mic clipped to his shoulder.

Within a few minutes, in which neither the man nor I had broken our glare on each other, the cop turned back to us.

"Sorry, ma'am, but we don't have a Theodore Drago on file for ownin' anythin' here. This here house and lot belongs to a Maury Mastich." He turned toward the guy and held out his I.D. "And I see that's you."

"Yes, sir," the guy said.

My jaw dropped. *This can't be happening!*

"Ma'am, you need to vacate the premises," the deputy said to me. "The owner don't want you here. If you resist, I'll have to arrest you for trespassin'."

"There has to be a mistake," I protested, panic starting to seep into my voice. "I've lived here for over two years."

"Not according to your driver's license, you don't. Says here you live on Peach Blossom Street." He held my I.D. out to me.

Crap. I'd never changed my address when Mom and Dad moved away.

"Still," I said, flustered. "My uncle has owned this house for . . . forever! You must have the address wrong."

"The address and deed filed with the county have been verified, ma'am," the cop said. "You can go to the courthouse tomorrow to see for yourself."

"I'd like to go right now," I said indignantly.

"It's Sunday, ma'am. The courthouse ain't open."

I huffed out a breath, fighting the urge to stomp my foot like a child. "Ask the neighbors, then. Mrs. Gingham right next door will tell you."

"Mrs. Gingham is who called me to say a strange girl she'd never seen before was snoopin' around my place," Maury Mustache said.

I glanced toward her window again. She didn't have the decency to drop the curtain this time, but stared at me as if I'd tried to break into her house and murder her. Mrs. Gingham whose dog I'd walked every time she was sick or out of town looked at me as though I was a complete stranger, and a dangerous one at that. What the hell was going on?

"Can you at least tell me where my uncle is, then, if he doesn't live here?" I asked, trying to preserve some dignity although I really wanted to scream and throw an all-out temper tantrum at the absurdity of this afternoon.

"Ma'am, we have no record of a Theodore Drago. He's not in any Georgia database."

"He hasn't had a driver's license for a few years. Look back some."

The policeman took a step forward and bowed his chest out further. "Ma'am, our databases go back several decades. There is no record of Theodore Drago and when I say *no record,* I mean no record. No driver's license. No vehicle titles. No house deeds. No utilities. As far as the State of Georgia is concerned, Theodore Drago don't exist. Now, please, ma'am, this gentleman would surely like to get back to his Sunday dinner. You must leave the property, or I *will* arrest you."

He fingered his handcuffs. I swallowed the lump that had grown in my throat as he explained, then nodded. I'd never been to jail—never been in real trouble in my life—and wasn't about to break that streak now. Besides, I needed to focus on finding Uncle Theo and then resolve this tomorrow at the courthouse, which I couldn't do if I were sitting behind bars.

I picked up my bags and lugged them over to my truck, neither of the men offering to help as I threw them into the cab. Where had all their southerly manners gone? Before I climbed into the driver's seat, I turned to Mr. Mustache.

"Was there anything at *all* in the house when you took possession?" I asked, my polite way of demanding where our belongings were. I, at least, could retain some manners.

He shook his head once, but then stopped himself. "Well, hold on. There was this book."

He opened his car door and dug around inside a bit, then popped out, holding a heavy-looking, brown-covered book in his hand. He held it out toward me.

"I tried to open it, but couldn't get through the clasp," the Mustache said. "Couldn't even cut through the leather strap. It's useless to me, so you can have it if you want it."

I'd never seen the book—which I could see now looked like a leather-bound journal—in my life, but if he'd found it in Uncle Theo's house, I certainly wasn't leaving it in his hands. Fuming with embarrassment and anger, I stalked over to him, snatched the book and stomped back to my truck, where I tossed it to the passenger side floor. I got in, turned the engine over and revved it. The truck was old, but in decent condition.

"You'll have to move if you want me out of here," I yelled over the noise.

Massive Mustache and the cop jumped into their respective cars and pulled them out of my way. Controlling my urge to floor the gas pedal and peel out, I drove off without a backward glance in my rearview mirror.

I headed straight to Mira's, but no one was there, either. Her curtains were drawn closed, so I couldn't see inside her little bungalow. I couldn't imagine where else Uncle Theo and Mira would have gone. Perhaps the lake, although the likelihood of that was near zero considering Mira refused to drive on highways. None of this made sense, and my brain became slower and slower at trying to figure it out. I considered going to the lake anyway, but there was no way I'd make the hour drive without falling asleep at the wheel. Besides, somewhere deep inside, I knew I needed to stay here. So I went to the only hotel in town. As I crashed, my sleep-fuzzed eyes stared at the tattoo on my wrist.

I didn't have a tattoo.

CHAPTER 4

Jeric 2012   Renting a car as a deaf driver wasn't the easiest thing in the world to do, but not entirely impossible either. I knew Atlanta well enough to know where to go, and several hours after landing, I had a cheap little compact I could barely fold myself into. At least I had a vehicle, and although sleep tried to shut me down, I managed to make the drive to the small town outside of Atlanta. The caramel-curled girl at the airport hadn't looked back once, and by the time I'd passed through customs, she was gone. Just as well. The girl was driving me insane, the last thing I needed right now.

The sun was still in the mid-spring sky when I crashed in the hotel room, and it was dark when I woke. 3:49 a.m. A little too early to be knocking on someone's door, especially when I was already the last person they'd want to see. Some people said I was crazy, but I wasn't stupid. I went for a run then pushed through my sit-up and push-up routine, though I hardly worked up a sweat. Maybe when life returned to normal, I could step up my routine. As if I'd ever have a normal life.

After a shower and breakfast at the hotel's free buffet of simple carbs that tasted like ass, I searched through my journal for the last known address and plugged it into the rental's navigation system. It wasn't even nine a.m. when I pulled up in front of the small, one-story house. After a long pep talk, I forced myself out of the car and up the walk to the door. Jabbed the doorbell button. Again. And again. Pounded on the door with my fist because I couldn't hear if the doorbell worked. Nothing. The curtains were pulled tight against the windows, so there was no telling if anyone moved around inside.

The neighbor's curtain, however, parted, and an older woman, probably in her seventies, peeked out, then came out her front door. Her mouth moved, but I shook my head and yanked on my ear. I brought up my typical "I can't hear" screen on my phone to show her, but she was already inside and out again with a paper and pen.

"Nobody lives there," she wrote with a shaky hand. "Been empty for some time now."

"How long, exactly?" I wrote. Her mouth moved, and she probably didn't know I could read her lips as she debated with herself—was it a few months ago or before her hip surgery? Before, but the first one or the second one? The first one was over a year ago. She didn't think it'd been that long.

She finally shook her head then wrote: "About a year ago?"

As if I could trust her assessment. I scrolled through the photos in my phone to a picture I'd taken of another picture, the only one I had left of that life. I showed it to the older woman and asked if she knew the people in it.

"Oh, yes," she started to speak. I nodded and let her know I could read her lips. It would be much faster than waiting for her to write it all out. "I think I do. I haven't seen them in years, though. Did he die? I think he did. Oh, no, maybe that was her son."

I cringed, but she rambled on without notice, and it became clear she didn't remember much unless it happened at least fifty years ago. But she was quite vocal about me.

"I don't understand ya'll and your doodles on your skin. Doesn't make sense why you'd want to ruin what God gave ya, bless your heart." She cocked her head as she looked up at my face. "Did you fix my TV, sonny? That jumpy screen will drive an old woman mad. You're the cable man, right?"

She grabbed my arm with surprising strength and dragged me inside. Without understanding why I was even doing it, I looked at her cable box, tightened the connection, and was on my way. She tried to give me five dollars, but I left it on her end table and pounded pavement to get out of there. She was a sweet old lady who probably shouldn't be living alone, but we'd wasted enough of each other's time.

I drove aimlessly around the small town, circled the town square, then pulled into an empty parking spot and stared ahead without seeing. Where had the woman I'd once called Grams gone? Had she been the woman the neighbor said had recently moved out? And what was "recently"? She'd never clarified if it had been a few months or a few years, although surely the place wouldn't have stayed empty for long. Maybe Grams had gone back north, to where I'd grown up. But what about the old man, my gramps? Well, he'd been my gramps at one time. Until he decided I was no longer anything but a bad memory to him, and I decided the feeling was mutual. Was he really dead? Was Grams dead, too?

A lump formed in my throat, and the urge to punch something nearly overcame me. I needed air. I jumped out of the car and started walking. I had no destination in mind, but a head of curls drew my attention to the diner on the other side of the square. I made my way over and although the curls were gone, I ducked inside and slid into a booth, the only customer there. It was a little early for lunch, but my bio-clock was so whacked, I didn't care.

A Georgia-peach of a waitress took my texted order in stride and brought me chicken-fried steak with gravy and mashed potatoes and bottomless cups of sweet tea. She even went so far as to give me her number. Surprise, surprise. I left it on the table, which didn't escape her notice—her lower lip stuck out in a pout as her eyes followed me out the door. No reason to lead her on. Tempting, but I was still on a mission.

To where, I wasn't sure. My gut told me to hang tight here, even when this little town seemed to be a dead end. Of course, my gut had been wrong about Italy, so maybe it had lost its touch. Maybe I shouldn't trust it so much. But without facts or even clues, what else did I have to go on besides instinct? Besides, to be honest, it was more than normal instinct or a vague sense of what I should do. This was a gravitational pull as if I had a huge magnet in my ass moving me beyond my control. Or more like a barbed trident hooked into my insides, yanking me around, to and fro, and if I fought it, I'd have one helluva hole in my gut. So I didn't fight it.

After stopping at a barbershop for a much-needed haircut, I returned to the hotel and paid for another night. Once in my room, I pulled out my tablet—the only computer I still had—and tapped into the hotel's Wi-Fi. Maybe I was supposed to stay here because this place really wasn't the end. There must still be something—a clue, a lead, a person—I might find here.

Hoping to find a new address, I searched my grandparents' names, but found nothing. Not just no known address, but nothing at all. I'd found this address for Grams on the Internet two years ago and had confirmed it right before leaving for Italy. There had also been the obituaries with their names listed as survivors and articles about the accident, but now there was nothing. Zilch. Nada. Even the obits were gone.

I scrubbed my hands over my freshly buzzed head. What was I supposed to do now? Sit here and wait for another clue? Another pull on my gut? What kind of plan was that? It wasn't one. I threw myself back on the bed and stared at the ceiling, trying to develop a new plan, but my mind drew a blank. I had nothing to go on. I was done. My mission for the last two-plus years had ended.

Anger began simmering within me, but jetlag won out.

The room was dark again when I woke, and my mood foul. I needed a drink. Turns out, the hotel bar was the hopping spot of the town. By the time I made it there, it was already half-full and a country band was setting up on stage. Yee-fuckin'-haw. I slammed back a shot of tequila. And then another. And more until all thoughts of my screwed up family, of the failed goal to find my *real* family, even of Leni were obliterated. And lucky for me, the little peach from the diner showed up, and she wasn't nearly as mad as she'd pretended to be.

Unfortunately, her boyfriend was. Unfortunately for him, that is.

A few more drinks and he and his friends might have had me, but they didn't know whom they were messing with. I used to get paid to fight much uglier and much meaner dudes than this. So when I saw the fist flying at me out of the corner of my eye, I ducked, then threw a punch of my own. Someone must have said to take it outside, because two large hands shoved me until we were through the door. Adrenaline pumped through my system, giving me a high I hadn't felt in years, and I jumped around on the balls of my feet. I wished I could speak—speak normally, anyway—but my taunting came in other ways.

The three douchebags fell for it and came at me all at once. Not a single fist touched me, but I landed several punches on them. I danced around as they swung, ducking and dodging when necessary, then answering with my own fists. A small crowd poured out of the bar, gathering around us. As much fun as I was having, I'd have to end this soon or someone would call the police. Cops were a buzz-kill. With three more punches and a knee to a face, all three of the fuckers were down. The crowd quickly dissipated, leaving the dudes on the ground, me and my peach.

"Your boyfriends?" I mouthed to her. She wrinkled her nose at the guy directly at my feet, then held her index fingers in a cross: ex. Then she wrapped her arm around my waist and insisted on accompanying me to my room to make sure I was okay.

She inspected every inch of my body and not only with her baby blue eyes. I let her think she had control—a game her type liked to play—but only for so long. There was only one reason she was in this room with me, so when my turn came, I gave it to her like she'd never had it before. I didn't have to hear to know she screamed, but each time the wall vibrated as the bed slammed into it, Leni's name reverberated in my mind. I grabbed a fistful of straight, black hair, but felt curls. When I squeezed my eyes shut, green eyes and honey skin swam behind my eyelids. I couldn't shake her, even as the peach and I went on and on, making a mess of the extra bed. There was a reason hotels came with two beds—one for sleep and one for play. I never did both in the same place. Jeric Winters did not sleep in wet spots.

When I was about to blow during our second round of the night, my gut clenched as though I'd been punched.

The instinctual pull that had led me halfway across the world and back to here hooked into my insides and reeled me in like a carp. Only stronger than usual. More urgent than ever. *Outside.* I needed to get outside. The reason I was in this God-forsaken town sobered me instantly. Was *she* out there? The one I'd been searching for all this time?

Something was seriously wrong, and I . . . *needed* . . . to be out there. The feeling overwhelmed me, took command of my muscles. Without giving the order a second thought, I jumped off the peach, barely registering her confused daze, and grabbed a towel as I headed for the door.

When I threw it open, a few cuss words slipped out of my mouth right before I hurdled the railing and sprinted for the parking lot.

CHAPTER 5

 I lay in bed with my arm securing a pillow over my head, although it did no good. I should have gone to the lake. Why *didn't* I go to the lake? The drive would have been worth it to sleep in my peaceful camper, surrounded only by nature. But no. For some idiotic reason, I thought it'd be better to stay close to town. I had things to do tomorrow. Places to go. Phone calls to make.

Today's visit to the courthouse did nothing but confirm what Officer Unfriendly had told me yesterday—Theodore Drago didn't exist according to the State of Georgia. But the court clerk, doing her best to show her southern hospitality, said if I brought in some paperwork of his, maybe we could get to the bottom of this mystery. Unfortunately, that meant making a phone call I really didn't want to make. Tomorrow morning I would have to, though. It was time, anyway. I'd hoped to find Uncle Theo along with a perfectly sound explanation and not have to worry Daddy, but apparently that wasn't going to happen.

But all of this wasn't what had me still awake at one a.m. Neither did the fact that a strange tattoo of a flame had mysteriously shown up on my inner wrist. I didn't have to think about it all day when my stack of bracelets covered it, but when I took them off tonight, the mark and where it had come from confounded me. But not enough to keep me awake when jetlag should have claimed me hours ago.

I missed Italy. More specifically, at this very moment, I missed the ancient inns where I stayed with their thick, heavy walls separating the rooms. The walls here could be sliced through with a box cutter. Earlier, it had been a baby in the room to the left of mine, crying its poor little heart out. For hours. When she finally settled down, the television in the room above mine blared some kind of musical show, and I think the occupant was dancing along with the people on TV. And they must have been clogging. That went off at eleven, and my room had fallen blissfully silent. I relished the peace, thinking I could finally go to sleep. As I drifted off, though, the giggles and the squealing began next door, right next to my head, followed by groans and moans and a rhythmic pounding against the wall. It went on for seemingly ever. What guy could even go that long? Judging by the girl's screams, which were now reaching a crescendo, he must have been an animal. Or maybe unable to ejaculate? *Ugh. Just finish already.*

But they didn't. I couldn't take one more bang against the wall, one more shout of "yes!" I sprang out of the bed, grabbed my key-card while stuffing my feet into my cowboy boots and charged out of the room. My initial intention had been to go for a walk, hoping by the time I returned, the couple would be worn out, but being the middle of a dark night and near the highway, leaving the hotel's well-lit property probably wasn't such a good idea. I thought about going for a drive, but if I was going to do so, I may as well drive to the lake.

Why not? Good question. Why shouldn't I go to the lake and make the drive back when I had the paperwork I needed? Besides the facts that it was 1:30 a.m., I was exhausted, and if they were done, I could be asleep in minutes here, nothing stopped me. I made a deal with myself: one lap around the hotel and if the wallbangers were still going at it, I was packing up.

The first-floor rooms opened to a sidewalk encircling the building, with a railing on the outside to keep anyone from traipsing through the landscaping to the parking lot. After passing several rooms, I reached the outlet that spilled onto the blacktop, where I felt a little more comfortable than being so close to people's doors. My imagination pictured someone grabbing me as I walked by and yanking me inside their room to do all kinds of disgusting acts.

When I nearly completed my lap of the parking lot, though, I wished I'd stayed closer to the building. An eerie feeling raised the hairs on the nape of my neck, then out of nowhere, two big, black shadows flew at me.

Literally *flew*.

They soared through the air, shapeless like obsidian mist, and joined together over my head. They swirled into a cloud, and the black vapor spiraled down and around me, like some kind of tornado, though no wind blew. Not a single hair on my head stirred, but a screech of, "We always find you" filled my ears. I threw my hands up as shields, and I tried to scream, but my heart had lodged in my throat, blocking any sound. My mouth clamped shut before I sucked any of this craziness into my body, and I shot my arms out in a sort of karate-chop. For the briefest of moments, not even a nanosecond, my hands hit something solid, but then the mist disappeared completely. Gone. As if it had never been there.

I glanced down at myself, wiped my hands over my t-shirt and pajama bottoms, expecting to find them damp or covered in black dust, but there was nothing. When I looked up, a man ran at me, wearing nothing but a towel and spewing a series of slurred profanity.

And my breath sucked back in all over again.

He stopped dead in his tracks five yards away in front of me, and his fist grabbed at the towel's corners before it came loose, while his deep blue eyes popped wide open. A bazillion thoughts jumbled in my mind. What was he doing here? Did he follow me all the way from Italy? Was that *him* causing the bed to bang against the wall? What happened to his hair? This was too wild to be a coincidence. Maybe he had something to do with everything going on. It should be illegal to look so hot. Were those *piercings* in his *nipples*?

Jeric and I stood there staring at each other as if caught up in some kind of surreal warp where time stood still. His mouth hung open, and he was clearly as surprised to see me as I was to see him. His hands twitched to say something, and the towel began to slip. He caught it in time, although the terrycloth now hung much lower on his hips. I couldn't stop staring at those hips, where his muscles began to form a V that ended behind the fabric. My thighs trembled, and my throat went dry.

"What's going on?" a female voice called from behind him.

Of course, he didn't hear her, didn't react, but I broke my stare and looked up. A woman with raven hair, only her hands and arms covering her girl-junk, stood in the doorway next to mine, eyeing Jeric and then me. I thought I might puke. When a barely audible but still sickening splat hit the pavement in front of Jeric, and my gaze followed the sound to the used condom lying at his feet, I did throw up a little in my mouth.

I looked up at his red face, back at the girl who whined for him to return, then turned away, hoping to skirt by this unbelievable situation, go to my room and pretend none of this ever happened. A hand grabbed my wrist. My stomach tilted and whirled and fell off a cliff, leaving me even queasier than I already was. The word "*dyad*" wafted through my mind again, and once more I felt like I knew him. Really *knew* him like I knew myself. But I didn't. Not really. I shook my arm free and strode off, toward the other end of the breezeway so I wouldn't have to pass their room to get to mine.

My heart raced and my hands shook like an addict's as I tried to swipe the card and open my door. After three tries, I was finally in, slamming the door behind me, then leaning against it to catch my breath. I closed my eyes and inhaled through my nose, then blew the air out just as slowly. My heart eventually resumed its normal pace.

Why was I so upset? Was it seeing him again? Here, of all places? That had to be it because I had absolutely no right to have a single feeling about his state of nakedness or the pounding and screams keeping me up all night. He was a guy in an airport, a passing stranger, nothing that justified me to care what he'd been doing and with whom.

Except he was here, in my hometown. What were the odds? Although, that could explain why I thought I knew him. Just because he'd been headed to Miami didn't mean he was from there. Maybe I'd seen him around? But again, what were the odds? And why wouldn't he mention anything about it when I said I lived near Atlanta?

"Who cares about him," I muttered, trying to convince myself I didn't. I needed to care more about the attack, or whatever the black mist had been, although it felt so unreal now that I wondered if I'd imagined the whole thing.

A pounding on the door right behind me, as though directly on my back, made me jump and do a half-spin at the same time. I stared at the door with wide eyes. Was it Jeric or that . . . thing? Either way, did I dare answer it? The door rattled in its jamb as the force of the banging increased. I peeked through the peephole. Jeric's face molded into an expression of anger and worry as his fists continued to beat the door. If he didn't stop, he'd wake up the baby next door as well as the rest of the hotel. Reluctantly, I opened the door, right in time to hear his woman screaming profanities at him from the parking lot. Over his shoulder, I saw her flipping him off right before ducking into the driver's side of an older model T-bird. This satisfied me in a way it shouldn't have.

My eyes returned to Jeric, who at least had thrown on jeans, but nothing else. Unlike his arms, his perfectly sculpted torso was bare of any tattoos except one scripted sentence running up his side along his ribs. And yes, his nipples were decorated with little hoops pierced through them, I couldn't help noticing. In fact, they sort of fascinated me, and I had to force myself to tear my eyes away and up to his, where I found another, tiny loop at the end of his left eyebrow. Interesting. His reaction to me was even more intriguing. His stormy-blue gaze raked over my face, then took in the rest of me in my PJs and boots. His hands fluttered in front of me, not to talk but as though he wanted to touch me, but was hesitant to do so.

"You're okay?" he finally signed, and I nodded hesitantly, still unsure of him. "You looked like you were being attacked, the way your fists were flying, but I didn't see anyone. Otherwise, I would have pounded them."

I blinked at him. He hadn't seen the black mist? Had it only been my imagination?

"Um," I started to say. I blinked again, then signed, "Something startled me. It was nothing."

"Are you sure?" He peered at me as though he didn't believe me. He hadn't seen what I had, but was still concerned. Had he heard me scream? Of course not. I hadn't been able to scream, but even if I had, he wouldn't have heard it, and I doubted his bimbo could have heard me over her shrieking.

"How did you know?" I asked. "What brought you out?"

His face twisted in a chagrined grimace. He only shrugged, though, taking a moment before answering. "I was coming out for air and saw you out there, looking terrified as hell."

Ha. A breath of air. Geez, I wondered why he'd needed one.

"Your girlfriend left," I signed, nodding toward the parking lot that was now missing a T-bird. "She looked pretty pissed."

"I don't do girlfriends, unless they're someone else's," he signed with a cocky grin. "And she was mad I made her leave."

"Why'd you throw her out?" None of my business, but he was sort of making it so.

"I didn't. I told her to go home. I don't do sleepovers either."

"Of course not." He couldn't see sarcasm in my signs, but he must have sensed it.

"They usually don't get mad."

They. Ugh.

"Don't you have any respect for women?" I asked, distracted.

His cocky grin faded. "Sure. I respect those who want a boyfriend by staying away from them. And I respect those women who sometimes want a good lay and nothing more by giving it to them. No harm to either side. Just a good time."

I studied his face, then sighed. Girls I'd worked and danced with before had done the same thing, so I knew such women existed. I guess if it worked for all involved, it wasn't my place to judge. His sex life wasn't exactly any of my business anyway.

"I'm fine," I signed. "Like I said, something startled me. Probably a raccoon in the bushes or something."

He gave me a once over, hesitated, and then pushed past me, strode down the hall and to the far bed that was still made. He sat in the middle of it, stretched his legs in front of him and leaned against the headboard.

"What are you doing?" I asked.

"Making sure you're really okay. I don't feel it."

I stared at him with an open mouth. As hot as he was and as much as I wanted to wallow in his concern and cocoon myself in those muscular arms, this was too much. I flew into a tirade, glad he could read lips, although my hands moved, too, flying about to emphasize my every word. Mama would have been so disappointed in me for losing my temper. She would have told me to paste on a smile and kindly show the gentleman to the door. Except Jeric was no gentleman, and at the moment, I didn't want to be a lady.

"What do you mean you don't *feel* it? And who the hell do you think you are? You can't just traipse into my hotel room and claim a spot! Why are you even here in the first place? Are you stalking me? Did you follow me from Sulmona to Rome and now here? I'm not one of those girls who will spread my legs for you at your command, you know. I don't care if you *are* an underwear model. So get your ass out of here before I call the front desk and have you thrown out."

Jeric moved like a boa making a strike, and he suddenly stood right in front of me, his hands on each side of my face, holding me still. Effectively silencing me. Our eyes locked for a few pounding beats of the heart, then his gaze fell to my lips and his tongue slid slowly over his own. He was going to kiss me. I inhaled sharply. I was going to let him. At least, I was until the mix of perfume and booze assaulted my nose. He must have seen the disgust in my eyes because his smoldering eyes darkened, and he took a step back.

I stepped back, too, out of the alley between the two beds, and threw my arm out and pointed at the door.

"Out!" I ordered. He needed to leave. Whether he was stalking me or not, he was too dangerous to be around. I couldn't trust him. I couldn't trust myself.

He sat on the bed and crossed his arms. I narrowed my eyes.

"I said to get out. I'm *this* close to turning you in as a stalker."

He cocked his head, then unfolded his arms to sign. "Not until you hear my side. Trust me. I'm not stalking you. I had no idea you'd be here."

I stared at him when he didn't continue. He was waiting for me to allow it. I knew he hadn't expected to see me when he came running out into the parking lot, the only reason I hadn't called the cops yet. He'd been genuinely surprised. And what kind of stalker screws other women? Isn't that counterintuitive? It's not like she looked like me or anything, and she certainly wasn't being forced against her will. He could have been trying to make me jealous. Did stalkers do that to their victims? I had no idea—the ins and outs of stalking weren't exactly my forte—but that brought me back to how surprised he'd been to see me.

I nodded for him to go on.

"I didn't follow you here. Since I had to come to Atlanta, I thought I'd come see my grandmother. But she wasn't home."

Something prickled the back of my neck, making me roll my shoulders.

"Why did you say you were going to Miami, then?" I demanded.

"Because that was the plan until the weather changed it."

I didn't know if I should believe him, but I hadn't exactly been watching the Weather Channel to deny his claim. I rubbed at my wrist while pacing a couple of times. The rest of his story sounded plausible, and although I couldn't get a tone from his voice, his eyes and body language made me want to believe him. My gaze traveled over him once more, catching on the glints of the loops in his eyebrow and nipples. They weren't normally my thing, but on Jeric . . . *Damn, is that not hot.* I shook myself out of it.

"Okay," I finally said. "I won't call the cops. But you need to go to your own room."

He shook his head. "I don't feel right doing that. I . . ." His eyes moved about as he inhaled and exhaled, as though he was trying to find the right words. "I'm worried about you."

That was it? That was his line? Well, it *was* a little endearing. But not enough.

"I'm fine. Besides, I thought you didn't do sleepovers."

His mouth stretched into the best grin he'd given me yet, full dimples and all. My heart palpitated. "I'd make an exception for you."

I gulped. *Be firm. You can't do this.* No, I couldn't. My uncle was missing and here I was about to let some man-whore try to sweet talk me into bed. The last thing I needed now was regret for a one-night-stand piled on top of everything else. How could he even go again anyway? Wasn't he all sexed out? Ew. No way I was falling for this guy. He'd just had another woman in his bed! I drew in a deep breath, straightened my back and hardened my eyes.

"As charming as you are, you need to go. Now. Or I might have to change my mind about calling the front desk."

His hands went up to protest again, but he must have seen in my face I was serious. He pressed his lips together, nodded and, then signed, "I'm right next door if you need me."

Then he finally left. I locked all the locks on the door and double-checked the window before crawling under the covers. After realizing I'd spend the rest of the night with my knees drawn to my chest and my eyes wide open, I counted the hours on my fingers, then reached over to the nightstand for my phone. May as well make the dreaded call to Alaska now and get it over with.

As I dialed my parents' number, I wondered: How do you tell your daddy you lost his uncle?

CHAPTER 6

I'd hoped a run would work out my tight muscles and the crick in my neck after spending the night in front of Leni's door on the cold, hard concrete. If anything, the cool air of dawn rushing through my lungs should help to clear my mind, and then maybe I could explain to myself *why* I'd spent the night in front of some girl's door on the cold, hard concrete. But I already knew one part of that answer—Leni wasn't "some" girl. She was so much more.

That's why I couldn't follow through with the kiss last night. I'd wanted to get it done and over with since we both obviously wanted it. But she deserved more than sloppy seconds, even if it was just a kiss. I'd still had the Georgia peach's scent all over me and alcohol on my breath, too. Shit. Leni deserved so much more than anything I could ever offer her.

My mind knew I should leave town, that I should have been gone already. Usually my heart would be in agreement, cold and hard to any feelings for a girl who could only shatter it, but not this time. Something deeper than that gut feeling—my soul?— told me to stay. To watch her. To protect her. And I couldn't bring myself to argue with . . . myself.

Shit. I was losing it. *She* was making me lose it. The very reason I avoided girlfriends—they weren't worth the trouble. Except Leni. She was different. Which was why I really did need to let go, move on, forget about her, and let her go on with her life without me messing it up.

My mind was made up to do exactly that by the time I finished my run, but after showering and packing, I couldn't follow through. I talked myself into seeing her one more time to say goodbye, to make sure she was really okay, which she more than likely was. And then, no matter what, I would go.

But when I left my room with my bags on my shoulders and stepped over to hers, I found the door ajar and housekeeping inside. *Shit.* She was already gone. *Just as well,* I told myself. Unfortunately, that didn't mean she was gone from my mind. I had a feeling it would take a while to forget about her. Our run-ins had been brief, and she really wasn't my type at all, but there was something about her that insisted on sticking with me.

I dropped my bags in the back seat of the rental car with her still on my mind as I wondered where she had gone. She'd demanded an explanation from me, which wasn't unreasonable, but she'd never explained what *she* was doing here at this hotel. Didn't she say she lived near Atlanta? So why, after being overseas for so long, was she at a hotel and not at home?

Wanting a real breakfast before hitting the road, I skipped the hotel's continental crap and drove down the street to a Denny's. I hated eating alone and hoped another peach of a waitress might keep me company—and distract me—but when I walked inside, I forgot why I was even here.

Leni sat in a booth on the far side from the door with a coffee cup and a book on the table in front of her, though she ignored both. She stared out the window instead, but I knew she didn't really see what was outside. Her mind had gone somewhere else. She felt sad or hurt. I didn't know how I knew this. Her eyes weren't teary or red and swollen or anything. I just knew.

I pushed past the hostess and made my way down the aisle

to Leni's booth, the hostess trying to stop me with a hand on my arm that I easily shrugged off. Leni's head snapped toward us, and then she shook it as I slid into the seat across from her. She waved off the hostess, and I let out the breath I'd been holding.

"Why are you here?" she asked.

"What's wrong?" I asked, going right to the point.

She ran her thumbs under her eyes, as though wiping away non-existent tears. She was holding them back. "I asked you first."

"I'm hungry."

Her lips twitched, but for a smile or a frown, I wasn't sure. "I'm . . . lost."

Her chest hitched as it rose, as though her breath stuttered, but then she plastered on her extra-sweet smile I knew now to be fake.

"You're at a Denny's in BFE Georgia. Does that help?"

She laughed, but the lingering smile still didn't reach her eyes.

"That's not what you meant, is it?" I asked. She shook her head, and I leaned forward over the table. "Tell me what's wrong."

She watched me for a moment, her eyes glancing up at my brow-ring and then down, traveling over my arms. When they reached my wrist, she frowned and quickly looked up at me, something flickering in her eyes. Had she noticed the flame tattoo or whatever it was? The thing had shown up all on its own, driving me crazy and pissing me off at the same time. Yeah, I had ink, but every single tat meant something to me, and here appears this mark out of nowhere with no meaning whatsoever. But had Leni been observant enough to notice it was new? It was bright as ever now, the edges raised, so she probably had. But why did she have that bewildered look on her face?

I was about to ask when she slid the book to sit between us. The brown leather cover had some kind of design embossed into it, and a metal clasp locked it shut.

"I can't open this," Leni signed.

My brows pulled together. That's what had her upset? I pulled my pocketknife out, and when she didn't stop me, I put the blade's edge to where the clasp met the leather and tried to saw through.

I couldn't even make a notch into the leather. I swiped my thumb over my blade, and it was as sharp as always.

A waitress came by to refill Leni's coffee cup and took my order, too.

"I already tried cutting it," Leni's hands told me when the waitress had left. "I've tried everything."

"What is it?" I asked.

She shrugged. "I don't know. The guy who gave it to me said he couldn't open it either."

"Why did he give it to you?"

She looked up at my face and then away. Her shoulders sagged, and she bit her lip, then finally returned her gaze to me.

"Never mind," she said. "It's nothing. So are you taking off?"

I didn't like how she changed the subject. Something about the book had upset her, but now she was trying to blow it off? No, more likely, trying to tell me it was none of my business.

"Just needed some fuel first," I said, and right on cue, the waitress slid a plate in front of me, overflowing with eggs, bacon, sausage and pancakes loaded with strawberries and whipped cream. I stabbed a strawberry covered in cream and held it out to Leni.

The smile she gave me was a little more real this time, but she shook her head. "No, thanks. I'm allergic to them."

I shoved it into my mouth. She watched me eat for a while, rejecting everything I offered to share with her.

"So where are you off to?" I asked after cleaning my plate. "Home?"

I must have said something wrong because tears filled Leni's eyes. She blinked them away, though.

"It's time for you to go," she said.

"I'm worried about you," I countered. The disbelieving look on her face stabbed me in the heart. "You don't think I can worry about anyone except myself, do you?"

She shrugged.

"Three days ago, I might have agreed with you," I admitted.

"And something's changed?"

I nodded. "I have."

Her eyebrows arched. "And what has changed you, Mr. Winters?"

I leaned over the table again, closer to her, and mouthed, "You did."

Her eyes widened briefly, then tightened and became hard. "Forget it. Like I said. It's time for you to go."

"Like I said, I'm worried about you. I can't go."

"You have to."

"No."

"Please." Her eyes pleaded with me. "I can't do this now. There's too much going on . . . family issues . . . ."

"I have lots of those myself. I can probably help."

"No. I can't do this. You can't help, trust me. And I don't need it anyway. I don't need . . . this."

"You don't need a friend?" I pressed.

Her hands moved with dramatic flair. "I don't need *you*! Now please, just go."

Like last night, her hard expression told me she was done arguing. She may have affected me like no other woman had before, but I wasn't about to beg. She probably had no clue what real family issues were anyway. Not like I did. But she was right. It *was* time for me to go. Even if I could help her through this, in the end, all I could bring her was more grief. This was probably some passing phase with me, and I'd soon be breaking her heart.

I gave her a short nod, stood and pulled some money out of my wallet, and threw it on the table. Without anything to lose, I bent over and almost touched my lips to Leni's forehead, but then I remembered that crazy-good feeling she gave me when we simply touched. I didn't need that now when I was preparing to leave her. So I simply tugged on a curl as she looked up at me with silver-green eyes full of despair, no matter how hard she tried to blink it away. Then I turned and strode off before I changed my mind.

After pulling out of the parking spot, I couldn't help a last glance over my shoulder to our table at the window. Leni was already gone.

Eyes forward. Focus forward. Time to move on.

I rolled my neck and shoulders and blew out a breath as if I could blow Leni out of my system. But the harder I tried to not think about her, the more I did. Something had happened to her last night. I felt it in my bones. And if they—it, whatever had been in the bushes—returned and harmed a single curl on her head, I'd never forgive myself.

My foot jumped from the gas pedal with the thought of leaving her alone and vulnerable. When the car didn't seem to respond, I glanced at the speedometer and realized I'd only been going twenty miles an hour anyway, as if my subconscious was telling me not to leave. *Maybe I should stick around to be sure she's okay.* I pulled to the side of the road to consider this idea. My mind ran away with itself, lost in forming a plan until a truck blasted past me so fast it shook the car and jolted me back to reality. I *knew* better than to sit on the side of the road. *Shit, Winters, what the fuck is wrong with you?*

I was not a stalker type. I wasn't even an up-front-in-your-face-I-want-to-be-your-boyfriend type. I was losing my mind, and the best thing I could do for me and for Leni was to leave town. As I stepped on the gas pedal and merged onto the road, my decision made, the pull inside me protested. It screamed louder and louder the faster the car went and the farther away from Leni I drove. I tried to ignore the ache, using every bit of my self-control to keep my foot on the pedal and my mind focused forward.

She's just a girl, no different than any other chick. And with a lot of baggage. You really don't want to get involved with all that.

True. Girls with baggage—I'd dealt with enough of that. Nobody seemed to have more baggage than models and strippers, and I'd had my fill of both. My own bags were enough for one person to carry. I didn't need to take on Leni's, too.

Giving myself a mental pat on the ass for doing the right

thing, I turned up the radio until the beat pounded through me and guided the car toward the ramp for the interstate. But although I pressed harder on the gas, the car refused to accelerate. Then it lurched. Sputtered. And died.

I sat in the driver's seat, staring at the gray smoke pluming from under the hood. The music's bass continued pounding out a beat, so the battery still worked. Smoke like that meant the radiator or engine, neither of them a quick fix. I banged my fist against the steering wheel. Why now? Now that I'd convinced myself to go, I wanted nothing more than to get far away from here.

With a frustrated groan, I threw open the door. A body jumped out of the way. I looked up to find Leni standing in the middle of the road, staring at me.

"You okay?" she signed, her eyes wide. "All the smoke . . ."

"What are you doing? Trying to get yourself killed?" I jumped out of the car, grabbed her arm—ignoring the dizzying effect the touch had on me—and pulled her to the shoulder and into the grass. Far away from danger.

Her eyes widened more. "Is it going to explode?"

"I doubt it." I turned and stalked over to the car.

Leni followed me, which I didn't realize until I stood at the front of the car and saw her reaching inside the passenger's side. The pound of the music stopped.

"Spanish rap?" she asked. "It was killing my ears. And just about all appreciation for music."

I shrugged. How was I supposed to know? "Will you get back now?"

The girl was scaring the shit out of me. A ramp didn't have nearly the same traffic as a highway—this one had none, actually—but still. She made me nervous.

I pointed to the grass again before releasing the hood. More smoke billowed out, engulfing my face. I stepped back, coughing, waiting for it to clear. Through the smoke, I saw Leni's old truck parked on the road behind me, hazard lights flashing. At least she still stood in the grass, with her hands on her hips as she watched me. A quick glance at the engine and I knew this was nothing I could fix.

I jogged to the driver's side, leaned in to put the car in neutral, then pushed it to the shoulder, doing my best to steer and jumping in to hit the brake when the car was a good ten feet in the grass. During that time, Leni had moved her truck, too.

I shook my head at her as she came over to my passenger's side, where I stood with the door open, nervous as hell.

"Get back," I ordered. She backed up several feet. Better.

"What are you going to do?" she asked.

What the hell do you care? I wanted to say—actually I wanted to yell it, pissed that she actually cared right after sending me out the door. That she was here in the first place, risking her life. Why couldn't she be like other girls who made leaving easy? Since I couldn't yell at her, I ignored her and searched inside the center console for the rental company's paperwork.

"It's their problem," I finally signed after finding the pink and yellow papers. I strode farther off the shoulder until the grass began to slope into a ditch, pulled my cell phone out of my pocket to text them, sat down and set it on my lap so I could sign. "They'll send a tow truck and another car for me. No need to worry. I'm sure you have things to do."

Leni glanced at her truck while biting her bottom lip, then looked back at me. Without warning, she snatched the papers and phone from my lap. I jumped up to retrieve them, but she held them behind her.

"It'll be easier if I talk to them," she mouthed.

Before I could protest, she already had my phone dialed and up to her ear. I watched her lips carefully to gather her side of the conversation. After giving my name and other info from the rental agreement, her brows drew together and her mouth tugged into a frown.

"You're sure?" her lips said. A pause followed. "No Jeric Winters in your system?" Another pause and then her eyes changed, her whole expression morphing into confusion then suspicion and then fear. "Please tell me you didn't *steal* this car."

I jerked back. "Hell no!"

"They don't have a record of you renting a car," she said, the phone still pressed to her ear. "He's asking if it's under a different name."

I jabbed my finger at the contract, where everything was spelled out. She studied it, then shook her head slowly. I pointed more specifically at the VIN and she nodded. Her mouth moved, reciting the numbers and letters to the person on the other end of the line. After a moment, she frowned again and dropped the phone from her ear. She pressed the End button before looking at me.

"Not only do they have no record of you in their system," she finally said as she shook the papers, "but they have no record of this car, either. They say it's not theirs."

I stared at her for a long moment, trying to understand. Then I grabbed the paper out of her hand and studied it, making sure it really was the contract for this particular car. Everything was correct, and the VIN engraved on the car matched the one on the papers.

Leni tugged on my arm to grab my attention. "Sirens in the distance. The police or fire department's coming. Probably both. We should get out of here."

I cocked my head. "Run from them?"

"I don't have time to explain. Come on!" She started jogging to her truck.

With a glance at the smoking engine, I grabbed my bags out of the back seat and ran for Leni's truck. She spun out, surprising me with the power of the old truck. I watched out the window and as we turned a corner, the fire truck came into view down the road. Leni made a few more turns, then parked on the side of the street. Before I could ask anything, her hands moved as quickly as she could manage.

"I can't believe I did that," she said with a mischievous grin. "I actually ran from the cops!"

I eyed her with a brow raised. "Have you ever done anything bad in your life?"

She shook her head.

"Never broken any laws at all? Ever?"

Her shoulder lifted in a shrug. "I speed sometimes."

I laughed while shaking my head. "So why did you do it now?"

She shrugged again. "Maybe you bring the worst out of me."

Ah. That could be true. Wouldn't be the first time I corrupted a girl.

"And you ran for the thrill?" I teased, but then her expression sobered as she shook her head.

"There's no record of you having legal possession of that car." She paused and frowned. "There's something really strange going on. With both of us, I think." Her eyes flitted to my wrist again. "And I can't help but think it's connected."

Her gaze came up and locked onto mine again, and I saw in her eyes what I felt. What she didn't say. That *we're* connected.

"Do you have any ideas? A plan?" I finally asked. She shook her head, then chewed on her bottom lip. "Where were you headed before you found me surrounded by smoke?"

Her eyes broke from mine, and she looked out the windshield as her face flushed. "I don't know. I had the overwhelming urge to go for a drive after you left . . . and I felt pulled in this direction." She looked back at me with a sheepish grin. "Almost like I knew something was wrong. That you needed me. Weird, right?"

Normally, yes. I'd be calling the police—or the asylum—to turn *her* in for stalking *me*. She sounded like a lunatic, but the revelation came as no surprise.

"No weirder than how hard it was for me to leave this place. My car wouldn't even let me go without you."

Her mouth pulled up into a real smile that made my breath catch. Man, did I want her. I wanted to feel her soft skin under my fingertips and those full lips against mine. I leaned forward, but she doubled over the steering wheel, her whole body shaking. I pulled back with a groan, thinking she was crying. But then she threw her head back. Her laughter shook the seat. A smile spread on my own face as I watched her until she finally calmed down enough to sign.

"I'm sorry, but if I don't laugh, I'll lose my mind. What you said is so absurd, but . . . at this point, I could believe anything." Her chest heaved with what I assumed to be a sigh, then all humor fell from her face and sadness filled it once again.

"Leni—" I started.

"Yeah. I'm crazy."

What? I shook my head. "I don't think so."

"Then what was that sign? It looked like 'crazy' to me."

I thought back to what I'd just said. Ah. "Leni. That's what I'd signed. How we deaf people say names—the first letter plus something characteristic for the person. So L plus—" I twirled my finger in a spiral near my cheek.

Her eyes narrowed. "Looks like crazy to me. So I'm L plus crazy?"

"Curls," I corrected, and I showed her the difference between the horizontal crazy sign and the vertical swirl I made for her curls.

"So what's yours?" she asked.

I grimaced. I hated the name they'd given me at the deaf school—J plus an index finger to the cheek for my dimples. "Why don't you give me your own?"

She eyed me for a moment, then made a J with her pinky and pointed to the end of her eyebrow for my piercing. A lot better than it could have been, considering our rough start last night. But she was too good to reference the used condom or to thrust her hips. Though I wouldn't have minded seeing her do the latter. I'd have her signing my name all day long to watch that.

"That'll work," I said, imitating her sign for my name. Then I asked again, "So, where were you headed?"

"I have a camper at the lake a little over an hour away."

I nodded. "Okay. Is there a bus station around here?"

She looked away and out the window, but she had that look of not seeing what was in front of her. She appeared to be trying to figure out the solution to some unknown problem. Finally she looked at me.

"Do you have somewhere you need to go?" she asked. "I mean, where would you go on the bus?"

I shrugged. "No clue, to be honest. Probably go to Miami. I kind of feel the need to go south."

I hadn't really, but as if the signed words had planted a seed in my gut, I had a vague feeling south might be right.

"Would you . . ." Her hands hesitated in the air. "Would you still make an exception for me for a sleepover?"

Whoa. Not what I was expecting.

"No, no." She shook her head emphatically. "That's not what I mean. I was just wondering if you'd come to the lake with me for a couple of days. I am kind of . . . needing a friend."

I gave her the best smile I could conjure. "I'm not big on camping, but where else do I have to go?"

After a stop for groceries and another for fuel, Leni drove us up into the mountains, to a quiet lake hidden in a valley and surrounded by Georgia pines. She pulled up to an Airstream camper sitting near the shore's edge, the silver bullet shining in the afternoon sun, and we unloaded her truck. The inside of the camper had a funky style that perfectly repped Leni. To the right of the door, the part over the tongue, was a futon mattress with no frame, piled high with various colored pillows. Orange and yellow tie-dyed curtains hung in the windows and a big, blue paper lantern dangled over the little table like a blue moon hanging in the sky. There was a kitchenette directly to the left, then what I assumed to be the bathroom and on the other side of it, a doorway leading to what must have been a small bedroom.

"Your place?" I asked.

"Pretty much. My uncle gave it to me so I'd have a place to get away from him. I think it was more so he'd have a place to send me away."

I glanced around. "Sent you to Italy and gave you a camper at the lake." My eyes came back to her. "You have a good life, don't you?"

Her eyes flicked away, but only for a brief moment before she looked at me, smiled and shrugged. "Yeah. Guess I do."

She moved about the camper with purpose, expertly setting everything up, including an awning that she hung with a couple of strings of colorful Christmas lights. A cat joined us while we ate hot dogs and potato chips at the picnic table outside, the colorful lights making a pattern of blue, pink and purple on its white coat. Leni said she'd never seen it before, but the cat seemed intent on hanging out with us.

"Why did you bring me here?" I asked her after dinner. She hadn't trusted me before. What had changed?

She didn't answer, but went inside for a moment, returning with the leather-bound book in her hand. She placed it on the table, sat down next to me and, to my surprise, grabbed my hand in hers. The world tilted a little like it always did, but the intensity was lessening with each touch. With her free hand, she ran a finger over the picture embossed in the leather cover—a weeping willow tree surrounded by fish and dolphins. Her finger pointed to an image engraved in the tree's trunk: a phoenix on fire. Then she lifted our clasped hands to rest on the table and pressed our arms tighter together.

I noticed for the first time she'd removed her bracelets. And I also noticed she had a flame tattoo exactly like the mark on my own wrist. When our arms were pressed together like that, the tattoos looked exactly like the phoenix's wings.

What. The. Fuck.

I yanked my hand out of hers and sprang to my feet. She caught my wrist in her hand before I could bolt, though, and pointed to the clasp. What had once been smooth, blank metal now had the same phoenix image engraved in it. She stroked her finger over it, and the clasp sprang open.

On the first page, in neat, girl's handwriting, were the words Jacey and Micah and a sketch of the flamed wings without the rest of the bird. On the next page were a date and the beginnings of what appeared to be a long-ass journal entry.

✳ THEN ✳
1989

CHAPTER 7

The singer of Bex's boyfriend's band screamed profanities into the microphone, supposedly singing some intense lyrics on a makeshift stage in the basement of an abandoned building. When pleading with me to come with her earlier, Bex, my roommate, had sold the band as "The Clash meets The Cult with a little Sex Pistols thrown in." As stupid as it sounds, I'd thought at the time her description had created the intense lure to see the show, because I'd been stoked to go. The band sucked, although the crowd either loved them or was simply too drunk to care because they turned the entire space into a mosh pit. Exchanging my Converse high-tops for my Doc Martens before we'd left had been a smart choice—my toes were thankful for the steel tips.

My nerves had been strung tighter than the bassist's guitar, and everything grated on them. The band's assaulting melody, sweaty bodies crashing into me, the warm beer that spilled over my hand, and all the smells that came with the scene . . . I couldn't take it anymore. I tried to chug my beer but the first swallow made me gag, so I tossed it before pushing my way up the stairs and outside. A rush of icy air hit my face as soon as I stepped through the door, and I pulled my black leather jacket tightly around me, wishing I had on more than a measly t-shirt underneath. When the January wind bit through the holey leggings under my denim miniskirt, I wanted nothing more than to magically appear in my bed at the dorm, snuggled under my comforter with a charcoal pencil and sketchpad in hand.

Normally, I'd have been so screwed up by then, I wouldn't have cared about anything—the band, the chaos, the cold. Any other time, I'd have been thrashing in the mosh pit myself. A rad buzz would have given me the false sense of warmth everyone else outside must have had as they swapped spit and smokes. A fragrant mix of menthol, cherry tobacco hand-rolls and the distinct smell of weed wafted through the chilly air, more palatable than the cloudy haze inside that tried to bring back memories I didn't want.

For some reason, though, I'd had no desire to drink myself to oblivion, my nerves too high on anticipation. Of what I didn't know. But whatever I'd been expecting, it hadn't happened, and the desire to go home grew into a desperate need. I was two hours away from campus, though, and my ride planned to stay until the last song finished. *I totally should have driven*, I thought as several people came bouncing through the door.

I watched for Bex, wondering if I'd have any chance of talking her into leaving early, although I was pretty sure of the answer. At least, until I saw her new boyfriend—what was his name? I couldn't remember—stumble outside, his arms around two chicks and their mouths all over his neck. Neither of them were Bex. In fact, where was Bex? Still in the bathroom, where she'd gone when I came outside? My gaze flicked between the door, still watching for Bex, and the boyfriend with his bitches. They huddled together near the wall opposite me, not even trying to hide their mini-orgy.

"Oh, hell no," I muttered, pushing myself off the wall I'd been leaning against as a light drizzle began to fall.

Maybe I'd had enough beer for liquid courage after all, but probably not. All I could think about was seeing Bex's face when she came out. Although she asked for most of her boy troubles, the poor girl didn't deserve *this*. Edgy, disappointed, and now completely pissed off, I stomped over to the trio.

"What the fuck, you dickwad?" I yelled as I grabbed the collar of one girl's jacket and, ignoring the pierce of the metal studs in my palm, yanked her away while my right hand swung, nailing what's-his-name in the jaw. While he gaped at me, stunned and rubbing his face, the other girl stepped into my space, her flabby boobs nearly touching my chin as I glared up at her. The ring in her nose wobbled as her lips lifted in an ugly smirk.

"What are you—psycho?" she snarled. "Well, you picked the wrong bitch to mess with."

Her hands twitched at her side, but not waiting to be hit first, I drove my knee into her stomach. She doubled over briefly, but before I could punch her in the head, her hand came up with a knife in it.

"Bring it on," I taunted, my hands out, fingers wiggling at her. I rolled my shoulders, trying to ignore the icy drizzle making trails under my coat and down my back.

The girl swiped her knife out, the streetlight bouncing off the silver blade as it swung toward me. I jabbed my fist out to knock it from her hand, or at least to keep it from slicing open my face. The knife never connected, though. Something yanked me backwards, out of its reach.

Not something. Some*one*. And as soon as the large hands clamped onto my upper-arms, the breath flew out of me. As though I'd been socked in the stomach, but nothing had hit me. I gasped, trying but unable to catch my breath as those hands dragged me farther down the alley, the touch searing through my leather jacket, into my skin, down to my bones. Every nerve zinged in my body like they did when I touched one of Pops' badly wired lamps. The pounding in my ears barely drowned out the stupid tramp screaming at me, the sound of her voice fading as someone dragged her in the opposite direction. But the pounding didn't drown out the word, "*dyad*," a voiceless whisper floating around my mind as if I should have known what it meant.

My body finally stopped moving, and as the hands turned me in place to face their owner, my fists balled, and a whole slew of profanities prepared to launch out of my mouth.

But they never made it out.

My breath caught in my lungs once again. My brain went numb, any thoughts becoming an incoherent jumble. The whole world disintegrated around us as my gaze met the darkest, most haunting pair of eyes I'd ever seen returning my stare, filled with the same expression I must have held. One that said with no trace of doubt, as if it were a self-evident, unquestionable truth decreed by the gods (if they actually existed):

"I. Know. You."

I know you. The words almost tumbled from my mouth, would have if my tongue hadn't been so tied.

Except . . . I'd never seen him before in my life. Trust me, I wouldn't have forgotten this face. A perfect, heart-stopping, I-want-to-know-what-it-tastes-like face framed by chin-length, wavy hair as dark as his eyes. My lips ached to brush over his chiseled cheekbones, and my fingers twitched with the thought of tangling themselves in his silky locks.

Oh, for God's sake. What is wrong with me?!

I didn't know how long we stood there, staring at each other, that zing sparking between us. Seconds? Minutes? Longer? No clue. The sound of flapping wings and the sudden rising of black shapes from the shadows around us jerked me back to reality. Too big to be bats, some kind of huge black birds rose to the sky, and I stared after them, my jaw hanging open.

"Jacey," Bex snapped from behind me, "what the hell is wrong with you?"

I spun around and blinked at her. "Did you . . . where . . . I mean . . ."

I shook my head, trying to clear my thoughts, and water spattered outwards.

"Why are you still out here?" Bex demanded. "It's fuckin' cold! And wet!"

My eyes took Bex in for real now. Her hot pink Mohawk was beginning to droop, some strands already plastered to her head, and her black eye makeup made trails down her powdered-white face. She looked like the poster-child for teen runaways. Water dripped from my own bangs and slid down my nose and cheeks. The drizzle had turned into an all-out downpour. When had that happened?

I glanced around, looking for the crowd that had just been out here, who had surely witnessed everything. For the *guy* who had turned my body into a vibrating thrum and my mind to mushy oatmeal. Who I felt like I knew almost as well as myself, but didn't know at all. But everyone had disappeared. Bex and I were the only idiots standing in the freezing rain. How long *had* I been out here, apparently alone?

"I'm totally ready to scat," Bex said. "If this gets any worse, the roads will be hell, and I don't want to deal with it. You ready?"

"Um . . . yeah," I mumbled as my ears ached with cold and my teeth began to chatter. I followed her down the street to her hand-me-down white Pinto we called Beanie, both of us silent as we slid into the car, and she cranked the engine over. We sat there shivering as she let the car warm up. "Bex?"

She looked over at me. I couldn't tell if the streaks on her cheeks now were still from the rain or from tears.

"I'm sorry," I said softly. "About, you know . . ." I squinted. "What's his name again?"

She swallowed, and I saw a brief flash of a thank-you in her eyes before they turned hard. "Who the hell cares what it is? We'll just call him 'asshole' from now on. Or even better, let's never talk about him again, okay?"

I nodded. I'd known Bex since move-in day of freshman year. Her room had been down the hall from me, but since my hair was jet black, I wore Doc Martens, and I hung a poster for The Cure over my bed, she found me in the sea of chunky sweaters and pegged jeans on our first day. We simply didn't fit in with the rest of the girls on our floor. We had even bonded over our names, somewhat unusual among the Trishes, Susans and various forms of Michelles. I couldn't imagine Bex as a Rebecca or even Becca, and she loved the story of how I'd insisted on being called Jacey ever since Pops moved me right before seventh grade. Altering my name had been my first act of rebellion, although he wouldn't let me change my last name. He told me Burns, both the name and the scars, were badges of honor—an honor to my parents. They were more like painful reminders. Anyway, Bex and I had pretty much clung to each other ever since.

I knew her well enough to know she didn't need a play-by-play of what happened.

"So, is he asshole number eight or nine?" I said as we pulled onto the highway. "Just so, you know, if you *do* ever talk about him again, I know which one you mean."

She shrugged. "I don't know. I've lost track myself."

We broke into laughter, which helped to lighten the mood, at least for a few minutes.

"What you did tonight was totally bitchin'," she said.

I stared out my window, not wanting to make a big deal out of it for Bex's sake. I was surprised she'd even said this much. "You would have done it for me, right?"

"Damn straight," she said. "But you never need it."

"Someday I might."

"I doubt it." She let out a sigh, then muttered, "What the hell's wrong with me?"

I could tell she didn't want an answer, so I remained silent.

Somehow Beanie got us back to school in the cold rain that turned to sleet, but I barely remembered the ride. Strange, yet familiar mocha-brown eyes haunted me all the way home, and still as I changed into sweats and climbed into my top bunk, finally able to snuggle under the covers.

"Bex?" I said right before falling asleep.

"Yeah?" she asked, her voice muffled as it came from her bed underneath mine.

"There's nothing wrong with you. You're just too good for all those jerks."

She didn't answer at first, unless you count a sniffle. Then she said, "Yeah, you're right. I deserve better. We both do."

I didn't expect a thanks from Bex—that was as close as I would get—but I hadn't expected those last words either. I'd never really thought about what kind of guy I deserved. I'd had one on-again-off-again boyfriend in high school, but he'd been killed in a car accident, taken away from me like everyone else in my life. Except Pops and Bex. At least I had them. Unlike Bex, boys weren't a top priority for me as I tried to figure out my place in this cruel world.

The next morning, I awoke to snow on the ground and a strange ache on my left wrist. I massaged it as I stared out the window from my bed, trying to remember what had happened last night that would have caused the ache. The brief fight with the slut? The mysterious guy? I glanced down at my wrist and gasped. The outline of a flame was . . . *tattooed* . . . on the inner edge, right below the wrist bone. It was light, barely visible, but there nonetheless.

"Is this some kind of sick joke?" I muttered as I licked my fingers and rubbed at it. It still didn't come off. A few minutes later, I stood at the sink in the communal bathroom for our hall, washing it with soap.

"What's that?" Bex asked, peering at it closely. "Ah, man, Jace! You got a tattoo and didn't tell me about it? We were supposed to get our first ones together, you skank. When did you do it?"

I shook my head and tried to explain I hadn't, that it had shown up overnight.

"Whatever," she said with a snort. "But if Joe did it, you better pour some alcohol on it. His needles are dirtier than Jenna's cootch."

Jenna, Bex's old roommate, came out of a bathroom stall right then and glared at Bex. She didn't say anything, though. Probably because one of her hands held a tube of prescription-strength anti-itch ointment and the other a pregnancy test box. With a huff, she turned for the bank of sinks.

Ignoring my denial about the tattoo, Bex made a face behind Jenna's back, then left me in the bathroom. I stared at the stubborn mark, finally admitting to myself it wouldn't wash away. *Where did you come from?* I tried to think if I'd been playing around with permanent markers last week. I had a habit of drawing on myself when I was bored . . . although the skin around the mark was slightly raised, like a brand-new tattoo. *So weird.* Besides, not in a million years would I draw a flame, of all things. Not on myself. I hoped it would fade. At least winter meant I could wear long sleeves to cover it without looking suspicious. But then I couldn't help but pull up the sleeve enough to stare at the flame because every time I did, those dark eyes came to mind, perfectly clear.

I couldn't stop thinking about the guy and why I'd felt so strongly that I knew him. Every time I made my way across campus to classes and while sitting in the dining hall, my eyes roamed, constantly looking for him. As I walked the halls of our dorm, I would glance into open doors, hoping to find him sitting at a desk inside one of the rooms or splayed out on a bed. Something, anything, that would explain why I thought I knew him. He consumed every waking thought for nearly a week.

Then I got The Call and totally forgot about him and pretty much everything else in the world.

CHAPTER 8

 "Jacey, I hate to be the one to tell you this," Trudy, Pops' neighbor, said on the other end of the line, "but your grandfather has left this world for the next one."

Why do people say such stupid things when someone dies? "Moved on." "Passed on." "Gone on to the next life." They're dead. End of story. They didn't go anywhere except six feet under.

That's what I thought about when Trudy dropped the bomb on me. The stupid phrases had irritated me as a little girl when my parents died, and now they abraded me like a cheese grater, shredding me into ribbons. And the reality of her words, no matter how nice she tried to make them, pushed me to the dorm-room floor and folded my body into a tight ball, wrapping itself around my heart and shielding it from the pain. And my brain—it refused to process her meaning. It only wanted to focus on the stupidity of hope for another life after this one.

Because to understand the true meaning behind her words—my grandfather was dead, gone, only a memory now—meant also understanding how completely alone I was. Pops had been the only family I had left. Now I had no one. Nineteen years old and no blood ties to this world. How does someone cope with that?

I didn't. Bex found me crumpled on the throw rug next to her bed, a heaving, snotty mess. She enveloped me in her arms and rocked me back and forth. I centered on the pain of her metal-studded bracelet piercing into my shoulder, trying to ignore the agony of my heart breaking. She'd left our door open, as we and everyone else did when we weren't naked or cramming for a test, and girls from our hall came and went, expressing their condolences. Some even stayed, sitting on Bex's bed or crawling to my top bunk, or leaning against our desks and dressers, trying to come up with something to say to make me feel better. But it was all awkward shit, stupid words everyone says because we don't know what else to say because, dammit, there just aren't the right words to express ourselves when someone dies. Our brains and mouths aren't equipped with the right tools to communicate what our hearts feel.

I wanted to yell at them, scream at the top of my lungs to shut the hell up, to get out of my room, to go to hell. To tell them that unless they'd lost their parents, *and* their Pops, the one person who had served as their parent *and* best friend for the last eleven years, the closest person in the world to them, then they had no effin' idea what I was going through. *I* had no idea what I was going through yet, the only reason I managed to keep my mouth shut and tune them out.

Eventually our room emptied. Eventually my face dried and I could breathe without a hitch. Eventually the realization that I had to go home hit me. Needing something to do, needing to move, to not dwell, I began to pack.

"Take only what you need right now," Bex said as she helped me. "The rest will be here when you get back."

I nodded, trying not to break down again. "What am I going to do about school?"

She patted my hand, the motherly instincts I never knew she had kicking in. "No worries. I'll take notes for you and tell your professors you'll be gone a while, okay?"

I nodded again even as tears burnt the backs of my eyes. Pretending I would return in a few days or a week was just that—pretending. I wouldn't return. Not this semester anyway. Somewhere in the recess of my mind, I knew I had things to do at home. Business to take care of. Pops had a house, belongings, things to be dealt with. But acknowledging this meant admitting to the terrible truth that I was the only one who could take care of the estate. That I was Pops' only living relative and he'd been mine. And I still wasn't ready to go there.

"You wanna get drunk?" Bex asked a few minutes later.

"Fuckin' A, I do."

✵ ✵ ✵

The next morning I stared out the dorm window at the campus with its limestone buildings covered in ivy, the big clock tower rising above the quad, the freezing classrooms and cranky old professors. I would miss the energy found on a college campus, the buzz of youth as they lived new experiences, both inside the classroom and out, but as much I enjoyed it here, it would never be home. I was beginning to wonder if I'd ever find "home," a place where I truly belonged.

With a heavy heart, I said goodbye to the friends I'd made in the dorm, lugged my overstuffed duffle bag down the stairs and out to my Jeep. Bex followed me out, lighting a cigarette as we crossed the parking lot.

"Love ya, girl," she said as she hugged me for the hundredth time in less than twenty-four hours. "I'll see you soon, right?"

I gave her a weak smile. "Yeah, sure."

After the four-hour drive home, I entered Pops' house and the wave of grief I expected to knock me over didn't come. In fact, I didn't feel any different than I usually did when I came home from school—that I didn't deserve Pops and all he did for me, including the home he'd tried to make for me and Sammy, my dog. He'd stayed with me in my parents' house for a couple of years after they died, not wanting to bring on too much change at once, but before I started junior high, he decided it time to return to his own home. He tried to make it my home, too, but it never would be. I never let it be.

After growing up as a perfect child, never in trouble and always earning good grades, I was rewarded with the loss of my parents and then moving to a new town and a new school. I'd decided being good hadn't worked out so well for me, so I thought I'd try being bad, which I excelled at, too. Besides my name, I took on a whole new persona at my new school—the cool girl who cared about nothing, especially not school. The wrong kind of boys liked my attitude, though, and I didn't want them to see what was under my clothes, so I made myself ugly. Well, different. I chopped off my long, red hair, and eventually dyed it. Then, when I found a new group of friends, came the face covered in white powder, the heavy black eyeliner and the wardrobe change. Along with an even worse attitude. And drinking binges.

I'd had never made it into college if not for Pops and the guilt I'd felt by junior year. I'd barely had time to turn my grades around, but he'd stuck with me, pushing me hard. If he'd only known I'd wanted it so bad just so I could get away and allow him to live a peaceful life. He'd barely been able to enjoy it.

The grief stayed away until I came into the living room and saw Pops' armchair, the ugly brown corduroy one where he should have been sitting, waiting for me to get home. And the fireplace that hadn't seen so much as a spark since I'd moved in— Pops had kept the hearth cold for me, even on the most blustery days. Because he knew that's what I'd needed. All I ever did was disappoint him, and for some reason, he'd loved me anyway.

I retrieved a bottle of whiskey from his liquor cabinet along with two shot glasses and sat in his chair.

"To you, Pops," I said, my voice cracking on his name, then I threw the shot to the back of my throat. The burn of the liquor felt good. I eyed Pops' glass. "Well, I guess I need to take that one for you, huh?"

I threw back the second shot, then poured two more. Rinse and repeat, until I could no longer focus on the glasses, so I pulled straight from the bottle. I drank until I passed out. And did so again the next night and the one after that. Then I didn't even wait for night.

"Jacey!" Trudy's voice came from far away, but at the same time boomed in my ear.

I sat up with a start. Well, sort of. I could barely keep myself upright. I blinked up at Pops' neighbor who stood over me, her round face barely visible beyond her rounder belly, and scratched my head. "What?"

The word came out gruffly, as if I had cotton in my mouth. Did I? I pushed my tongue out and smacked my lips. It *felt* like I had cotton in my mouth.

"My goodness, girl, it's freezing in here. Why don't you have a fire going?" She bustled over to the fireplace and bent over to peer inside it, the back of her dark gray dress riding up, exposing the tops of her stockings.

"No!" I yelled. At least, it sounded to me like a yell.

She clucked her tongue and waddled over to me. "You and your pops and your aversion to burning trees. Never understood that." She peered more closely at me, then crossed her arms over her full bosom. "Are you drunk again?"

"No," I said, wondering why she wore such a silly black hat. "*Still.*"

Trudy shook her head, then reached out and grabbed my hands, trying to pull me to my feet. I'd apparently passed out on the braided rug in front of Pops' chair. "It's time to go to the funeral."

"Oh, yeah!" I nearly squealed. "No wonder you're dressed so funny."

"Yes. And you need to hurry up and get dressed, too." She clucked her tongue again. "If you were mine, I'd give you a good whoopin'. That's what you need."

I ignored her and forced myself to my feet and upstairs to my room, then nearly crashed down the steps after I was dressed. Trudy drove me to the chapel, barely able to hide her outrage. *Fuck her*, I thought. I wasn't hers. I wasn't *anyone's* anymore.

"Miss Burns, are you okay?" the pastor asked me as I weaved my way to Pops' coffin sitting in front of the pulpit. Although I'd given up on God the night my parents died, Pops had always been pretty involved in the church.

"Just peachy," I slurred, squinting at him. Not exactly the truth, obviously, but I wasn't about to get into it with this guy. I just wanted this funeral to be done and over with so I could go home and drink myself unconscious.

Fortunately, Pops, the meticulous man who was always prepared for anything, had already planned out his funeral years ago. He'd even bought the plot! So I hadn't really had to do anything but show up, which was a good thing because I realized now, I was barely capable of handling even that. I nearly ate carpet as I tripped over my own feet, making my way to the front pew. Pops lay in the open coffin not ten feet away, but the thought of going up there now made me queasy. I didn't want to remember him pale and pasty, not like himself at all.

The funeral passed by in a blur, and when I thought no one was looking, I snuck swigs from Pops' flask. My only clear memory of the service was walking up to the pedestal to say a few words about Pops, trying like hell not to look at him lying in the box. So I focused on the crowd instead, which I regretted nearly as much. They all stared at me, not expectantly or sympathetically. Rather, their expressions showed shock, shame and even disgust. Eyes roamed over me, not appreciating my funeral outfit of a black turtleneck, miniskirt, fishnets and combat boots. Heads shook in disapproval, and it was all I could do to keep from telling them all to eff-off. I rushed through my speech without remembering what I said, wanting nothing more than to escape those judging eyes. Trying hard not to ralph.

After the service ended and everyone had finally left, the funeral director was about to close Pops' coffin once and for all.

"No!" I nearly screamed, and I stumbled for the coffin. "He won't be able to breathe!"

The man stared at me, likely wondering if I'd really said that.

"He can't breathe," I said as sobs worked their way up my throat. The reality that once he closed the lid I'd never see my Pops again finally hit me. "He'll never breathe again."

He'll never again sit in his ugly brown chair. Or smack his lips as he ate his bran flakes. Or light up his God-awful tobacco pipe. He'll never again look at me with a frown on his mouth but a gleam in his eye that told me he knew I could do better. He'll never again call me "little bird."

I suddenly regretted not spending time with Pops sooner. This was my last chance. As I stared at him, looking as much like a wax figure as I'd expected and not like himself at all, the tears finally came. And I felt so ashamed. Not for crying, but for my behavior. I'd disgraced Pops the one last chance I had to make him proud. I'd made a fool of myself. Of him. How can one person be such a shitty granddaughter?

"I'm so sorry, Pops," I said as I pressed my lips to his cold forehead. "So, so sorry. I'll make it up to you, okay? I'll make you proud from now on. I promise, Pops. I promise to be the person you always wanted me to be."

Although I knew he was gone, I could practically hear his reply: "Don't do it for me, little bird. I love you no matter what. Do it for yourself. Always stay true to your heart and soul."

Watching the coffin being lowered into the ground and then the groundskeepers shoveling dirt on top of it sobered me up. And I knew what I had to do. I went home, poured all the liquor down the drain and even tore up and threw away all but my least extreme clothes. If I didn't do something then, I knew I could let the punk lifestyle take me. I had found my escape in the hardcore-ness of it all. I was allowed to be angry and bitchy and those people didn't mind. In fact, they encouraged it. And we all drowned our poor-me sorrows in alcohol, or smoked them out, then banged against each other so the physical pain would outweigh the misery in our hearts. Right now, I could have used such an escape more than ever. But I knew I would lose myself completely in it. I was already on the verge.

I didn't want to be that person anymore. I didn't know who I truly was, but it was time to grow up and find out.

✿ ✿ ✿

Pops died in January. He'd left his estate nice and neat, as if he knew the time was coming although he was only sixty years old and had seemed in perfect health only two weeks earlier when I'd been home for Christmas break. Apparently his heart had given out, and he'd slipped away in his sleep. At least he hadn't suffered.

Even with everything nicely organized, it took me months to finalize it all. I sold the house, wanting to leave this town and all its bad memories behind for good. Everything inside also had to go, as did Pops' car and various banking, investment, and insurance accounts. I was able to pay off the house's mortgage and have some money left over for next year's tuition, books, and rent. I'd planned to return to college in the fall.

Bex had kindly packed all of my things at school at the end of the semester a few weeks ago. She'd sent me the must-haves while keeping the rest in storage until we moved into the apartment we would share. I'd lost a semester but if I worked diligently, I could make up the classes and still graduate on time. That had been the plan anyway. The universe laughed at my plan.

See, Pops had pretty much taken care of everything except one small matter: a piece of property he owned in Florida. I hadn't even known it existed until I went through his papers, and all I still knew was I'd inherited a structure on a piece of land in a small town right on the Gulf of Mexico. I called the real estate agent on the business card in the file so I could put the property on the market, but the jerk refused until I came down and looked at the place first. He even said, "Your grandfather insisted you see it before making any decisions. I swore to him I wouldn't list it until you signed the papers in person, and I'm a man of my word, ma'am."

So once everything else had been settled, here I was in early June, packing up my Jeep and preparing for an unwanted trip to

Florida. I stood in the doorway of Pops' house, now empty, just like my heart. As a child, I'd been constantly afraid of losing Pops since I'd lost my parents, but I'd never truly imagined this day to become reality. Leaving this house made me feel so old at only twenty. In the last five months, I'd had one birthday but aged ten years.

"Are you sure you don't want me to come with you?" Bex had asked me for the sixteenth time last night.

"I'm sure," I said, twirling the kinky phone cord around my finger as I leaned against the kitchen wall. "I need some alone time."

I didn't think I was ready to face Bex and all that she was yet. I hadn't told her my decision to grow up and clean up. I'd hoped a few months away from it all would put enough distance between me and that way of life so it wouldn't be so hard when I returned to school. Maybe once I cleaned myself up, I could be an example for Bex rather than her being a temptation for me. Besides, she needed to keep her job and her own plans for the summer, even if she had sounded disappointed on the phone last night.

"Ready to go, Sammy?" The words came out as only a whisper around the lump in my throat. The Labrador-retriever-mix nudged his head against my hand, and I dug my fingers into his soft fur. I'd left him behind to keep Pops company since I couldn't exactly have a dog in the dorm, and he'd been over at Trudy's until I'd sobered up. I'd never leave him behind again. "It's just you and me now, boy."

He let out a bark before bounding over to the Jeep, jumping into the passenger side and sitting on the seat, facing forward: *Ready*, his bright-eyed expression said. You'd never believe he was twelve years old. He still looked and acted like the overgrown puppy Pops and I had rescued from the pound about a year before Mom and Dad died.

As we merged onto the highway headed south, I vowed out loud to never look back. Mom and Dad and Pops, they were all in the past. I needed to tuck them into a safe place in my heart, and move on with my new life. Otherwise, the reality of being totally alone in this big world would send me back to booze and drugs. It would end me. I knew this as a certain fact, and a part of me felt as though I deserved it, which terrified the hell out of me.

However, I refused to let the idea of surviving on my own scare me. New me. New life.

"We're on an adventure," I said to Sammy as I squared my shoulders and focused on the road before us. Deepening my voice, I gave my best Bill-and-Ted impersonation. "Jacey and Sammy's Excellent Adventure. Totally rad, fer shur."

I gave him a pat on the head, pushed a mixed tape into the cassette deck, and sang along with The Ramones at the top of my lungs. Sammy returned my smile, his tongue hanging out, as the wind whipped his ears behind his head. Somehow, I vowed to myself, I would find a way to make it. After I tied up this one last loose end. If only it had been an easy square knot.

✼ ✼ ✼

The location was gorgeous, and as soon as I turned onto the road running parallel to the Gulf of Mexico, an unexpected sense of peace washed over me. Seafood restaurants, boutiques, hotels, and condos lined the road with occasional empty lots that provided a pristine view of the beach and water. Although everything was shinier than I usually liked—a little *too* pretty—I fell in love at first sight.

This had to be why Pops insisted I see the place before selling it. But had he expected me to move here? I'll never know. When I first pulled up to the address on his paperwork, I thought he must have known. The place sat right on the main road and across the street from the Gulf in one of those exact spots where there was nothing but beach and water on the other side. It looked as though he'd had it all prepared for me.

I sat in the paved driveway, waiting for Buck the real estate agent to meet me. I'd called him from a pay phone at my last stop for gas in Tampa, and he'd accurately estimated I was thirty minutes away. He would arrive any minute.

"It's . . . nice, isn't it?" I asked Sammy as I slid out of the Jeep, never taking my eyes off the property as he hopped into the driver's seat, then jumped down and immediately began exploring.

The house itself, quite a large one, wasn't exactly what I'd imagined Pops buying for himself or thinking I'd want, but for some reason, I did kind of like it. With its Asian-style architecture, it felt out of place among all the modern and Spanish-style homes I'd seen so far, which was probably what made the house perfect for me. After all, I was usually out of place, too, wherever I was.

I waited impatiently for Buck, unable to keep myself from climbing the wide, covered front porch and peeking into the glass doors and windows. The place was furnished! Not exactly my style— it looked as though a Swatch watch had barfed all over the inside with tacky modern geometric patterns and lots of pastels— nor Pops', but probably typical for the area. It would be fine for the summers, the only time I'd be able to spend here, if even that. And the view across the street made up for it all. Still peeking into windows, I began to wonder if Buck had forgotten about me as I circled the house, astonished to find a smaller version of the home at the rear of the property. A guest house?

And was someone inside? I thought I saw movement through one of the windows, possibly a renter, but a voice from behind me made me spin around.

CHAPTER 9

"Well, there you are." The familiar voice unmistakably belonged to Buck, a thin man, average height, his head balding with patches of yellow on the sides. Sammy ran to my side and stood with his ears up, his whole body on alert. Although he didn't growl, I sensed he didn't like Buck very much. "Since you didn't show up when I thought you would, I was a little concerned something happened to you, but thought I'd check over here before I got too worried."

I cocked my head as I approached him. I'd been here almost exactly the time he'd expected. He was the one who hadn't shown up on time. "Um . . . sorry?"

"You're Jacey Burns, right?" Buck asked, holding his hand out to me, his fingernails yellowed, probably from years of smoking if the smell of stale tobacco enveloping him meant anything.

"Yes." I reluctantly shook his hand, letting go as soon as politely possible, and casually wiped my hand on my jeans. "But I've been here for nearly an hour, waiting on you."

"Oh, yes. You were on time, I suppose, but so was I. Only, I was at the right place, and you aren't."

I looked at the unusual but pretty house and back at him, my eyes narrowing. "What do you mean?"

"You're on Gulf Drive *North*. You want to be on Gulf Drive *South*. When you crossed the bridge, you should have turned left, not right."

My heart sank. "So this isn't my place?"

"Nope. Follow me and I'll take you there." He looked me up and down, as though studying my black Psychedelic Furs concert shirt, ripped-up jeans and Converse high-tops. "Your place is more suited to you. I'm sure you'll love it."

My eyes narrowed tighter. What did he know about me? I happened to love the oversized Asian house, even if it was a little . . . pretentious. Biting my tongue, I called Sammy to the Jeep, and we followed Buck's ugly gold sedan back the way we'd come, passing the bridge I'd crossed from the mainland. Although only a bridge separated the two areas, I felt as though we'd crossed into a whole different world. Pink, green, bright blue and lavender houses, inns, shops, bars, and cafés lined the road here, with side streets turning to the left that were clustered with small homes—beach shacks was probably a better term for them. And although I hated Buck for judging me, he was right.

"Well, the other place was awesome, Sammy, but this is more our speed, don't you think?"

My dog, standing in the passenger seat as he leaned out the window, wagged his tail in agreement. But I'd spoken too soon.

Buck pulled into a sand pit of a driveway that appeared to have had room for at least four cars at one time, but overgrown bushes had taken over two full spaces. And the place the little parking lot served? It wasn't big and shiny, that's for sure.

Buck later called it a four-plex and said it had lots of potential. All I saw was a run-down hellhole that couldn't possibly have belonged to my grandfather.

"I think there's a mistake," I managed to say once we were out of our vehicles. I'd barely been able to close my mouth after it had hung open for several minutes as I sat in my Jeep staring. "My grandfather would have never bought this kind of place, let alone let it sit like this. No, not my Pops."

"Well, he did. He's owned it for many a year, actually. For a while there, I had the occasional investor or couple wanting to buy it and fix it up, but your granddad kept telling me, 'No, I'm saving it for Jacey.' I gave up even asking him several years ago."

I shook my head. "I have no clue what he was thinking, except it must be worth a lot of money? Maybe it'd been an investment for me?"

"Possibly," Buck said with a noncommittal shrug. "But I doubt it. There was a reason he wanted you to see it first."

I couldn't imagine why. To me, it looked like nothing more than an eyesore.

"Well, I've seen it. And I sure as hell don't want it. What's it worth and how quickly do you think it can be sold?"

Buck's eyes cut toward me. "Why don't we go in and check out the units?"

I blew out a frustrated sigh. This trip had been a complete waste of my time, and I didn't want to spend anymore. I needed to find a place to stay for the night, get the paperwork taken care of tomorrow, and then figure out what I'd do until the piece of shit sold. Bex said the lease on our new apartment didn't start until August, so I had two months with no place for Sammy and me to live.

Buck was already at one of the first-floor doors, pushing it open. Four units made up the structure, with the top two served by outside, rusty metal stairs on each side of the building. The top-floor units each had a tiny balcony out front, facing the main road and a bar across the street. *They might have a nice view*, I thought, but I doubted it.

I reluctantly followed Buck inside the ground-floor, right-side unit, entering into an efficiency with a living area, a kitchenette, a bathroom, and a small area behind it with barely enough room for a full-size bed. The unit was actually larger than I expected, and even more disgusting. The place had apparently flooded at some point, and although no mold stained the walls, the room smelled as though mildew had tried to grow but someone had doused the place with bleach.

"We have someone come in once in a while to make sure the place hasn't become a hazard," Buck said, confirming my theory. "It's actually in pretty good shape, considering. Just needs a little TLC."

"A *little*?" I asked, wrinkling my nose.

"It's really all cosmetics," Buck said. "It'll take a little work and some cash, but you're really better off fixing it up than selling it right away. I think that's what your grandfather had in mind."

Yeah, right. Pops knew me better than that. I was far from being the fixer-upper type. On the other hand, Pops always told me not to be afraid of a little work, or even a lot of it. Was he still trying to teach me a lesson from the grave?

"How better off?" I asked skeptically.

"If you listed it now, you'd be lucky to get enough to pay my commission and all the fees and taxes. You might end up with ten grand in your pocket, at the most. If you fix it up, though, restore it to how nice it could be, you could wind up with five to ten times more, even after the cash you put into it."

Five to ten times more? That would not only pay my tuition until graduation, but also give me a nice sum to start off with afterwards. But ... I looked around. Ugh, that was a lot of work. Could I even get it done before I had to be in Virginia for the first day of classes?

"I have no idea where to start," I admitted. "I have no clue how to fix up a place and not a lot of time either."

"I can recommend whatever you need. I know all the contractors around." He pulled a stack of business cards from his front shirt pocket, shuffled through them, then handed me a few. "The one on top is my best recommendation. He's pretty busy, but if you tell him I sent you, he'll take care of you."

My suspicion radar piqued at this. Why did Buck push this idea so hard? Some kind of devotion to my Pops' wishes? I highly doubted it. Pops hadn't even mentioned he owned this place, let alone knew anyone here well enough to care. Were Buck and this contractor in on some kind of scam?

"Look, the more you sell it for, the more commission I make," Buck said, apparently sensing my paranoia. "Besides, I think your granddad saved this place for you for a reason. I don't know what, maybe for the money after it's fixed up and sold, but I do know that's what he'd hoped for. It's cut-and-dry to us who are older and wiser, and if I left a place for my granddaughter like this, I hope that's what she'd do. Why don't you give it some thought, at least?"

I glanced around the unit, taking in the peeling wallpaper, the threadbare shag rug and stained linoleum, the rusted kitchen faucet and metallic gold, itty-bitty fridge. Sucking in my courage, I made my way to the bathroom, afraid of what I would find, but it wasn't as grody as I expected. The pink paint of the sink and tub was chipping and mildew grew in the corners, the toilet definitely needed to be replaced, as well as the flooring, but not as nasty as it could have been.

"Are the other units like this one?" I asked.

"Pretty much. The upstairs ones are a little better off since they didn't flood with the last hurricane. We don't have to treat them for mold but once a year, which is normal for an empty place down here with nobody cleaning and maintaining it every day. You want to see them?"

I blew out a breath. "I guess, but I can't take long. I need to find a place to stay tonight. You know anywhere that takes dogs?"

"Why don't you look at the rest of the units? If you don't mind sleeping on the floor, you might decide to stay in one upstairs. I had the utilities turned on yesterday. You'll have to run the water a while to get the rust out of the pipes, but at least you'll have running water, air conditioning and a place for your dog."

The thought of sleeping on a floor that who knew how many people had traipsed over disgusted me, but I had, admittedly, stayed in worse. And I did have a sleeping bag and blankets with me. Then when I entered the upstairs, left unit, I thought maybe there was hope for this place after all. It appeared as though Pops, or maybe the previous owner, had started remodeling with this unit at some point, but never made it to the others. There was no wallpaper, the carpet appeared to have been replaced though it was already outdated, the kitchen was all white with no ugly appliances from the seventies, and the bathroom was bearable. With a little scrubbing, I might have even sat my bare ass on the toilet seat.

The two upstairs units were set up a little differently than the downstairs ones. The kitchenette, bathroom, and a closet lined the rear wall and one large room made up the front, which could easily be split in half with a curtain to separate the living area from the sleeping part. Both sides had big picture windows with French doors in the middle leading out to the little balconies I'd seen from the ground. I peered through the grimy windows to find a spectacular view of the sun in the western sky over the Gulf. Of course, the bar across the street was also part of the view, but it didn't completely ruin the scene.

Uh-oh. The potential was definitely growing on me. This place could actually be really cute, a perfect little beach getaway for college kids or couples on a budget. Definitely not the big beach house down the road, but who needed all that space anyway? And the money to be made was becoming more and more tempting. It would be nice to know I didn't have to work throughout college and I'd still have money to live on while I launched my career. Hell, maybe I could even take a break first. Or better yet—make my dream of being a professional artist come true!

My mind ran away with these thoughts, almost convincing myself right there as Buck watched me. But the practical side of me kicked in right in time. Before I made a decision, I needed to find out how much this would cost me. I had money from the rest of Pops' estate. It was supposed to be for next year's tuition and rent, but this could be an investment with great returns. Was it enough, though? And how long would this take? If it couldn't be done and sold by the time classes started, I'd be screwed, my tuition and rent money tied up in this place. And what if there's more wrong with it than meets the eye?

"I'll get back to you, okay?" I asked Buck as I rubbed the back of my neck. "There's a lot to think about."

"Of course. I think your grandfather would be happy to hear that. Nothing like seeing our offspring making smart decisions." He gave me what he probably meant to be a grandfatherly smile, but I found it a little creepy. "Give that contractor a call as soon as you can. To be honest, I already told him you were coming, so he's expecting to hear from you. I hope that's okay. I promised your granddad I'd help out however I can."

He winked at me, which definitely grossed me out. I walked outside with him, cringing as the metal stairs creaked under our weight. Buck swore they were safe and Sammy didn't worry, bounding up and down them with no troubles, but I did. If I went through with this, they would be the first thing to be replaced. Because I definitely wanted to stay in the top-left unit while I was here.

Once Buck finally drove off after giving me a quick run-down of where I could find dinner, breakfast, and a store, I unpacked the Jeep, carefully trudging up the stairs.

"Well, Sammy, I guess this is home," I said as I poured a bowl of food for him. "For now anyway."

He stood on his hind legs, placed his paws on my shoulders and licked my face. His seal of approval. And if Sammy, the smartest dog in the world, liked the place, and Pops, the smartest man in the world, had kept it for me, then who was I to question it?

The bar across the street served food, and although it wasn't one of Buck's recommendations, it was close and I could bring Sammy so I wouldn't look like a total nerd eating by myself. The rear part of the bar had a large patio area that spilled onto the beach, and we sat out there as the sun lowered in the sky, Sammy keeping me company while I ate a burger and fries. The food wasn't bad and the atmosphere righteous, but when people— couples and groups—began filling up the place for cocktails and the live band setting up to play later, I took my cue to leave.

I used their pay phone out front to check in with Bex.

"I'm sorry, who is this?" Bex's mom asked, catching me off guard.

"It's me, Jacey. From college?"

"Oh, huh. I don't think Rebecca has ever mentioned you. Does she have your number, honey?"

Bex had always talked about her mom losing her mind, but this was the first time I'd ever heard it for myself. How many times had I met her? Stayed at their house for the weekend? Shaking my head, I simply said, "No, I don't really have one right now. I'm in Florida. I'll call back another time."

"She's not here much, dear. She's moved into her apartment at school and spends most of her time there with her roommate. But I can tell her you called."

And before I could say anything, the line went dead. Bex's roommate? She had to have been lying to her mother. That was the only explanation, which was better than the alternatives—Bex was pissed at me and had found someone to replace me or her mother really had gone over the deep end. The first one sucked for me and the second one really sucked for her. But as it was, I worried about her. She hadn't said anything two nights ago about going anywhere else or moving in with anyone for the summer. So where was she really?

The question gnawed at me as Sammy and I took a walk before heading back to our new place. Well, our temporary place. I still wasn't sure whether to trust Buck's suggestion. While Sammy ran up and down the white beach and nipped at the gentle waves sliding onto shore, I squished my butt into the soft sand and shuffled through the business cards Buck had given me. Only half of the sun showed over the horizon, streaking the sky with pinks and purples and providing barely enough light for me to study the cards.

I couldn't help my suspicion of the first one, bright orange paper with black ink, because Buck had been recommending him so highly. Maybe that makes no sense, but I didn't quite trust Buck himself. The second card, white with metallic gold lettering, made me think of high dollar signs. The last wasn't a card at all, but a scrap piece of paper with the name Humphrey and a phone number handwritten in blue ink. This one piqued my interest—probably cheap and perhaps a little rebellious of the "professional" establishment. Just my type. If I decided to do this, the handwritten number would be the first one I called.

Probably the smartest thing I should do, though, was talk to another real estate agent and make sure I wasn't sinking a bunch of dough into something that would never sell for what I put into it. That would be the mature adult decision, and whether I had wanted to or not, I'd been forced to become a mature adult.

When Sammy and I re-entered the upstairs unit, I sure didn't feel like one. My gaze slid over the dark room and I suddenly felt like a little girl, lost and alone. Completely alone. I barely made it through the door before the grief slammed into me. I curled into a ball on the pallet I'd already made with my sleeping bag and blankets, and I bawled. Sammy lay against me, trying to lap up my tears, but he gave in when they fell too fast for him to keep up.

I hadn't cried like this since Trudy had called me at the dorm to tell me about Pops. In fact, I hadn't cried at all since the funeral, constantly keeping myself busy, moving, looking to the next thing to be done. The tasks were brainless, no tough decisions to be made since Pops had already made them. All but one, anyway. Now nothing more remained to do except take care of this rundown apartment building. And I had to make a decision without any idea of what Pops really wanted—if this place was so important to him, why had he never mentioned it before?—and without anyone I knew to give me advice I could trust.

"Pops," I said aloud when the tears dried, "I don't know if you're there, if you can hear me. I never thought so, and you probably aren't. You're dead and gone and I have to accept that. But ... but if there's any chance you are ... can you please help me? I don't know what to do. I have no clue what you would want me to do. Please, Pops, if there's such thing as souls and spirits and you have any way of still being here in some kind of form, please tell me. Give me a sign. I can't do this by myself."

Of course, he didn't answer. He was gone. The ideas of souls and spirits and "next lives" were simply comfort tools used to help people cope with the death of loved ones. Pops was gone. No part of him remained to give me answers or even a sign.

When I was ten, an old lady ran a stoplight and T-boned Pops and me, slamming into the driver's side. Pops suffered a couple of broken ribs and we both had some scratches and bruises, but at the time, I believed he was going to die. "Don't worry, little bird, I'll never leave you," he'd promised but even then I knew better. After all, my parents had left me, hadn't they? Everyone dies. I dreamt of that accident, the screech of the brakes and slam of metal against metal ringing in my ears, but in my dream, Pops never looked at me to say he'd never leave me. Because he already had.

I awoke slowly, the sounds of the accident still reverberating in my mind. It took me a few seconds to realize they weren't in my dream or my head. The horrible sound of metal scraping against metal and concrete came from right outside, followed by a loud crash. I rushed to the door and threw it open.

Three things happened simultaneously:

My gaze landed on the metal staircase to my door laying on its side on the ground where a dark-haired man stood frowning at it.

I yelled, "What the hell?"

And my body remained on its trajectory through the door ... and into nothing but empty air.

CHAPTER 10

My arms flailed. My stomach fell faster than the rest of me, and a scream ripped through my throat and out my mouth. And the next thing I knew, I slammed into a hard body, strong arms catching me without a waver in their owner's stance. My breath heaved out and didn't return. A jolt of energy ran through my body, a tingling sensation hitting every nerve. With eyes bugging out of my head, I looked up into my savior's face. He stared back at me with astonished—and familiar—eyes.

"I know you." This time, the words flew out of my mouth before I could stop them, even while the word *dyad* whispered in my mind.

Something sparked in his own brown eyes—the same sense of familiarity. Neither of us seemed to be able to break the lock we had on each other.

"I don't think so," he muttered gruffly. "Are you okay? Can I put you down?"

His gaze scanned my body carefully as though he studied every freckle for injury, leaving a trail of goose bumps in its wake. Embarrassed, I struggled in his arms until finally he set me on my feet. The sound of Sammy's bark from the doorway registered in my brain. I gave him the *silence* sign, and he quieted.

"Looks like you'll live," the guy said, and his sarcasm hit me the wrong way.

"How did you do that?" I demanded. Sure he had a muscular form—a very nice, delicious form that made him the epitome of "tall, dark, and handsome"—and I weighed no more than a buck-ten, but still. "How did you catch me so easily from a two-story fall?"

He smirked. "It's not exactly two stories. If you were on the roof, that would be two stories."

I narrowed my eyes. "You know what I mean. How did you do it?"

"Honestly, I don't know. You were falling. Someone had to catch you, and since no one else was around, I volunteered." He shrugged. "It was my fault anyway. Guess I felt obligated. Don't make me regret it, okay?"

He returned to the staircase, studying the braces that had been anchored into the wall not five minutes ago.

"Ah, man! What the hell did you do to my stairs?" My astonishment and embarrassment quickly turned to anger and frustration.

"Seems I did you a favor."

"Excuse me? You ripped my stairs from the wall! Nearly killed me!"

"An eight-foot drop likely wouldn't kill you. And they *fell* from the wall."

"You said it was your fault I fell. What did you do?" I put a hand on my hip, shook a finger at him and ranted on. "And I do know you. I recognize you, anyway. Your hair's shorter, but it's only hair. Not much of a disguise. You were at the show in Charlottesville. You pulled me out of the fight. All the way up in *Virginia*. And now you're *here*, right where I am. Again. You better start explaining, or I'll call the cops."

He smirked again, eyeing my wagging finger. I didn't know whether to admire the grin—a hint of dimples showed when his full lips lifted like that—or hit it right off his face.

"You're a feisty one, aren't you? Especially for such a little thing," he said, and my hand balled into a fist in natural reaction to his condescending tone. He lifted his hands in the air in surrender. I couldn't help but notice his smooth, tanned skin stretched taught over the long and strong muscles of his hands and tried not to think about what they would feel like against my body again. I shook my head, erasing those errant thoughts.

"Explain," I repeated, now through gritted teeth.

He rocked back on his heels and crossed his arms over his chest, the muscles straining against his black Guns N' Roses t-shirt.

"I heard you wanted to know what it would take to fix this place up. Thought I'd check it out to get an idea of what it needed." His dark gaze darted over to the old, rusty staircase lying on its side, then back at me. "I'd say the stairs need to be replaced, for starters."

"Is that your game?" I spewed. "Come over and wreck everything so I'll pay you to fix it? What kind of split does Buck get? He probably told you to start with the stairs, knowing I was up there and now have no choice but to fix them. I mean, my stuff and my dog are up there. Oh, man." I turned to look up at the door. "Sammy? You okay, boy?"

Sammy wagged his whole body and let out a happy bark. I pushed my hand through my tangled hair and realized for the first time I still wore what I slept in—an old t-shirt and boy's boxer shorts.

"I'll get my ladder," the guy said, turning for his truck parked in the overgrown lot. He returned with a long ladder and leaned it against the building's side, having no problem with reaching the door upstairs.

"Hold up a minute," I ordered. He started up the ladder even as I continued. "Is this part of your charges? Because this is totally bogus. I didn't ask for any of this. I don't even know if I want to fix anything. I'm not sure I can even afford it. So don't be—"

He reached the top, pulled Sammy under one arm like an oversized football—and Sammy *let* him—and shimmied his way down one-handed.

"No charge," he said, setting Sammy down. "I dig dogs."

My arms fell limply to my side, and no words came. His dark eyes gleamed as he surveyed me, making my thoughts go to inappropriate places, especially under the circumstances. Then he cocked his head, and it was all I could do to not become putty in his hands.

"Can we start over?" he asked. He held his hand out to me. "I'm Micah. I do a little work for the locals here and there. They call me the village handyman. You won't find anyone better—or cheaper—but if you want me to go, I'll go."

I looked at his hand and back up at his face. "And what about my stairs?"

His hand remained in the space between us. "I gave them a shake before trusting my weight on them to go knock on your door. They fell right off the wall. They were about to go any time, so you're lucky it didn't happen while you were on them. Or, worse, someone else who would be happy to sue you."

"And what'll this cost to fix?"

He rubbed his square chin covered in dark stubble, as if he hadn't taken the time to shave this morning. "Tell you what. You buy the supplies, and I'll put up the new stairs for only a thank-you for saving your life."

"And why would you do that?"

"Guess I feel a little guilty, even if they were about to come down anyway. Besides, you'll get a sample of my work before deciding to hire me." He stuck his hand out again, and a real smile spread across his face, fully displaying dimples more heart-stopping than I'd expected. His grin grew even wider at my expression.

Blowing out a breath of both reluctance and embarrassment, I reached up for his hand. As soon as our palms touched, that strange jolt flipped my stomach and my head spun. Micah must have felt something, too, because his eyes widened, although his hand tightened around mine.

"Um . . . fine," I choked out, extricating my hand from his before the bones in my legs began to melt.

"Excellent." He seemed to recover himself, and the smirk returned. "Of course, your other options are a retired dude from New York who charges you as if he were still there although he prefers fishing to working so he never shows up, and a sixty-nine-year-old who's usually drunk and likes to work in his speedo and nothing else."

My nose wrinkled involuntarily at the visual. If this were a beauty pageant, I didn't have to see the others, even if they weren't old, swindling wrinkle-bags. I doubted anyone here—or anywhere, really—compared to Micah. He was the hottest guy I'd ever seen. *Ever*. But this wasn't a pageant and even though I felt like I'd known him before—really *known* him, not just recognized him—I still questioned his intentions. If he thought he could take me for a ride, he had another thing coming. Well . . . unless it was a ride of the naked kind . . . . I blinked. Man, where were these horn-dog thoughts coming from?

"If we book it to the lumberyard, I can probably have your stairs done by the end of the day," Micah said as Sammy came running up to him after doing his business. My dog nudged his nose against Micah's hand and received a scratch behind the ears. Sammy loved this stranger. *Traitor*, I couldn't help but think, although I knew if Sammy liked Micah, the guy couldn't be too bad. "You can use the ladder to get your things, though." His eyes scanned me from head to toe. "Like some clothes, maybe?"

I looked down at myself. Awesome. I was totally nipping out through the thin fabric of the t-shirt. I crossed my arms over my chest and my face heated to the temperature of hell. I made a beeline for the ladder.

"I mean, I don't have a problem with what you're wearing," Micah called after me. "Could even get us a discount at the lumberyard. Up to you."

My face flushed even hotter, and I nearly missed the first step of the ladder. Then I rushed the whole way up, once again angry and embarrassed, now with myself because I let him get to me. No guy had ever affected me like Micah did. I was reacting like a schoolgirl, and I hated it. The fact that he hadn't explained how we'd "coincidentally" run into each other in two different states at two different times had even slipped my mind, which was unacceptable. Whatever Sammy thought of the guy, it was a little creepy he'd show up again so randomly.

After an awkward sponge bath since I had nothing to clean the shower insert or even a shower curtain, I dressed and returned to the ground, my mind changed. I had decided last night if I had any work done, it would be by someone I trusted, not some dude who freaked me out so much, let alone was the one sleazy Buck pushed so hard on me. Micah probably made up those bogus lies about the other two so I wouldn't even think about them, but I wasn't falling for it. No, I would make my own decision, not be forced into this. So when my feet touched the ground, I pulled the two business cards and scrap paper out of my jeans pocket, and turned, ready to announce my decision, only to find Micah playing fetch with Sammy.

"He's an awesome dog," Micah said as Sammy ran up to him with a stick in his mouth. Micah sank into a squat and scrubbed Sammy's neck and patted him on the back. "Aren't you, boy?"

Sammy licked Micah's cheek.

"Sammy," I said, trying to sound stern because he wasn't supposed to lick people's faces, but the word came out as more of a jealous whine. Sammy came bounding over to me, sat at my feet and looked up at me with a smile in his eyes. I dipped down and hugged him. "Of course you're a good boy. You're *my* boy."

Micah eyed me again. Making me feel self-conscious. Again.

"*What?*" I asked.

"You just, uh . . . never mind. You'll figure it out soon enough."

"What?" I demanded again.

"You're a little overdressed is all."

I'd put on another pair of ripped-up jeans (I didn't have any other kind), a loose, black top and a black tank under it, which was necessary because the top often slid off one shoulder or the other. I wasn't into showing off bra straps. Since destroying most of my punk clothes, not much remained of my wardrobe, and this was one of the last clean outfits left.

"Overdressed? For the lumberyard?" What kind of place was this?

"No, for the heat. There's a reason most people around here wear as few clothes as they can get away with."

I cocked my head. "You're wearing jeans." Which he looked very good in.

"I'll be working. Trust me, those clothes will be coming off you soon enough."

My cheeks heated again.

"Not likely," I muttered. I wasn't like the locals with their deeply bronzed skin. I had typical redhead coloring with fair skin and freckles, and others would be blinded by the sun reflecting off my flesh if I exposed any more of it. This had always been my excuse anyway when the talk of bathing suits ever came up, and I stuck to it now. Micah didn't argue, but simply shrugged, as if he knew he'd be proven right soon enough. Whatever.

"You ready? We'll take my truck," Micah said.

I waved the small papers in my hand. "We're not going. I changed my mind."

Micah stopped in his tracks, and his lovely smile slid off his face, replaced by disappointment. Dammit. I didn't like that look on him. I had to mentally kick myself, because I shouldn't care. He was only disappointed because he wouldn't be taking my money.

"Okay, then," he said amicably enough. "So which one are you going with? Butch? His orange card matches his speedo. He also happens to be Buck's brother. He's your real estate agent, right? I'm sure he really talked Butch's work up. Or will it be Paul, the one with the fancy card? He's probably already out on the boat, so you'll have to wait until this evening to even get a quote."

"Neither," I said all smart-assish as I waved the scrap paper in the air. "This one. Humphrey. So you can—" I paused as his words fully registered. "Wait. You're not orange-card-dude?"

Micah wrinkled his nose and forehead. "Not even." Then he held his hand out again. "Once again. Micah. Micah Humphrey."

His dimples showed as he took in the expression on my face, then pulled his hand back to his side. Were we both a little scared of what happened when we touched?

"So," he said, once more moving toward his truck. "If we put Sammy in the bed, will he stay?"

I didn't answer at first, but nibbled on my inner lip. The coincidences were stacking up, making me wonder if this was good kismet or bad karma. I *had* asked Pops for a sign last night, but never expected to actually be given one. Getting into a truck and going somewhere with a guy I'd met less than an hour ago didn't seem very smart. Not something Pops would condone.

"Your Jeep won't fit everything we need," Micah said, noticing my hesitation. "And it's a bit of drive to take two cars. If you'd rather Sammy get in front with us, that's fine. I just thought it'd be a little crowded."

When Micah opened his truck door—the passenger side, as though being a gentleman—Sammy followed him over and jumped right in. As if to say Micah could be trusted. *Jeez, Pops, if I didn't know better, I'd say you're really screwing with me.* With a sigh, I climbed in after my dog. At least Sammy was big, creating a decent barrier between Micah and me. I only hoped he hadn't gone completely traitor and would still protect me if Micah made a suspicious move. I tried to ignore a certain part of me that envied the dog because he got to sit so close to the hot dude on the other side.

"So . . . UVA?" I asked as we turned off the road the bridge was on and into the traffic of "town."

"UVA what?" Micah asked, not taking his eyes off the road.

"Guess not," I muttered. I didn't think so—he didn't appear to be UVA material. Probably not James Madison either. "Radford? Virginia Commonwealth? Um . . ."

I wracked my brain for other colleges I knew within an hour-or-so drive from Charlottesville. Of course, he could have come from farther away like Bex and I had, but I doubted it. Only girlfriends and groupies did that, especially in the dead of winter.

"Should I know what you're talking about?" Micah asked.

"Just trying to figure out where you go to school. You never said what you were doing in Charlottesville that night and now you're here, so I figured you go to school around there, and you're down here to work for the summer. You from around here?"

"No. Across the board."

"What does that mean?"

"Not from around here. Not from Virginia either. And do I really look like the scholarly type?"

"Do I?"

His eyes cut over to me, and the corner of his mouth turned up in a half-smile. "Touché."

"But you're not? You don't go to college?"

"Not exactly. Do you?"

He was being evasive, so I thought I should be, too. "Not exactly."

It was true—I'd basically dropped out last semester and still hadn't finished registration for the fall—even if the plan was to return in a couple of months.

"So what were you doing there?" I asked.

"What were you doing there?" he countered.

"Seeing the band, of course." I didn't go into details about why that particular band. He didn't need to know anymore about my life at this point of our, er, relationship. Or whatever you call it. "Wanted to check it out."

"Yeah, me, too." Micah didn't elaborate either, and my frustration grew.

"How'd you get from there to here?"

"I drove." He patted the dashboard as I let out a groan of frustration. Before I could complain, though, he continued. "You have Sammy. I have Ginger. This truck is my best friend. We've been through a lot together, including a lot of states."

"So you're a drifter?"

"You could say that."

"But why here?" I pressed.

"I heard there was work. Was hooked up with a cool place to live. So I've been here for the past few months." He peered sideways at me again. "I could ask you the same, you know. What you were doing there and here, right where I happen to be."

"I have good reasons. For both."

"So do I."

"Well, you know mine. I didn't show up here for the hell of it. I didn't have a choice. You know that. So what are *your* reasons?"

He looked at me full-on now, over Sammy's back, with a big smile on his face and a gleam in those mocha eyes. My stomach dropped like it had when I'd fallen from the door this morning. "You show me yours and I'll show you mine? Is that what you want to play? Because there are much more fun versions than this."

My mouth might have fallen open a little. His grin growing wider, Micah turned his attention back to the road.

"Last I checked, coincidences aren't a crime," he said. "That's all it is. A weird coincidence."

Reluctantly, I nodded in agreement. What else could I do? He obviously wasn't going to give me any other answers, and I certainly didn't want to piss him off since Sammy and I were currently at his mercy. Who knew what he could to do to us? Sheesh. What had I gotten myself into? I needed to be very wary. Alert. I patted my pockets for my switchblade and pepper spray I always kept with me. Both were in easy reach.

"So, didn't like the skinhead thing?" I asked, changing the subject.

"What the hell are you talking about now? Do you ever speak English?"

"I am! The last time I saw you, you had long hair. Now it's extremely short, as if you'd gone skinhead but changed your mind."

He snorted. "Definitely not skinhead. Those guys are assholes."

Agreed. I'd never met one I liked. "Then what? Some kind of makeover?"

He chuckled. "Once again, I could ask you the same. You look different, too."

I swallowed. He was right, and for some reason, I felt the need to explain. Maybe something inside me wanted to trust him. I ran my fingers through my straggly hair that barely reached my shoulders. Trudy had helped me return the color to natural, but we'd had to cut it pretty short. At least I hadn't shaved any of my head for over a year, or she probably would have sheared it all off and given me a wig. Apparently, Micah had noticed the change, as well as the lack of heavy eyeliner. In fact, I'd been going with the natural look lately, trying to be as inconspicuous as possible these days. I inhaled a deep breath and let it out.

"My grandfather was my last living relative." I swallowed again to keep away the lump trying to form in my throat. "When he died, I wigged out at first. Practically drank myself to death. When I finally came out of it, I knew I couldn't go back to that whole punk scene. So here I am, trying to be a grown-up."

Micah's right hand left the steering wheel and made the smallest move toward me, but then he pulled it back, as if changing his mind. Yep. He'd definitely felt something when we touched.

"I didn't know about your grandfather," he said quietly. "I'm sorry. I know how you feel."

Now it was my turn to snort. "I hate it when people say that. *Nobody* knows how I feel. Not really."

"Well, maybe not exactly. You still have your friends, right? The girl you were at the show with, at least?"

"Bex? Yeah, I guess."

"Well, there you go. You have someone still."

I peered over at him. His face resembled a stone statue's, and his knuckles shone white, his hands gripping the steering wheel so hard.

"And you don't?" I asked.

"There's a reason I'm a drifter, as you put it. Nothing to tie me down."

"No parents? No brothers or sisters?"

"I grew up in foster homes and couldn't wait for the day to escape. Closest I've had to real brothers was in the Marines Corps. But, well, shit happens." He clammed up then. I was surprised he'd even told me as much as he had. Not normal for a guy, especially with a girl he just met. Then again, maybe he'd felt the same as I had—that we somehow already knew each other.

"So ex-military, huh? That explains the hair. You finally had the chance to grow it out and didn't like it?"

His hand ran over his short dark hair. "Pretty much. Old habits die hard."

"How long were you in?"

"A little over four years. I enlisted the day I turned 18."

"And?"

"And what?"

"Well, you obviously didn't enlist for the education benefits. You already said as much. So not a good career choice?"

His face hardened again. "You ask too many questions. I've answered more than I should."

As if on cue, he turned into a parking lot of a large building with a fenced-in lumberyard to its side. Time to focus back on the business at hand, but my last question burned my curiosity. Actually, Micah's reaction was what ate at me. Had something happened? It must have been something bad. Had he been dishonorably discharged? Ah, man. Maybe trusting him had been a bad idea after all.

"I'll go put the order in for all the supplies, then you can go in and pay," Micah said, sliding out of his door and slamming it shut. He strode off, leaving me with Sammy.

I watched the smooth way his body moved as he headed for the store's doors, admiring his physique while absent-mindedly rubbing at my arm. When he disappeared inside, the ache in my left wrist fully registered in my brain.

"What in the hell?" I shrieked, startling Sammy. The flame mark, which I'd forgotten about when it had faded to nearly non-existent, had returned, much brighter and more defined than before.

CHAPTER 11

I rubbed frantically at my wrist, licked my fingers and rubbed some more. "Oh, my god. Oh, my god. What *is* this thing?"

I jumped out of the truck, completely freaked out, and paced up and down the side of it, grinding my wrist against my jeans the whole time. The flame only brightened.

"This is so bogus. What am I going to do?" I whined to myself. I had no way of hiding the mark, which had become pretty damn conspicuous now. Would Micah notice its sudden appearance? Maybe he'd think it had been there all along. Not likely, though. It practically glowed—no way he could have missed it before. *Who cares what Micah thinks?! I have a fucking tattoo that's NOT a tattoo!* Where did the thing come from? Why?

"Your stuff is ready and waiting for your money," Micah huffed behind me. I turned around with my hand behind my back, but he'd already made it to the other side and was sliding into the truck.

I didn't know what to do, but figured I better act nonchalant or he'd think I was a freak and leave me stranded there. I hurried inside the store and immediately searched for the bathroom. But like before, the mark wouldn't wash away. After several minutes with no success, I knew I was pushing my luck, so I went to the counter and paid. I thought I'd taken too long when I first walked outside, my left arm held tightly against my body, because the truck was gone. The faded red color flashed in the corner of my eye, though, and I found Micah loading the back with supplies and Sammy hanging his head out the window that slid open to the bed.

Reluctantly, I headed for the truck's tailgate to help Micah load, although I didn't know how I'd keep the bright red and orange flame hidden.

"Don't worry about it," Micah said roughly. "I'm almost done."

"I can—"

"Just get in the truck, okay?" he barked, making me jump.

I let out a low growl, not liking his tone with me, but went to the cab without a word. Micah climbed in a few minutes later, and we drove the fifteen miles to my place with the radio blasting heavy metal, drowning out any chance for conversation. I couldn't for the life of me figure out what had put him into such a bad mood so quickly. Maybe he remembered another job he could have done— one that actually paid? Well, I could certainly pay him, if that's what he wanted. The stairs had needed to be replaced anyway. And I didn't need his bad attitude—my anguish capacity had already reached its max as I fretted about the glowing mark.

"I gotta go take care of something," Micah said, his voice still gruff. He'd stopped on the road, not bothering to pull into the parking lot. "I'll be back later."

"I can pay you, if that's the problem," I said.

"A deal's a deal," he growled.

"But I can—"

"It's not a problem!" he nearly yelled. He inhaled through flared nostrils, then added more quietly, "Really, it's not you or this. I'm just going to grab some lunch."

I almost laughed. "Wow. You sure get grumpy when you're hungry."

He grunted in response. I led Sammy out the passenger door and watched Micah take off, his wheels throwing sand and other debris on the road. I knew this couldn't be about a growling stomach. Something else was wrong.

A strange sensation washed over me once he left. A sense of something missing, as if I were no longer complete. As weird as it sounds, I felt as though a part of me had left with him. *That's not just weird. It's wrong! You've only known the guy for a few hours.* Or had I? Why did I feel like I'd known him for longer . . . forever? Actually, an odd feeling deep inside me, in my very core, hinted it was about more than *knowing* Micah. Whatever connection we had, it went way deeper.

Which was totally whacked out.

This line of absurd thinking would make me crazy, so I concentrated instead on my own lunch. I'd skipped breakfast and had no food in the fridge. I also needed cleaning supplies, so Sammy and I climbed into the Jeep and headed for the local store.

Not knowing how long Micah would be gone, I hurried through the Safeway, grabbing snacks and junk food and a case of Diet Coke, along with sponges, detergents, bleach, and a cheap plastic shower curtain, trying not to care about its transparency. Except for Sammy I lived alone, but my stomach still fluttered uncomfortably at the small chance of someone seeing me naked.

"Interesting tattoo you have there," said a male voice from behind me as I stood in line. Having nearly forgotten about it already, I didn't realize he spoke to me until he added, "Does the flame mean anything?"

I looked up at him in shock. For some reason, my heart burst into a gallop. In his late twenties maybe, with blond, spiky hair and inky black eyes, he looked like a Billy Idol wannabe, but instinct told me his good looks lay precariously on the surface. Something ugly and dark churned underneath, waiting for the opportunity to shed its pretty skin.

"Um . . . no," I said breathlessly. The man tilted his head as he looked deep into my eyes, and I swore, if we truly had souls, he tried to peer right into mine. The hairs on the back of my neck rose, and my palms became clammy. I spun in a hurry and quickly pushed my cart out of line. "Forgot something," I mumbled.

Bandages. I'd forgotten bandages, the only way I figured I could hide the bright mark until it hopefully faded again. Thankfully, the spooky guy was gone by the time I returned up front to the checkout.

Hauling the goods up the ladder wasn't easy, but taking several trips, I managed. After putting everything away, I took my switchblade out and went into the bathroom to perform minor surgery. I couldn't wait for the mark to simply fade, especially since it seemed to be growing and brightening even more. If for any reason someone pulled off the bandage—someone as in Micah—the questions would fly, and I had no answers. At least, no sensible answers. And most importantly, if I could make the flame go away faster, I'd be a lot less wigged out myself.

So I sterilized the blade with a lighter I'd found in my Jeep (probably dropped by Bex a long time ago), gritted my teeth, and began dragging it across my skin. I'd been personally introduced to real pain before and I wasn't into inflicting it on myself, so I hoped scraping off a layer or two of skin would be enough. Tiny beads of blood popped up on my forearm. Excellent. Even if I couldn't make the mark disappear completely, a good scab would keep it hidden. I cleaned the "wound" and wrapped it in a bandage.

Now I needed a story to go with it. I tried to think of one as I began cleaning, but nothing came to mind. I considered purposely breaking the bathroom mirror, one of the few things in the efficiency that needed absolutely nothing done to it. At some point, noises that sounded appropriate for construction came from outside, so Micah had returned and set to work without even a hello. This disappointed me more than it should have.

After a few hours, I couldn't take it anymore. I'd tried to ignore the desire to see him again, but it had only built up into an urgent need that possessed my body like a demon. If I didn't go downstairs, my crackling nerves might cause me to climb the walls and hang from the ceiling, projectile vomiting green slime all over my clean kitchen. Okay, maybe not so bad I needed an exorcist, but before my brain caught up with my body, I'd already begun hedging my way down the ladder, a plastic cup filled with ice and water in one hand.

"Thought you might be thirsty," I said once my feet landed on solid ground and the electric saw had turned off. Four wooden posts stood upright in newly poured cement in the ground, and Micah was now standing at some kind of portable saw contraption, cutting boards for the stair treads.

"Thank you," he said, not bothering to remove his work gloves before taking the cup from me. He downed the whole cup then refilled it from a nearby thermos. *Idiot.* Of course he had his own water. This was his job after all. "I'd buy you a six-pack instead, but I'm not old enough. But maybe food would be better anyway? Wouldn't want you getting all grumpy again."

That sexy smirk of his made an appearance. "Sorry about that."

"No problem. I've been warned now. So, uh, I'll make sure there's a pizza here waiting before you're done tonight."

The smirk disappeared and something flashed in his eyes before he looked down at his hands. "As good as it sounds, I'll have to pass."

Well. He'd pretty much told me he didn't have a girlfriend or any friends for that matter, so he probably didn't have much in the way of other plans. Which meant his rejection of my offer was a nice way of rejecting me altogether. Not that I'd been asking him on a date or anything. I thought it'd be nice to buy him dinner since he wouldn't let me pay him.

I forced a weak smile. "Guess I'll have to eat alone then."

"I don't think you'll be alone," Micah said.

Man. How patronizing. "Of course not. I always have Sammy."

His eyes darkened. "That's not all. Seems you have a guest."

His head moved in the very slightest of nods toward the bar parking lot across the street. I had no idea what he meant at first, but something instinctual made my eyes zero in on a blue Ford Taurus sitting in the middle of the lot. A light blond, spiky head could be seen through the windshield.

Micah's voice dropped to nearly a whisper. "He's been sitting there since I got here. Never went inside. No one's come out to him. Any idea who he is?"

"I can't really see him, but I think he might be the guy I ran into at the store." A chill tingled at the base of my spine as I remembered those inky black eyes. "I can't believe he followed me. What a creep."

"I'll try to keep an eye on him," Micah said. "I don't like it. But I guess I'm not surprised. A young girl who looks like you do probably attracts all kinds."

I looked at him with my head tilted, not sure whether to take his statement as a compliment or not. He returned my gaze, and his face broke into that sublime grin, dimples and all.

"Especially when you run around like that." He eyed my bare shoulders. As he'd predicted, I'd taken off my top and only wore the tank now. "Wish I would've been wrong. You're quite the distraction."

Compliment. Definitely a compliment. His husky tone sent my insides into a hot, swirling mess. I smiled like an idiot until I remembered his rejection not two minutes ago. He was a flirt, nothing more.

"Yeah, well, I'm sure he'll go away," I said, referring to the perv across the street. "Come up when you're done, and maybe he'll think you're not only here to build my stairs. I promise I won't make you stay for pizza or anything."

The words came out a little bitchier than I'd intended so before I made a bigger fool of myself, I hurried up the ladder and went back to my cleaning.

"He's gone." Micah's voice came from my doorway a few hours later, right as I finished scrubbing every nook and cranny of the bathroom. I now felt comfortable taking a shit and a shower in there, and my kitchen shone, too.

"Told ya," I said as I came out of the bathroom, pulling the cleaning gloves off. "He just needed to realize I'm not an easy target." Then I frowned. "Hopefully that doesn't mean he's off to another victim."

Micah glanced out the front French doors. "Yeah. Hopefully." He looked back at me, and his gaze immediately fell to the bandage on my arm. I'd been able to keep it hidden earlier but had forgotten just now. His brows furrowed, and his voice came out thick with concern. A little too much concern, if you asked me. "What happened? Are you okay?"

"I, uh . . ." *Quick! Think!* I still hadn't invented a story. I glanced around, avoiding his eyes, until my gaze fell on the darkening space behind him and the doorway. "I slid down the ladder a little when I was bringing groceries up. Caught my arm on the edge. It's no biggie. Really."

Micah's eyes narrowed as he studied me carefully as if looking for a different answer. I hoped my face wouldn't give my lie away. Finally he shook his head.

"Maybe I need to get you a pair of work gloves," he muttered as his fingers smoothed down the hem of his glove against the bulging muscle of his forearm. "Well, since he's gone, I'll get going, too. You want me to bring Sammy up for the night?"

"Guess that means the stairs aren't done?"

"The cement footings need to set overnight. I'll finish in the morning."

"Well, crap. What *am* I going to do about Sammy? I can't ask him to go from now until morning without going potty." I glanced down at my dog who waited at the bottom of the ladder. He'd stayed outside all day, keeping Micah company. He'd probably hold it all night in fear of otherwise disappointing me, but that wasn't fair. I sighed. "Maybe I'll sleep in my Jeep tonight. I certainly can't carry him up the ladder. He weighs almost as much as I do."

"What about downstairs? Is there a reason you picked the unit with the deadly steps?"

"This one's in the best shape, especially now that I spent five hours cleaning it. Those down there . . . just no way. I'd rather sleep in my Jeep."

"Not exactly safe," Micah muttered. He ran a gloved hand over the short hairs on the back of his head. "Look, I can come by later and bring Sammy up."

"What? No! I can't ask you to do that."

"It's no problem." Micah made his way to the first rungs of the ladder, as if trying to escape any further argument from me. Then he muttered something I wasn't sure he meant for me to hear: "I'd feel better checking on you anyway."

I chose not to respond because in a way the words prickled me—I can take care of myself! I wanted to protest—but on the other hand, I was kind of glad he'd be coming back. Just in case the stalker-dude did, too.

After Micah left, I gathered some money and my keys, shut the door and made my way down the ladder. Sammy and I walked to the pizza parlor down the street. Although I'd bought a bunch of food, mentioning pizza to Micah had set off a craving I didn't want to fight. Besides, I couldn't bring myself to sit upstairs, eating, while Sammy was stuck on the ground by himself. He wouldn't run away or even go exploring without me—he was a good dog and loved me. I wanted to show him I deserved his loyalty, so I spent the evening outside with him, sitting on the beach and watching the waves as the sky pulled its glittering blanket of night over the world.

Eventually, however, I had to return to the apartment to get a drink and use the bathroom, which meant leaving him for a few minutes. As luck would have it, that's when all hell broke loose. I was still buttoning my jeans as I ran out of the bathroom at the sound of Sammy's frantic barks and growls. I'd never heard my Sammy sound so vicious.

"Stay up there!" Micah's shout boomed from the darkness below, followed by the sounds of some kind of fight. Sammy was still barking and growling, and I could see his light fur as he bounced around. They weren't fighting each other. So who?

When Sammy let out a yelp of pain, I pulled my switchblade out of my pocket, turned in the doorway and set one foot on a rung. The whole ladder trembled. I looked down to find a shaved head already halfway up the ladder. Not Micah's dark hair on that head. Rather, Micah and Billy Idol-dude came into a patch of light on the ground, throwing blows at each other. Even as he punched the other guy, Micah's foot swung out and kicked the bottom of the ladder. The whole thing slid to the side, then tumbled to the ground, baldy on top of it. I hopped back inside just in time.

Stuck, I could only watch as Micah fought with both men down below. Sammy helped, biting baldy's leg and yanking as hard as he could until his man went down. Then he went for the man's face, but baldy's fist plowed into Sammy's head. I screamed as my dog flew to the side, but he shot right up and charged again. This time he went directly for the balls. The guy fell to his knees, screaming, trying to push Sammy away but unable. I couldn't have been prouder of my baby. Micah's guy, also severely beaten, twisted out of Micah's grip and dove for the overgrown bushes at the side of the property. Sammy finally let go of baldy, who also jumped into the foliage. Then two black shadows rose from the shrubs and flew off. Very similar to those in the icy alley in Virginia.

Micah let out an angry yell.

In a split second, he had the ladder up and Sammy under one arm, and he was flying up the side of the house. We both dropped to our knees by my dog, checking him for injuries. Blood matted the fur by his shoulder—a cut made by a knife. It wasn't bad and had already stopped bleeding. Thankfully, we found no other injuries. As we rose to our feet, I couldn't help but inspect Micah.

When he grabbed my shoulders and pushed me against the wall, I figured he wasn't hurt.

"Who the hell are they?" he barked. "Who are *you*?"

I shook my head, my eyes wide. "I don't know! What do you mean?"

"Something's going on here, and I want to know what." He let go of my shoulders, only to grab the bandage on my wrist and yank. I gasped, half at the pain of the little hairs being ripped out and half at surprise. "What the fuck is this? Huh, Jacey? How do you explain it all?"

I pulled my arm across my body. "I told you. I scraped it going down the ladder."

What was wrong with him?

He leaned closer to me, his face right in mine. "Don't. Lie. To. Me. That's not a scrape."

"What do you—" I held my arm out, and my jaw fell open. He was right. The scrape—the scab I'd so painfully created—was gone. The flame was more defined and brighter than ever.

"Explain it," Micah ordered. He held up his own arm. "Explain this!"

If my jaw could drop any farther, it'd be bruised from hitting the ground. A flame, identical to mine, marked Micah's skin directly under his right wrist.

"I . . . I don't . . ." I shook my head as my mouth stammered over the words. "I have no idea. Where did you get it?" More words began to fight their way out. "And what do you mean, 'explain'? *You* explain. You tell me what's going on, because I have no idea!"

Micah threw his arms up in the air. The open door must have caught his attention because he reached over and slammed it closed. Then he turned back to me and placed one hand against the wall on each side of my head and leaned even closer than before, forcing me to press my back against the wall.

"You give me flack for being here, but you showed up after me. You could have followed me here. Brought your screwed up henchmen with you, pretending to stalk you but it's really me they're after, huh? And this mark? It showed up this afternoon out of nowhere. Nowhere! And it won't go away. What the hell is going on?"

My throat worked at a swallow while my lungs tried to draw in air at the same time. Both functions failed. I stared into Micah's eyes, drowning in them, completely losing myself in their dark pools, in *him*. I fought the urge to close the gap separating us, to press into him, become *within* him. The word *dyad* tumbled around my head once again.

"Jacey!" His hands were on my shoulders again, shaking me. "Breathe."

His voice sounded so far away although his eyes were still right there, pulling me in. Pinpricks of light flashed across my vision. My body softened, and I was okay with that because it was only a physical presence that mattered little. My soul was what mattered now. I *did* have one. We both did. And they were meant to be one. Our souls were two halves of one whole. I believed this with an absolute certainty.

"Jacey, please," Micah pleaded, his voice coming closer, begging me now rather than yelling. "Just breathe."

I realized his voice sounded so close now because his lips were against my ear. His muscular arms wrapped around my shoulders and cradled me against his hard chest. His breath caught, and now *he* seemed to be losing it. His body sagged into mine, and we barely held each other up. He wouldn't let go of me, but held tightly, and we both fell against the wall, then slid down it. We settled into a heap on the floor, legs entangled, arms wrapped around each other, foreheads pressed together. His eyes still never left mine, but they widened and deepened, and somehow I knew he was experiencing the same thing I had. His hands came to my face, holding me still. We both panted, breathing each other's air as something both magnificent and terrifying exchanged between us.

Something within me rose, more burning than physical desire, an overwhelming urge straight from the core of my existence. A primal, desperate compulsion to close the space between us until there was nothing, until we became one, indistinguishable mass. The need to bond.

"Jacey," Micah whispered. His eyes broke away from mine and stared at my lips as his tongue swiped over his own. "I need to . . . Can I . . . ?"

I nodded infinitesimally, and his mouth pressed against mine.

Our eyes closed, but the connection didn't break. It strengthened. He was gentle at first but only momentarily as the need for more exploded in both of us. His lips parted, and his tongue traced mine before pushing them open. Our tongues danced playfully, his darting in and out, barely brushing against mine, but then I opened my mouth more and let him in. And it was as if I let *all* of him in.

An intense rush flowed through me, filled me completely as though I'd been an empty vessel, made me feel whole although I'd never felt incomplete before. What I can only call our souls coming together.

I'm not the greatest writer. I don't know how to explain it. I don't even know if I could draw or paint what happened to us. Nobody would understand. Like the grief of a loved one's death, maybe those feelings weren't meant to be captured. All I can say is I'd never before believed in souls and spirits until then, but I can't deny ours greeted each other and bonded, *melded*, became one like they were supposed to be.

The feeling shook me to the core, turning everything I believed in upside down, freaking me out some, but filling me with crazed wonder, too. *The dyads are whole again.* With this nonsensical thought, a sense of peace washed over me.

It didn't last for long, though.

CHAPTER 12

 Our hands slid over each other's faces, necks, shoulders, daring to go further in exploration. The need for each other became more physical than anything, and when this thought registered in my mind, I forced myself to pull away before we went too far. Micah's eyes opened, and we stared at each other for a moment that lasted an eternity. In my peripheral vision, I saw Sammy sitting behind him, watching us, his head tilted to the side, his ears up, and his tail wagging. I blinked. Micah sucked in a breath. Our connection broke, and in an instant, he was on his feet.

"What the hell was that?" Micah breathed, staring at me like I was some kind of freak. As if I had attacked him or something. The accusation in both his tone and his eyes hurt, and I immediately became defensive.

"Most guys call it the best they've ever had," I snapped. "Most" guys as in three of the four I've ever even kissed, but that was beside the point.

"You know what I mean," he growled. His hands flew up and clasped together behind his head, and he began to pace. I slowly rose to my feet, hoping my noodle-like legs would hold me.

I did know what he meant, but I swallowed my pride. "Don't get your panties in such a bunch. It was just a kiss," I muttered.

My lips and chin felt swollen and rough, as if it was more than a simple kiss, though. His sexy stubble had done quite the number on my face for just a kiss. I glanced at the clock and couldn't believe over two hours had passed.

He was suddenly in front of me, his hands on my face gently but firmly. "If it was just a kiss, I'd be begging you for more because that's all I've wanted to do all day. *That*—what happened just now—was more than a kiss, and you know it." He let go of me and began to pace again. I leaned against the wall, my legs too wobbly to hold myself up. "So what was it? What's going on? First the mark . . . tattoo . . . whatever it is. Then those men. And now that . . . not just a kiss thing. You doing some kind of voodoo punk magic shit on me?"

I chuckled darkly. "As if such a thing existed."

"Then what is it, Jacey?" he yelled.

Adrenaline shot through my veins. I pushed off the wall and stepped in front of him.

"I don't know," I said through clenched teeth as I glared up at his face. "But it's not *me* doing this, so I'd appreciate it if you'd back the hell off me. This is wigging me out, too, you know."

He studied my face for several moments, waiting for my expression to break and show my lie. But I wasn't lying, and he eventually must have realized this. The sharp pierce of his mocha-brown eyes softened before he turned away from me. He walked over to the French doors and stared out into the blackness beyond. Or maybe he watched the bar's parking lot.

"Why don't we start with those men?" I suggested, hoping that talking this out would lead to some answers. "What happened?"

Micah heaved out a breath before turning around to face me. "I came over to bring Sammy up. When I came around the corner, he was at the bottom of the ladder, the hair on his back raised and his teeth bared at two men dressed all in black. When I asked who they were, the blond said he was a friend of yours.

Sammy started barking like a mad-dog, startling them, and they went into attack mode. The blond came after me while the bald guy ran for the ladder. You know the rest."

"They're definitely no friends of mine," I said. Micah's eyes showed he wasn't sure whether to believe me. "Look, the guy was behind me in line at the grocery store. That's the first time I've ever seen him, I swear. He creeped me out, so I left the line."

"They said something about how they should have made the hit in Virginia."

I threw my hands in the air with exasperation. "What do you want from me, Micah? I've never seen them before. I swear it! And why are you so paranoid? Maybe they meant a hit on *me*. They were at *my* place, after all."

"And who would want to kill you?"

The word sent a chill up my spine, and at the same time deflated my bravado. "I . . . I don't know. None of this makes sense."

"You're telling me." Micah walked over to the living room wall, slid down it to his butt, rested his elbows on his knees and dropped his head into his hands. I went over to my bedding by the opposite wall and sat down with a pillow in my lap, suddenly feeling exhausted. But I knew I wouldn't be able to sleep a wink.

"So who would want to kill *you*?" I asked. "Why are you so paranoid? Does it have something to do with the military?"

Micah lifted his head to look at me. "Whoever they are, they didn't expect me to fight back so hard. They acted surprised by my combat training."

"So why are you so worried? Why do you think I'd do this to you? Do you have some kind of riches you're hiding? Did you commit some kind of crime?"

"None of the above." He rubbed his hand over his head several times. "Look, I'm sorry I blamed you. But all of this started with you."

I peered at him. "I could say the same, you know. For me, this all started with you."

He chuckled, though the sound held no humor. "Yeah, I guess you're right. So what does it all mean? What do *you* think is going on?"

I'd never forget the odd yet awesome feeling of our souls bonding together, but now that it was over, the idea sounded ridiculous. I wanted to know if he'd felt it, too, but was too embarrassed to ask.

"Do you know what dyad means?" I hedged instead.

His head jerked up. His eyes widened, then narrowed tightly. His voice came out in a whisper. "You heard that, too?"

"Duh. I didn't pull it out of my ass. So do you know?"

"No idea. You're the college girl. No dictionary around?"

I was about to shake my head when I remembered I kept a pocket dictionary in my school backpack. Pops had given it to me, telling me to keep it in my bag in case I ever needed it while in class or study group. I crawled over to the pile of stuff I'd taken out of my Jeep and pulled out my backpack. After a few seconds of digging around through all of my important papers, I found the little dictionary stuffed into a bottom corner.

"Totally weird," I muttered once I'd flipped through the pages to the D section, then found *dyad*.

"What?" Micah asked, still sitting on the far side of the room and making no effort to come to my side.

"The official definition says, 'a group of two people, a pair, such as husband and wife.' But someone's scribbled in the margins." I frowned. "Pops gave this to me new. How did this get here?"

"What does it say?" Impatience colored Micah's tone.

The lines and swirls appeared to be nothing specific at first, but then I was able to make out the words. I swallowed hard and looked up at Micah.

"It . . . um . . . here." I tossed the book across the room. Apparently, neither of us felt comfortable getting too close to the other. For me, anyway, I wasn't sure which I feared more—what was going on or losing control again and jumping his bones.

Micah thumbed through the pages until he found the right

one. His eyes squinted as he focused on the handwriting. Then he looked up at me, his straight, dark eyebrows high on his forehead. "Twin Flames?"

Simultaneously, we both looked at the other's wrist and then at our own. Then Micah threw the book across the room, with more force than necessary. I ducked before it nailed me in the forehead.

"Sorry," he muttered.

I reached for the dictionary and, by chance it was defined, I looked up Twin Flames. No definition given by Merriam-Webster, but another note scrawled in the margin referred to the Appendix. Flipping to the end of the book, I found no official appendix. Instead, ballpoint ink covered the last page of the book. The handwriting was easier to read as I became used to it. I read it aloud.

"Twin Flames: A deeper connection than soul mates. While soul mates are two souls made for each other, Twin Flames are two halves of a single soul that has been divided. The halves pull to each other until they are finally reunited. When they are once again bound to each other, they are stronger than the sum of their parts."

By the time I dropped the book to my lap, Micah was on his feet and striding for the door.

"I gotta get out of here," he said. "I can't do this."

And then he was gone, pulling the door shut behind him.

I didn't have to ask if he'd felt the same truth about our souls bonding during the kiss that was more than just a kiss. His reaction to what I read told me. I couldn't blame him for walking out—the flame tattoos, the definition of Twin Flames, the incredible connection we'd made during the kiss was all a bit much for me and I wasn't a guy—but it took everything I had to keep from begging him to stay or lashing out at him and calling him a coward. I wasn't that type of girl and wasn't about to become one. If he wanted to go, I wouldn't force or guilt-trip him into staying, even if it meant never seeing him again.

Based on what I felt as he left, though, I didn't think he'd go far or stay away for long. I could *sense* him—as in, I could feel his presence as he moved across the yard to the parking lot and climbed into his truck—and I was sure he could sense me. When he pulled away, my heart, or maybe it was my soul, felt like a rubber band being stretched from the other end. The sensation wasn't exactly painful, but it didn't feel good either. I could only hope if he did decide to take off, one of us would figure out how to break the bond. Maybe enough distance and time would cause it to disintegrate or even snap on its own . . . but I doubted it.

I had no idea what to think of all this. I wanted to call Bex and tell her everything, but she would think me totally whacked. The whole scenario was completely nutso. Besides, exhaustion kept me from making the trek to the bar's pay phone, and, admittedly, a little fear did, too, with those two guys somewhere out there. Micah wouldn't be here to rescue me this time. Hell, as far as I knew, he could be headed out of town for good. The pull on my soul remained.

So I stretched out on my makeshift bed and tried to think things through. Sammy snuggled beside me as I picked up the dictionary and investigated it. Although the cover was scratched and marked and bent at the corners, you could tell it hadn't really ever been used. I had always used the full-size dictionary in my dorm room, one of the things Bex had packed and kept in storage for me. The spine on this one was pretty smooth, having been cracked open only twice before—the day Pops gave it to me and tonight. So how did those notes get in there?

I surely would have noticed them when I first received the gift and fanned through the pages. The "appendix" couldn't have been missed, written on a blank page facing the inside cover. But the book had been at the bottom of my backpack for nearly two years. At least . . . I thought it had. The notion of someone taking it out to add these little notes then somehow stuffing it all the way back to the bottom was silly. Who would do such a thing? Why?

"I don't get it, Sammy," I mumbled. He nuzzled his head against my arm, making me drop the book.

I tried to think harder on the dictionary and the mysterious definitions, but my body shut down, overwhelmed by the day's insanity. When I woke up in the middle of the night, my first thought was the pull had disappeared. I crawled over to the French doors and peeked out the window. Micah's truck sat outside in the parking lot, no lights or engine on, and from what I could see through the windshield, his body was splayed out uncomfortably in the seat.

I fought the urge to go down and tell him to go home, that I didn't need a babysitter, but based on the little flip my heart made when I saw him down there, I didn't trust myself. I'd probably ask him to come upstairs instead, which could be disastrous, regardless of his answer. I didn't want him to leave again, but I also didn't want to do anything I'd regret in the morning. So I pretended I didn't know he'd come back and returned to my crappy bed on the floor. Knowing he was nearby allowed me to relax completely, and I slept soundly until the noises of construction were right outside my door.

This morning was one of those times I was glad Sammy couldn't talk. Nobody needed to know about the celebratory dance I may or may not have done while still in bed when I knew Micah hadn't bailed on me. I was ridiculously stoked to feel him right outside, and if Bex were here, I'd never hear the end of it. She'd never seen me even slightly interested in a guy—boy-crazy was her thing, not mine—and what I felt had to be beyond anything she'd ever experienced in her life. After all, I don't think it's every day someone goes through what we had.

The weight of this thought slowly settled within me, and my excitement turned dark. What *had* we gone through? What did it all mean? Was it even real? The flame on my wrist and the feeling in my gut, in my very core—the feeling of Micah—meant something had definitely happened. I was tied to him in some inexplicable way, which terrified me. Would I always have these weird feelings now? My chest heaved and tightened, and the air clawed at my lungs and throat as the thought of losing control over myself sent me into a panic attack.

A persistent pounding on the door jerked my thoughts out of the downward spiral. "Jacey! Let me in!"

Oh, my god. I can't let him see me like this. I drew in deep breaths and exhaled slowly—*in, out, in, out*—trying to quell the pounding in my chest that echoed the one on the door.

"Now, Jacey!"

In, out, in, out. My lungs and heart finally settled into a more natural rhythm when the wood jamb cracked and the door flew open. Micah was on his knees in front of me in a heartbeat.

"Are you okay?" he panted, his hands hovering over my shoulders as if he wanted to embrace me but feared the touch. His overwhelming concern flooded over me, nearly suffocating me again. Why did he care so much? Too much. Way too much. And I knew why, but I didn't want to admit it. Rather than panicking again, I became angry.

"I'm fine," I snapped, tugging the blankets to my chest. "My stairs yesterday and my door today? How do you plan on waking me up tomorrow?"

His hands fell to his thighs, and the worry left his eyes, leaving them hard as stones. "Of course you're fine. I'll fix the door."

He rose to his feet and walked out the door, trying to close it behind him but he'd broken the latch, so it sort of just hung there. I growled to myself, then rose to begin my day. Sammy bounced around, and I swore under my breath. After that brief altercation, I didn't want to bother Micah, but Sammy had needs. As soon as I opened the door—well, opened it further—Micah was already there, taking Sammy without a word to me, but talking to my dog all the way down the ladder and even as Sammy ran to the bushes and peed. I watched them play for a few minutes until my own needs became urgent.

"He loves my dog," I muttered on the way to the bathroom. "And Sammy loves him. He can't be the worst person to be bonded to."

But still . . . the idea of being tied so closely to another person was too much. Surely that's not what Twin Flames meant. Maybe all of the gibberish in the dictionary was just that—bullshit. After all, it had been handwritten, not officially defined by the experts. I needed to find a library.

After a scalding hot shower that didn't wash away the freaky vibes running through me no matter how hard I scrubbed, I gathered my things to head out for some research. I was pleased at the progress outside my door, although I still had to use the ladder. Without a word to Micah, I headed for my Jeep, Sammy on my heels.

"Where are you going?" Micah called out. I stopped in my tracks but didn't turn around.

"To find a library. I don't assume you know where one is?"

He snorted. "Of course I do. But I'm not telling you."

I spun on my heel. "Excuse me? Why not?"

He strode across the yard closer to me, spiking my heart rate. His voice came out lower. "There are a couple of guys who are apparently stalking you, remember? I don't like you running around by yourself."

My jaw dropped. Part of me thrilled at his protectiveness, but another balked at it, raising my hackles. "I can take care of myself, thank you very much."

"Probably, but I still don't like it. I can't, in good conscience, let you go. I'll be done by lunch time, and then I'll be happy to take you myself."

I opened my Jeep door and threw my bag inside. "I don't need a babysitter."

"More like a bodyguard."

"I don't need that either," I said petulantly.

He cocked his head. "Are you sure about that? The same Ford Taurus from yesterday has driven by here at least half-a-dozen times this morning. It's the main drag, so a couple times is expected. Not six, though."

My gaze drifted over to the road, where several cars drove by. Were those guys waiting for me to be alone? Was I going to let that possibility keep me prisoner?

"Surely they wouldn't attack in a public place in broad daylight," I scoffed as I moved to get in the Jeep. "Can you watch Sammy for me?"

"No."

I turned to look at him. He was serious.

"I can't let you go," he added, pushing the Jeep's door closed in front of me.

That set me off. "How dare you! You can't order me around like this. Who do you think you are? What do you even care? Last night you bolted, said you couldn't handle this, and now you're treating me like a helpless little girl?"

"I feel . . . this need to protect you. I always have, since that night in the alley in Virginia." His hand lifted toward me, but it stopped in mid-air and went to the back of his head instead. His gaze traveled over my face and when his eyes came to mine, I tried to look away but I wasn't fast enough. Our eyes locked and that intense rush swirled through my veins. "Look, I want to know more, too. Just wait for me to finish here so I can go with you."

Did he have any idea what he was doing to me? Did he do it on purpose? I couldn't deny him when I was like this. I wanted him to come with me, too. I wanted nothing more than for him to be my side. Constantly. Forever. I shook myself out of it and forced my eyes from his.

"Fine," I muttered. "As long as you don't bail again when shit gets freaky."

"Jacey," Micah murmured, and I couldn't help but look up at him, into those dark, mysterious eyes. His hand moved toward me again, but he didn't pull back this time. He cupped my chin and ran his thumb over my bottom lip. My whole body vibrated like a tuning fork. "I don't think I *can* bail on you."

He dropped his hand and walked away. He'd probably felt the heat pouring out of my body, licking at his skin. I drew in a deep breath to slow my stuttering heart. When I was calm again, I reached into my Jeep and grabbed my change purse, then headed across the yard.

"Hey," Micah called out. "Where do you think—"

"I'm just going across the street to the pay phone. Right there." I pointed at it. "I'll still be in your eyesight, warden."

His eyes narrowed for a moment, then he nodded. Whew. I thought he was going to insist on standing right next to me while I made my call, which wouldn't be cool because I needed to talk to Bex. About him. I no longer cared about the harassment she would give me. I only hoped she'd be home this time or her mother would at least remember me and give me a phone number.

"Hello?" Bex answered on the second ring.

"Bex! You're there," I nearly squealed.

"Who's this?" She sounded genuinely perplexed.

"Duh. It's me. Jacey." The words poured out of me. "Dude, I'm so stoked you answered. I've been trying to get ahold of you, but your mom was like whacked out, I should have taken you up on your offer to come with me because I could totally use a friend right now, you'll never believe what's happening down here—"

"Whoa! Take a breath there, chicky. Now who is this again?"

I rolled my eyes. "Bex, this is long distance. I don't have a ton of quarters on me, but I do have plenty to tell you. Please don't play games."

"Dude, seriously. If you don't tell me who you are, I'm hanging up."

"Um . . . Jacey?" Why did it sound like a question?

She chuckled, and I let out a relieved breath. "I guess you have the wrong number. I don't know a Jacey."

"Very funny. I know it's been too long since we talked, but not *that* long."

"I'm serious. I *don't* know a Jacey."

I huffed into the phone, tired of her game. "Your roomie. Your best friend at college. I miss you horribly, and I'm really, *really* sorry I didn't let you come with me. I would kiss your feet or whatever else you'd like me to kiss if I was there. Now please cut the bullshit."

"Fuck you, weirdo! Don't ever call here again!" She hung up

with that. I stood there in shock, staring at the pay phone for several moments. Then I waited a little longer for her to call back. Her parents had a fancy service called Call Return or something, which let them dial the last number to call them.

"And that's how it begins, young Guardian," said a vaguely familiar voice behind me. The voice of the Billy Idol dude. "It starts with the people you know and love, and before long, your whole existence will be completely forgotten by this world."

I spun around, but there was no one there. Only a bush between me and the bar's door and nothing in or behind it. Except . . . I peered closer. *What is that?* A large, dark shadow suddenly rose from the branches.

My mind silently screamed for Micah, but I had no time to actually call for him as the dark shape flew at me. I ducked and threw my hands up to protect my face and head. A heavy weight collided into my hands, but as soon as it made contact, the shadow shattered into a thousand pieces. A swarm of black birds rose into the sky in a whir of flapping wings and a cacophony of angry screeches.

"You okay?" Micah asked from right next to me.

I jerked upright and blinked at him.

"How did you get here so fast?" I breathed as my mind tried to wrap around what had happened. He'd been at least fifty yards away, on the other side of a busy street, but had appeared in a heartbeat. "And how did you *know?*"

He frowned. "I felt your fear, and then I was here."

He looked away as if embarrassed by this admission.

"Yeah, I'm okay," I said in an attempt to ignore what his admission may mean. "I think."

"Didn't expect you to be so afraid of birds," he scoffed in his own attempt to skirt the issue.

"They, uh, surprised me, I guess. That was weird." I didn't want to tell him about how the birds had been a black shadow with the creepy guy's voice. Too much for me to handle, let alone him. Besides, he'd probably want to accompany me everywhere, even to the bathroom, if he knew the guy had come so close. Which he probably hadn't. I'd probably imagined the whole thing in my shock. "Actually, it's not the birds. The phone call . . . it, um . . . never mind."

Micah peered at me with concern. "What about it?"

I shook my head and forced a smile. "Nothing. Not important. Just a little tiff with my best friend."

This seemed to be enough to satisfy Micah's unusual curiosity and concern. After waiting for a couple of cars to pass, we crossed the street to my place, and he went back to work. Sammy ran over to me, knocked me to my knees and licked my face as though he hadn't seen me in months. You'd think he'd been as worried as Micah.

✳ NOW ✳
2012

CHAPTER 13

Jeric
2012

Too much. It was all too much, and I couldn't read another word. I needed to get out of here, away from this freak show my life had become. My feet carried me away in a brisk run, down the road that looped the small lake. Campsites lined the shore on my left and hills rose to my right with houses overlooking the water. The light of the full moon filtered through the pine trees lining both sides, smattering the gray of the asphalt road with patches of silver.

What was happening to me? Who *was* this Leni chick? No, not Leni. She couldn't have been doing this. Her body had been trembling when I left her on the picnic table in front of the Airstream. She was as disturbed by all of this as I was. So who was this Jacey chick? And this Micah? Was this really her journal? Was she even real? Or was someone dicking with Leni and me?

The vague familiarity of the whole thing as we read, as if I'd been told this story before, made me think it was all true. Then again, maybe the similarities fed this belief—the flame tattoos, the feeling of knowing Leni before I'd ever met her, the word *dyad*, which I'd already Googled and knew what it meant, echoing in my mind the first few times Leni and I touched.

How could this be happening?

I should have run far away, escaped while I could, leaving this fucked-up shit behind and never thinking about it again. But I wasn't a runner. I was a fighter. And Leni was involved in this, too, and I couldn't abandon her. Not anymore. Everything had changed.

The entrance to the state park came up, which meant I had nearly completed the circle around the entire lake. Granted it was dark, but I remembered little about the landscape around me. How far had I run in such a short time? Not far enough. I slowed to a walk and found a log by the water, where I sat and leaned my elbows on my knees. I pushed my hands through my short hair, trying to calm my temper before returning to Leni. She had to be freaking out, too.

A bright light shone over me. A vehicle turning into the area.

I watched as a light-colored cargo van shut its headlights off, even as it continued down Lake Road. A little suspicious, but maybe the driver was being courteous, not wanting to shine lights into any of the campsites this late at night, despite the fact the sites were mostly empty. About a hundred yards down the road, the van's brake lights shone, then it turned right into one of the driveways that climbed its way up the hill. *Yep, a courteous neighbor.*

I unfolded myself from the log and stretched, rolled my neck and shoulders and headed for a tree to take a leak. I'd just pulled my zipper down when two figures, dressed darkly to look like nothing more than shadows, darted out of the same driveway the van had entered, and ran down the road away from me. *Now that's definitely suspicious.*

I couldn't piss fast enough. After a couple of hurried shakes, I began jogging through the trees while still zipping and buttoning up. Chasing after these guys who were obviously up to no good might not have been my brightest idea, but I couldn't help myself. All I could think about was Leni in her camper alone. The pull in my gut was greater than it'd ever been.

Since I couldn't hear if my steps snapped twigs as I ran, I stayed on the sand near the water's edge, but as close to the cover of the trees as possible. They passed an old RV that was closed up and battened down, apparently vacant tonight. That wasn't their target. Somehow, I knew what was. Another half-a-mile down, they cut off the road and into the trees. They slowed their pace, and I slowed as well, keeping my eyes trained on the moving shadows in the darkness. As expected, they stopped on the edge of Leni's lot, with its camper aglow from the inside and the Christmas lights twinkling from the awning. They paused only for a moment.

They split off, sticking to the shadows as they crept around her trailer in opposite directions. While they were on the far side, I seized the opportunity to plant myself behind her truck, hoping to God they hadn't heard my footfalls. Sweat rolled down my back as I crouched down and peered around the bumper. They both returned to the front and stood at the door. I was at the perfect angle. When one raised some kind of tool to jimmy the lock, I bolted from my hiding spot and sprang at them.

The element of surprise allowed me to bowl both of them over at once, all of us crashing onto one of the folding chairs Leni had set out earlier. We jumped to our feet at the same time. Hoods made of a thin, black material hid their faces. One of them held a small knife out at me while the other simply held up fists. My heart pounded against my ribs, pumping adrenaline through my veins. Except for the occasional bar fight, I hadn't seriously fought in a few years—a black eye or a swollen lip could have breached my modeling contract—but the cage-fighting instincts immediately rushed back to me and took over.

With a sidekick, I knocked the knife out of the guy's hand, my first priority. The other guy's fist flew through the air at my head, but I jerked away in time so it only grazed my temple. I shot my own fist at his gut, and he doubled over. As I kneed him in the chin, the first dude's foot came toward my ribs. I grabbed it from the air and twisted, flipping him over. He fell hard against the ground. While he was down, I focused on the other guy. Blood dripped from under his hood, but he wasn't deterred. With one swift motion, his fist smashed into my cheek and his foot swept into my calf, knocking me to my knees. With a hard shove, my face planted into the ground, my arms pinned underneath my torso.

He drove a knee into my back, dug his fingers into my forehead from behind and yanked my head backward. He crouched over me, twisting my head back and forth as he seemed to be looking for something on my face or neck. When he didn't find whatever it was he sought, his head twisted, as if trying to get a better look at my shoulders and arms. Something grazed down my spine, feeling almost like a tickle, and then my shirt fell away from my shoulder blades. He shifted his knee from my middle-back to my ass and sat there for a long moment. Then he sucker-punched me in the kidney before springing to his feet and yanking me up to my knees by my neck.

My muscles tightened as I prepared to do a backwards head-butt into his groin, but I froze at the sight in front of me. The other fucker had Leni by the back of her neck, the point of a knife skimming down her bare arm. She wore sweats cut into short-shorts and a thin top with only strings over the shoulders, what the female models had called a cami. Her eyes caught mine, then darted away, down to my right. My gaze followed hers to a shotgun halfway under the camper. She must have heard the ruckus we'd created and come out to stop us, but was easily overtaken. Foolish girl.

Her captor seemed to have the same fascination with her head as mine. He moved his hand from her neck and dug his fingers into her curls, grabbing a fistful close to the crown of her head. He jerked her head side to side and pulled it back, also searching for something. Also not finding it. My muscles bunched, prepared to fight again, as he moved the knife to one of the cami's strings and flicked it in half. The front fell loose, exposing the top curve of her boob. An angry fire burst within me.

Before I could move, a white blur shot through the air and landed on the douche's head.

He immediately released Leni, his hands flying to the cat, but its claws attached to his head and face. I didn't waste the opportunity. Using the strength of my whole upper body, I threw myself backwards and my head slammed into my captor's gut. I used the momentum to get my feet underneath me, then jumped upwards. Pain shot through the top of my head as it met his chin. I spun, ready to throw a punch, but his body was already sagging to the ground.

I turned back to the other guy, who still fought the cat on his head. Long tears ran through his hood where the feline had clawed him. I didn't particularly like cats, but this one rocked. While the white ball of fur distracted the guy with another claw across the chin, I punched him in the ribs. As if the cat knew I had this, it sprang from the guy's head and out of sight.

The asshole fought back, apparently skilled in martial arts, but not fast enough or strong enough to take me down. But he still remained a tough opponent. My breaths came harder as we continued trading punches and kicks. Then, with a good shove from his shoulder, I stumbled backwards and right into the other guy's arms. He'd apparently regained consciousness. The first guy lifted his fist to aim for my face, and I felt a blow, but not from either of my assailants. They both suddenly froze. I didn't understand for a long moment, until the smell of burnt gunpowder filled my nose. In a heartbeat, the two men were gone.

I turned toward Leni as she lowered the shotgun's barrel from pointing straight up into the air to pointing at me. My chest and shoulders heaved as I panted, and I didn't think my heart could race any faster, but the gun pushed it a little more. "Put the gun down," I finally signed. "They're gone."

She shook her head violently, but the barrel remained trained on my chest.

"What are you doing, Leni?"

"Did you bring them here?" her lips demanded.

"No! What are you talking about?"

"Then how did they find us?"

I shook my head. "I'm sure it was random. Some thugs looking to rob us."

"No. They came after *me*, Jeric. *Me.* They basically said as much. And you weren't here when they did. You disappear into the darkness, and they suddenly show up. What do you expect me to think? Has this all been some crazy set up? What do you want from me?"

"I want answers, just like you do. But this isn't me. If I'd wanted to hurt you, I've had all kinds of chances. You know I could take that gun away from you right now if I wanted to."

"I'd like to see you try," she said, but then she lowered it to her side.

I took a step toward her, my hand reached out for her, and the gun was back up, pointed at my chest again.

"You're bleeding," I signed.

I hated that she was hurt. I hated those guys for making her bleed. I hated myself for leaving her alone in the first place. But more than anything, I only wanted to make her better, to hold her and tell her I would make everything okay again. I didn't know if and how I could keep such a promise, but I would die trying.

Her stormy eyes softened as she watched me, then her face crumpled, and the shotgun fell to the ground. Tears pooled in her eyes, and she wrapped her arms around herself, but that didn't stop her from shaking like a leaf. I stepped forward once more and pulled her into my arms. Trying to ignore but also enjoying the way my body reacted to her, I held her tightly against me and pressed my cheek against the top of her head. The fruity scent of her shampoo made my head swim. She eventually stopped shaking and stepped out of my hold. My heart jumped when I saw the blood smeared on her top.

"I'm going to get some towels and ice," she signed. "You're bleeding, too."

I looked down at my bare chest and found a couple of shallow cuts. Nothing serious. At least a ring hadn't been torn out. Now that would have been some real pain. I was fine, more worried about her. Leni dialed her phone on her way inside, probably calling the police. I sat on one of the folding chairs to wait, and the white cat jumped into my lap and curled up.

"Best cat ever," I signed to Leni when she came back out. I took a towel and a bag of ice from her.

She sat in the chair next to me, only a plastic table between us. One plastic table too many, as far as I was concerned, but I wouldn't push it with her. The cat jumped off my lap and brushed against her legs when I leaned over and pressed the cloth to the cut on her head. An ugly little bump was already rising, a murderous rage rising within me along with it.

"So you have no idea what that was about?" I asked.

She shook her head. "They were looking for something, but I don't know what. One kept saying, 'It's gotta be inside. We gotta get in there.' Whatever they wanted, though, I wasn't about to let them in my camper."

Before we could discuss it more, red and blue lights flashed across her face. The police had arrived . . . and did little, as I'd expected, except take our reports and say they'd keep an eye out for the white van. I had a feeling they'd never find it.

"Where did you learn to fight like that?" Leni asked after the cops had left, and we were seated in the folding chairs again.

"It's a long story. You sure you're up for it?"

She watched her finger pick at something invisible on her shirt before she looked back up at me. "I have to be, don't I? We're both involved in this crazy shit. We should probably learn as much about each other as possible. Don't you think?"

Getting her meaning, I glanced over at the picnic table for the book. It was gone. I sprang to my feet. I'd wanted to burn the thing an hour ago, but that would be stupid. We needed it—hopefully it held answers for us—and we definitely didn't need it falling into the wrong hands.

"Relax," Leni signed. "I put it away as soon as you left. I didn't want to be tempted to read ahead." Her eyes widened. "You think it was the book they were looking for? They kept talking about the brand, too."

My brows lifted. "The brand?"

She tapped her finger on her bracelets that hung together like a band, hiding the flame on her arm. Did she ever take them off?

"These?" she asked.

"But they were searching our heads and necks."

"One said, 'It's always on the torso.' He thought maybe we weren't the ones they were looking for."

"Then maybe we're not. Maybe it's a coincidence."

We stared at each other for a moment, neither of us really believing it.

Then Leni nodded and put on her fake grin. "Yeah. We're probably just being paranoid, with everything going on. So you going to tell me your long story or what?"

Before taking my seat again, I stepped inside to my bag and fished out my half-full bottle of whiskey. This could be a long night, and I needed something to take the edge off. I easily found two cups in the kitchenette, brought it all outside and set them on the table between us. Leni shook her head, but I poured her some anyway in case she changed her mind, which could be very likely. I picked up my own glass and threw the liquid to the back of my throat.

"So, I wasn't always deaf," I began, and Leni nodded because I'd told her this already. "When I was fourteen, I had an awesome life. I was the lead singer and guitarist in a band, and we were pretty damn good. Everyone thought we were so cool, coming to our gigs at local bars and everything. School was no problem for me—was easy, even the advanced classes—and teachers loved me. Life was good. Perfect. Then there was the accident, and I woke up from a coma with no family and no hearing."

Leni interrupted me. "Wait—you can sing?"

I gave her a sad smile. "I used to."

The smile she returned was as sad as mine. "It must be horrible to lose that."

"You have no idea." Hell if I didn't miss singing and music more than anything else, even more than hearing girls scream my name at the shows. Except for one girl . . . I scrubbed my hand over my face, then continued. "So when I finally got to go to school—I was held back a year because I'd missed so much—I wasn't so cool anymore. The rumor mill kicked up and for some, I was the poor orphan who lost his family, and others blamed me. Nobody knew how to act around me. My ex-band mates, my best friends, became the biggest dicks, and I went from being the cool kid to being a loner and the weird deaf guy. My home life sucked, and kids picked on me all the time. I tried to fight back, but I'd always been a music geek, not an athlete. I got my ass kicked I don't know how many times."

"Why didn't you just run from them?"

I gave her a look. "I. Don't. Run. But I did get tired of the bruises and the nosebleeds, and my grandparents calling the bullies' parents and embarrassing me even more. Their parents never did a damn thing except fuel the fire. So I decided to do something about it." I took another swallow of whiskey before continuing. "I began lifting weights, bulking up and learning how to fight. I got pretty good at it, to the point where parents were now calling my house to whine about how I'd broken their kid's arm or nose. So my grandparents took me on a Sunday drive in the country, where we conveniently ended up at the state's deaf school. My grandparents said being around people like me would help, but they were trying to get rid of me, the reminder of all they'd lost. They dropped me off and never came back."

I poured more of the amber liquid into my cup and took another drink. "I didn't belong there, either. I'd been taught Signed English after losing my hearing, which had been hard enough. The school wanted me to learn ASL, but I refused. The kids and teachers never did accept me."

"I thought the deaf community was close-knit and very accepting, though."

"Close-knit, yes. Accepting, no. Not when you don't want to be like them. Hell, I was 17 by then, pissed off at life and the world because I'd lost everything. But most of them didn't see deafness as a loss because they'd never had hearing to begin with. They didn't understand me, and I didn't want to understand them. I just wanted out of there. As soon as I could leave on my own, I did. Street fighting—kind of like that movie Fight Club?—was how I supported myself for a while, then I got involved with MMA and the UFC."

Leni looked at me for a long moment, and I was glad to see no pity in her eyes. Empathy maybe, but not pathetic pity. She reached for her cup and took a swig, then kindly moved the conversation along without harping on the painful parts. This. This was what I liked about her. This was what made her different than other girls who'd be all teary and "poor baby this and poor baby that." She was so laid back, accepting and non-judgmental. This was why I told her when I'd never told anyone the full story.

"Do you still fight?"

I shook my head. "The further I went in the UFC, the harder the poundings and the less fun it was. And there's no purpose except for bragging rights. Not the same as defending yourself or someone else who can't." I shrugged. "Something else with a lot better money and much less pain came along, so I took it."

"Modeling?" she asked.

I peered at her knowing smile. "How'd you find out?"

"I saw an ad in a French magazine on the plane the same day I first met you."

"Must have been an old magazine. I haven't modeled in over a year."

"And it happened to be in the hands of the lady sitting next to me. Isn't that a . . . coincidence?" She rolled her eyes as she signed the word. "So what have you been doing for the last year?"

"When I had enough money put aside, I began the search for my mother."

"But . . . I thought your mother died?" She lifted her eyebrows with the question.

I tried not to cringe and fought the urge to change the subject as I normally would do. Leni was right—we needed to get the truth out there. "My adopted mother and father died in the accident. That's why it was so easy for her parents to blame me and then forget I ever existed. I don't think they ever truly accepted me as one of their own. Especially my grandfather."

She reached out and placed a hand over mine.

"I'm sorry, Jeric," she mouthed, and she had no idea what that meant to me. It wasn't the pitiful, poor-baby kind of look she gave me or an insincere touch to get my attention. She was genuinely sorry I was the toilet life shit in. Nobody had ever given a damn about me before. Not like this.

I about drowned in the sea of her eyes again, but then she sucked her bottom lip between her teeth and now all I could think about was kissing her. I wanted to suck on that lip myself. Know what she tasted like, every bit of her.

Her hand retreated to her lap. "Your birth mother?"

I told her about how my grandmother had kept in touch with me as long as her husband didn't find out she was aiding and abetting the delinquent who had killed his daughter. I'd thought at first leaving me at the deaf school had been her idea, but then she'd sent me a birthday card and another at Christmas, each of them containing a little cash. Not much, but every bit helped. When I got out of the deaf school, she wouldn't let me come see her, but she'd give me little hints about the adoption. Maybe she thought if I went looking for my birth mother, I'd leave them alone.

Her little clues had planted a seed that grew into an obsession. I honestly didn't understand why I was so determined to find my biological mother. She gave me up. Why would I possibly want to know her? But something inside me told me I needed to do this, so I did. I went up to New England, to California and Louisiana, even to Alaska, and I was about to give in and come here, had even posted about it on Facebook for the few people who cared. Then I got an email advertising trips to Italy, and I remembered Grams once mentioning something about the Italian countryside. And I *knew* I had to go.

I paused to take another drink while thinking about how to explain to Leni this intense pull I'd been feeling all of this time without sounding like a damn lunatic who needed to be locked up. A sudden realization caught my breath and nearly choked me. *Oh, shit.* The draw hadn't been to my mother after all. I hadn't been "feeling" her only to reach dead end after dead end. I'd thought my gut had failed me, but it hadn't. All this time, it had been leading me to Leni.

And that was all sorts of fucked up.

CHAPTER 14

Leni 2012   *THUNK... THUNK... THUNK...* The sound of wood chopping greeted me as I opened my eyes to a gray light filtering through the blue and green tie-dyed curtains of my camper's bedroom. My groggy mind refused to clear as the thud, long pause, thud, long pause, thud, played in the background, and my heart felt thick and heavy in my chest. My life had completely changed yesterday. Well, it had started before then, of course, but yesterday it really spun topsy-turvy and flipped over a few times, landing upside-down.

I didn't know what to believe anymore. Everything I'd ever known and understood had been destroyed, and new ideas, thoughts, and beliefs took their places. I would have never brought a guy I'd only known a couple of days to the isolated camper with me in that past life, but here he was, outside chopping wood. I hadn't been able to watch him go when he left the Denny's yesterday morning, feeling what Jacey had when Micah had left her after their trip to the lumberyard. Like a piece of me had gone with him. I'd chased after him, and as bad as it sounds, had been secretly glad when I saw his car going up in smoke. Jeric and I had a connection that went deeper than I could possibly understand.

And his story . . . my heart had broken for him several times last night as he told it, though I tried not to let him see. I'd wanted to know more, especially about the accident, but I could tell he'd been avoiding the details for a reason. He'd had a hard enough time telling me as much as he did, which I had a feeling he'd never shared before—nobody knew the real Jeric Winters except for me. The image he projected wasn't a front. He was the real deal, every bit of it justified.

I wanted to tell him everything would be okay now, but really, we were both worse off than ever. Still, it had taken nearly every ounce of control I had to keep from crawling into his lap and wrapping my arms around him.

He must have sensed my desire right before I asked him about his birth mother. He'd paused, and I was scared he was going to clam up completely, maybe even leave, so I had prodded him to go on. He didn't have much to say about her, though, explaining he only wanted to know who she was. I had a feeling he'd been looking for her acceptance after his adopted family had rejected him so harshly. Maybe that's what he needed to accept himself and to allow other people into his life. Like, perhaps, a girlfriend.

I chuckled darkly at myself. I shouldn't have been thinking about such a thing. There were too many other problems to worry about. Besides, although I felt like I did about him—more than I should have—I knew better about his type. Trying to be the one who could change the bad boy was futile. My brain knew this, but my heart and body wanted to ignore it. Especially when I sat up and peeked out the window to find his god-like body down by the lakeshore, clad in only black workout pants hanging low on his hips and white running shoes. Even my mind faltered then, going to one fun but naughty place. His back muscles rippled and his biceps bulged as he swung the ax down.

I needed a cold shower.

No, I needed music. I needed to dance, to work this tension off before we continued our quest for answers. We had lots more of the journal to read, and, of course, I still had to tell him my story. It was pretty boring compared to his . . . at least, up until three days ago. I still hadn't told him about Uncle Theo and the phone calls with my parents. My so-called "parents" . . .

Music. I needed music. Loud enough to drown out the phone conversations trying to replay in my mind.

I jumped up from the bed, took the one step to the bathroom to pee, then the two steps to the living area where the iPod docking station was. I selected my favorite dance playlist and turned the volume up. My body responded immediately.

The music took control, and I moved to it in the tiny space, dancing on the futon mattress up front where Jeric had slept, spinning in the kitchenette, using the table as a prop. My muscles loosened. My mind went blank. My soul lost itself in the music and the movement. This was exactly the release I needed. Jeric ran to relieve stress; I danced. The space wasn't big enough, though. After a luscious move with my legs and hips I'd used often in the club, I did a half-pirouette to the door to find more space outside.

And I froze mid-movement.

Jeric stood in the doorway. Well, actually, he leaned against the jamb, his arms crossed and the screen door propped against his bare shoulder. His blue eyes smoldered as he stared at me, a sunray glinting off his brow ring. How long had he been watching? Why did he look like that? Was it the music? He could probably feel it, especially as loud as I had it. And me dancing and enjoying something he could never hear again had to be salt in his wound.

"I'm sorry," I signed before reaching behind me to turn it off.

He shook his head, and my hand paused in mid-air.

"Don't stop," he signed, but I stood there, feeling self-conscious as he continued to watch me.

When I still didn't move, he did. He straightened up and took a half-step inside, the screen door banging closed behind him. He placed his hands on my hips and gently pushed them one way and then the other. His touch electrified me, and the music embraced me, and self-conscious or not, I couldn't help it. My body moved on its own as it always does, swaying and swinging and moving to the beat. And my eyes never left Jeric's, even as his filled with heat. I finally turned and pressed my back to him, still moving to the music, and he grew hard against me. His hands on my hips again, he turned me around and jerked me to him.

One of his hands slid up my side, over my shoulder and to my face. I arched my body up and into him, and his piercings rubbed against my own hard nipples poking through the measly cami I wore. His erection pulsed against my belly. His eyes held me hostage. His thumb skimmed over my bottom lip. My mouth parted.

This wasn't the first time I'd moved like this with a guy and not the first time I delighted in the feeling. But it was the first time I felt it was right. That acting on my desire was not only good, but, with Jeric, necessary.

Apparently, he didn't feel the same.

He closed his eyes and released his hold on me. I stumbled backwards, hitting my butt against the counter.

"I'm sorry," he signed as he opened his eyes. "I can't . . ."

I sucked my lower lip between my teeth and nodded. "You mean you don't want to."

His eyes filled with incredulity. "Are you kidding me? I want nothing more! I can't stop thinking about splaying you out on that mattress, feeling you under my hands, knowing what you feel like *inside*."

My eyes widened, the visual taking me by surprise.

"See?" he signed. "You deserve better. You deserve someone who can treat you like a lady."

"And you can't?" I taunted. I knew otherwise. He already had treated me with more respect than any guy ever had. The way he had looked at me last night right after those men had left, worried about my bleeding head—no man except Daddy and Uncle Theo had ever looked at me with such kindness and caring. He hadn't even tried to come to my bedroom last night.

"I don't know how," he said. "It's hard as hell to keep my hands off you. I don't know how to do this, except to keep going on runs and chopping wood. I mean, look at you in those short shorts and . . . all that."

He looked down at my braless chest and away.

"You drive me crazy, Leni," he continued. "And you think I don't *want* to?"

I swallowed hard. "And that's why you won't even kiss me?"

He shrugged. "You deserve to choose. I don't want to force anything on you, especially not me."

Ah. Huh.

"I'm just talking about a kiss." I had no idea why it had suddenly become so important to me. Where were my priorities? Why did I feel like this *was* a priority?

He chuckled, a small smile showing a hint of his dimples, although his eyes burned once again. "I don't think I can do just a kiss. Not with you."

His words reminded me of Jacey and Micah's first kiss. Would a kiss with Jeric feel the same way? Maybe that's where this was all coming from. I wanted to know. *Needed* to know. My heart pounded with the thought. I took a step closer to Jeric.

"Try," I said aloud, his eyes on my lips.

"Leni . . ." He warned.

"I'm asking. Isn't that what you want?" I took another step, now up against him again. I looked up at him through my lashes. "Don't make me beg."

He groaned, then the next thing I knew, his hands returned to my hips, pushing me backwards until my butt hit the counter again. Then they were on each side of my face, and his mouth was crashing down on mine.

My stomach jumped into my throat then did that crazy plunging feeling as soon as our lips touched. I couldn't breathe, forgot I even needed to as his mouth pressed harder. And then his tongue flicked out, over my bottom lip, wanting in. I pushed myself against him, welding my body to his as I parted my lips and met his tongue with my own.

Oh, my God. Jacey was right. The feeling was indescribable.

My soul tugged and pulled as if trying to escape my body. Pulled toward *him*. And at the same time, I felt his coming for me, and they met in the minute space between us and danced and mixed and bonded together, creating the most amazing and unbelievable sensation I'd ever felt. I'd almost call it an out-of-body experience except I still physically felt every nerve ending in my body, and each one was on fire from head to my curling toes.

Jeric's hand slid down my back as he pulled tighter, our mouths and tongues still moving together. His fingers slid under my shirt, pressing into the skin over my ribs and sending a thrill throughout my body. I moaned with pleasure, wanting more, more, more, but instead, I pushed him away because no way could my body handle more. Otherwise, it might burst into flames.

He took several steps back until he was against the screen door again, and we both stared at each other, gasping for breath. I wished I knew what he was thinking. He had so much more experience than I did. Had he felt the same thing I had, or was that just another kiss for him?

"Not just a kiss," he signed, and he shook his head as a smile slowly crept over his face. My favorite one with all the dimples. "Not with you. Now I understand what that Jacey chick meant."

"You felt it, too?" I asked aloud with disbelief.

His smile widened, then became a grimace as he shifted his hips. "I need to go chop more wood."

My lips quivered with a smile of understanding.

"I guess I shouldn't take a swim in the lake, then?" I teased, not really planning on it although the cold water sounded appealing to my heated core.

He cocked a brow. "What would you be wearing?"

"It's the lake. What do you think? Nothing."

He made a face that looked like a grimace was fighting off a grin. I thought he might actually be in pain. "I think I'll go for a run then."

I laughed. "Kidding! A swimsuit, dumbass."

"A bikini?"

"Of course."

His eyes slid over me, to my feet and back up, sending a wave of chills over my skin and a flame of heat inside. "Yeah. I'll go for a run."

He took off before I could stop him. Feeling bad that he'd left for no reason, I changed into my bikini to sit in the sun. The water would be too cold this early in the season for an actual swim. I pulled my shotgun out, too—last time Jeric left me, I'd been attacked. And now that I thought about it, the ambush felt strangely similar to the one Jacey described in her journal. *Another so-called coincidence?* I wondered as I opened the screen door. A buzz from behind me made me jump.

Jeric had left his phone on the counter, and it vibrated as a new text lit up the screen. I couldn't help but see it when I glanced over: a girl wondering what he was doing and when he'd be around. Ugh. Was this something I wanted to deal with? How many, exactly, would be texting? As I stared at the phone, curiosity got the best of me.

I wouldn't normally spy like a crazed girlfriend, but really, how well did I know this guy? I mean, in a way, I felt like I knew him as well as I knew myself, but I didn't really *know* him. In fact, everything he told me last night could have been lies for all I knew. I didn't feel that was the case, but a girl couldn't be too careful, especially since I'd brought him to my camper, let him sleep in the only home I had left. I deserved to know more, didn't I? And the fool didn't have his phone password-protected, so he was asking for it.

With all of that justification, which really didn't justify anything, I swiped the screen to open his phone. The text message app came up first, but except for the one that had just come in, the cache was blank. His contacts list only contained business numbers and email addresses. He had a Facebook app, but his last status update was over a month ago, saying, "Leaving for Italy. See ya later, haters." His email inbox was empty, too. So either he wiped out everything regularly, which could mean he had something to hide, or he didn't have many life connections. My phone was pretty empty for that very reason, so it was possible. When I tapped on the photos app, however, all benefit of the doubt disappeared.

My hand shook as I stared at the first photo that came up. The sound of footsteps on gravel outside made me nearly drop the phone, and I spun around to look out the window. Jeric quickly approached the backside of the camper.

With the phone still in my hand, I picked up my gun, went outside and leaned against the picnic table, waiting. Jeric stopped by my truck and stared at me, a mischievous grin tugging at his lips. I glared back at him, and his expression shifted into bewilderment until his gaze fell on his phone in my hand. He rolled his eyes and walked toward me.

"You looked at my phone?" he signed. I didn't answer. "You can't be mad at what you found. This thing between us is new, and I know lots of people, including girls. I can't help it if they text me."

"And the pictures?" I asked aloud, unable to sign since my hands were full.

He sighed. "I'll delete them if you want. They mean nothing to me."

"Oh, really? Even the one of Mira?"

All color drained from his face.

"That's what I thought," I said, and I shifted the gun, very close to pointing it at him again. He stepped backwards until he was by the truck. "How do you know Mira? Why do you have a picture on your phone of her? What have you done with her and my uncle?"

His brow furrowed. "Leni—"

"What have you done to them?" I yelled. I inhaled a deep breath, trying to keep my cool. Stupid tears of anger burned my eyes, but I blinked them away, taking control as Mama had taught me. But all of this had meant nothing to him. None of it. It had all been part of his psycho plan, whatever it was, and, if he got into my pants, so much the better. I couldn't believe I'd fallen for it all. Red-hot rage burned in my chest, but I refused to let him see it and was glad he couldn't hear the waver in my voice. "Where are they?"

"I have no idea what you're talking about. You know Mira?"

I wanted to spit fire at him, but if I didn't say my words clearly, he wouldn't understand. "Of. Course. I. Do. She takes care of my uncle, as if you didn't know that already. One more time: where are they?"

A swirl of expressions passed over his face. "Mira's my grandmother. The one I came to see, remember? Except I couldn't find her. She'd moved or . . . something."

"Yeah, missing with my uncle. Except in the two years she's been helping Uncle Theo, she never mentioned anything about having a grandson."

"No, she wouldn't, would she?" The hurt in Jeric's face almost made me regret my words.

"She never even mentioned being married, either. No family at all."

Confusion flickered in his eyes. "Nothing?"

"No. Nothing. Just a guy she used to take care of before my uncle, but she didn't even like that guy. Said he was a cold-hearted bastard who drank himself to death."

"Sounds like my gramps," Jeric said. His middle finger stroked at the ring in his brow for a moment. "She never did seem to love him, but how could anyone love that asshole? But to forget the rest . . ." His head tilted, and his eyes narrowed. "Wait. You say she's missing?"

"Not just missing. Gone! At least, my uncle is, and I'm assuming she's with him. Everything about his very existence has been wiped out. As if he never even lived."

Jeric's eyes filled with concern. "Why didn't you tell me?"

"Why didn't *you*?"

"I did."

"You never said your grandmother was *Mira*." Ah, shit. I

nearly dropped the gun as things began to clear. "Everything's starting to make sense. Sort of."

I tossed his phone to where he still stood by the truck and took the bullet out of the shotgun's chamber before laying the weapon on the table. I wanted to pace while I thought out loud, but Jeric wouldn't be able to see my hands or my lips. So I walked back and forth a few times under the shade of the awning, thinking hard, then stopped in front of the truck, where he leaned against the bumper.

"The voice had told Jacey her existence in this world would disappear. With everything else we have in common with her and Micah, that must be what's happening to us."

"She wasn't even sure she heard it."

"Like I'm not sure I heard, 'We always find you.' Except they found her, and they found me last night, and it's all too . . . coincidental. And my uncle is gone. Everything about him wiped out. Your grandmother has disappeared, too, and for all we know, her existence has been obliterated. The rental car company, Jeric. They had no record of you. And you said you'd rented from them a few times, right?"

"It's been a couple of years. Maybe they clean their database." By the look on his face, he knew this theory was weak, especially since he'd had a current rental. He blew out a breath. "Unbelievable."

"Doesn't matter. It's happening." I turned away and paced a couple more times, then faced him again. "There's more."

And as much as I'd wanted to pretend they'd never happened, I told him about the calls to my family the other night.

"We don't have a daughter," my mom had said after I explained who I was since she claimed to not recognize my voice. "We don't have any children."

We hadn't talked in a while—had no reason to anymore—but her words had been a knife to my heart. No matter what I'd said, how much I pleaded with her to speak the truth, she denied my existence.

"I recited everything I knew about her and Daddy," I told Jeric as fresh tears rose. "About their marriage, her miscarriages and then being so happy when they got pregnant with me. She demanded to know how I knew everything, even called me a stalker. For the first time in my memory, she lost her cool. She screamed at me, saying, 'We don't have any children! I couldn't have babies!' Then she hung up on me, so I called my daddy. He said he didn't have any uncles, only aunts, and denied any relation to Uncle Theo or me."

Realization dawned on Jeric's face.

"That's what had you so upset at Denny's," Jeric said.

I grimaced, then nodded. "You could tell?"

"I *felt* it," he said, his eyes soft. "You think you hide your feelings well, but not from me." His brow lifted. "You give this front of being so laid-back and carefree, but I don't think that's the real you."

Maybe he didn't intend for his words to be an accusation, but my body stiffened and my hands signed sharply. "What do you know?"

He shrugged. "Not a lot, but I know what I saw in your hotel room, when I wouldn't leave. And I've seen other glimpses."

"Maybe because you bring the worst out of me," I snapped.

"Maybe because I bring out the real you. Because I think *that's* the real you. The one who feels and cares and sometimes wants to scream her head off. All those fake smiles you give—you make them look genuinely sweet, but I know they're not. I think behind all those smiles is a lot of hurt and anger."

I inhaled a controlled breath, trying not to reveal how close to home he'd hit. "Who are you and where is Jeric Winters? You're a guy. You're *you*. What makes you think you know anything?"

"Because I used to know a girl who did the exact same thing. The only other girl I've ever loved." He cringed and dropped his hands for a moment. There were lots of things in that statement I didn't want to think about and apparently neither did he because he took a step closer to me and continued. "You *should* be angry right now, Leni. You should be fucking pissed off. You should be throwing things. Punching things. Flipping off the world."

I rolled my eyes. "Just because that's how *you* deal with life doesn't mean we all do."

His brows raised. "I feel the anger simmering underneath your surface. I feel the real you wanting to break free. As crazy as it sounds, I *feel* your feelings, Leni. Why don't you let it out?"

"What good would it do?" I'd learned at a young age that throwing a tantrum didn't get you anywhere except in trouble. "Yeah, I do smile through everything whether I feel it or not. Like my mama always said, nobody cares what you really feel. Why bog them down with your troubles? Why bog *you* down with mine?"

"Why not?" he countered. "Shit, we're in this together. And one of these days you're going to blow up like Mount fucking Saint Helens anyway if you don't let yourself be you. Try it some time. Try to let all that anger out. I bet you'd like it."

I couldn't help but chuckle. Uncle Theo used to tell me the same thing. He'd hoped I'd find the real me in Italy, and maybe I had, but Mama's teachings were too ingrained in me. She'd had a way of making sure of that.

I blew out a sigh and put on the smile that came automatically, then scowled because it did come so automatically. This made Jeric's lips pull into a crooked grin.

"That's improvement," he signed. "So why didn't you tell me sooner about all of this? About your parents?"

"How could I? It's so messed up."

He pointed to his chest covered in little beads of sweat. "Disowned, remember?"

Right. But, although I'd been worried at first Uncle Theo had told my parents about the club incident and they were disappointed—again—this wasn't quite the same.

"They haven't disowned me. They didn't say, 'We don't like you. Go away.' They don't believe I ever even existed. Don't you see? Everyone who has ever known us has either disappeared or believes we don't exist. If this goes on, we'll be like Uncle Theo—every government record wiped out, everything we own lost—"

Jeric stopped me. "Do you have money in the bank?"

"Yeah. It's college money, though. Why?"

"If we don't get our cash out now, we might not ever."

I closed my eyes, wanting to scream and being very tempted to accept Jeric's challenge to let it all out, because that one statement made it all so real. Old habits die hard, though, and I couldn't bring myself to do it. Another dance session would have been better anyway, but I didn't have time. We had business to take care of. So I counted to ten, stood up and grabbed my gun to put it away and get dressed so we could go to town. Jeric stopped me once again.

"For the record," he signed, "I don't think I've ever seen anything sexier than you in a bikini holding a gun."

I shook my head. "I'll keep that in mind."

Feeling like our lives were slipping between our fingers like sand, we each hurriedly showered and dressed, then rushed to town. I used a check to withdraw all of my money, but Jeric's bank didn't have a branch in town, so we drove around to every cash machine we could find, withdrawing the maximum amount until his bank put a stop to it. It was the best we could do, but not bad. I had plenty to live off of for a while, thanks to my side-job at the club—the one that had led Uncle Theo to send me off to Italy when he found out about it.

While in town, we grabbed some more groceries and Jeric bought more booze, then we headed "home"—the only home either of us had anymore—and sat down to read again.

At this point, Jacey and Micah seemed to be our only hope for answers.

✳ THEN ✳
1989

CHAPTER 15

Jacey
1989

The phone call, the voice, the birds—they'd all freaked me out. Sammy and I sat in the overgrown grass in front of my building while Micah nailed down the last boards of the deck at the top of the new stairs. My mind chewed on my phone call with Bex and the voice I'd heard afterward as fervently as Sammy gnawed on his rawhide bone. How could my best friend possibly forget who I was? We'd talked to each other only five days ago when she'd offered to come down here with me. And now she denied knowing me? The voice in the bushes was wrong—Bex must have been on something. She had no problem experimenting with drugs. I needed to get her out of that lifestyle.

Unfortunately, I had my own troubles to straighten out here, and not only this Twin Flames predicament.

"Stairs are done," Micah announced as he bounded down them and over to me.

"Bravo," I said with only a hint of sarcasm that he met with his irresistible smile. I hadn't seen those dimples since yesterday, and they got to me again.

He dropped to his butt next to me, and we both studied his handiwork.

"So do I have a job?" he asked.

My smile morphed into a grimace as I let out a sigh. "I don't know what to do. We have this . . . whatever it is with you and me . . . to figure out, but I really need to get back north. I think something's wrong with Bex."

"The phone call?"

"Yeah."

"Mmm." He nodded, then he cocked his head as he looked at me. "Can I show you something before you make up your mind?"

His dark eyes glinted with mischief, making me a little nervous. "I guess . . ."

He lifted his chin toward the front of the building. "I was peeking in the windows to get an idea of what all needs to be done. I wanted to be sure I could handle the job."

"Buck wouldn't have called if you couldn't," I scoffed.

He tugged at his ear before saying, "Buck didn't call me."

"But . . . then how did you know?"

"It's a small town. I heard the owner might want to fix the place up. Not normally my type of job, but for some reason, I felt the need to check it out."

"Hmph. 'Some reason'?" *Some reason* seemed to be ruling my life, and intuition told me our matching tattoos and Twin Flames triggered all these inexplicable motives.

"Yeah, well . . ." Micah cleared his throat. "Anyway, did you wonder why the bottom units are long and narrow and the top units are wider?"

"Not really," I admitted. "I thought they just looked bigger upstairs because of the arrangement."

"Usually, all the wet areas—your kitchens and bathrooms—line up to keep the plumbing close together. You know how units in hotel or apartment buildings are mirror images of each other? It's so there's less pipe to run. The same walls are used all the way up the structure."

"Except in mine."

"Right. Even if there were a firewall between each side, it

would only make sense for all the plumbing to be in the rear, like with the top two units. But the lower two have the plumbing on the interior wall."

"Okay. So there's no firewall between the sides?" I still wasn't sure where he headed with all of this construction mumbo-jumbo.

"Jacey, the downstairs units don't share an interior wall at all. They're too narrow."

"What?" Why hadn't I noticed? I stared hard at the building, as if it had done something to offend me. "So there's a space between them?"

"Exactly. And not a small one. At least six feet wide, and the entire length of the building."

I rose to my feet, walked over to the left window and peered inside, then looked through the right window. Then I eyed the front of the building. No way did those two walls butt against each other, and there was definitely quite a bit of area between the two.

"Well, why would they do such a thing? Why make the units smaller than necessary?"

"Good question," Micah said from right next to me. "And why is there plumbing on those interior walls?"

"Does it matter? I mean, does it affect the building? Is this another thing I have to fix?"

"Probably not. But you might be able to add a laundry room, which will increase the value of this place. You don't even need to put the machines in. We just need to put a door in the back, and put in the plumbing and electrical, which shouldn't be difficult. Looks like there could be room for storage, too, like for bikes or beach chairs. Also more value to the place."

"Yeah, I don't know." I pushed my hands through my hair. "Sounds like a lot of work, and this whole building needs so much already. I have no clue if it's worth it." Which reminded me—I'd been here nearly two days and still hadn't contacted another real estate agent for a second opinion.

"Oh, it's definitely worth it."

I snickered. "Of course you'd say that since you want me to hire you."

His shoulder lifted and dropped. "Whether you use me or someone else, you'll triple the value of the place."

I pulled back at this. "No way! You really think it's worth *that* much? If it were your decision, what would you do?"

He stroked his chin as he studied the front of the building. "Yeah. Even if I had to pay someone else, it'd be more than worth it. From what I've heard from the locals around here, a place like this, all fixed up and ready to rent, you'd make out whether you sold it or kept it. You could easily make a few grand a month renting out the units."

"A few grand a *month*? Who would pay *that* for a measly room?"

"Tourists. $300 a week per unit, no problem."

"Wow," I breathed, looking at Pops' gift with a whole new appreciation. "Buck never mentioned this."

"Why would he? He doesn't make commission if you don't sell it."

So Buck's so-called promise to Pops was really just about the potential to make a higher commission. And to shovel more work to his brother. I *knew* I couldn't trust him, the conniving scumbag.

A jolt rushed through my hand and arm, jerking me out of my anger at the skeevy salesman. I pulled my hand up to find it enclosed in Micah's, and a thrill swirled in my belly. His face flashed with something unreadable, but then he began tugging me toward the rear of the building.

"Let's at least see if we can figure out the mystery," he said.

"Which one?" I muttered, looking down at our clasped hands, and then I stopped, pulling Micah to a halt, too. I lifted our arms, pressed my forearm against his and gasped. "Dude! Check it out."

With our wrists smashed together, the bases of the flames nearly touched, and they resembled fiery wings of a bird.

Micah's fingers sprang open as he tried to release my hand. I squeezed his harder.

"You promised you wouldn't bail," I said, looking into his eyes.

They flickered between anxiety and ease before he narrowed them. "You were the one just talking about leaving."

I had, but when he said it like this, my insides compressed into a tight little ball, and once again, I plunged into the depths of his mocha eyes. My stomach dropped and my heart sped at a gallop as the part of me that was not my physical self wrapped around him, blended into him, clung to his every fiber. Our eyes still locked, I felt him—some part of him—reach into me, too, fortifying the diaphanous cloth our souls had woven together.

"I . . . I don't think I can leave you either," I finally said in a hoarse whisper. I licked my lips, and my bottom lip caught between my teeth.

"Dammit, Jacey," Micah grumbled as his free hand wrapped around the back of my head, and he pushed me against the building wall with his body.

He didn't hesitate this time. He didn't ask. He dove down and delivered a soft kiss that rapidly became urgent. His tongue slid over his lips, and I parted mine, welcoming him in, pulling him in, wanting every bit of him inside me. He extracted his hand from mine only to clamp it onto my waist while deepening the kiss even more. Our lips and tongues danced together as he kissed me in a way I'd never been kissed before. An exciting thrill vibrated through my body, making my breasts tight and hard and my thighs clench.

His hand slid over my jeans to my ass, and he lifted me, putting me at eye level so he wouldn't have to crouch. I wrapped my legs around his waist, and he pressed harder against me. We moaned into each other when his erection throbbed between my legs. My heart pounded, and my belly quivered as butterflies danced inside.

I swear my soul was dancing, too. I'd never felt such joy, such elation, such emotional bliss. Every part of my being, physical and otherwise, wanted this. Wanted us completely and totally together in every sense of the word. Wanted him. Micah. *My other half.*

My mind pricked at this. Okay, maybe my brain didn't want it. At least, not yet.

"Micah," I panted against his lips. "Too . . . fast."

He didn't stop kissing me.

"Please . . . Micah." I placed my hand on his hard chest. I didn't push, but I did press. "Slow. Please."

He did slow the kiss down and eventually pulled away enough to look at me. His brown eyes smoldered with heated desire, sending another thrill through me. My throat worked to swallow.

"Um . . ." I gave him a weak smile. "We're moving a little fast."

He returned my smile, dimples and all. When he spoke, his voice came out husky. "I can't help it. You . . . if you had any idea what you do to me . . ."

He kissed each corner of my mouth.

"I know," I said, closing my eyes as a new wave of desire rushed through me. I forced my eyes open and squirmed against him. "You do it to me, too. But, this is all . . . just . . ."

He grazed his teeth over my bottom lip then pressed his forehead against mine. "Too much. I know."

His hands grasped my hips, and he took a step back. Reluctantly, I unglued my legs from around his waist so he could set me on my feet. My knees nearly gave out, and I stumbled. Micah caught me with a chuckle, making me blush.

"Wow, a little light-headed," I mumbled.

"Mm-hmm." His lips danced with a teasing smile.

I blushed harder. "I haven't eaten anything today."

He nodded. "I'm sure that's what it is." He winked at me, then took my hand. "I'll take you to lunch, and the library, but first, what we were doing before . . . before you did that thing you did to me."

I smiled as I followed him around the corner. "And what did I do to you exactly?"

"We'll just say you found my soft spot."

"It felt pretty hard to me."

He laughed, then shook his head. "See? That. That's what you do to me."

"Ah, smart-ass, ex-punk girl makes tough Marine a little soft?"

"Not exactly."

"Oh, so any girl does?" My elation dropped a few levels.

He stopped and turned his full burning gaze on me. "No, only smart-ass, ex-punk girls named Jacey, who has managed to make me nearly lose control as I've never done before."

I rolled my eyes. "Please don't try to convince me you're a virgin. I'll never buy it."

"Of course not." He pulled me closer to him, our bodies nearly touching again. "But I've always been in control of the situation. I've always known what I was doing. With you . . . it's one surprise after another. Half the time, I have no clue what I'm doing. And even though I sometimes think I'm losing my mind, I can't say I don't like it. Which is the biggest shock of all."

His eyes flashed, his hand dropped mine, and he walked off, as if afraid of what he'd admitted.

"So you're a control freak," I said as we stepped up to the center of the building's rear wall.

"A *self*-control freak," he corrected as he squatted down to inspect where the building's siding met the concrete foundation.

The way he'd ordered me around earlier and became so overprotective, I wanted to argue the point, but didn't.

"So is being a self-control freak why you went into the Marines, or are you like that *because* you're a Marine?"

"I grew up in foster homes, bouncing around from one shithole to another, most people only taking me for the state aid money." His fingers grasped onto an edge of the siding, and he yanked. The aluminum protested loudly before pulling away from the building. "The few I actually liked either had kids of their own and decided they couldn't foster anymore, or had other issues, and I was pulled out and placed into hell. My childhood was chaos." He pulled on another piece of siding and dragged it back. "I couldn't wait for the day I could take control of my own life. My last foster mother was pretty cool. I still talk to her now and then. But I enlisted on my eighteenth birthday. And yeah, the Marines helped me learn the control I wanted so badly."

Whoa. That was heavy. Imagining him as a young boy with no parents and having to grow up with virtual strangers made my chest ache. I'd lost my parents at nine years old, but at least I'd always had Pops. I now understood what he'd meant when he said he had no one.

"And then I came along and ruined it all?" I teased in an attempt to lighten the mood.

Micah peeled one last piece of siding out. "Yeah, something like that."

He had pulled away about five feet of siding, leaving the pieces pried back perpendicular to the building, revealing a six-foot-high rectangle of plywood. He began knocking around on it until we both heard the hollow sound.

"What does that mean?" I asked.

"It means there's nothing solid behind there."

"I know that," I huffed. "I mean what you said—*something like that*. You were all nomadic before I came along. Or were you a *controlled* nomad?"

"Yeah, I was." He turned to face me and put his hands on his narrow hips, right where his jeans hung. "After my discharge, I had a few places to visit. People I owed a personal thank-you to. That part was controlled. And then I had the uncontrollable need to go to Virginia and make a stop at that god-awful show that night. I don't know why, but I knew I *had* to go. How can you listen to such noise?"

I chuckled. "Yeah, it sucked, didn't it?"

"Sid Vicious must have been rolling in his grave. Anyway, I hung around for a week or so, but the need to be there disappeared. I started heading north again but stopped in Northern Virginia, having no idea where to go next. I had no home, no job, no purpose."

"Wait. You were in Northern Virginia? Right after the show?"

"A week after."

"Whoa. That's when I'd gone home for Pops' funeral."

His eyes tightened as he stared at me for a moment, then he gave a slight head shake before he went on. "I decided to give Angie, my last foster mother, a call, and she suggested I come down here. Said she had a widowed friend who needed someone to watch her house over the summer while she went north, and she even had a place for me to stay. I wasn't sure about the idea when Angie first mentioned it, but eventually I couldn't ignore the urge to come here. As soon as I got to town, my new neighbor asked if I knew anything about fixing his roof, and then more work fell in my lap. And right when I finished my last project, you showed up." His gaze drilled into me. "Any control over my life I thought I had . . . it was all just an illusion."

I wrinkled my nose. "Well, isn't that how life is anyway? Anytime you think you have control, life waves its big magic wand and poof! Everything around you has changed. *Life's* an illusion."

He lifted his hands in the air. "Do you get what I'm saying, Jace? The last several months were all about you. As if I was *drawn* to you. Or pushed to go where you would be."

The description of Twin Flames echoed in my mind, causing chills to slither over my skin.

I broke eye contact with Micah and looked at the plywood. "So, uh, are you going to find a way in or not? If not, I think we need to get to the library."

"I'll get my saw. It shouldn't take long."

Ten minutes later, Micah had cut a door into the back of the building. The long and narrow space was about eight feet wide and seemed to stretch all the way to the front of the building, as expected, although the other end receded into dark shadow. While Micah went to retrieve a flashlight, I stepped inside. And became completely disoriented.

I still stood in the dark, empty space, but at the same time, I felt like I was in an entirely different structure. Like an image overlaid onto my vision, I also stood in the hallway of a big house with shiny hardwood floors and pale yellow walls. In front of me, a curved, sweeping staircase with a wrought iron and wood banister rose to the second floor ahead. Sunlight poured through a large Palladian window at the second level of the foyer up front, and a pair of gorgeous, dark wooden doors stood open, exposing a manicured lawn shaded by royal palm trees and oaks dripping with Spanish moss. The view beyond, however, was obscured by a bright, white light.

"Jacey?" Micah's voice came from a distance. The vision faded, but the disoriented feeling lingered.

"Did you see that?" I asked. "Do you feel it?"

Micah's eyes darted around. "It does feel strange in here, but all I see is an empty space."

He shone his flashlight over the gray concrete walls.

"This is unexpected," he said as he walked farther inside to inspect. "I'd hoped the pipes would be exposed."

The light careened over the area, glancing over an object in the far corner.

"What's that?" I asked. Micah moved the beam back, and it landed on a rectangular, brown object lying in an otherwise empty room that shouldn't even be here.

I rushed over to it. A book. My fingers caressed the soft leather cover before picking it up. Micah stood behind me, looking over my shoulder as he directed the light on the front cover. We both gasped.

An intricate picture was embossed into the leather—what appeared to be a large willow tree with fish and dolphins swimming underneath it. A clasp secured the book closed, like a journal, but there was no keyhole, no knobs to squeeze together, nothing. I turned the book over, only to find the same image embossed on the back, but still no way to reveal the pages inside. Looking at the front again, I swiped a finger over the clasp, feeling for something, anything, but only found smooth metal.

"I wonder what's wrong with Sammy," Micah said, distracting me. Sammy stood at the makeshift door Micah had cut open, barking in our direction but not coming in. "We better get going anyway. We have a lot to do, including buying you a new door."

When we returned to full daylight, I inspected the clasp more closely and ran my finger over it again, but still nothing.

Micah set the plywood into place, kind of leaning it precariously, then half-assed pushed the siding over it.

"There's nothing for anyone to bother in there," he said as we walked around the corner. Then he glanced up toward my door. "But your place is a different story."

We went upstairs, and Micah fiddled with the door enough so it would close. The latch wouldn't lock and the door would be easy to push open, but at least it wouldn't be hanging ajar, an open invitation to anyone passing by.

"Sammy, be a good boy and guard our stuff, okay?" I said, scratching him behind the ears. "Don't let anyone in. Bark like crazy and scare them away."

He wagged his tail, as if he understood.

"I could really use a shower," Micah said as we headed toward his truck. "Do you mind if we swing by my place for a minute?"

Trying not to let my imagination carry away at the thought of Micah in the shower, I could barely manage to say, "No problem."

"Why'd you bring that?" he asked when I slid into the cab.

"Oh." I looked down at the book still in my hand. "No idea. Didn't realize I had."

I placed it on the seat and pretty much forgot about it when we pulled into a familiar driveway.

"You live here?" I asked with a laugh.

"Yeah, back here. Why?" He drove up to the guesthouse that sat behind the very house I'd first pulled up to when I came to town. The one where Buck found me right when I'd thought I'd seen someone moving around inside. The "someone" had been Micah!

"Um . . . no reason," I said, my voice wobbly. Adding this "coincidence" in with everything else made me want to break into laughter—hysterical, likely maniacal laughter. "Trust me. You don't want to know."

I felt kind of weird being in Micah's little home. After all, I'd only met him yesterday. But I was also curious to see where he lived. *How* he lived. He left me in the small living room with its adjoining kitchen while he went into the bedroom. He didn't bother to close the door, and it was all I could do to not follow and watch. Instead I poked around a little, though there wasn't much to see. The owners had obviously furnished the place, and whatever personal belongings Micah possessed, they weren't out on display.

Just as he grumbled something incomprehensible then turned the shower on, the knob of his front door wiggled. My breath caught, but before I could move, the door swung open. A tall woman, only a little older than me, wearing a bikini top and a beach towel around her waist, stood in the doorway. She sucked in a breath and glared at me with slits for eyes and fists on her hips.

"Like, who the hell are you and what are you doing in my house?" she demanded.

CHAPTER 16

Jacey
1989

So Micah had a girlfriend. And not just a girlfriend, but a *live-in* girlfriend. Awesome. Totally fucking awesome. So much for him being all alone. His entire sob story was probably a crock of dung.

"I don't need this," I muttered as I headed for the door. But the woman wouldn't move.

"What? You think you're gonna, like, mosey on outta here without an explanation?" she said. "Think again!"

"Geez, take a chill pill. I had no idea. Really." I tried to shoulder my way past her so I could run far away from there before I either broke into sobs or busted my hand as I put it through something. I couldn't believe how stupid I'd been. Of course someone like Micah had a girlfriend. He was no different than any other jerkoff who had his looks, playing me like the dumb, naïve girl I was. And it didn't help that she had a perfect body with bodacious curves and honey-colored, smooth-as-silk skin bared for all to admire. I wanted to put my hand through *her*.

When she shoved me back inside, I almost did.

"You think I'm, like, stupid or something?" she nearly yelled. "Nobody steals from me and walks away from it!"

My hands balled into fists at my sides, and I was about to take a swing.

"Who the hell are you?" Micah and the woman said at the same time.

Wearing only a towel around his waist and dog tags, he stood dripping wet in the bedroom doorway, and oh my god, was he a sight to see. But I was certainly glad I wasn't on the receiving end of the glare he had for this woman. *Okay, I've misjudged things.* But if she wasn't his live-in girlfriend, who was she?

"Did you just, like, take a shower in my house?" the woman screeched.

Micah strode several paces toward her. "You mean *my* house."

"Excuse me? I'm so sure!" Her eyes traveled down Micah's wet body and up again, and her voice went from salty to sweet. "I, like, think I know where I live, but if you'd, like, want to stay . . ." *Oh, gag me.* Then she looked over at me and back at him. "Just put the dog out first."

I flew at the woman, but Micah's arm darted out and wrapped around my waist. Oh, my god, I was up against his nearly naked body. The woman's eyes narrowed, and she made a sound of disgust.

"I suggest you leave," Micah said, his voice low and threatening. "You have no right coming into *my* place and treating my guest like this."

The woman lifted an eyebrow. "Leave? Are you kidding? You both need to leave *my* place, or I'll call the cops. Or better yet." She turned and glanced out the still open door. "Here comes my Aunt Gracie. You, like, totally don't want to mess with her."

Micah's arm around me loosened but didn't let go. "Grace Jones? She's your aunt?"

The woman recoiled with surprise. "You know her?"

"Of course. I'm watching her house for her. Taking care of the grounds."

The woman chuckled and rolled her eyes. "I'm so sure. Are you high or something?"

"Martha? I heard all kinds of racket in here. What's all the fuss about?" An older woman, about sixty years old and the kind of soft and plump you wanted to hug, appeared in the doorway. "Oh. Who's this handsome young man? You didn't tell me you met anyone."

"I haven't," Martha said through clenched teeth as she folded her arms over her chest. "I, like, came home and found her in here and he was taking a shower in my bathroom."

"I'm sorry, Mrs. Jones," Micah said, "there must be some kind of misunderstanding."

The older woman tilted her head as she peered at us. "Do I know you?"

Micah's arm completely released me, and he took a step forward, holding his hand out. "Yes, ma'am. I'm Micah Humphrey. You hired me to take care of your place for the summer, remember? We met in March."

Mrs. Jones smiled and shook Micah's hand. "You're right. There must be some misunderstanding." Both Micah and I relaxed. "Martha's my only house sitter. The only person I'd ever trust. I've never met you before in my life, young man. I think I would remember. You're very handsome and charming."

"Ma'am, I assure you we've met before. Angie introduced us, remember?"

"Angie?" Mrs. Jones' eyes glassed over for a moment, then she shook her head. "No, I'm afraid I don't know an Angie. I'm sorry for whatever misunderstanding there is here, but you must leave now, young man."

"Mrs. Jones—" Micah began.

The sweet old lady pulled her glasses down her nose and peered over them, looking Micah squarely in the eyes. "Put some clothes on and get out of here now. If you do so quietly, I won't call the police. I see you're a soldier and not pressing charges for breaking and entering is my way of thanking you for your service. Do you understand?" She pushed her glasses up her nose and smiled sweetly again, though her eyes meant business.

Micah stared at her in disbelief for a long moment. Then his gaze went to Martha, and then came to me. He gave me an infinitesimal shake of his head before turning on his heel and heading for the bedroom.

"Excuse me," I said softly. "I'm totally sorry for . . . this."

I made a beeline out the door and for the truck, but then I wasn't sure what to do. The old me would have kept on walking. My place was only about a mile away, and a walk on the beach sure sounded better than listening to excuses of a psycho who had been mooching off some poor old lady, living in her guesthouse without her even knowing it.

But things were different now. My life had become a Rubik's cube, with new twists and turns every day creating a bigger, unsolvable mess. My own best friend and roommate had denied knowing me, so how hard was it to believe an old woman who'd met Micah only once would have forgotten him? Except she wasn't *that* old and seemed to have her wits about her. And Micah was definitely unforgettable.

"*It starts with the people you know and love, and before long, your whole existence will be completely forgotten by this world.*" The shadow-man's words echoed in my mind.

I had to give Micah the benefit of the doubt. After all, we were apparently in this together.

"Thank God you're still here," Micah said as he came jogging up to the truck, a huge army-green duffle bag in his hand. He swung it over the side of the bed and dropped it into the back. "I thought you would have booked by now."

"Oh, I was tempted."

He came around to my side of the truck and placed a hand on each of my cheeks. "I have no idea what just went down, but I'm going to find out. I need to make a phone call. Please believe me, Jace. I'm not some weirdo breaking into people's houses and lying about it."

His eyes told me his truth. "This is totally bogus, whatever's going on, but, yeah, I believe you."

He pulled me into his arms, and my heart went into overdrive.

"Thank you," he said with a breath of relief. He kissed the top of my head, then let me go and opened my door for me. "We'll go to the library first. I can use the pay phone there to call Angie. She was my last foster mother, the one who told me about Mrs. Jones. They'd been friends for years, according to Angie. Maybe she can explain what's going on."

When Micah tried to call her, though, her line had been disconnected. He called directory service for her state and all the ones surrounding it. Realizing he was grasping at straws, he slammed the phone into its cradle, making the bell ding. He braced his hands on the side of the phone booth, and his head hung as he glared at the ground. His jaw muscle twitched.

"Micah, don't have a cow, but I have something to tell you," I said from right outside the folding door, and he looked over his shoulder at me with anger sparking in his eyes.

The events from this morning might piss him off even more, which I didn't exactly want to do, but he needed to know. What had happened to me was apparently happening to him. I told him all about my phone call with Bex and then what the Billy Idol dude's voice had said afterward.

"What the hell does that mean?" he growled.

I could only shrug, because, like with everything else going on, I had no idea.

"Well, let's see if we can find out." He pushed out of the phone booth and strode for the library's front doors.

As soon as we walked inside, I drew in a deep breath, loving the musty fragrance of old books and leather bindings. But this little place resembled a home library compared to the one at school. The university library had several floors of nothing but books, with a few computers in one section for students to write papers, although I never used them. The machines scared me, except for the one where I could look up books by author or subject and the screen would tell me what section the book was in, which was pretty convenient. Here, they only had the standard card catalog. And not much of a selection, especially non-fiction. So much for doing extensive research.

Not that we had time anyway. We still needed to return to the lumber store and buy me a new door, and Micah wouldn't leave me alone and vulnerable. As everything became more bizarre by the hour, I really didn't want to be alone anyway. So together we found a couple of promising books, and Micah checked them out using his card, since I didn't even have a local driver's license. I was pleasantly surprised he had a library card.

By the time we arrived home, the sun dangled low over the Gulf, my door hung open, and Sammy was gone.

"Anything missing?" Micah asked from behind me as I gaped at the mess from the doorway.

The nice, neat pile of suitcases and bags I'd brought in from the Jeep was now strewn throughout the main room, my stuff dumped out of them.

"Yeah. My dog. Who cares about the rest of this stuff?" I pushed past him and ran down the stairs, yelling Sammy's name.

When I paused for a breath, a scurrying sound came from the overgrown bushes. My stomach flipped and my heart stuttered with the thought of the two men from last night diving into those same bushes.

"Sammy?" I said, my voice a little shaky with trepidation as I slowly moved toward the sound. A twig snapped and a puppy-like whine came from the bushes. I inched closer, worried he was hurt, but also afraid I was walking into a trap. "You okay, boy?"

Silence answered me. I moved closer then crouched down, trying to peer into the bushes. I reached a hand out to move a branch to the side. A large, dark shadow flew at me, a lot like the one this morning by the pay phone. I screamed, and tried to jump to my feet and run, but terror made me clumsy. The object plowed into me, knocking me on my back. The breath flew out of my lungs as stars wavered in my vision. Something wet dragged over my cheek.

My eyes focused on the square, yellow head, dark brown eyes and black nose hovering right over my face. A pink tongue darted out and covered my cheek again.

"Sammy!" I shrieked with joy this time and threw my arms around his neck.

My joy at finding him safe, though acting a little funny,

quickly changed to disappointment when we entered the efficiency. Sammy had never misbehaved so badly, but it explained his strange, timid behavior right now.

"Sammy, did you do this?" I said accusingly. His head sunk and his tail drooped between his legs.

"Not unless he can work zippers," Micah said as he squatted over one of my bags and a pile of clothes next to it.

My gaze slid over the mess. Every bag and suitcase remained intact, gaping at the zipped or snapped openings, and my stuff was in fairly neat piles, as if dumped, rather than each piece being pulled out one at a time and strewn around the room. The clothes weren't folded—they'd definitely been rifled through—but this wasn't the kind of mess a dog would make. My skin crawled, and I felt dirty and grimy. Violated.

Micah took my hand and dragged me across the street to the pay phone to call the police because he refused to leave me alone even for a few seconds. I staggered in a daze after him. All I really wanted was a shower. The police came, briefly investigated and took our reports.

"You didn't notice anything missing?" the blond cop asked me.

I shook my head. "I don't think so. I don't have anything of much value."

"Anything they'd be searching for?"

"No." I shook my head again. "And who? Nobody knows me here. What would they think I had?"

The cop chuckled. "Everybody—the locals anyway—knows you're here. It's a small town, ma'am. Unfortunately, we do have our riffraff. They were probably looking for jewelry or other valuables. I'm sorry this happened to you." He nodded at my door. "I suggest you fix the door and put a good bolt lock on it. Doesn't look like that mutt of yours is much of a guard dog."

I frowned, but bit my tongue from defending Sammy. My dog had done an excellent job of protecting me last night, so whoever did this had scared him. Badly. And it took a lot to scare Sammy.

"Why did you bother calling them?" I asked Micah after the police left into the night with absolutely no evidence. "You know who did this, and I doubt a couple of small-town cops can do anything about what's going on. Those guys aren't normal run-of-the-mill thugs."

"No, but it doesn't hurt to have patrol cars driving by every now and then and keeping an eye out."

While Micah hung the new door and added a bolt lock to it, I took a long, hot shower. Funny how this morning I attempted to wash away the feeling of Micah in my veins, and now, twelve hours later, I tried to scrub off the violated feeling of some grody dudes pawing my clothes. My bras and my underwear. Yeah, real funny. Maybe this was a sign I needed to get out of here, go back north, take care of Bex and forget about the gnarly mess here.

But when I walked out of the bathroom, I knew I couldn't do such a thing.

I held a towel wrapped around me and stared at my clothes still in their strangely neat piles. The thought of putting a single scrap of those things on my body right now gagged me. Micah came through the door then with his big military bag. He dropped it next to the door and began fishing through it, then he handed me a t-shirt and a pair of boxers.

"They're clean, don't worry," he said with a crooked smile. "We'll wash all your stuff tomorrow."

I blinked away the tears threatening to fall because of his kindness. He understood. How could someone so rough be so sweet? How could someone who barely knew me care so much? Deep down I knew the answer to that one, which was why I knew I couldn't leave.

I hadn't realized I'd been trembling until Micah came over, wrapped his arms around my shoulders and pulled me tight against him. I buried my face into his chest and fought back the sobs. He held me for several minutes, not moving as I breathed in his now familiar scent, as I felt his presence once again swirl within me, warming me from the inside out. Once he felt me calm down, he stepped back and took the t-shirt wadded up in my hands. I tightened the towel around me, an automatic reaction, when he pulled the shirt over my head and down over the terrycloth. Then he took the boxers from me and helped me step into them, then pulled them up and under the towel.

"Um," he said when they were halfway up, his voice rough, "if I go any farther, they'll end up coming back off."

The sound of a strangled laugh came from my throat, and I reached under the towel to pull the boxers up, then dropped the towel to the floor. The shorts barely hung on my hips, but the t-shirt came to my thighs and practically covered the boxers anyway. Micah stared at me—well, my body in his undergarments—for a long time, then turned away, his tongue swiping over his lips. I wondered if he'd be reacting the same way if he saw what was underneath his clothes I wore, or if he'd wrinkle his nose in disgust.

He proceeded to bunch up my pallet of blankets and then tossed them onto one of the piles of clothes before spreading his own out on the floor.

"I'm not trying to say I'm staying here," Micah said as he made me a new bed. "Honestly, I'm not presuming anything. Except . . . I didn't think you'd want to sleep on those . . ."

"Micah?" I said, my voice soft. He stopped what he was doing, inhaled a deep breath, then turned to look at me. "Please stay with me. I don't think . . . I don't want to be alone tonight."

"You're sure?"

"Totally." Strange how comfortable I'd already become with him, considering we'd only known each other for two days. Or had we? How long had we really known each other? Were we really the same soul split in two?

Micah's dimples flashed. "Guess I don't really have anywhere to go anyway, do I?"

I reheated leftover pizza for dinner, but although I hadn't eaten anything all day, I had no appetite. Micah did, though, so in addition to pizza, I brought out some chips and dip for him and strawberries for me, about the only thing I could stomach. We munched while starting in on the books we'd brought home from the library. They told us nothing more than what we already knew.

The one book we'd found specifically on Twin Flames described the phenomenon the same way as the handwriting in the back of my dictionary had—one soul divided into two and the two halves constantly searched for each other—but most of the book was dedicated to finding your own twin flame, as if everyone had one. Maybe they do, but not everyone went through what Micah and I were dealing with.

"But what does it all mean?" I asked when we finished skimming through all the books and realized we had nothing useful. "What's the purpose of it all? What's causing everything to happen? And why *us*?"

"Obviously nobody's experienced what we have, or someone would have written a book about it. We must be unique. Or someone's screwing with us. Maybe there isn't a 'why' or a purpose."

I considered this. "But I feel like there is. In my gut. Don't you?"

Micah tossed the last book on the floor, pushed to his feet and began pacing. "I'm not sure I can trust my gut right now. It's been acting all kinds of crazy lately."

I looked up at him and said, "It brought you to me. Do you think that's a mistake?"

He threw his arms in the air. "I don't know, Jacey!"

Oh. Dude. Did he really say that? I didn't know whether to be hurt or angry. Something must have shown on my face because when he made his turn and saw my expression, he was instantly on his knees in front of me.

"Ah, shit. I'm sorry, Jace. That's not what I meant." He wrapped me into a hug. "I'm glad I met you. This . . . this holding you in my arms right now . . . I never would have imagined a feeling like this. This feeling of being whole. I only meant I don't know if following my gut has created all this other fucked-up stuff or if all this other stuff was happening anyway, causing me to follow my gut. Am I making any sense?"

I pulled back a little. "Yeah. Like the chicken and the egg?"

"Exactly."

"So I don't scare you? I mean, this whatever it is between us?"

"Well, I didn't say that. You kind of scare the hell out of me, actually, even if we didn't have all this whatever it is between us."

I swiped my finger over his nose and chuckled. "How on earth do I scare you, Marine?"

"I told you. You cause me to lose my self-control. These feelings I have for you . . . *already* . . . they scare me." He gripped my chin between his fingers and thumb, and his eyes bore into mine. "But more than anything, the thought of losing you . . . that would break me, Jacey, like nothing in my miserable life ever has."

The sincerity in his eyes showed the truth of what he said, and my heart flew into a panic. He'd stepped right up to the line of saying those three words, and if he crossed it, I might punch him. This was all too much, entirely too fast. I felt the same way, and he was right—the feeling was scary as hell.

I pulled away from him, and now it was my turn to pace, but I wasn't much of a pacer. I stopped in front of the kitchen counter, the only indication of where the living room ended and the kitchen began, and stared down at the leather-bound book we'd found this afternoon. Something in the embossed image caught my eye.

"Micah, this may sound crazy—"

"Define 'crazy' because it'll take a lot to impress me now."

"Well . . . I think this book may have our answers." I took it over to him and sat down beside him, then placed the book in my lap. I pointed to the image carved into the trunk of the tree that neither of us had noticed earlier, then clasped his hand again so our tattoo-marks matched up. The little carving in the tree trunk was a bird with flames for wings. Flames exactly like our tattoos.

"Nice. Hooray. If only we could get it open." He lifted the book from my lap with his free hand and inspected the clasp closely. "Maybe a sharp knife? I have one in my toolbox."

He moved to stand up, but I didn't let go of his hand. "Wait. Look. That wasn't there before."

The same fiery bird had appeared on the metal clasp that had been perfectly smooth. I ran my finger over the clasp. The book fell open.

And every page was blank.

CHAPTER 17

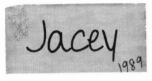

"You're hired," I told Micah the next morning before popping the last strawberry into my mouth.

He looked at me across the makeshift table he'd created out of the scraps from my stairs. "You want to fix the place up?"

I shrugged. "May as well, right? Looks like I'll be here for a while anyway."

"Cool beans," he said with a smile. "What about Bex?"

My shoulders sagged. "Maybe I'll fly up there for a couple of days to make sure she's okay."

"Not alone, you won't."

"You have to stay here and work."

"You're not going alone, Jacey," he said more firmly.

I considered arguing with him, but chose to drop the subject for now. I'd awoken in a relatively good mood—the first time in a long time—and I didn't want to ruin it. Maybe I had accepted this fate of ours overnight and realized I must make the most of it, or maybe waking up in Micah's arms had put me in high spirits.

I'd been a little worried when we first lay down together last night, since we possessed little control over ourselves with each other. Neither of us were virgins, of course, and we were both adults, and we seemed to be more permanently bound than any married couple, considering the bonds our souls had made, so sex didn't have to be a big issue. But I'd learned too late what people meant when they said relinquishing your virginity to someone was a gift, and I'd regretted every sexual encounter I'd had to date. Not that there were lots, but in hindsight, one time had been too many.

I'd hung around enough guys since then, had been exposed to enough porno and seen enough sex in public to learn guys worshipped the cootchie. They talked about it frequently and thought about it even more. They wanted to see it, touch it, taste it, master it. As if once they came out on the day they were born, all they could think about was how to get back in. They may take you out, treat you like a princess and maybe even really care about *you*, but as soon as you give them access to the jewel between your legs, you've made their dreams come true. You've given them a slice of heaven. And not every guy deserves to have that, not my slice of heaven anyway.

Like I said, I'd come to appreciate this too late to keep my virginity, which was the most precious slice of all, but now I knew better. I decided a long time ago I would only give my little gift to a man who deserved it, and I wasn't sure yet if Micah was that man. My heart and soul felt certain, but my brain still questioned this unbelievable connection we had. What if this was all a fluke and a few months down the road, we went on our separate ways? Or even in a few weeks or *days*? The thought pained me, but I couldn't see the future. And since the craziness had only started a few days ago (not counting our meeting in Virginia), it could end just as quickly. I wasn't ready to go all-in yet. Not in that way.

We *were* able to control ourselves, though, basically by not starting anything in the first place. We didn't even kiss goodnight. I settled into the "bed" with my back to him and he did the same, and we lay there awkwardly for a while as the charged energy around us settled. We didn't talk. We barely breathed, afraid any movement would set us off. And somehow, we'd both fallen asleep.

Sometime in the night, we'd become entangled, though, and I'd awoken to his arms around me and my back pressed against his chest. And it felt alarmingly right.

"So, anyway," I said to drop the subject of going north, "I want to start with this apartment, if possible. I want to make it more comfy for us to live in while we work on the rest of the place."

He lifted an eyebrow, but I didn't know if it was for the "*us* to live in" or the "while *we* work." Both had been slips of the tongue.

"Um, I mean, if you want to stay here. Just, uh, thought it would be more convenient . . ." I stood up, my face flushing, and walked over to the French doors. I turned my back to him, presumably to gaze at the fog hanging over the beach side of the street, but more to hide my face. "Actually, this place is livable enough for now, I guess, so we could start on one of the others, and you could stay in that one as soon as it's done. It's the least I can do for you."

He didn't say anything, so I glanced over my shoulder. His beam showed nearly all of his pearly whites. I narrowed my eyes, using the façade of anger to hide the flush.

"Actually," he finally said, "I was more intrigued by the idea of you helping me."

I stiffened even more. "Yeah, I didn't, like, mean that either. Even less than . . . the other thing I said. I can draw floor plans or whatever you need, but I'm clueless about construction. It could be totally dangerous."

"I can't do everything by myself, but I'll try to keep you out of it as much as possible, okay?" he offered. I nodded. "As for the other thing . . . whatever you feel good with. I don't expect anything, but I do have this need to be close. You understand, right?"

I nodded again. "More than I should."

He glanced around the one-room unit. "It won't take much to get this one up to your standards. Why don't we start with it and go from there?"

So we did. He inspected the efficiency more closely, made a list of supplies, and we went shopping together. We went everywhere together because he'd hardly let me out of his sight. While he worked, I began keeping a journal in the book we found.

"What are you doing?" Micah had asked me when I'd first sat down to write.

"Well, it's totally meant for us, with the mark and everything, and since there's nothing in it, I guess we're supposed to put something in it. So I figured I'd write down everything happening to us and maybe somehow it'll help. Why else would we be given a blank book?"

I'd considered the idea Pops had left it for me, and it was the reason he needed me to come down and work on the place. A far-fetched idea, but at this point, I could almost believe anything.

Micah shrugged. "If you think it'll help . . . .. It's not like there's much else we can do about it right now."

"Maybe a clue or lead or something will come up, but yeah, in the meantime, I'll write our story down while you're working."

We fell into a routine. Micah worked, and I wrote in the journal and helped him when he needed an extra set of hands. In the evenings, we took Sammy for walks on the beach and ate dinner, and then I told him about the day's journal entry, leaving out some of the embarrassing details and hoping he'd never actually read the thing. We became more comfortable with each other and our trust in ourselves grew. We could even have a heavy make-out session and bring ourselves to stop. It wasn't easy, but we found a way. At least, I did, still unsure of whether I was willing to give him my gift.

"What's this?" Micah asked one evening as he stared at the open journal.

I'd wanted him to see this page—a drawing I'd felt compelled to add of a beachside Victorian mansion with gingerbread trim, a second-floor balcony wrapped in wrought iron railings, and a sweeping front lawn with royal palm trees and oaks dripping with Spanish moss. The outside of the place I'd envisioned in the secret space downstairs. I didn't remember ever seeing such a mansion in person, but I felt like I'd actually been there before.

"How did you know?" Micah asked.

"Know what?" My brows pushed together.

"I've dreamt about this place."

"I . . . I didn't." A chill waved over my skin, raising goose bumps. "I've been picturing it in my head ever since we found the space downstairs. That's why I felt like I should draw it in the book."

Micah's eyes traced over the sketch. "I can't believe the detail you captured. Do you know where it is?"

I hesitated because I did kind of have an idea, but I felt ridiculous for believing it. I finally blurted it out. "Not exactly, but I sort of want to say Tampa or Saint Petersburg."

"Yeah . . . me, too."

"Do you think . . ." Again, the idea was silly, but I said it anyway. ". . . maybe we should try to find it?"

"Without an address, we have no way. Tampa/St. Pete isn't exactly a small area."

Good point. "Well, who knows? Maybe the address will magically come to us."

Micah harrumphed, knowing that could very well happen. We let the subject drop, for the time being anyway.

Time became a funny thing since Micah and I met. We spent hours a day asking questions, trying to get to know each other better, but at the same time, we already felt like we'd been together for eons. Literally. Sometimes we already knew the answer to our questions as soon as we asked. Things that were basic to our personalities, like he knew I was creative before I even told him about my dreams of being an artist, and I knew he was the logical type, having to analyze a situation before diving in.

"You're like bright fire," he said one night as he wrapped a lock of my red hair around his finger.

We lay on our makeshift bed, facing each other, but I had to roll on my back and stare at the ceiling, blinking against the sting behind my eyes. He propped himself up on an elbow to hover over me.

"What's wrong?" he asked.

I shook my head, but a lump had formed in my throat and the tears welled, threatening to fall. I squeezed my eyes shut.

"I don't like fire," I managed to say, and it sounded totally stupid. Not at all what I felt inside.

"I just meant you're warm-hearted, and you have this sometimes explosive personality when you're outraged and a charge forward attitude. You brighten the room you're in and you seem to be lighting my way."

I gulped, trying to swallow that lump away, and opened my eyes to find his warm ones studying my face.

"I meant it as a compliment," he said. "Your heat is consuming me, and I like it."

I forced a small smile, but the tears wouldn't stop. I didn't want to be fire. I hated fire. Fire had ruined my whole life.

"Jacey, what's wrong?" He moved closer to me, his face filled with worry as he wiped the tears from my temple.

"Fire . . . kills," I finally choked out.

He studied my face with those warm, dark eyes of his, his forehead wrinkled with concern and bewilderment. Then his eyes widened before his hand came to my cheek. He kissed each side of my quivering mouth.

"Your parents?" he asked. I nodded. "Tell me."

I inhaled a deep breath, and it shuddered out of me. "There's not much to say. We were at our cabin in the mountains. The fire in the fireplace popped and sparks flew out of the hearth. The cabin ignited like a Christmas tree. Mom and Dad . . . they couldn't get out."

"And you did."

"Barely. The ceiling caved, and I thought I was going to die, but . . . ." I let my voice trail off.

"How?" Micah pressed.

I turned my head toward the side of the bed where Sammy lay and buried my hand in his neck fur. "He was barely more than a puppy, but Sammy pulled me out."

Micah looked at my dog, and a grin spread over his face. "I knew there was a reason I liked you, Sammy. You're a hero." He reached across me to give Sammy a pat on the head, then returned his gaze to me. "Kind of ironic your last name is Burns."

"Yeah. Ironic." I chuckled, the sound hollow. "I guess you're right, though. I am like fire."

His eyes narrowed for a moment, then he leaned down farther and pressed his forehead against mine. "You are brave and strong and passionate, especially about the people you love. I can see it in how you worry about Bex. I can hear it when you talk about your Pops. I know you love your parents, but don't blame yourself for surviving, Jacey. You were *meant* to."

He stopped me from arguing by planting his mouth on mine, and he kissed away any coherent thoughts about my parents, the fire . . . about anything but him and me.

I always tried to do the same for him when he'd thrash in the night and wake up screaming. I'd hold him in my arms until he settled down, but he never explained anything except to say, "Real-life nightmares." Guess we both had those. Quite a couple we were.

We had so many things in common, it was scary, but we were also polar opposites in many areas, as if we filled in each other's holes, making us complete. After a week, it felt like a lifetime or two had passed. We were already finishing each other's sentences like an old married couple, which was how we felt—except in that one area.

And we could physically *feel* each other's presences, even miles away.

Well, the farthest Micah tested this pull to each other was a mile, but that didn't mean we couldn't go farther. He didn't like being so far away from me, though, in case those men returned. We hadn't seen them at all, but when we walked Sammy, especially at night, we both *felt* someone following us, staying to the shadows because we never saw them. I started calling them Shadowmen.

I grew more and more concerned about Bex. Two weeks went by since she'd called me a psycho and hung up on me, and I hadn't been able to get a hold of her or her mom since. Nobody ever answered the phone except an answering machine. Today I would try once again, and I was prepared to continue trying all day long until I spoke to someone. I needed to know Bex was okay. A queasy feeling in my gut told me she wasn't.

When I picked up the cheap little princess phone I'd bought, however, the newly installed line was dead.

"Dude, what's up with the phone?" I called to Micah. He was supposed to be installing new flooring in the bathroom, closet and kitchen today, the last part of renovating my unit before moving on to the next one. "Did you cut the line or something?"

"No," he answered from inside the closet. "Something wrong?"

I crossed the ten steps to the closet in the corner of the apartment, an unusually large space, although it was the only storage area in the efficiency. Micah was on his hands and knees in the corner, his perfect ass facing me, dimples showing above the waistband of his acid-wash jeans.

"Um . . ." What was I here for? Oh, right. "There's no dial tone. I'm going to go across the street and call the phone company. And Bex while I'm over there."

He leaned back on his heels, then stood and turned toward me, so now his bare chest was in my face. My tongue ran over my lips, wanting to lick it. He cleared his throat. I looked up at his face, faking innocence, but he'd caught me.

"I'll go down with you," he said with a curve of his lips. "I think I might have found something here, but I need a crowbar."

A crowbar? Yeah, right. "If you insist."

He probably planned to wait in the yard so he could keep an eye on me. I didn't mind his overprotectiveness for the most part. I sensed the malicious presence, too, and although I wasn't afraid of much, the Shadowmen made me edgy. Having a Marine watching out for me wasn't a bad thing.

Micah headed for his truck as I hurried across the street and called the phone company.

"I'm sorry, but I don't show service at that address," the lady on the other end of the line told me.

"I've only had it a couple of days. Unit D," I clarified.

"No, ma'am, there's nothing in our records. Would you like me to place an order for new service?"

What the hell? "No! I just got new service two days ago. Can you check again?"

"I'm looking right now, but I don't see anything." She rattled off the address to me, and I confirmed she had it right. "And you say you've had service?"

"Yes," I said through gritted teeth, my nerves beginning to wear.

"I'll look into this and send someone out."

"Thank you," I said as pleasantly as I could muster.

"And your name again?"

With a groan, I gave her my name—again—and my address—again—even though she should have had both in their system. I'd already made long distance calls, so I was sure they'd suddenly find me when they decided to bill me the measly ten cents a call for reaching an answering machine.

I hung up with her, dropped in several quarters and called Bex's Mom's number. Finally, someone answered.

"Hey, Mrs. K, this is Jacey, Bex's roommate," I said, feeling the need to qualify myself after the last conversation I had with her. "Is Bex there?"

"Excuse me?" she demanded, her voice a mix of disbelief and horror. "Is this some kind of sick joke?"

"Um . . ." What was that supposed to mean? Her tone terrified me. She must have been off her meds again. "No. I just want to speak to Bex."

"How dare you!" she screamed. "Who do you think you are, sicko?"

I cleared my throat and tried to speak calmly and softly. "Mrs. Kelly, please, calm down. It's me, Jacey. Bex's roommate. Is everything okay?"

"Darcy?" she asked, and her voice completely changed. "Oh, my God, honey. I'm sorry. I'm not myself. It's true, honey. The message you got is true."

"Jacey," I murmured, relieved she'd at least come close to

getting it right, which meant she remembered me. Then I spoke up, confused. "What message? Where? What's going on?"

"The message my brother left you on your answering machine. I'm sorry I couldn't call you myself. I'm just . . . so . . ." Mrs. Kelly broke into a fit of sobs.

"I'm sorry I didn't get the message," I said. "I don't have an answering machine."

She sniffled. "Of course you do, honey. I bought it for you and Rebecca just last week, for your apartment. You two had that sweet message, 'Hi, this is Darcy and Bex,' each of you saying your name. Oh, dear God, I'll never hear her voice again." And she had another meltdown.

I considered hanging up and calling back later when she was off the sauce or on her meds or whatever had her so screwed up was fixed, but her last words and the grief in her sobs sent a ripple of fear up my spine. Before I could say something, a new voice, a male came on the line.

"Who is this?" he demanded, the anger and accusation in his tone catching me off guard. I recognized Bex's older brother's voice—it's not one you could forget, baritone and bold although he wasn't much bigger than Bex or me.

"Ronnie, it's me, Jacey."

"We don't know a Jacey."

Here we go again. Maybe I could make him remember, though. "Of course you do. You stayed in mine and Bex's dorm room. Threw up all over my pillow after drinking a bottle of tequila, remember?"

"Bex has always roomed with Darcy, so whoever you are— Wait a minute. This is the same number. You're calling from the same number that keeps calling here, aren't you?" His voice rose with anger and more accusation. "Did you do that to her? Are you the sicko who took her? I'll fucking kill you!"

A shudder ran through me, and my stomach clenched. "No. No, no, no. Ronnie, please settle down. I have no idea what you're talking about. I'm all the way in Florida. What's going on?"

"Yeah, that's what this Caller ID shows, but how do we know? Maybe you're in on it! Bex told me about the psycho pretending to be her best friend. You better have a good alibi, miss, or a good lawyer because we're going to trace this call and—"

"Hang up and call the police," Mrs. Kelly yelled in the background. "We need to tell them about this call."

"Ronnie, stop!" I shrieked, panic gripping me. "What's wrong with Bex? Please just tell me."

"She's dead!" he roared. "Murdered!"

CHAPTER 18

 "If you had anything to do with it, lady, so help me God—" Ronnie continued, but the phone slipped from my shaking hand before I heard his threat.

I lurched forward and my feet caught on something, making me stumble a few steps before taking off into a sprint. I paid no attention to any possible traffic as I ran across the road and ignored Micah as I bounded up the steps two stairs at a time.

My clothes were already stuffed into bags, ready to be taken to the laundromat. I grabbed a couple, not knowing what was in them and not caring, as well as Sammy's dog food and leash.

Micah blocked the door.

"Where are you going?" he demanded. "What's wrong?"

"I have to go north. To Virginia." I tried to push past him but he was a boulder.

"Not alone. You already know that."

"I'm going," I said through clenched teeth.

"Jacey—"

"Just stop!" I yelled. "Forget about me. I have to go north. I have to go to Bex. She . . . she's . . . she needs me."

I couldn't repeat what Ronnie said. I couldn't believe it. Not until I saw for myself.

"Right this minute?"

"YES!" I screamed. "Now!"

He took a half-step back, startled by my ferocity, and I seized the opportunity to push past him. He flew inside, and I soared down the stairs and for my Jeep. I stopped dead several feet from it. Something was taped to the driver's side window. A newspaper clipping, about half a page actually. The picture and headline seemed to burn brightly from the page, ensuring I could see them:

MISSING COLLEGE STUDENT'S BODY FOUND

Bex's picture.

My stomach heaved as though I'd been punched.

Something large slammed into me from behind. Micah caught me before I hit the ground, but his eyes were glued on the same thing as mine. With two strides forward, he ripped it off the window.

"He said she was murdered," I whispered without really knowing what I was saying. "But it can't be true. It's a lie. Right? How could they even accuse me of such a thing?"

Micah's head snapped toward me. "What? *Who?*"

I stared at him with unseeing eyes, my mind boggling. "It's not true."

"They accused you, Jacey?" Micah demanded, his voice rough. Large hands grabbed my shoulders and shook me. I lifted my eyes to his face. "Who? What did they say?"

My mouth moved without my brain registering half of my words.

"Her family. They acted like they didn't even know me. Said I was some sicko in on it. But it doesn't matter, Micah," I said. "It's not true. She's not even dead. My Bex . . . she can't be . . ."

I shook my head, as if I could shake away the last few minutes of my life like an Etch a Sketch drawing.

He pulled me into his arms. "I'm sorry, babe. She is. And you can't go up there."

"I have to. She needs me."

"She's dead, Jace."

I shook my head. My throat thickened. "She needs me."

"She doesn't. She's gone. And if you go up there, you could be, too."

I didn't understand, my brain trying to block out the truth and the grief and the reality of it all, which meant blocking out everything.

"I have an alibi. They *know* I called from Florida," I said. "It's on their Caller I.D. thingamabob."

"That's not what I mean," Micah said, his voice low and soft. "How do you think this article got on your Jeep? It's from *The Roanoke Times*."

"That's the newspaper I had to subscribe to for current events class last year," I said absently, then his meaning started to seep in. "What's the date? How did it get all the way down here?"

"Today's date. And good question."

The hairs on the nape of my neck rose. "The Shadowmen," I whispered.

"Probably. And they had to have done it in the three minutes we were just upstairs, because it wasn't on your Jeep when I came out to my truck."

I let Micah lead me back upstairs and into the relative safety of my apartment. Not that it resembled Fort Knox or anything, but at least we no longer stood outside in broad daylight with Shadowmen nearby. My bags slid off my shoulders and fell to the floor as I stood dazedly in the middle of the room.

"Do you think they . . . Bex? Is she really . . .?" My brain was less effective at blocking things out up here in the comfort of my home, and the truth began making its way in.

"I'm sorry," Micah said again, and I couldn't deny the sorrow in his eyes.

I swallowed. I nodded. And I doubled over with full-body sobs.

Micah caught me when my knees gave out and carried me over to the pile of blankets we called a bed. He sat down against the wall with me in his lap. My tears and snot stained his shirt as he silently held me tight against him, knowing there was nothing he could say to heal my broken heart.

Time passed. Minutes? Hours? I had no idea, but the light coming through the window had changed before I could finally breathe again. I remained in Micah's arms, my cheek pressed against his chest, his heart pounding in my ear, and my eyes closed. Memories of the last two years with Bex replayed, and guilt flooded me.

"I should have gone up there before," I finally said, surprised at how hoarse my voice sounded. "I could have brought her down here. I should have let her come with me in the first place. Then she'd still be alive."

"You can't blame yourself," Micah murmured. "Don't take this on."

"How did she . . . die?" I asked, hiccupping on the word. "What does the paper say?"

He didn't answer at first, and somehow I knew he wondered if I was ready to hear it. "Somehow" as in the way we frequently seemed to know what the other was thinking. Bex's death must have been bad.

"Just tell me," I said.

"Well . . . it looks like her car broke down on the highway, and they think someone must have stopped to offer her help but had other plans. There were bruises around her neck, as if she'd been choked, and her body was in the woods only thirty yards from her car, but they didn't find it for nearly three days." Micah paused, the gulp of him swallowing sounding in my ear as his hand slid up my back and squeezed my shoulder. "They're investigating to see if she was raped."

I gasped. *My poor Bex! My poor, poor Bex.* I tried to block the image of her last minutes, but the vision of her struggle—I *knew* she fought—came to me too vividly, followed by the life leaving her eyes. New tears flowed. I should have been there. She should have been here with me! "Do they have any idea who?"

"No one they're reporting publicly. They're only saying there were two sets of footprints around her car and another set of tire tracks besides hers."

"The Shadowmen," I said.

"Maybe," Micah said. "But maybe they only knew about it and know she's important to you. Taping the article where you could see it might only be another way to mess with you. You said she hung around a lot of shady characters, right?"

I simply nodded. Regardless, her blood was on my hands. The Shadowmen obviously wanted something from me and had some sneaky plan of getting it, possibly by hurting me through Bex. And if it wasn't them, if it was one of those assholes she often ran off with for days at a time, then that was my fault, too, because I hadn't been there to protect her. I hadn't gone up there when I should have two weeks ago. A fresh round of tears built in my throat and behind my eyes until I could fight them no longer. I crawled off Micah's lap, curled into a ball and sobbed again.

I lay in bed most of the afternoon, crying or staring at the wall, wishing the boulder of guilt would crush me already and put me out of my misery. But that's not how guilt works. That's not how life works. We have to suffer with the regret of everything we meant to do for others, but never did. It's always too late for good intentions. Actions matter, not intent, and I hadn't acted fast enough to save my Bex. Or my Pops. Or my parents. And although I'd felt alone before when Pops had died, I'd had Bex. And Sammy. Now Bex was gone, too.

Sammy lay next to me, and I hugged him fiercely. He whined from the pressure I put on his shoulder, still sore from the cut the Shadowmen had made, and I released my hold. Why hadn't the wound healed yet?

"You need to get better," I said. "You can't leave me, too. You're all I have left."

Micah cleared his throat from the other side of the bed. Although I'd pretty much ignored him most of the afternoon, he hadn't left my side. I rolled over to face him.

"You have me," he said simply.

I couldn't look at him, but kept my eyes on my hand as I traced a pattern into his jeans-clad thigh. "I barely know you."

"You know that's not true."

"I mean, we just . . . it's only been two weeks. How do we—"

"Don't do this, Jacey." The sharp tone of his voice brought my gaze to his face. Determination filled his eyes. "Don't question it. You have me."

"I don't know that for sure. *You* can't say that for sure."

"Yes. I. Can."

I sat up, and little lights flashed in my vision, I'd been horizontal for so long. "No, you can't. Look at me, Micah. Look at my life. Everyone I've ever loved is gone."

"And what? You think it's some kind of jinx? Are you really going to pull that? Leave it for the books and movies."

"But maybe it is! I'm fire, remember? And fire kills. Maybe I'm some kind of death warrant for everyone I love. Your life could be on the line, and I can't risk—"

Micah had been piercing me with narrowed eyes, but now his lips twitched as if fighting a smile.

"What?" I asked with exasperation.

"Did you just say you love me?"

"No."

"Maybe not in so many words . . ."

I shook my head. He cocked an eyebrow. "So you deny loving me or deny saying it?"

"Neither. Both. I mean—"

He didn't let me finish, which was just as well because I really wasn't sure what I meant. Yeah, I loved him. Already. And it was more intense than any kind of love I'd ever felt before—more than the love I'd ever had for Bex or Pops or even my parents and definitely more than for any guy—saturating every cell in my body from head to toe, into my core. Into my soul. But I didn't want to admit to it. Not to him and not to anyone, because then the universe would know and come after him, too. Because one person could not lose everyone in her life unless she was a harbinger of death. Maybe I was even the grim reaper himself. Herself. Whatever.

It should have always been me. Not them.

Micah braced my face in his hands. "I don't get it either, but I love you, too, Jacey. I'm not afraid to say it, and I'm not going to keel over and die because I do. Please don't fight it. Please don't fight us. We need to be together. You're all I have, too, you know. We're all either of us have. And if loving you does by some fucked-up chance kill me, I'm okay with it. I couldn't die a better way, Jace."

"Easy for you to say. You're not the one left behind with a broken heart." And a fractured soul.

"Well, if you want to look at it your way, I could say the same thing. Everyone I've ever cared about has died, too. So it could just as easily be you who d—" He broke off, unable to finish his sentence. He swallowed, then simply ended with, "We don't know who will go first, but for now, we have each other."

When my gaze lifted to his face, I felt like I was seeing him for the first time all over again. Touching him for the first time. Falling into his eyes. When his mouth lowered onto mine, I kissed him back fiercely, and I don't know what overcame me. Maybe the feeling of our souls once again coming together was too much for me to handle this time in my vulnerable state. Or maybe it was the need to know I did still have him. That there was still someone on this earth who cared about me, who made me feel like I mattered, who acknowledged I even *existed*.

Who loved me.

I gave in to whatever it was, and so did Micah. Our mouths moved together, kissing and sucking. Our lips separated and I inhaled him and he inhaled me and our tongues flicked and tasted and tangled with each other. Our hands moved from face to head to neck to shoulders. Down the back, the sides. Under the shirt. Muscles pulled taut under our touches. Fingers tugged at hems. Micah's shirt came off. He began to lift mine, but I rerouted his hand to the button on my jeans instead.

It had always worked before. I wasn't flat-chested—I had enough to not look like a boy, but not enough for guys to be infatuated with my bodacious ta-tas. I'd always been able to get away with keeping my shirt on, easy enough when you're in the backseat of a car or in someone's closet at a party, when it was all about fucking and not about making love.

But it didn't work with Micah.

He lifted his head and looked at me, questions in his eyes.

"I want to enjoy all of you," he murmured.

"No, you don't," I said, shaking my head. "Trust me. It's not all enjoyable."

He cocked his head. "Yes. I do. I love every bit of you, so how could I not enjoy it?"

He pushed my shirt up barely enough to expose a strip of skin, where his lips planted soft kisses. My stomach quivered under his touch, which he took as encouragement, raising my shirt even more. I clamped my hands on his.

"Micah—"

"If you're not ready, tell me," he said between kisses, his breath hot against my skin. "We'll stop right now."

"I don't want to *stop*. I just—"

"Then let me love all of you."

He pushed my shirt up farther, and I stiffened. That was far enough to see. But instead of stopping and recoiling in horror, he lifted my shirt all the way up and over my head. Then he gazed at my ugly body. At the gross, puckered burn scars across the top of my stomach and over my ribs. My body began to shake. I moved my arms to cover my midsection, but he clasped my wrists and held them out to my sides.

His eyes lifted to mine, and I expected to see disgust or pity in them. Instead, I only saw love.

"You're beautiful," he said. "Every inch of you."

He leaned down and peppered my scars with gentle kisses. Overcome with emotions, I grabbed his head and brought it up to mine, needing to kiss him. To show him the same love he'd shown me. His mouth didn't leave mine as his hands pushed to my back to undo my bra. He slid it off, one arm at a time, then his lips moved from mine and I let out a sigh as he kissed his way over my jaw and down my neck. His hand found my bare breast and squeezed softly, and my whole body ignited. No one had ever seen me like this, let alone touched me. Heat consumed me as his mouth trailed over my collarbone and down, and then flamed hotter when his tongue wrapped around my nipple. His lips pulled my breast into his mouth, and my back arched into him as a moan burned in my throat.

My hands slid over his muscular torso, one exploring the valleys and ridges of his pecs and abs, the other digging into his back. My hand slid down, over his jeans, and stroked his erection. My God was he hard. And huge, at least to me. He groaned against my breast, then moved out of my reach as his mouth traveled to my torso, leaving a trail of kisses over the scars again and down, until he reached the waistband of my jeans. He stopped and looked up at me with scorching eyes. Asking for permission. I lifted my hips, giving it.

He pulled my jeans off, then his fingers lightly stroked around the edges of my panties, the tickling sensation making me tremble. My whole body ached for more, but he teased with feather-light touches and kisses over the top of my underwear and on my thighs until I practically ripped my panties off myself. And finally, *finally* he touched me in the hottest place of all, sending a ripple of pleasure through my core. His fingers and lips and tongue did things no one had ever done to me before, making me writhe and buck against him until I soared into the first real orgasm I'd ever had, although I hadn't realized it until then. Nothing I'd ever experienced before compared to this. I finally understood the big deal about sex.

And Micah wasn't done. Not even close.

My fingers digging into his hair, I had to pull him up before I shattered into so many pieces that I'd never recover. I wanted to pleasure him, but he wouldn't let me.

"I don't think I can last," he whispered hoarsely, "and I want to be inside you the first time."

Holy shit, no one ever said anything like that to me. I lifted my legs and hips, and grabbed his hard ass and pulled him into me. We both cried out as he entered. And immediately our bodies burst with an urgent need that took completely over. At least, I thought everything was purely physical, sensual, sexual, even animalistic as he pumped into me and I rocked against him. But then we both climbed higher and higher until we hit our peaks and came together, and that's when I knew my soul was still in the moment.

Utterly and completely in it, but then . . . not.

Our first kiss didn't compare. Our souls hadn't really bound then. Now. *This.*

Oh. My. God.

What was happening? How could this even be possible?

I didn't know. I didn't care. I didn't ever want it to end. I'd never felt so removed from my body, literally, yet so whole. So complete.

We are one.

Together.

Again.

Night blackened the window when we finally collapsed from exhaustion. Sammy's whining and barking jerked me awake when I began to doze off in Micah's arms. My dog frantically scratched at the door as if trying to tear through it.

✷ NOW ✷
2012

CHAPTER 19

Leni's hand moved from her flushed neck to her mouth, her elbow bumping my arm because we huddled so closely together, leaning over the book on the table. Her body had tensed up next to mine, and heat radiated from her skin. I couldn't help but wonder if her panties were wet after reading Jacey's detailed description, and the more I thought about it, the more the urge grew to find out. So I bolted from the table, and walked several paces to the truck, needing to put some distance between us. I placed my palms on the truck's hood and dropped my head between my arms.

What the hell was she doing to me? The old Jeric wouldn't have given a second thought to finding out. He would have wrapped an arm around her, grabbed a tit with one hand and slid the other between her legs, and if she wasn't wet yet, he would have made her so until she begged for him to take her. The old Jeric would have already had her in the sack, one head or the other buried between her legs.

But the old Jeric then would have sent her on her way, everyone content with the sexcapade.

I'd never let girls get to me like this. I had fun with them. We drank, we partied, we laughed, we played in the sheets, and then they went home. I felt nothing else for them. Friends, with benefits. No female had ever slid under my skin like Leni had.

And she hadn't even tried. She didn't seem to know what she did to me. So many girls had wanted from me what I couldn't give them, but Leni had no idea she was the exception. The only one who could make me want to give her everything. The world. Myself. Whatever she wanted. For the first time ever, Jeric Winters was whipped. Already. What the hell was I supposed to do about it?

Nothing. Live with it. That's all I could do.

Because Leni wouldn't put up with the old Jeric. She'd be the one sending me on my way and that thought hurt worse than a kick to the ball sack. I'd rather that spine-curling pain than the agony of losing her. Which brought me to my original question: What the hell was she doing to me? How could I feel the way I did about her? I didn't think it possible to ever feel like this about someone again. But this was different and so damn strong, I couldn't imagine *not* ever having these feelings for Leni. Like they'd always been there, buried, just waiting for me to meet her.

I closed my eyes and breathed deeply, trying to get ahold of myself. When I turned back, Leni was up, too, leaning against the table, her eyes glazed over with thought as her hand stroked her throat. The late-afternoon sun glowed fiery orange over the lake behind her, creating silhouettes of the pine trees on the far bank.

"Do you think their Shadowmen are the same guys who attacked us?" she signed as her eyes focused on me. Not exactly where my mind had been, so it took me a moment to understand what she meant.

I shrugged. "That was twenty-three years ago."

"Maybe it's the same group, if not the same men."

"Who? What kind of group? And why us?" The questions made me edgy, and my hands moved sharply as I signed. "Who are they to us, this Micah and Jacey?"

Leni chewed on her bottom lip then looked at me. "I have a theory about that." She hesitated for a moment. "What if they're your parents? Your biological parents?"

Fuck. I wasn't expecting that. The idea hadn't even crossed my mind. "*You* found the book. Why would you think they'd be my parents?"

"Maybe Mira had had it. Maybe it came with you, as a baby."

I didn't like this idea. It didn't *feel* right.

"Maybe they're yours," I signed.

Her face showed the same look of surprise I'd felt when she suggested they were mine, but then her brows drew together.

"The story *does* feel vaguely familiar, like I've been told it before," she said. I'd been thinking the same thing as we read—like I'd heard this story a long time ago. "But it's impossible. I mean look at me. They both sound very white."

"Jacey, yes, but we don't know Micah's background. Maybe he's mixed like you—brown eyes, dark hair . . ."

"She would say something in the journal, especially back then. She even asked if he'd been a skinhead, which would make no sense." The way her hands flew about, she didn't like the idea any more than I did. "Besides, they can't be. Not unless everything my parents ever told me about how they met and got married is a complete lie."

I watched her for several beats, waiting for her to realize the irony of her words. But she didn't. "From what you've said about them—disowning you like that—I wouldn't be surprised."

Her eyes hardened as she glared at me.

"You know nothing about my parents!" she signed angrily, and I expected her to flip me the finger, but instead her hands fell limply to her side and the fire extinguished immediately. Her gaze dropped to the ground, and her toe pushed at a rock stuck in the dirt for a minute, until she looked up at me again with her damn fake smile that looked authentic if you didn't know her like I did. Already.

"Why did you do that?" I demanded. "You have a right to be angry. Get mad for once, Leni. Let yourself be *real*."

The grin fell from her face, but confusion filled her eyes. "Why? It won't accomplish anything, except to make a fool of myself."

"So what? It's only me here. Lash out if you want to. Yell and scream. I can't hear you, but it's not like you'd hurt my feelings anyway. I can take your anger."

She tossed her hands in the air. "But you're right. After the way they treated me on the phone the other night, they're not who I thought they are. But I'm not going to take it out on you."

"I'm asking you to. I'm *begging*. Let it out before you explode like a damn time bomb."

"No. It's stupid."

"Then be stupid. Don't you ever do anything dumb or wrong? Do you ever put yourself out there? Take any risks?"

She hesitated, but then shrugged. "I'm not much of a risk-taker."

"Of course not. You've never had to be, have you?" My gaze traveled to the Airstream, then to her truck and returned to her. "You've always had everything done for you, haven't you?"

She shrugged again. "My mother's a control freak. She didn't want anyone—including me—to screw things up."

"So you simply did everything she wanted? She told you what to do and you obediently followed her orders?" Agitation built between us and that's what I wanted from her, but she refused to play my game.

"Well, yeah," she said easily. "She's my mama. She took care of me. So did my daddy, and Uncle Theo when my parents moved."

I nodded. "Of course they did. I'm sure teachers, the police, the authorities have always treated you well, too."

"Yeah, they've always been fine." She paused, then added, "Until the past couple of days anyway."

"And now you're seeing a different side of everyone, are you? Getting a little taste of disappointment from the adults in your life? And you don't know what to do. Do you have any idea how to take care of yourself when there's no one to boss you around?"

She threw her hip out and lifted her chin, the only reaction to my jab. "I went to Italy by myself, didn't I?"

I gave her a rude smirk, pushing her harder. "A trip your uncle planned, paid for and sent you off to, where'd you be with people he knew, who told you where to sleep, what and when to eat and how to dance. Did you even want to go or was that more of everyone wanting to control Leni?"

"Yes, I wanted to go. It was a dream come true!"

I felt her giving in, ready to let loose the real Leni, so I kept prodding. "What? To dance in Italy? That was your dream?"

"To dance at all. Professionally."

"Then why aren't you? Why aren't you dancing here in the States? Too afraid to put yourself out there where it matters?"

Her cheeks pinked, and I hoped to see a spark of fire in her eyes, what I was looking for. A hint of anger flashed, but disappeared just as quickly.

"I wanted to stay to take care of my uncle."

"Bullshit," I said. "That's an excuse. What's the real reason you didn't go to New York? I saw you dance in Italy. I've seen you dance here, and you're damn good. So what happened? Why are you here and not there?"

She stared at me for a long moment, her chest rising with a breath. "Why are you doing this?"

"Because you need it."

"Need what?"

To stop being a damn puppet. To let you be you. But saying so would derail the progress I was making.

"You're avoiding my question," I accused. "Why aren't you in New York?"

She didn't answer except to cross her arms over her chest.

"Why, Leni?"

"My uncle needed me."

"So much that he sent you halfway across the world for a month? And now he's run off with my grams. For all we know, they're whooping it up in Vegas."

She shook her head.

"It's an excuse," I said again. She stood her ground, but I kept pressing. "Unless your parents made you stay? Could your control-freak mom not let you leave?"

She scowled. "She wanted me to go as badly as I did. It was her dream, too. She'd always wanted me to be a ballerina. Put me in dance when I was four years old."

Ah. I'd seen the moms in the modeling agency and at the studios with their kids, with bright eyes of hope and longing, wanting their kids to be a star since they never were.

"Was it even *your* dream?" I taunted. "Or just mom's?"

She narrowed her eyes at me. Her body began to tremble. *Yes.* I was getting somewhere.

"Did you even *want* it?" I pressed.

Her fists balled at her sides, and her nostrils flared.

"Did you, Leni? Or were you only doing what Mama told you to do?"

"Yes! No! I mean, yes, I wanted it. I just wanted to dance." She inhaled a deep breath and again snuffed out the real Leni. "I didn't get in, though, okay? Yeah, Mama arranged the audition with the ballet company, but *I* put myself out there. *I* was the one on stage. *I* auditioned and they said no. End of story."

I knew by the way she held herself that was not the end of the story.

"So one audition and you gave up?" I asked, pushing her further.

She shrugged and looked away.

I moved to her line of vision. "You gave up because of one person's opinion for one dance company out of how many?"

She didn't take my bait, but remained calm. "What they said . . . why they didn't take me . . . *Nobody* would take me, Jeric. Not in New York, not for ballet. I'm not cut out for it."

My own anger clawed at my gut. I didn't know if it was on behalf of her or because of her refusal to bite or because I'd had my own dream yanked out from under my feet.

"What could they have possibly said to make you give up?" I demanded.

Something flashed in her eyes, but again, only for a nanosecond. "I don't have the right body, and I never will. I'm not long and willowy. Quite the opposite and there's nothing I can do about it. I'll never be what they're looking for."

The resignation her body language showed turned my anger into rage, and still, I didn't know if it was on behalf of Leni—who the hell were they to say such things?—or because she'd given up.

"*That's* your excuse?" I asked, my hands punching the air with each sign. I tugged on my ear. "*This* is an excuse for giving up on a dream, Leni. Not that! How could you let them do that? How could you let them make you stop dancing?"

"Because they're right, and I can't help the way my body's shaped. It's my heritage, and I'm proud of it. Besides, they didn't say never dance again. They suggested other genres. Better for my body type and the moves I could do. Like what you saw this morning."

I couldn't disagree that her body was definitely made for those kinds of moves. Better than any stripper I'd ever seen, even in the highest-class executive clubs. She'd left my head spinning, all of the blood flowing to my dick.

"So why didn't you do that? Why not audition with other dance companies that aren't ballet?"

She stared at me for a long moment, a storm churning behind her green eyes, and I waited with anticipation for her to let it out. But then she blinked and squared her shoulders.

"It doesn't matter anymore," she said, controlled as ever. "That's a past life."

"Right. Because you gave up. Which tells me it wasn't your dream to start with."

She narrowed her eyes. "Let it go."

"You were only doing what Mama wanted all along, weren't you? Not what you wanted at all."

"I said to let it go!"

But I didn't. I was onto something. "And what does Mama think about you giving up? Looks like she lost control, didn't she? A little disappointed, is she? Oh, yeah. She doesn't even admit you exist!"

Leni's eyes widened with shock as though I'd hit her. Yeah, I really said that and already regretted it. But she recovered quickly and simply raised a brow.

"I'm done with this conversation." She crossed her arms over her chest and put on that stupid, sweet smile, teeth showing and all.

I stared at her for a long moment, then shook my head. "I don't understand you. I just pushed every button I could find on you. And still you're calm as shit."

"And I don't understand you. It's over. I'm over it all. Why are *you* so riled up?"

"Because I'm pissed," I admitted, kicking the folding chair and knocking it over. Ghost, the cat who'd been curled in a ball sleeping in the other chair, lifted his head and glared at me before returning to his nap.

"And what does that do for you, being all pissed?" Leni asked. "Punching the air and kicking at chairs? What's the point?"

"Because I want to! It's a release and it feels good! Dammit, don't you ever do anything for you just because it feels good?"

She flinched, and then her face reddened even more than before. I'd hit a new button without realizing it was there. And it was as good as her mother button, if not better. Maybe she'd let herself go now, be the real Leni that I knew lurked under the surface waiting to break out. There was no way she was this laid back for real.

"I said I'm done," she said, and she stalked off toward the lake.

That was the best I was going to get? Shit, with everything going on, if she didn't release soon, I would regret being around when she finally did blow. Nobody could keep everything she had to be feeling in check for long.

I watched her stroll down to the shore, wondering if I should follow her but her ass distracted me—I'd never seen anything so perfect. Those dancers could fuck off. What did they know? I'd been with enough models and dancers to know what they felt like—my hands were bigger than their asses, and I was afraid my cock would literally break them in two. But Leni. She had the talent *and* the soft curves. Not too much, but just right.

Dude. Again.

Shit. What was happening to me?

Anxious energy rushed through my veins, but I didn't want to go for another run to work it off. To be honest, running wouldn't have done the trick anyway. The anger that had been building while egging Leni on had already evaporated. The need to go, however, to move went deeper. The same gut feeling that had led me to Leni pulled at me again, wanting to go south now, with Leni at my side. And it had been strongest when I saw Jacey's drawing of the old Victorian mansion in her journal, and laced with an edge I didn't like. An edge that made me think the lure was dangerous.

Figuring Leni wanted to be alone, I went inside to retrieve my own journal, bringing Jacey's with me. I set them on the counter side by side and flipped through the pages of both until I found what I was looking for—nearly identical drawings, although Jacey's was much better than mine, sketched by an expert hand. Like Jacey and Micah, I'd somehow known when I drew it several months ago it was in the Tampa/St. Pete area. Unlike Jacey and Micah, I had the Internet, but I still hadn't been able to find the house online. I stared at the two drawings, and as always, the mansion gave me a sinister feeling, as though the house itself might open up and eat us alive.

An hour or so passed as I researched the Internet for Jacey and Micah, but nothing came up on Google or any of the social media sites. No proof they ever existed, which really wasn't so surprising, was it?

I pushed away from the counter and went back outside. Night had settled in. Leni's form was silhouetted against the moonlight on the lake as she still stood by the shore. I wished I knew what she was thinking. My muscles jumped with the need to move again, and I reconsidered going for another run. But I couldn't leave Leni, now that it was dark. When I did last night, the Shadowmen had come. I wasn't letting her out of my sight in case they returned. Shit. I sounded like Micah.

That dude and I had way too much in common. Why was that? Why did I feel like I knew him as much as I felt like I knew Leni? He and Jacey couldn't be my parents. I'd know, wouldn't I? But could that explain the connection I felt to these strangers? Had I heard their story before? But where? From who?

Our lives had become a big, fat riddle. I'd always hated riddles.

Leni eventually made her way to the campsite, pushed past me and inside. When she didn't come out after a few minutes, I went in to see what she was up to. She lay huddled on her side on her bed in the darkened end of the Airstream. She'd gone to sleep? Her form trembled. Damn. She was crying. Yeah, I wanted her to release the pressure valve, but I'd been hoping for a fiery burst. Not tears. I didn't do tears. I didn't know how.

After locking up the camper, I went back to her and tried to get her to sit up and talk to me, to at least let me apologize, but she grabbed my hand and pulled me down to the bed. I lay next to her, and she curled herself into me, tucking her head into my shoulder and burying her face against my chest. I guessed that meant she forgave me. I wrapped my arms around her and held her close while she cried herself to sleep.

CHAPTER 20

 My stealthy attempt at disentangling myself from Jeric's arms without waking him didn't work. He squeezed me tighter and moaned against my neck. One hand slid down my side and came to a rest on my hip, his fingers pressing into the sensitive area where my panties met my leg. I wondered if he was fully awake and knew whom he lay next to, or if I was just another girl in his sleep-fogged mind.

"Leni," he murmured right by my ear, and my body froze. He'd spoken! Said my name! And, whoa, did I not love the sound of it, the way it wrapped around my heart. I lay still, hoping he'd say it again, but he didn't.

The quiet of being with him was sometimes unnerving. Uncle Theo had his hearing aid, but when he didn't put it in, he'd have the television blaring at its highest volume. With Jeric, there was nothing. A rare groan or grunt, but nothing more. Until now. He must have still been asleep. His rhythmic breathing next to my ear confirmed this.

I let out a sigh. How had this man affected me the way he did? How could I feel what I did for him? Already? Jeric Winters was so not my type. Well, not really. Okay, so there may have been a few bad boys at the club who had intrigued me. Maybe all who walked through the door. But it was only curiosity. Something to fantasize about in my mind, but not to act on. Bad boys equaled broken hearts. Lots of them, strewn around like shattered beer bottles because girls meant nothing more to these guys. If I fell any harder for Jeric, I'd be one of those broken hearts.

But dammit, if I hadn't already fallen for him, regardless of whether I wanted to or not. What I felt for him went beyond the edgy outer shell that protected the hurt he felt inside, beyond the warm heart I knew he kept hidden, and deep into his soul. My soul greeted his like we were longtime lovers waiting for this reunion. Like we were Twin Flames, separated before, but finally together again.

Goodness, girl. Get ahold of yourself.

We weren't Jacey and Micah. There were lots of similarities and coincidences, but that didn't mean we were exactly the same. Nothing had said Jeric and I were Twin Flames. Except the marks. And my soul when it met his. But those were hearsay, as my daddy would say. No hard evidence. Jacey and Micah's story may be like ours, but it wasn't ours. Besides, from what I'd found on the Internet, the idea of Twin Flames sounded like a crock of New Age crap. Did I even want to be bound so tightly with Jeric?

Yes, my heart whispered and my soul echoed.

Ugh. I needed to get up. I struggled against Jeric's hold again, but he still wouldn't let me go. He was so stubborn, even in his sleep. He'd been trying hard last night to piss me off, intent on making me explode, and he actually had come close—he had no idea how spot-on he'd been with some of his accusations—but I could be stubborn, too. Mama would have been proud of how well I kept it together. How I hadn't broken. Except I had. I'd cried.

Jeric was probably right—I did have too many emotions pent up and I should have just let it all out in an angry outburst. Mama said it was better to cry behind closed doors, but I didn't know anymore. I hadn't been able to go behind closed doors. No, instead I'd cried myself to sleep in his arms. Now he probably saw me as weak.

But he already did anyway. Saw me as a child who couldn't do anything on her own. And that was one thing he'd nailed, right into my heart. I'd never realized it before, but he'd been absolutely right. Unlike him, or Jacey or Micah, I hadn't had a horrible life with all of its lessons. The grown-ups who had raised me weren't perfect, but they had taken care of me. Had always followed through for me. Even when I was caring for Uncle Theo, he was taking care of me, too. I could always rely on the adults in my life. On the authorities to do their jobs.

Until now.

And Jeric was right again. I hadn't known what to do.

But I did this morning. The draw I felt to go south had to mean something, and it was time to follow my own instincts. With another tug against his hold, Jeric finally flopped over onto his back, and his arm released me. I slid out of the bed, letting him sleep.

The morning sun hung low in the sky. The clock read 7:06. A little early for me. But it wasn't jetlag or Jeric or Mama still getting to me. I'd woken up two hours ago with a vague memory persistently nagging at the edge of my mind. The house. The one in Jacey's journal. I'd seen it before and now I knew where.

After a stop in the bathroom, I pulled my mass of curls into a ponytail, then began searching the camper's storage spots. The Airstream wasn't big by any means, but it contained all sorts of secret hiding places. I only wished I could remember which one I'd seen that postcard in. At least my banging around wouldn't wake Jeric. That had to be a plus side of being deaf.

As I reached up and dug around in a cabinet in the so-called living room, the cubbyhole above the futon Jeric had slept in the first night, my fingers finally closed on a stiff piece of paper. I pulled the postcard out, rocked back on my heels and stared at it for a long moment, then strode over to the kitchen counter. Jacey's journal lay open at her drawing. Another journal—Jeric's, I assumed—also lay open to a nearly identical drawing. I set the postcard down between them.

They all depicted the same Victorian mansion.

The nudge to go south grew stronger.

A pair of hands clasped my waist and a shock jolted through my neck. Jeric's lips pressed against my skin right below my ear, sending a shockwave through my body and making my heart burst into a gallop. He stepped back, a chuckling sound emanating in his throat. The little bit I'd heard of his voice made me ache to hear more. He must have been a fantastic singer. But I'd be happy just to hear my name again.

He stepped to my side, an arm lingering around my waist, and gazed at the pictures on the counter.

"You drew that one?" I asked him, pointing to the second journal. He nodded and picked up the postcard to study it closer. "The postcard's been in here since Uncle Theo gave me the camper. I remembered seeing it a long time ago. I wasn't sure if Uncle Theo wanted it, so I'd left it where I'd found it."

Jeric flipped the card over, and both of our bodies tensed at the words scrawled on the other side: *You will find your answers here.*

That was all. No address for either a sender or a recipient. No postmark. No other message or even tiny print captioning the picture on the other side.

Jeric set it down right where I'd placed it before, and we both stared at the three images. More memories danced at the edge of my consciousness, but I couldn't grasp at them. I felt, however, as though I'd been to that house before. Or, at least, near it. As though I'd seen it in person. I shook my head. It had to be because I'd seen the postcard before. After all, I'd never been to Tampa . . . if that's where it actually was.

But I felt drawn there now.

"Maybe we should pack up and head down there?" I suggested off-handedly. I wasn't sure I believed the message on the back of the postcard—at least, I didn't know if it was meant for us or if it had been for Uncle Theo—but as soon as I signed the words, I knew they were right. We needed to find this house.

But Jeric stiffened next to me. His hand left my waist, and he signed, "I don't know. It feels wrong to me."

I peered at him, and his gaze was on his journal. He reached out and flipped through the pages until he settled on one. I stared at a sketch that made my spine go ram-rod straight. That was me, no doubt. He'd sketched me before he ever met me, based on the date scribbled next to the drawing. Which meant . . . had he been to the club? I stepped away, shaking my head but staring at the floor, unsure what to feel or think. He slid his finger under my chin, lifting my face to look at him.

"I dreamt about you before I ever knew you," he said. "I had to sketch this when I woke up because I didn't want to forget what you looked like."

Whoa. Okay. Not what I thought. Whew. For some reason, I didn't want him knowing about my little stint at the club.

"I told you how I'd been searching for my birth mother? I was wrong. I realize now I'd been searching for you all that time. Something in me was pulling me to you." He flipped back to the page with the mansion. "I dreamt about this place, too, and had to sketch it."

I understood what he was saying.

"You feel the pull to go there, too, don't you?" I asked. He nodded. "Like Jacey and Micah did. And me. What does it mean?"

He shrugged. "I don't know. But I don't think I want to find out. That place . . . ever since I drew it months ago . . . I don't like it."

"What? Are you scared?" I teased.

He rolled his eyes. "There's something about it . . . . The house, the pictures of it anyway . . . they piss me off. Make me hate it with a vengeance."

"You hate this house? Have you ever been there?"

He didn't answer me at first, but eventually shook his head. "Not that I know of. But . . . I feel like I have, though."

I let out a sigh. "Me, too. Maybe that's all that's bothering you about it."

He shook his head again. "No. It's something more. The house feels . . . sinister. Like bad things have happened there. Terrible things."

I studied the pictures. I thought they were beautiful. The house gave me a warm feeling. And the message on the postcard—maybe it really did have the answers we needed. Another jolt in my gut confirmed this idea.

"I think we should go," I signed again, and the feeling to move out instantly strengthened. "I don't think we're really safe here, anyway. The Shadowmen could come back any time. And if we're both feeling the pull there . . . if the card says it has answers . . ."

Jeric looked at me with his brows raised. "You're going to listen to a card that's how many years old? We don't even know if the message is for us."

"I think it is. I *feel* like it is." Again, the feeling I was right strengthened. Became more urgent. "I *know* it is. We have to go there, Jeric."

He peered at me, as if gauging if I was actually serious. But his face disappeared from my sight. Flashes of images took over my vision—dark eyes full of worry and fear; huge shadows flying through the air; blurred faces I somehow knew were Uncle Theo and Mira; then a huge body of water with lights on the far side, a chill rising from the surface and into my bones, and a bright light beyond the water, sending warmth, beckoning me, offering shelter, safety, *love* . . . then complete blackness.

When my vision returned, I was staring up into Jeric's face, the camper's ceiling behind him. I lay on the floor, his arm underneath me. No, not on the floor. In his lap. Relief washed over his face.

"What happened?" I asked.

"You passed out. Are you okay?"

I struggled to sit up, and he lifted my shoulders, but held me in his lap.

"I think so. That was weird. Those visions—they almost felt like memories."

His brow wrinkled. "Visions?"

"Just now. But they were more real than visions. As if I'd actually experienced it all before."

He eyed me for a moment, skepticism filling his face. "Are you sure you're okay? Did you hit your head?"

I pushed my way out of his arms and off of his lap, up to my feet. He rose with me, his hands out in case I collapsed again.

"I'm fine. No, I didn't hit my head." I rubbed it, in case I was wrong and had hit it on my way down, while the visions played in my mind. I didn't find any bumps. Still, I leaned my hands on the counter, bracing myself just in case. The postcard lay backside up now. My heart rate spiked again, and I picked the card up, holding it close to my face. The more I squinted at the handwriting, the more it looked like Uncle Theo's. "He left this as a message, maybe before he was taken."

"Who?" Jeric asked.

"My uncle. Maybe Mira, too. Oh, my God! That's it. They're at the house." The warm feeling of the visions overcame me again. This was right. I knew it. "We need to go there. Right now."

I turned away to glance around the Airstream, making a mental inventory of what to take. Maybe we should pull the whole camper? It sure beat staying in motels on our way down. On the other hand, we should probably drive straight through. If my truck would make it.

Jeric grasped my shoulders, grabbing my attention. When he knew he had it, he let go and signed, "We're not going."

His expression was firm, and his hand motions deliberate.

"I felt it, though," I insisted. "In the vision, or memory, or whatever it was."

"That's exactly why we're not. I don't trust it."

"You don't trust what? Me?"

"No. The house. What just happened to you. It will only get worse."

I didn't understand him, but it didn't matter. "We *need* to go. Mira is there. Maybe you feel bad about the place because you know they're keeping her there." My breath caught. "What if the Shadowmen are holding them hostage? What if they plan to do what they did to Bex?"

Jeric gave me a look as if I should know what he was thinking. When I didn't, he said, "Then they're probably already dead."

My breath caught, and I shook my head in denial. "They would have told us. Left an article taped to my truck. They could be torturing them instead. Jeric, please. We have to go. It's where our answers are!"

His hand shot out, waving at Jacey's journal on the counter. "What about that? Our answers are in there!"

"We can read it on the way."

"Not together. We can't even read aloud to each other." His eyes flashed anger at this.

Being able to read aloud while the other drove would have certainly been more convenient. I, too, wanted to know more about Jacey and Micah. But I needed to solve my own mystery, find Uncle Theo and personally take him to Alaska, if I had to, to bring my parents back to reality. Or at least to get the truth out of them. Sure, Jacey's journal might have had answers, but so did this old house in Florida. The pull to go was too strong to ignore.

"I'm going," I said. "If you don't want to go, fine, but I am. You were right—I was pretty clueless before. But not anymore. I won't take the risk that my uncle and your grandma are locked up somewhere, and we're the only ones who know where."

I crossed my arms over my chest and waited for Jeric's answer.

CHAPTER 21

 Leni had no clue what she was doing to me, making me choose like this. She may as well have asked me to choose between watching her murder or her rape. Either one would kill me, and something about the mansion made me feel like either one could likely happen if we went. I had mixed feelings about Mira—wasn't sure if I cared where she was—but Leni loved her uncle and I wanted her to find him. But why did it have to be there? Bad vibes. The place gave me bad fucking vibes.

Everything inside me screamed not to go, but I couldn't let her go alone, and I had to help her. I had to protect her. Maybe her truck would break down right outside of town when she tried to leave me, like my rental car had, but I had a feeling that wouldn't stop her. My Beautiful Girl was stubborn as a damn mule. Even more stubborn than me. Which only confirmed the real Leni wasn't as carefree and laid back as she put off.

I slid both hands over my head, then tossed them in the air with frustrated resignation. "Fine. Let's go find your uncle."

Her face broke into a grin, and she threw her arms around my neck and planted a kiss on my lips. Oh, hell yeah, this was worth putting up her with stubbornness. I leaned in for more, needing to taste her sweet mouth. She parted her lips and gave me a teasing swipe of her tongue before pressing her hands against my chest and pushing me off. Her face flushed as she looked at me with those silver-green eyes.

"That will lead to things we don't have time for right now," she signed.

"Just a kiss . . ."

Her mesmerizing lips turned up in a smile. "More than a kiss, and you know it."

She glanced down at the bulge in my pants. Damn, she'd turned me into a freakin' middle-schooler who got hard as a rock from a simple lip-smack. But maybe if I could distract her, she'd change her mind about going.

"We could make time now and leave tomorrow," I suggested with my best smile. Her reaction was palpable—my scheme almost worked—but she shook her head, her curls flopping in their ponytail.

"I can't decide whether to take the camper or not," she signed. "It hasn't been farther than the dump station in years, and I don't know how my truck will do pulling it."

I sighed. So stubborn. "The Shadowmen also know it."

"Right."

"But motels require IDs."

"Except if we drove straight through . . ."

I lifted an eyebrow. "I'm pretty sure your truck can't handle that."

She grimaced. "Probably not. But it'll go farther than with a camper on it." Her chest heaved and her brow puckered as she glanced around again, then her face became resolute. "We're taking it. Besides my truck, it's the only thing I own and who knows if it'll be here when we get back."

"*If* we get back," I corrected.

She ignored this statement.

Prepping the camper to be hauled on the road for the first time in years ate up the rest of the morning. I tried once more to convince her to wait—if I could delay her one day at a time, maybe she'd drop the idea of going altogether. But she wouldn't give in.

By noon, we were on the road headed south. By four o'clock, we were stranded on the side of the road.

Well, not exactly. We'd crossed the state line into Florida and pulled off the highway for gas when the truck decided not to start. Leni popped the hood, and we both peered at the engine compartment, but I saw nothing obviously wrong. Nothing that would be a quick fix, or even a temporary one to at least move the truck away from the island of gas pumps.

"It's a sign we should go no farther," I suggested. Leni flashed me a dirty look.

"This isn't funny! Now what?" She kicked the truck's tire in an uncharacteristic show of anger, then strode off for the truck stop's entrance. I kept my eye on her through the glass wall as she spoke to the attendant inside and then to another guy, and she stomped back to the truck several minutes later, her angry strides betraying her stoic expression.

"They can't look at it until tomorrow, and there's no rental car place for seventy miles, so we're stranded," she signed. At least, I thought that's what she said. Her hands jerked with anger, skewing her signs. They moved slower and more fluidly with her next sentence as she once again gained control. "But there's an RV park across the street. A truck driver inside said he'd pull the camper over there for me."

Yeah, I'm sure he did.

The truck driver looked none too happy to see me climb into the cab with Leni after her truck had been pushed over to the mechanic's bay and he'd hooked her camper to his rig. His expectations for a special thank you must have been ruined when he realized she wasn't alone. I returned the driver's scowl with a toothy grin as I swung my arm over her shoulders and pulled her close to me.

A small building with only a tiny window and a wooden door housed the RV park's office. I couldn't see inside from the truck cab, so I followed Leni into the building, too paranoid to let her out of my sight. A chick about our age with cherry-red hair looked up from a magazine spread open on the counter. Something about her felt vaguely familiar, but I was pretty sure I'd never met her. If so, I would have definitely banged her, and I'd never forget that red hair. She was the right type for the pre-Leni me, but now she was just another girl, making it easy for me to pretty much ignore her so I could focus on our surroundings and remain alert for any problems.

Every time I looked at Leni, however, her brows were pushed together as she stared at the redhead, who was filling out a registration card. Leni looked to be in deep concentration.

"Bex?" Leni finally mouthed. At least, that's what her lips seemed to say. Her face flushed, and I figured she must have blurted it out. Red's head snapped up, and her eyes squinted.

"Uh, no. Bethany," her lips said. "But close. How did ya know?"

My eyes returned to Leni. She seemed to be stammering, and her face reddened even more.

"A, uh, a wild guess," her lips said before she offered her signature smile. "Actually, you remind me of someone named Rebecca, but she went by Bex."

"Went?" Bethany asked, catching the past tense.

Leni became obviously flustered, and I felt bad for her, but there was little I could do. The fact that she spoke about Bex—who I could only take to mean Jacey's Bex—freaked me out, too.

"I, uh, never really knew her myself. Someone I met in passing." Leni looked up to me, obviously wondering if I caught the conversation.

I couldn't help but bring it up later, once the camper was dropped on its site and the truck driver had skedaddled, probably off to prey on some other pretty girl.

"Bex?" I asked Leni as I leaned against the kitchenette's counter while she opened a can of cat food. Ghost had leapt out when we opened the camper door, surprising both of us. We hadn't known he'd been inside when we locked up before leaving. "What was that about?"

She set the food on the floor for the cat, then shrugged. "No idea, really. She just . . . she felt so familiar and Bex's name popped into my mind. Weird, right?"

"You could say that."

"She could barely take her eyes off you. I'm surprised she managed to give me correct change."

I shrugged. "Didn't notice."

She gave me a crooked grin. "Yeah, it must happen all the time. You probably don't notice it at all anymore."

Actually, I did. I used to anyway. "Before you, I noticed everything about every girl around me, especially if they were looking at me. All I can tell you about that girl is she had red hair and her name's Bethany. Which I only know because of you."

She eyed me for a moment, as if considering whether to believe me. I grasped her hips and pulled her to me. I pressed my finger to her chest.

"All I see anymore," I signed with one hand before leaning down and grabbing that taste of her I'd been craving all day.

She reacted the way I was used to—arching her body against me, opening her mouth for my tongue, allowing my hands to finally explore. I didn't know if it was the connection we had or if she really was better than everyone else I'd ever been with combined. She kissed me expertly, her mouth and tongue moving exactly the way I liked. Her hands rubbed the back of my head and she may has well have been stroking my other head, it felt so good. And her body. Damn, it was perfect. When she allowed me to pull her top over her head, I thought I'd lose it right then. I wanted to rip her bra off with my teeth, feel those soft tits of hers, suck on them until her nipples were as hard as my dick. I forced myself to go slow, to enjoy every second, every inch of her dark honey skin. Trying not to scare her away with how bad I fucking wanted her.

I clamped my hands on her waist and lifted her to the counter. She wrapped her legs around me, holding me close while I reached back and pulled my shirt off. Her gaze heated as she stared at my nipple rings, and her pink tongue slid over her lips. She didn't even have to touch me, and I nearly exploded.

My hands tightened against her back, sliding up and down, one grasping at her curls and the other at her bra clasp. She let me undo it. Let me caress her, let me lick and suck at her, arching her back to give me better access. Damn, she tasted better than I imagined. My free hand slid down. My fingers dipped inside her shorts, and all I could think about was that if she felt this good on the outside, how was I ever going to live through feeling her on the inside. My fingertip bathed in her warmth and wetness as my hand barely grazed over her sweet spot.

She jerked backward and pushed me away.

I froze and looked up at her face, already flushed with heat but now reddening even more. Her green eyes were wide. Frightened. She was scared? I stepped back, holding my hands in the air.

"I won't hurt you," I signed. She nodded, but still held herself away, her arm over her tits. Hiding them. Oh, shit. I rubbed my hands over my head, not able to ignore the smell of her on my finger. Which didn't help my effin' hard-on. "You're a virgin, aren't you?"

She didn't answer, but the way she pressed her lips together— and everything else—was answer enough.

I blew out a frustrated breath. "I knew it."

Now her face hardened. Keeping herself covered with her arms, she spoke with her mouth. "Knew what? That I'm not experienced enough for you? Not good enough?"

She grabbed at her bra, pushed her arms through and yanked it on. "This was wrong. I should have never . . ."

I grabbed her hands, stopping her, and shook my head. We stared at each other in a standoff for a long moment, then I finally let her go, only so I could speak.

"*I'm* not good enough," I signed, and her hard expression softened. "You're pure. Pure perfection. And here I am slobbering all over you like a dog."

Her body shook with what must have been a chuckle, the way her mouth held a small smile. "I want you to slobber all over me. I *want* you, Jeric. All of you. Just . . ." She glanced away from me, then back. "I need patience, that's all. I know you're not used to girls holding out on you, but that's not me. I'm not like that."

I returned her smile. "I don't want you to be like them. You'll drive me up the damn wall, but I'll be patient. At least . . . I'll do my best. Don't get too mad if I screw up, okay? I can't help myself with you."

Her eyes darted to my nipple rings, and her hand floated up to touch, but she pulled it back at the last second. "Yeah, me, too."

I took another step away before I lost control already and dove into her. I held her top out at arm's length.

She pulled it over her head, and when her face came into view, she seemed to be trying to decide something. Then she looked me in the eye and signed, "I'm not all that pure, you know. You don't know me as well as you think you do."

Her eyes gleamed with a sinful secret, but then she shrugged.

"Just thought you should know," she added, "in case it makes a difference with whatever's going on with us. If we need a snow-white, pure-of-thought princess to save our asses, I'm not her."

I shook my head, then gave her a teasing smile. "Someday you'll tell me those wicked thoughts in that head of yours."

"Someday," she said, returning my devilish grin as she hopped off the counter. "For now, we should read."

"There's a bar and grill across the street. Can I take you out for something to eat first? If I can't have you, I need something else in my mouth."

✳ THEN ✳
1989

CHAPTER 22

 "I think Sammy needs to go out," Micah said as he rolled onto his elbow and squinted at Sammy, who desperately tried to claw his way through the front door.

"Sammy, stop!" I ordered, but my dog ignored me. "He's never acted like this before."

"Maybe he's embarrassed." Micah grinned as he pushed a damp strand of hair from my face before brushing a kiss over my forehead.

A glance at the clock showed several hours had passed, so no surprise Sammy had to go. But I still should have known his behavior was more than a need to pee. I must have been too hyped up on what had happened—the most totally radical, righteous, *awesome* experience I'd ever had—to notice, though. I smiled giddily at Micah, a thrill of pleasure running through my body, and although part of me wanted to lay here with him, naked and content—no, *more* than content and not even self-conscious anymore—another part of me wasn't sure I could, even if Sammy didn't insist on a trip outdoors. When I rose to my feet, I felt surprisingly strong, powerful even, and full of energy.

Micah rose, too, and wrapped his arms around me, pressing me against his naked body. His lips skimmed over my neck and collarbone.

"I'll take him out. I don't want you to get dressed," he murmured against my skin.

I turned my head to catch his lips with my own, and the kiss alone about sent me into another orgasm.

"I don't want you dressed, either," I said, running my hands over the perfect lines of his chest. "We'll go together. Just a few minutes then we can be naked all night, if you'd like."

His fingers trailed a feather-light line down my spine, then he grabbed my ass, making me squeal. "Oh, I'd very much like."

He kissed me hard and long, and I about gave in when Sammy started barking. With a groan, we pulled apart and dressed hurriedly, paying little attention to what we actually wore, or to Sammy, who was tearing up my brand-new door.

"Okay, okay," I said to Sammy as my hand clasped the knob.

As soon as the door opened, Sammy bolted through it, a yellow shot of lightning blasting into the night. Micah and I stumbled after him, still wrapped in each other emotionally and physically, our arms encircling each other's waists. At least, until we heard the collision of Sammy's body into another form and the grunt of a human voice followed by a ferocious canine growl. My arm dropped from Micah's waist and his from mine as we both stiffened.

Adrenaline, not fear, shot through my body when I took in the many shadows surrounding us. The Shadowmen outnumbered us three-to-one, but I felt confident we could take them on. My muscles coiled, ready for a fight. And when they attacked, my body moved like it never had before. My temper had driven me into previous fights, but those hadn't even been real. They'd been catfights, as much as I hated to admit it. But this—this was real. And I thrived in it.

The Shadowmen charged us, four on Micah, two on me, and Sammy still fighting with the one he knocked down when he flew out of the apartment. Billy Idol-dude tried to grab me from one side and a guy with dark skin, hair and eyes reached for my other side, as if they thought they could snatch me and run. They had another thing coming. My elbows came up, knocking both of them in their chins, and I twisted away from their grasping hands. I spun and clocked dark-guy with my fist in his jaw, making him stumble backwards. A kick to his groin brought him to his knees. Another to his head knocked him out. His form shattered into a million pieces that flew upwards, tiny shadows headed for the sky.

Before I could draw a breath, Billy Idol-dude grabbed me from behind, his arms encircling me and caging mine to my body. I squirmed and flailed and kicked my heels against his shins. His grip on me didn't loosen. With a full body thrust forward and down, I flipped him over my head, but he held onto me and took me with him, making me land face up, laying on top of him. In a swift motion, he rolled us over, flattening me against the deck. The sweet, woody smell of the new lumber filled my nose.

With one arm still around me and his body pinning me to the deck floor, the guy's other arm slid from underneath us. His elbow jabbed and pushed between my shoulder blades as he released his other arm. I bucked against him, trying to pull my knees under me as he jockeyed for a new position, but his weight suddenly felt as though it had tripled, holding me down. A large hand—larger than it should have been with long, spindly fingers—grasped the back of my head and jammed my face into the rough wood. The man's weight shifted, and then his face was close to mine, hot, rancid breath huffing against my ear.

Something pointed and sharp grazed along my temple and cheek, and a two-inch long, purplish-green claw came into view in the corner of my eye. What was this thing, this Shadowman? His fingers had been normal when I saw him at the store. At least, I thought they had. I hadn't really looked that closely at him, but surely I would have noticed this.

"Your friend was . . . delicious," he drawled in my ear, his breath curling down to my nose and making me gag. "I bet you are, too."

"Fuck you," I snarled. I tried to throw my head back to head-butt him, but his hand tightened, and his claws dug into my scalp.

So I jerked my elbow up, landing a blow into his ribs. With a grunt, his weight shifted on me enough to change his center of balance. Faster than I thought possible, I threw my arm up again, putting my whole body into the move. My elbow connected with his face this time, pushing him more to the side, and the inertia of my body threw him off completely.

I jumped to my feet, swinging out a sidekick as I did. His hands flew up and latched onto my foot, bringing me down to my knees with a painful thud. I kicked my foot back at him and broke free from his grip. My heel landed hard against his temple, making his head snap to the side. I sprang to my feet again and landed another kick to his ribs, right where I'd elbowed him earlier. The sound of a breaking bone cracked through the night. I went to kick him one more time, now in the groin, but when my foot should have connected, it met nothing but smoke.

Shock and then elation filled me. Strength, ability, speed . . . I'd never fought with such power before. I spun around to help Micah, but he'd just swung a fist at his last guy, and before it collided into the side of the Shadowman's face, the form disappeared like the others. We shared a stunned look, then we both turned for Sammy. My dog sat on the far side of the deck, his tongue hanging out the side of his mouth as he panted. His tail switched with the smallest of wags. A black dust darkened his golden fur, and his guy was gone, too.

"We did it," I gasped, and I grinned at Micah. His mouth began to pull into a smile, too, but then his eyes darkened as he stared at me.

"You're hurt," he said, grabbing my hand and pulling me inside to the bathroom.

A glance in the mirror showed a trail of blood dribbling from my hairline.

"It's only a scratch," I said, inspecting it more closely.

Micah still took great care in cleaning the wound, for which I was grateful because the thought of the germs in that guy's discolored fingernails—or claws, whatever they were—sickened me. We investigated the rest of our bodies, and Sammy's, too, but the small cut on my head seemed to be our only injury. Although I felt fine, pumped even at how I was able to kick not just one guy's ass, but two, Micah's earlier thoughts of getting naked again had disappeared.

"I don't want to hurt you," he said as we lay snuggled in bed.

"But I'm fine," I protested. "And you would only make me more fine."

In fact, I felt sure making love to him would be good for me, but he wouldn't listen.

"We have the rest of our lives ahead of us," he said.

I sighed, liking the sound of that. Whatever qualms either of us had had with each other were gone now. Our out-of-body experience while making love had brought us even closer together, proving we belonged to each other and nothing could tear us apart.

"Tomorrow, then," I relented.

"Absolutely."

I eventually fell asleep and into a fit of dreams. They started as a nightmare, first of Bex fighting for her life and losing and me watching her die. Then Shadowmen chased Micah and me down the street, then the beach and even across the water. We ran and ran, and at first I had no idea where we were going, but then the Victorian mansion came into view. Micah and I had found it, nestled on a tiny island. We tried to run for it, the Shadowmen on our heels, but as hard and as fast as we ran, we never came any closer. Like we were running in place, going nowhere.

"We can't get there from here," Micah said, giving up.

"Make love to me," I responded, and the statement didn't feel odd at all, a perfectly normal reply in a dream although our lives were on the line. Micah took me into his arms, and the dream became spectacular.

Right when it came to the good part, though, my subconscious returned to the other dream. One moment, Micah and I were naked and thrusting against each other, the next moment, the Shadowmen surrounded us, and then suddenly, we were standing on the front steps of the mansion. The door flew open, as if welcoming us, and as soon as we entered the luxurious house, warmth and the sense of safety enveloped us. We were home.

"We made it," Micah kept saying, over and over again.

"The Shadowmen can't get us here," I replied every time. "This is where we need to be. This place will heal me."

That last statement made less sense to me than the one about making love. I glanced down at myself, looking for injuries, but found none. Then my head started pounding, a quiet drum in the background at first, but it escalated to a loud bass right in my ears.

When I awoke, the bliss of last night had disappeared, replaced by a dull headache, sadness about Bex, and an epiphany.

"We need to go to the mansion," I said aloud before I even opened my eyes. "I know right where it is."

"I think I do, too," Micah murmured next to me.

My eyes flew open, and I turned my head toward him.

"Did you dream about it, too? Did you see where it is?"

His brow wrinkled. "No. I feel a pull in my gut. The feeling to where is more distinct than before, more specific."

I rolled onto my side to face him. My head ached with the movement. "We should go there. At least check it out. There has to be a reason we're both dreaming and envisioning it."

He lifted his hand to my temple and pushed my hair away from my forehead to inspect my injury. I winced. He frowned.

"What?" I asked.

"I've never seen anything like it. Do you remember how it happened?"

"He dug his gnarly fingernails into my head. It's just a scratch. Really."

"I guess . . . kind of looks like there's a bruise around it, too."

"What?" I moved to get up and see for myself, but my head felt like the Terminator's robotic hand crushed my skull, worse than any hangover I'd ever had, which was saying a lot. I lay back down. "Ugh. I have a bitchin' headache."

Micah brought me a glass of water and some aspirin, then he took Sammy outside. After a few minutes, I couldn't hold it anymore and had to get up to pee. The headache seemed to be subsiding already—or was at least masked by the aspirin. Unfortunately, the ugly mark on my head that looked like a blackening bruise didn't go away so easily. Neither did my heartache over Bex.

I moved like a slug throughout the morning as I loaded our bags into Micah's truck to take to the laundromat, while he finished the flooring in the kitchen since he hadn't been able to yesterday. The pain in my head hadn't gone completely away, but remained as a dull ache, more annoying than anything, though it seemed to be growing, into my neck and over my shoulders.

"Are you sure you're okay?" Micah asked as we headed out the door to do laundry. "You look a little pale."

"I'm fine," I said with a sigh. As fine as could be expected, anyway. I really wanted to curl up on the bedding and sleep. To escape the pain in my heart even more than the one in my head.

"I'd do this myself, but I'm not leaving you alone," he said. "Not after last night."

"I know. That's fine." I couldn't argue with his overprotectiveness anymore. I kind of felt the same about him—I didn't want to leave him alone in case he was attacked while solo—but wasn't about to say so. Not exactly a boost to his macho Marine ego.

When we hit the ground at the bottom of the stairs and rounded the building's corner, we found Buck's sedan in the parking area and his reedy frame closing the driver side door. Sammy, who had followed us down, growled lowly, but I gave him the silence sign. His ears remained perked and his eyes alert as we approached the real estate agent.

"Did you ever tell him you hired me?" Micah asked, keeping his voice low enough so only I could hear him.

"It's not really any of his business, is it?"

"Looks like he's making it his business."

"Hey, there," Buck said when he turned to see us approaching. He glanced at me, but Micah kept his interest. "Are you looking to buy the place?"

Micah chuckled, though it sounded a little hollow. Did he plain not like Buck or was he getting the same weird vibes I was?

"No, not me," he said.

"I hired Micah to do the work," I said, and Buck finally looked at me as if I might matter, though he looked none too happy about my announcement. "He gave me the best offer."

Micah's mouth twitched at this, hinting at a smile, but Buck's turned down in a deeper frown.

"I'm sorry," the agent said, "I don't really understand. Who are you?"

I blinked at him. "Jacey. Jacey Burns, remember? I own this place."

Buck scratched his head. "Jacey, you say?"

Micah and I exchanged a knowing glance, then I tried to remind Buck that he knew me. "My grandpa passed away and left this place to me, and you insisted I come down and see it, remember? Well, I'm fixing it up. You can take it off your books and not worry about it anymore. I'm not even sure if I'm going to sell it."

Buck scrutinized my face, his brow puckered. "You say you inherited it now?"

I let out a breath of exasperation. "Yes."

"And you said your name is Jacey?"

"Yes."

"Hmm . . . no, I don't remember. I could have sworn . . ." He glanced at Micah, probably feeling the burn of his glare, then cleared his throat and looked back at me with a false, creepy smile. "I guess I have my properties mixed up. I thought it was this one the Baker couple had bought and stopped by to check on things. You're not the Bakers?"

Micah and I exchanged another look. Buck couldn't have sold this place out from under me, could he? Surely I would have had to sign something.

"Are you sure the Bakers bought this place?" I asked. "Maybe you should go check your records."

Confusion filled Buck's eyes, mixed with something else. Suspicion? Then he narrowed them as he rubbed at his ear.

"You're right," he said. "I probably do have everything mixed up."

He turned for his car and gave us one last befuddled glance before climbing in and pulling away.

"What a dick," Micah muttered.

"I don't feel good about this," I said. "It's too much like what happened with Grace Jones . . . and . . . and B-b—" My throat tightened around her name. I forced it out. "Bex." I swallowed. "Like the Shadowman said—our existences are disappearing."

"Maybe not," Micah hedged. "Buck's old and a drunk. It wouldn't be the first time he screwed up. Maybe when he gets to his office, he'll realize he made a fool of himself."

"Since when did you become so optimistic?" I muttered. He didn't answer.

I sat in Micah's truck while he started the laundry in the washing machines, and when he came back out to join me, I lay across the seat with my head in his lap. I drifted off for a while, strange images filling my head. My heart ached to dream of Bex, to make sure I never forgot her, but she's not what my subconscious brought. Instead, I dreamt of a strange place with strange people—even I was strange.

I wasn't only me. I was us—Micah and me as one, like when we'd made love. One soul, one being. We shared thoughts and feelings and even a body, and although it sounded awkward, I felt as though we lived the most natural, most perfect existence. Like we were beyond human, above the selfish and greedy self-centered ways of this world. We were about *us* and *them*. There was no *me*.

Micah woke me as he moved to leave, and I sat up to watch him enter the laundromat and move our clothes to the dryer. Although I saw him clearly through the windows and he watched me carefully while he worked, his physical absence left a cold spot next to me. The chill crept over my body and settled like a fog, and by the time Micah returned to the truck, my teeth chattered.

"I don't feel so well," I said as he wrapped his arms around me and rubbed my back and arms.

"You don't look so well, either. You're even paler than you

were this morning." He pulled me tighter against him. "I'll get you home as soon as possible."

Micah did his best to take care of me, but I missed my Bex. Although she wasn't normally the motherly type, she at least seemed to know exactly what I needed when I was sick or when Pops had died. Probably because we were alike in that way. We took care of each other through our colds and flus that were inevitable while living in the dorms, bringing each other soup, tissues, and cough medicine. Leaving the room so the sickie could sleep, but also knowing when to stay.

Back at the apartment, I lay on the pallet of clean blankets and finally I dreamt of Bex. She was more alive than ever, laughing with her whole body at the awesome joke she'd played on everyone, but a part of me knew it hadn't been a joke, that she wasn't real. I tried to squash that part of me, to push it out of my dream, but she became louder and louder, and Bex's face drifted away, replaced by Micah's. We were in the mansion, and he was shaking me.

"Sorry, babe, but you need to wake up," he said. "Come on, Jace. Wake up. Now!"

My subconscious jerked out of the mansion, and I awoke to Micah actually shaking me. Darkness filled the apartment, someone pounded on the door, practically breaking it down, and Sammy ran around like a mad-dog, barking.

"We gotta get out of here," Micah said. Whispered. Why?

"Police!" a voice yelled from the other side. "Let us in. You have no right to be here. You are trespassing on private property."

My brows came together, and Micah nodded at the front window. "Buck's out there, too. You were right. He must have found nothing about you or your ownership, so he brought the police to kick us out."

I bolted upright and a wave of nausea slammed over me.

"Shit," Micah said, his eyes tight with worry. "You're in no condition to go anywhere."

CHAPTER 23

"Get my backpack," I told Micah, massaging my aching head as the police pounded on the door again. "That's where I keep the important stuff. The papers from Pops should be in there."

"Open up now or we're coming in," the police yelled.

"Right, but Jacey," Micah held up my backpack, which appeared to be empty, "all of your documents—they're all gone. There's only a few sheets of blank paper in here."

My heart stuttered and my eyes widened. More pounding on the door jump-started the beat in my chest. The door shook in its jamb. They were going to bust their way in and find us here with no proof I owned this place. With no proof I was even me. Where had my papers gone? My birth certificate, my Social Security card, all of my college paperwork . . . everything had been in that backpack. My existence truly had disappeared.

"We have to get out of here," Micah said.

Of course we did. With no ID, no proof of anything, the police would take us in, probably turn us over to the courts or something. What would happen to us then? I didn't want to find out.

"How?" I asked.

He tugged me to my feet, and I swayed as the room spun around me before settling into place. Micah had apparently already gathered some of our bags and grouped them around his feet. He picked them up and slung them over his shoulders, then took my hand and tugged me toward the closet. I staggered like a drunk after him.

"Remember I told you I thought I found something?" He kneeled down on the closet floor and pried up a trapdoor that opened to the hidden space below.

When the front door shook more violently, I didn't hesitate to go through the trapdoor. As soon as I landed on my feet, I looked up to find Micah dropping Sammy through the hole. He landed in my arms, but I went down on my tailbone with the force, clamping my mouth shut against a shriek from the pain that shot up my back and across my hips. Tailbones hurt worse than elbows. Micah dropped bags around us, then pulled the door closed as he dropped to the floor. Barely in time. A loud crack of shattering wood came from the apartment above as the police busted through the door.

Micah, Sammy, and I crouched in the corner of the hidden space, waiting silently. Footsteps above creaked the floorboards, and then more footsteps came from outside. My heart picked up speed again as someone moved close to the hole Micah had created in the building's siding. A light shone beyond it and seeped through the cracks around the plywood Micah had propped into the hole he'd made, although the illumination didn't quite reach us in the far corner. Still—shouldn't the police have checked it out more thoroughly? They simply walked on, as though they found nothing suspicious at all about the bent siding or hole cut into the wall.

As the immediate threat seemed to lessen and I relaxed a bit against Micah, the space's play on my mind returned. Although I knew we sat in a dark corner, I felt the mansion all around us. As if I didn't already feel sick enough, the disorientation made my head dizzy and my stomach churn.

"We need to get out of here. We can't stay," Micah whispered.

"The mansion," I replied. "We have to go there. It's the only place we'll be safe."

I felt that truth as sure as I felt Micah's strong arms around me.

We waited for what felt like several hours but was probably only one or two before Micah crept outside to see if the police had left. He returned in less than a minute, moonlight following him in.

"All but one are gone, and he's across the street, watching," he said. "Looks like they impounded my truck, but your Jeep's still out there."

My heart sank. Ownership of our vehicles must have disappeared out of their system, too.

"They'll come back for it as soon as they check the tags with the Virginia DMV," I said.

Micah nodded. "We need to make a run for it now. Are you up to it?"

"Do I have a choice?"

He grimaced. "Not really."

We stayed low to the ground as we snuck out of our hiding space and along the rear of the building. Even Sammy walked in a crouch as if he understood. Micah and I angled our heads to peek around the corner. My Jeep stood in the parking area about twenty yards away, and beyond it and across the street sat a marked car under a street lamp. The cop, however, didn't sit in his car on a stakeout, but spoke animatedly to a man at the bar's door, his hand gesturing in our direction. He was probably questioning the employees to find out if any of them knew who Micah and I were. Thank goodness they didn't—not for our sake, but for theirs. If we'd made any friends in this little town, they could have wound up dead.

Micah held his hand out in front of me, and the streetlight glinted off of my keys. I pointed to the one for the Jeep, and he nodded. As soon as the officer turned his back to us, we ran for it. Adrenaline overcame my weakness and carried me across the overgrown weeds and grass to the Jeep. Sammy jumped in the back and Micah threw our bags back there, too, as I clamored into the passenger seat. Micah peeled out, and I looked over my shoulder—the cop shouted after us as he ran to his car.

Micah sped down the road and barely slowed enough to avoid tipping the Jeep as he made the turn for the bridge to the mainland. Sirens wailed in the distance, but we had enough of a head start. When we crossed the bridge, my lungs released the breath I hadn't realized I'd been holding. I couldn't believe we were running from the police. This wasn't the same as bolting from a party when the cops showed up. We were probably considered honest-to-God fugitives, but it looked like we actually might make it.

Until a huge, dark shadow flew at Micah's window. A sound cracked through the night. Breaking glass. Micah jerked to the side, and the steering wheel spun in his hands, careening us off the road and down the embankment. Micah's arm flew out, pressing me against the seat. The Jeep flipped once. Twice. Landed upside down on the edge of the water.

"Are you okay?" Micah gasped as his hands already worked at his seatbelt.

"I think so." My head ached even more, and the seatbelt dug into my shoulder, but I otherwise seemed uninjured. I fumbled with the clasp until my belt freed me, and I fell to the roof. "Sammy?"

My mind registered his barking outside of the vehicle. *Oh, thank God.* He'd already made it out, and he sounded okay, though jumpy. I wasn't sure if the roll bar would have saved him. As I army-crawled my way out of the wreckage, though, he darted into an alleyway, still barking.

"Sammy!" I called.

"He's probably scared," Micah said from right next to me. He squatted over where I lay on the ground, not letting me up until he fully inspected me for injuries.

"Sammy," I yelled again when Micah finally released me, and I'd pushed myself to my feet.

A dog's cry sounded from the alley.

"Shadowmen," I whispered in horror.

Micah moved faster than me, already sprinting for the alley. Sammy came out, though, limping toward us. Relief and exhaustion brought me to my knees, and Sammy came over and laid his head in my lap. Another deep cut jagged through his other shoulder—whether from the accident or the Shadowmen in the alley, I wasn't sure.

The wail of sirens grew louder.

"We have to get out of here," Micah said. "We're out in the open."

He gathered our bags and half-carried me up the embankment and into the alley Sammy had come out of, my dog limping along at our side. A cold sweat broke out on my forehead—at least one Shadowman, the one who'd probably flown into the Jeep, had just been down this alley—but we had nowhere else to hide. The police must not have seen the Jeep upside-down by the water, because their cars flew right by, red and blue lights flashing across the buildings beyond the embankment.

"Come on," Micah said, his voice barely loud enough for me to hear.

His body threw off a blanket of tension that locked my own muscles tight. I stumbled at his side, my weight too much for my legs to carry, as we made our way to a residential street. Micah pushed me into the first vehicle he found with an unlocked door—some kind of older model American sports car. I was too tired to care what kind. Too tired to care when he hot-wired the ignition and drove us out of there.

"It's not very far," I mumbled, my head lolling against the passenger side window. "I feel it. Right up the road."

Micah rested his hand on my knee. "I'll get us there."

"The mansion, right? You know where?"

I dozed off before hearing his answer.

"Damn." Micah's huff of exasperation brought me out of unconsciousness.

"What's wrong?" I asked, trying to peel my eyes open.

His hand patted my thigh. "Nothing, babe. Go back to sleep. I'm going to take us around Tampa Bay to the other side."

My eyes finally cracked open—well, one did anyway—to see a huge body of water in front of us, the moonlight glancing off its rough surface as Micah hightailed it in reverse. Several black shapes flew over the water. More Shadowmen.

The mansion pulled at my gut from the distance, but we couldn't get there from here. Too many shadows for us to fight, especially when I couldn't even lift my head from the seat. My eyes closed as I prayed—*prayed* for the first time since my parents died—that Micah would get us to safety. To the mansion.

The next thing I knew, Micah was pulling me out of the car seat and into his arms.

"Are we there? At the mansion?" I asked, my voice thick with grogginess and my eyes still closed as I lay my head against his shoulder, and he carried me away from the stolen car.

"We can't drive there," Micah said. "I don't think we're going to make it there at all."

"We have to," I mumbled with a tongue that felt like dead weight in my mouth. Although my whole body felt numb, useless, my heart spiked with panic. "It's the only place . . ."

"Shh. Don't worry. You just need to rest right now. I'll take care of things."

"But—"

"Over here," an unfamiliar voice called out, no more than a whisper, though it sounded miles away. "Get her in here."

I had no clue who she was or where she beckoned us or if she was even real because blackness overcame me.

I awoke in an unfamiliar bed, but an actual real bed that was soft and comfortable after weeks of sleeping on the floor. Except Micah wasn't in there with me. I tried to sit up, but my body remained numb and heavy as a truck. I peered around the dark room—a motel room, maybe?—to see Micah's form silhouetted against a large window as he gazed out of it. He must have sensed I'd awakened because he didn't look my way.

"There's at least twenty of them," he said quietly. "Maybe thirty. We'll never make it."

I pushed myself up enough to see out the window. I could make out the water with tiny lights on the far side of it, probably Tampa Bay, and felt the pull of the mansion—our refuge—somewhere out there. It must have been on an island, just out of reach. Dozens of shadows flew in the night sky and hovered over the water. I wondered if everyone could see them, or only us.

"We have to find a way," I said. My elbow buckled, and I collapsed against the pillows.

"I'm not taking you into that," Micah said. "It's way too dangerous."

"We *have* to, Micah."

I blacked out again. Well, not really blacked out, because I dreamt. Except it didn't really feel like a dream, more like past experiences, memories. Micah and I were one again, our souls united into a single being, and we were in that other world, the one where *I* and *me* didn't exist, but only *we* and *us*. Even for the others in this world, so many others, life was about all of us.

The world itself was like Earth, but not. The sky appeared more teal than blue, and two yellow orbs shone in it—two suns, one big and seemingly close, the other much farther away and the size of our Earth's moon. A sweet fragrance filled the air, but not anything I'd ever smelled on Earth. Trees with twisting branches and purple bark and leaves lined the edges of a vast space in front of us interrupted by rectangular pools of fuchsia water. The scene reminded me of The Mall in Washington between the Lincoln Memorial and the Washington Monument. Except for the candy-like colors, of course. We stood with others like us at the top of the steps of a huge building I knew to be a castle. Its crystal-like walls reached high above, reflecting the aquamarine sky.

The people, for lack of a better word, around us revered Micah and me, as if we ranked high above them, although structured hierarchy meant little in this world. At least it hadn't really mattered until we'd come under attack. I tried to understand what that meant, but couldn't. We weren't being attacked now . . . although the sky—no, everything-—seemed to be darkening around us. Fading out. Disappearing?

I couldn't lift my head when I awoke, still in the bed in the dark room by the water. The pillow under me was soaked and so was my face—covered in tears. My chest felt an unequivocal emptiness, a hole even bigger than Bex's and Pops' deaths had created.

"Micah?" I whimpered.

A weight settled onto the bed next to me, and he pulled me into his arms.

"Right here," he murmured.

"I thought . . . I thought I lost you." I didn't know why—that's not what I'd dreamt at all—but the feeling was true. I was losing him. The hole in my chest was *his* absence. And in more than just my heart. His presence in my soul was disappearing, too. "Something's wrong. I think . . . we need to get to the mansion."

"We can't. I've been watching and studying, but there's no way with all those Shadowmen out there."

"We *have* to," I cried, fear sending me into a panic. My heart raced, and the dark room suddenly felt like a prison, but I was too weak to escape.

"It's too dangerous."

"I don't care! We have to get there. If we don't . . ." My chest tightened with the reality of what I was feeling. "I think . . . I think I'm dying, Micah."

He pulled back and stared at me for a long moment, and the same terror I felt filled his eyes. His arms tightened around me as he once again crushed me against him, eliminating any space between us.

"No. I won't let that happen. I'll take you to a hospital."

"They can't help!"

"They have to! I won't lose you, Jacey. You can't leave me."

"Just . . ." My constricted chest and tight throat left me panting for a breath. "Get me . . . to the mansion."

I passed out again, only to waken to Micah carrying me. But instead of holding me tight against him as he'd done before, his arms felt loose, as if he might drop me. His steps slugged heavily as he struggled to reach the door of the room.

"I'm gonna get us help, babe," he said, his voice hoarse and distant. My eyes rolled up to his face. A thin sheen of sweat covered his pale skin. He looked as bad as I felt. "It's just the flu. I have it, too. I'm gonna get us help."

He lurched. We both crashed to the floor, and neither of us had the strength to get up.

The door flew open.

"Crap," said a female voice. "They're not doing well at all."

"Let's get them to the bed," a male responded. "I've got him. You take her."

Thin arms slid under my shoulders and knees and lifted me, though not far off the ground. My eyes fluttered open. A young woman, not much older—or bigger—than me carried my lifeless weight with ease. The moonlight through the window shone off her light-colored hair and into her pale eyes as she laid me on the bed.

A weight settled next to me. I could only move my eyes to find Micah in bed with me, a black guy standing over him.

"You two need to re-Bond," the girl said. "Join up and get over there. Otherwise, you're gonna die."

"What do you mean?" Micah croaked.

"You're Separating," the strange guy said. "You need to re-Bond. Do it however you need to do it, but get it done or you'll both die."

"And if it comes to that . . . well, we can't let you just *die*," the girl added.

They left us alone with that cryptic message.

With the last bit of strength remaining in my body, I rolled over to face Micah.

"Who are they?" I asked.

He struggled to roll to his side, then to lift his hand as if to push my hair away, but weakness must have overcome him, because it rested like a dead weight on the side of my face.

"No idea. They said they could help us, but they haven't done anything but—"

My eyes popped wide open as a stabbing pain jolted through my body. A scream blasted from my mouth, and I clutched at Micah's hand and squeezed it to my chest. Another burst, like a spontaneous combustion inside me. Burning agony exploded through my racing heart, as though it were being smashed into pieces.

"Micah," I gasped.

"I'm here, babe." His voice came out thick, like molasses.

"It *burns*." I tried to pull in a breath, but my lungs could only muster a wheeze of air. "Micah . . . finish the journal for me . . . okay?"

"What?"

"Just . . . promise. Write this . . . all down. Okay?"

"I promise," he said as his fingers brushed against my cheek.

"I . . . love—"

He gripped my face harder, cutting me off. Panic raised his voice. "No, Jacey. Don't do this. Stay with me."

"I . . . love you."

"Help!" he yelled, the scream piercing my eardrums. "Hurry!"

My vision blurred at the edges. This was it. I felt death at my door. "Love . . . you . . . .. Always have . . . always . . . will."

"I love you, too, Jacey. But don't . . . hang on, babe. Don't do this." He yelled louder, "Get in here! She needs help!"

He tried to move away, but I held him to me tightly.

"Please . . . don't . . . leave me." I stared into his warm, brown eyes, falling into them like I had in the beginning as his gaze remained locked on mine, bathing in the love they now held.

"Never." His voice fell away, like a leaf carried on the wind, off into the distance.

A bright light blasted my vision, and the world faded out as fire consumed me.

CHAPTER 24

Micah
1984

June 24, 1984

Jacey's gone.
They killed her.
But it's all my fault.
I'm not far behind her.

✻ NOW ✻
2012

CHAPTER 25

Jeric flipped through the rest of the journal, but no more entries filled the pages. He slammed the book shut, making me jump, and bolted from his seat next to me on the futon at the front of the camper. His arms clamped over his head as if protecting it from a blow, and he turned in a wide circle with his eyes squeezed shut. He strode to the back bedroom then returned to the front. He glanced at me with storming blue eyes and an unreadable expression, swiped his hand over his face, shook his head, and charged outside.

I scrubbed at the tears on my cheeks as I stared dazedly at the door. Jacey was dead. I couldn't believe it. *Dead*. I'd come to know her so well, had grown closer to her than I ever had with a character in a book, I felt like a piece of me had died with her. And we'd put so much hope into her and Micah's story, and this was how it ended. How could this be it?

The way Jeric tore out of here, he was beyond pissed. I couldn't blame him. All of our hopes and expectations had been in that stupid book, and they'd died along with Micah's last words. Jeric would need a long run to settle down from this, but when ten minutes passed and he still hadn't returned, worry began to form in the pit of my stomach.

I finally rose from the futon and went outside, hoping to find him out there. No sign of him anywhere. I looked up the campground's narrow dirt road toward the highway, but the dim streetlamp fifty yards away cast a brownish-yellow pool of light only at its base. I glanced the other way, toward the rear of the park, but it was lost in darkness.

A shudder of fear ran up my spine.

I ran inside, grabbed my shotgun and headed out, with Ghost by my side, to look for Jeric. Why wasn't he back already? How could he have run off in the first place? Here we both were, traipsing around in the dark in a strange place with people . . . creatures . . . whatever the Shadowmen were possibly out here right now with us. There was a chance they weren't, a small chance they hadn't followed us from Georgia, but the prickly sensation on the nape of my neck told me they lurked nearby, watching. Waiting. For a time like this.

The campground's dirt road made a lopsided circle through the park with sites on each side of the path. Campers and RVs sat on most of the sites, nearly all lit up at ten o'clock at night, but plenty of sites remained empty between them. With Ghost trotting along with me, I jogged through these black spaces, keeping a tight grip on my gun. If anyone saw me, I'd probably be hauled off to jail. I came full circle with no sign of Jeric, only to find him sitting on top of the picnic table outside my Airstream, a half-empty bottle of whiskey in his hand.

I stared at him with my mouth hanging open. He returned my glare while taking a long draw of the amber liquid, his eyes hard and accusing. As if *I* had been the one who'd had a hissy fit and then disappeared. I took my gun inside and put it away, then came back out.

"So what now?" I asked with my hands.

Ghost sat on his haunches next to me and stared at Jeric, as if waiting for his answer, too. He didn't respond at first but took another drink before setting the bottle down next to him.

"Nothing," he signed. "I'm done."

"What?"

"I'm done."

When he didn't clarify, I signed, "Done with what? What do you mean?"

He threw his hands out in a sweeping motion. "With everything. Most of all with that fucking book."

"Yeah, we're done with it anyway, but that doesn't mean you can quit on everything else. We have to figure this out."

"There's nothing to figure out! I want nothing to do with any of it. *Nothing*. You should forget about it all, too."

I stared at him for a long moment, then pointed at the flame on my wrist. "What about this? What about Uncle Theo and Mira? We can't just give up! On us! On them!"

"Watch me." He picked up the bottle and took another swig and then another, as if determined to get drunk.

Something else was wrong. Something was going through his head that he didn't want to face. He couldn't have given up so easily just because Jacey and Micah had left us with nothing to work with. Did he know something more? Had something occurred to him and flipped a switch in his mind? If so, he apparently had no intentions of discussing it now, and the more pulls he took on the bottle, the less likely I would understand anyway.

"We'll talk in the morning," I signed, and I went inside, hoping he'd change his mind.

I dropped to the futon, crossed my arms and legs and waited for him to come inside. And waited. And waited. I peeked out the window. He still sat on the picnic table, his head hanging low, his hands clasped behind it, and his mouth moving as though he muttered under his breath. I sat down again, but couldn't stay still, so I paced the camper several times. From the bedroom, I watched him through the window again. Now his hands were planted on the table behind him, bracing him as his head hung back and he stared at the sky. Every once in a while, he pulled another swig until no more whiskey remained in the bottle.

Surely he'd be coming inside soon to pass out.

No such luck. I returned to the front and huddled down on the futon, still waiting, then ended up on my side and then my back. I'd been staring at the camper's cloth-lined ceiling and worrying about Uncle Theo and Mira, when Jeric broke into song outside. He was singing! His words were slurred, but good gravy did he have a voice. Pure as fresh rain, nearly smooth as honey, but a little rough from lack of use, giving it a sexy edge. He really could have been a rock star, even deaf. If he only knew.

I drifted off at some point and awoke with a start, sun streaming through the window onto my face. I blinked, momentarily disoriented. Yellow and orange tie-dyed curtains meant I was still up front, on the futon. I sat up and looked around. Ghost lay at my feet, but no Jeric. I looked outside at the picnic table, but he wasn't there either, so I rushed to the bedroom, throwing pillows and blankets around, although he'd obviously not slept there. My heart stuttered as panic gripped me full force.

Shadowmen.

What if he'd passed out on the picnic table and they'd attacked? Why hadn't I made him come in?

I ran outside, looking for signs of a struggle, but there were none. Running down the road, I searched for evidence of someone being dragged through the dirt, tire treads by our camper, anything, but I found nothing. These weren't normal people, though. Could they fly off with him? Could he be in the woods at the edge of the campground, his dead body abandoned like Bex's? My stomach rolled with that thought.

I dashed back inside and spun in circles, not knowing what to do. And then I noticed. All of his stuff was gone. His bag, his shoes, his tablet . . . all gone.

And a note I hadn't seen before, scrawled on a paper towel left on the counter, the handwriting like chicken scratch. Jeric's writing in his journal was pretty neat for a dude, so he must have still been drunk when he wrote this:

Leni,
I can't do this anymore. It's all bullshit.
I'm out of here. You should go home, too.
~~Love~~ Take care,
J

I swallowed the melon-sized lump suddenly blocking my throat and blinked against the sting in my eyes. The paper towel fluttered in my shaking hand as I read the note again, each word tearing a piece from my heart. No. He couldn't have left me. He was all I had left.

Wadding the note and stuffing it into my pocket, I sprinted out of the camper and up to the office. The bell above the door rang loudly, calling a giggling Bethany to the front. The stench of cigarette smoke followed her in. Her face fell when she saw me, probably because of my own expression.

"The guy I was with—did you see him leave?" I demanded, panic wavering my voice.

A crashing sound came from the other room, and Bethany glanced that way, then looked back at me with both worry and apology filling her eyes.

"Sorry," she said as she moved for the door connecting the front office to whatever lay beyond. An adjoining apartment, I thought. "But I—"

"Sorry to bother you," I muttered as I rushed outside.

With fists on my hips, I looked over at the truck stop across the road. My truck was still in the mechanic's bay, pumped up on a jack, but I didn't care about it now. I couldn't leave even if it was done. The need to go to Tampa had disappeared at the same time Jeric had, and all I felt now was the need to find him.

When traffic allowed, I jogged across the highway, through the large store and around the pumps and parking area outside, then into the onsite bar. I blinked at the sudden darkness, the cavernous room dim and empty except for a bartender and one guy wearing a cowboy hat sitting at the bar. Not Jeric. The mechanical bull sat still in its corner, unlike last night when we'd come in for hamburgers and fries before going back to the journal. I'd been tempted then to show Jeric my special talents, but had chosen not to. Maybe if I had, he wouldn't have left me . . . .

I shook myself out of it and hurried outside, thinking maybe he'd tried to hitch a ride from one of the truck drivers. As a guy old enough to be my daddy climbed down from his cab and leered at me, though, I gave up and ran across the street and to my camper.

Inside, I fell to the futon, hoping he'd change his mind and return. What else could I do but wait? I was stranded, no way to leave until my truck was done and nowhere to go anyway. And left completely and utterly alone.

I checked Jeric's Facebook page, although he didn't get on much. I admonished myself for the ridiculous thought that we hadn't even been able to update our status to "In a relationship." At least there would be no need to change it back. I couldn't find him on there, though. Not on my Friends list and not when I searched for him. Then my phone screen showed, "Please log in," and when I tried, it denied me access. None of my online accounts worked. Great. There went another part of me.

I texted Jeric several messages: "Where are you?" "Are you coming back?" When no answer came, I asked, "Did you really leave me?" And I waited for some kind of reply, anything, but none came. About two hours after sending the last one, I knew none would come—my phone showed "No Service" and nothing I did fixed it.

I tried not to panic, but my heart grew heavy in my chest and my stomach squeezed itself into a tiny ball as the reality of my situation settled in. I had no home except this camper stuck in a podunk, off-the-highway town in northern Florida where I knew nobody. My great-uncle was missing, and now that the pull to go to Tampa was gone, I had no idea where to look for him. He was probably dead by now anyway, murdered by the same "them" who had killed Jacey and Micah. My own existence had faded into the ether, and, if what had happened to Jacey and Micah was happening to us, scary Shadowmen, who might not have been real men at all, hunted me.

Jeric's presence had been a buffer to the chaos my life had become. Not only someone to share it with, but a connection that had given me hope. The inexplicable feelings I had for him hadn't seeped in slowly until they reached my heart, but had sprang from my very soul as if they'd always been there. They kept me optimistic that whatever was going on, however things turned out, I'd be okay because I had him here with me.

I shouldn't have put so much stock in him, in us. Foolishness, I knew. He asked if I ever took chances when he'd been my biggest risk of all. He had no idea how much I had put myself out there with him, inviting him to the camper and into my life. Like every other time I'd done something because I wanted to and because it felt good, as he'd put it, I'd made a huge mistake. There was a reason Mama controlled my life—I wasn't fit to make decisions.

Don't go there. I drew in a deep breath. No, I didn't need to go to that dark place I'd lived in for so long until Uncle Theo had helped me find a way out. Mama's hold on me reached far, all the way from Alaska to Georgia after she and Daddy had moved, but Uncle Theo tried to teach me to trust in myself. To live my life, not hers. And even when I'd disappointed him so badly, he encouraged me, saying I was bound to make mistakes and that was okay. Okay to make mistakes? To fail? The opposite of what I'd been taught for as long as I could remember.

"Life's about falling down and getting back up again," he'd said before I left for Italy. "This is your chance to get back up. And whatever you do, whatever happens, follow your own heart, little bird. Believe in yourself. In your instinct. That's your soul talking to you, and it's much wiser than your brain."

My soul, however, felt nothing but emptiness now.

Needing an escape, a distraction, I picked up Jacey's journal and read the last several entries again, hoping something had changed but, of course, it hadn't. "They" had killed Jacey.

But who were "they"? The Shadowmen? Or the people who were supposedly helping them? Micah could have elaborated a bit more. And did he mean he was about to die, too? Did he kill himself because of heartbreak?

What does it matter?

None of it mattered because the whole act of reading the journal had been completely pointless. There were no answers in this book. It was only a tragic story with a horrible ending. Nothing useful for us at all.

My gut wrenched at the reminder that we really knew nothing. If I went on without Jeric, the thought of which caused another twist of my insides, I could be facing what Jacey and Micah did—death. Maybe that's what the whole book was for, simply to warn us away.

But there had to be more to it, didn't there?

Like Jeric had last night, I flipped through the blank pages, but more slowly, looking for evidence of torn-out sheets, indentions pens had left from writing on another page, anything. When I returned to Micah's entry, I gasped out loud. New words had appeared, the ink faded to almost invisible and not in Jacey's or Micah's handwriting:

"You know the rest. Remember."

I stared at the two phrases. Had they been there before, but so light we hadn't seen them? They had to have been. Because otherwise . . . a chill brought goose bumps to my skin. There was no other explanation. Not in my world.

But what was I supposed to remember? I closed my eyes and concentrated on the individual pieces of the puzzle, trying to see how they fit together so I could determine which pieces were missing. Which ones I needed to remember.

My mind danced on the edge of consciousness as I tried to make sense of it all. I needed to figure this out.

This is important. Urgent. The meaning of it all.

"You know the rest. Remember."

�֍ THEN �֍
1989

CHAPTER 26

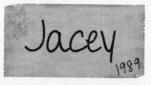 Darkness surrounded me as I drifted away from my body. And from Micah. The raw edges of my soul, where we had been wrenched apart, burned with agony, and I'd never felt so devastatingly alone.

Then my parents' smiling faces gazed at me and images of scenes from my childhood appeared. Was this for real? Was I dying and watching my life flash by? *You've got to be kidding me.* Scene after scene shuffled past, but eventually slowed. To *that* night. I watched myself as a girl, laying out my paintings by the fireplace at the cabin so the watercolors would be dry by morning and my mom could frame them to brighten the cabin's dark wood interior. But neither my mom nor the cabin would be there in the morning.

I sat on my cot in the corner of the one-room cabin with my knees drawn to my chest. A nightmare had awoken me and I couldn't fall back to sleep, so I watched long shadows dance across the walls. The yellowish-orange light of the fire grew brighter, and the wood popped and sparks flew out of the hearth. Some landed on my art, and the paper immediately ignited.

Mom and Dad slept on the pullout bed of the old couch. Right in front of the fireplace. A scream had barely worked its way through my throat before their blankets caught fire. Flames licked hungrily and smoke filled the air. Daddy called for me in the darkness, and I tried to find him, but my eyes watered, and I couldn't stop coughing to answer him. The entire log cabin lit up in seconds as though it were only dry kindling.

A dog barked outside, and I tried to make my way toward the sound, toward the door, crawling on my hands and knees like they'd taught us at school. I'd lost my bearings in the cabin when the roof collapsed, but I'd rolled over at the loud crash, trying to escape the fire raining down around me. A burning ember from a beam fell across my stomach and ribs. My scream tore through the night as the ember singed through my clothes and into my skin. But my throat was so parched, my lips cracked, and no tears came from my dried-out ducts. Smoke burned my lungs, and I gave up trying to breathe.

That's when Sammy found me. He barked and then grabbed my arm with his mouth and pulled. I could barely feel his teeth digging into my skin, my lungs, stomach and ribs searing with such agony. Somehow, he dragged me outside. Somehow, I managed to crawl several feet away from the cabin. Somehow, I lay on a bed of pine needles on the ground without crying or screaming, but silently watching as the flames grew bigger, as though trying to lick the clouds above, setting everything around me in an orange glow.

I screamed now. Screamed for my parents. For myself. Why did they have to die? Why not me? Why was I left in the world alone? I'd been a good girl. I'd done everything right as a child—obeyed my parents, earned good grades, received academic and art awards. What had I done that was so bad to be left behind? I understood the semi-boyfriend in high school, even Pops and Bex. I deserved for them to be ripped away from me after everything I'd done since my parents' deaths. But why Mom and Dad? Was I a bad person from the start? Born to bring only death and destruction? The Grim Reaper after all?

"No, Jacey, do not go into the darkness. Come to the light." The voice sounded from far away. "This way, child. To the light where your soul belongs." The soothing voice offered comfort. Lured me into its warmth.

Then bright light engulfed me.

The pain of being separated from Micah, of reliving the fire, of feeling so broken and lost and alone slid away. My soul seemed to grow, yet became lighter at the same time. Lighter as in the weight of the world, of mundane life, of love and loss and stress and fear, had lifted completely. I became weightless, drifting on the air of this place of white nothingness like a feather floating on a stream.

And I felt . . . free.

"Yes, you are a free soul," the deep but soothing voice sounded all around me again.

The white light I seemed to be drifting in faded and shapes of my surroundings grew defined edges. A room, like a cave, but not dark or dirty. Ribbons of color streamed through the walls and ceiling as if a rainbow river flowed through them, but a turn to my right showed that they reflected the vast, irregularly shaped pool in the center of the room. A pool of light, not water, although a mist rose and swirled along its surface, its colors constantly blurring and changing. Hundreds, maybe thousands, of orbs of blue light bobbed around the curving edges, and a figure in a white robe stood on the side directly opposite me, a hood hiding its face in shadow. I assumed the voice I'd just heard belonged to it.

"Am I dead?" I blurted out.

"By Earthly definition, yes," the figure answered, and I was right about the voice belonging to him. "But this is not Earth."

I swallowed. Well, swallowing was the sensation I felt, although I had no real body. I *knew* this—in fact, I was pretty sure I was another light orb bobbing by the pool—but I still felt like I had some kind of a defined shape with arms and legs and a head.

"Is this . . . is this Heaven?" I stammered because I never expected I'd wind up here. I hadn't even been sure Heaven or God existed, but I'd followed the *light* (was it a cliché or had all those people talking about "the light" really experienced death?). "Are you *God*?"

"More Earthly terms." The white robe chuckled. "But, goodness, no, I am not The Maker. I am the Keeper here."

"Where is here? Where are we if not in Heaven? We're not in Hell, are we?" The place held too much beauty and serenity to possibly be Hell, but maybe the ambiance was part of the deceit.

"Most definitely not what you would call Hell. We are in the Space Between."

I tilted the head I didn't really have. "The Space Between?"

"That is where we are. Welcome. We had hoped we wouldn't see you again quite so soon, but apparently, that was His plan all along. So here we are again."

"Again," I echoed. "In the Space Between. Between what?"

"Between Heaven and Hell, to use words you are familiar with. Between worlds and realms and dimensions. Between lives and between time. The Space Between it all. This is where all souls come when they leave their physical bodies in their respective worlds so their lives may be reviewed and their souls renewed before choosing their next paths and their next worlds."

"And you say I've been here before?"

"Oh, yes, many times. Since the beginning of forever."

And somehow, I knew he spoke the truth. The Space Between *felt* familiar. I felt suddenly certain I'd been here before, although I couldn't recall it ever looking like this—with a man in a robe and a pool of light and mist before me. Why did I feel like we were in an Earthly cave, albeit a surreal one?

"You see and smell and hear and feel this place in a way most familiar to you from your last life, your last world. You're putting the Space into terms you can understand from recent memory. It's different every time you return."

A series of memories flashed through me of thousands of lifetimes on thousands of different worlds, including the one with the glass palace reflecting the teal-green sky with its two suns. A darkness flickered through me with this last thought.

The Keeper suddenly stood right next to me, and a warm current washed through me. I formed the visual of him taking my hand, because that's how it felt to my soul.

"Come, child, we must hurry. You must remember it all before you go back."

"Go back?"

"Well, I assume that's what you will choose, but, of course, the choice is yours."

"Please explain."

I could feel his smile, although I still couldn't see his face. "I thought you'd never ask."

He tugged on me to follow him, so I did as we moved around the edge of the pool, the orbs bobbing out of our way.

"You have been many people and have gone by many names throughout the millennia of time, but your soul has always meant protector of the light. The one you currently know as Micah, the uplifted leader of armies, belongs to you and you to him. You are dyads. Your souls were created for each other in the beginning and, after many life cycles of learning and growing together, they became one. The Union is the highest form dyad souls can take. You have both always been warriors, and in recent lives you had reached the highest of the world echelons."

"Wait. What does that mean?"

The Keeper seemed to sigh. "We only have a short time. I'll explain briefly. The Maker created thousands of worlds, realms, and dimensions across the universe and beyond, and He created the souls to populate them, more than any Earthly human could comprehend. Souls travel to different worlds for different life cycles. Some worlds are in lower dimensions, where souls are challenged with the foundations of love and life. At the other end of the spectrum are the highest echelons, where Union souls can go to learn about the most complex truths—concepts only The Maker and those closest to Him, whom you would call the angels, truly understand."

As I processed this, one of the orbs by the pool changed from a bluish color like the others to a bright pink. The Keeper left my side to attend to the orb. After a few moments, the ball of light vaulted high above the pool and then dove down, disappearing into the misty swirls of light.

"So sorry to keep you waiting," the Keeper apologized. "She'd chosen her next destination, and I had to send her on her way."

"That's how souls go to the next place? Through the pool of light?"

The Keeper's hood bounced in a nod. "When physical bodies die, the souls inside detach from the corporeal world they'd inhabited and come here to the Space Between. They review their most recent life and how it affected their souls, then based on their growth—or lack thereof—they're given a choice of what comes next. They may be limited to a few choices, or I may be able to offer them many. Each soul and each life cycle is different, as are the worlds. Some, the highest levels, only allow Union souls. You had been on such a world before your trip to Earth."

I stopped in the path we were making around the pool. "If Earth is one of those higher level worlds, I don't even want to know what the lower ones are like. They must be in Hell."

"Well, no. Only the Dark worlds are in Hell, as you call it. But Earth is not a higher level, nowhere close to Heaven."

I blew out air I didn't really breathe. "That's a relief. So if Earth is a lower level and Micah and I were at the highest level before, why were we here? There—on Earth, I mean?"

"Yes, yes." Excitement filled his "voice." "This is the part you must try to remember for next time. The part we must deeply embed into your soul."

As if on cue, the memories began to return.

"Wait. I know this." I paused to gather the thoughts and images and clarify them in my mind, the thinking part of my soul. "We were warriors. Micah and me. Actually . . . we were one warrior, together, a mighty one, right?"

The Keeper nodded. "You have always been Guardians."

"We led an army on that world," I continued, still pulling the memories in one at a time. "We shouldn't have needed it, though. I remember a peace we'd never had on any other world, in any other realm or dimension. Except . . . darkness had come in. Darkness consumed us."

"Yes. Enyxa, ruler of the Dark worlds—Hell as you call it—had found her way into that world, forcing you to fight. Her Lakari infiltrated."

"There were too many dark spirits, and they overtook us." My soul filled with grief as more memories came. "Oh, my god. The *pain*. I remember the pain. And the screaming. They separated the Union souls. Ripped them apart!"

If I had an actual heart, it would be breaking with the agony. Like what I had felt when pulled away from Micah, but a hundred times worse. Although I had no physical eyes or tear ducts, I felt as though tears streamed.

"All of those souls . . ." I sobbed.

The Keeper placed a hand on my shoulder, and his voice came out low and heavy with grief. "Enyxa found a way to bypass the Space Between and sent those Separated souls to different worlds, where they'd never be able to find each other and rejoin."

I instantly knew what this meant. After several life cycles of not finding each other, Separated souls grew Dark, and eventually they succumbed to Enyxa. They became her Lakari. Or Shadowmen, as I'd called them in this last life.

"We were lucky the two of you made it here together, although you'd already been Separated."

I couldn't remember this part. The torture of our Separation eclipsed the memories of what happened next.

"And we chose to go to Earth?" I asked as a guess. "Why?"

"I don't think it was really much of a choice. You see, Enyxa has been working to destroy Earth. She's been sending more and more Lakari there, darkening the world with all that she offers—greed, power, and *self* over love, kindness, and *others*. Earth continues to slide into the shadows of heartache and hopelessness, and eventually, it will become hers. You and Micah, hurt and angry and the warriors you are, seized the opportunity to fight for the souls there."

"But how?"

"By once again choosing to be Guardians. For hundreds of life-cycles, you've both chosen this path—to be protectors of the Gates. On Earth, the Guardians are often Separated souls that have re-Bonded. They are called the Phoenix. Joining the Phoenix had been a natural choice for both of you."

"But . . . I'm here. I didn't fight at all. I didn't guard anything."

The Keeper let out a heavy sigh. "You were not strong enough, child. Neither of you. You lost your powers of the Union when you were Separated, and you fought the Lakari before you were Forged. Your souls were not ready for such a fight, and their darkness overcame you. Although The Maker has His plan and I don't know it, I assume you needed this life cycle to reacclimate yourselves to Earth and to living as the Separated. You didn't remember anything and were only beginning to put the pieces together. You'd barely started to re-Bond, let alone make it to the Gate to be Forged and receive your missions. Thank goodness you made it as far as you did!"

My mind tried to grasp at these elusive memories, but only became boggled. None of this sounded familiar at all. "A Gate? Forged? Missions? Re-Bond?"

An orb turned pink and the Keeper disappeared. He returned in a moment and picked up where we left off.

"You and Micah had a brief re-Bonding, but it wasn't enough. If you'd had more time or had come to remember and understand what you needed to do sooner, you would have known to strengthen your Bond and get to the Gate."

"But what *is* this Gate?" I asked again.

Instead of answering me, his head lifted and turned, and at the same time, a warm feeling swelled within me. "Ah. Here's the one you know as Micah now. That explanation will have to wait. We must hurry with him so you both can move on."

A blue light streaked toward me and collided into my soul. Micah's presence curled around and within me, a bittersweet feeling. I beamed to have him with me again, but my light dulled knowing the tough but sweet Micah I knew no longer blessed Earth with his existence. Our energies swirled together, but our souls weren't able to Bond as one, to become a Union again.

"That will take more than this one life cycle," the Keeper said. "You will have to grow into that level of completeness once again."

Micah didn't understand, so the Keeper patiently but hurriedly went through everything we'd discussed, and Micah's memories, like mine, eventually returned. As we continued to encircle the pool, the Keeper broke away every now and then to tend to another pink orb.

"And now it is your turn to choose," the Keeper said when he returned to us from one such orb. "You may choose to be a Guardian again, or you may choose differently. Just remember— Guardians lead the most difficult lives. No matter what world you choose, your life will be hard, preparing you for your service. You may return to Earth or you may choose another world."

He explained the other worlds that were our choices, including two I remembered and loved.

"This choice you must each make on your own," the Keeper said. "Heed well that if the two of you do not choose the same, your souls could forever be Separated. Only The Maker knows what you will decide, so do not ask me."

Like last time, the choice seemed obvious to me. We were warriors. We'd always been Guardians. And we needed to fight the dark spirits on Earth. But when I tried to share this with Micah, I couldn't. The direct thought, the words, even the feeling became imprisoned within me.

"We can't decide together?" I asked.

"No. I am sorry," the Keeper said.

"Why not?" Micah demanded. "If our souls are at risk of growing Dark . . ."

"It is called free will. An individual choice for one's future. Some may want to take the risk of going Dark in exchange for other benefits, while others would not. Each soul has the right and responsibility to decide its own fate without outside influence."

Whoa. That was heavy. And irrefutable. I could only hope Micah felt in his soul the same as I did. That he would choose the same future as me.

"You must choose simultaneously," the Keeper added. "Time and space here are different than in the physical worlds. If one of you goes and the other hesitates, even for only a click or two, years could go by in your physical world. If you're separated by too many years, you may never find each other again. And you must choose quickly. You've spent too much time here already."

"But we have more questions," I protested.

"Your answers will come at the Gate. We need as many Guardian souls on the worlds as possible, and since you are useless to us until you reach adulthood, the sooner you go, the better for all. Assuming you follow your previous decisions, of course."

Well, when he put it like that . . .

Within a short moment, Micah's orb turned bright pink. He'd chosen so quickly! I believed he'd want to be together and hoped his hasty decision meant he agreed with me—Earth needed us as Guardians. Knowing him, the goodness of his soul, that would surely be his choice.

The Keeper moved to the edge of the pool with Micah, but as much as I tried, I couldn't budge while they whispered to each other. I wanted to say, "Good-bye." No, "See you soon." But I was stuck, and panic began to rise because I had no idea when I would see Micah again. When we would be reunited, if ever. I needed to feel him in and around me one more time. I needed to say, "I love you."

Micah must have felt something from me because he returned a wave of love before soaring high into the air and then diving into the pool, his soul whooshing away from me into a sea of light.

"I'm ready," I said, not wanting to delay, and a bright pink light surrounded me.

"I'm not surprised he went first," the Keeper said as he returned to my side and guided me to the edge of the pool. "He'll always be your protector."

My pink light faltered. "What?"

"You are his light. He is your protector. You are a fiery soul, showing him the way, allowing him to lead in battle, but lighting the paths he must take. In this past life, however, you shone too brightly. You must learn to control the fire burning within you and use it for good. In turn, he will do whatever it takes to protect your soul, including going first to find you sooner, to keep you safe."

My protector. Micah had certainly been protective of me, without knowing about any of this. Now, with this knowledge and especially with what had happened to bring us here, he'd probably be even more so. What if he hadn't chosen Earth after all because of the dangers of Enyxa and her Lakari? What if he'd chosen to not be a Guardian, expecting me to do the same so we'd both be safe? What if he'd chosen one of the other worlds— like the one constantly blanketed with green mist that I loved so much? My pink light dimmed even more with my indecision.

A clicking sound rose from the pool. Time had gone by. I had no idea how much, but I had to hurry if we were even to have a chance.

But what if I chose the wrong world? What if Micah and I never found each other? What if I never saw him, felt him, loved him, held him, Bonded with him again? How could I choose when there was so much at stake? If I chose wrong, our souls would go Dark. Micah's beautiful soul would turn black and cold.

Always stay true to your heart and soul.

A whispered voice from deep within. And I knew where I needed to go. At least, I hoped I did. My pink light grew bright again.

As I prepared to make my own dive, the Keeper gave me final instructions, though I could barely stay still with anxiety. I needed to go.

Another click sounded.

Without waiting for the Keeper to finish, I jolted skyward, then sank into the pool with my choice, the Keeper's voice in my soul calling after me.

"Live well, Jacquelena."

✴ NOW ✴
2012

CHAPTER 27

Jacquelena. My name echoed in my head, and my eyes flew open.

"Oh. My. *God.*"

My breath caught in my lungs with the epiphany, and my heart paused before taking off in a gallop. Could it be true?

"No. Impossible." I shook my head, curls hitting my chin. "No freakin' way."

The idea was so absurd I couldn't believe my lame imagination had even come up with it.

Twin Flames. Separated souls pulling to each other like magnets. Reincarnation? *Really?*

I closed my eyes, needing to clear my head because this was insane. Strange, yet vaguely familiar images filled my mind, scrolling by as though I relived memories. Jacey had described her imaginary world with its castle and two suns so vividly, I felt as though I'd been there, too. Now I knew I *had* been there. My mind—my memory—traveled to yet another world, covered almost entirely in water and ice, its sole sun small as Earth's moon, but the people around happy and content. Visions of more worlds flashed quickly then slowed as I returned to Earth, but not the Earth I knew. Rustic villages and crudely built wagons and women in dresses of earlier times—centuries ago. And even farther back, of Ancient Greece.

Every time, every place, I felt Jeric right there with me. Different eyes, different faces and bodies, but the exact same soul within. I *felt* his *soul*. In some of those foreign worlds, our souls were entwined, united, a single entity. A Union. On Earth, however, we were separate, before the Union. Soul Mates then—two souls made for each other. His appearance changed as my mind traveled backward through the centuries, but he was always right there. Always by my side, always taking care of me. Always loving me.

He was Jeremicah.

I was Jacquelena.

He was Micah.

I was Jacey.

No wonder I'd felt such a deep connection to him from the very beginning. No wonder I felt this soul-bound love for him so soon. Because it had always been there, waiting for him. Waiting for his *return*.

I didn't have to deny my love for him, because it was too soon by normal standards. I'd loved him for eons. Forever.

Jeric must have figured this out last night—the reason for his freak-out. I couldn't blame him. The guy had kept people, especially women, out of his life for a reason. And now to know we were really soul-bound? To have it confirmed and to realize we'd been together forever? That we'd actually been one soul before? I could barely accept the ridiculous concept myself. But I knew what I *felt*, and he had to be feeling it, too. This kind of love would scare the hell out of him, especially when he was so sure no one could love him. It had probably set him off more than anything else and sent him running.

I sprang to my feet. *Jeric.* My heart—my soul—needed him. He needed me. I had to find him.

But how? I had no idea when he'd actually left, how long he'd been gone. A few hours, possibly all night. He could have taken off shortly after I'd fallen asleep. He could be anywhere!

No. You feel him.

A lump of fear that I'd never find him, never see him again, had formed in my throat, and I swallowed it down. Jacey and Micah had been able to feel each other's presence miles away. And they could feel the pull when the distance was too much. Could I? I didn't feel a tug. But when I concentrated, I *did* feel Jeric's presence still in my heart, in my soul. He couldn't be far. I tried to steady my heart rate so I could focus on locating exactly where I felt him, but failed. My emotions and thoughts were all over the place.

But I *had* to find him.

I shot out of the camper and down the dirt road.

"Jeric!" I screamed, knowing he couldn't hear me but maybe someone was with him. "Jeric!"

I darted down the dirt lane, zigzagging back and forth, calling his name. Like a madwoman, I pounded on an RV's door and when no one answered, I went to the next one. People came out of their campers, staring at me, but nobody answered my pleas for help. My legs pushed me toward the front of the campground, and I could feel his presence growing stronger.

The front office came into sight, and I sprinted for it, my mind, my heart, my soul focused on Jeric. And there he was, in the doorway of the apartment connected to the office, stumbling and squinting against the bright afternoon sun. I'd never been so happy to see anyone in my life.

"Jeric," I yelled again. He turned toward me as if he could hear me. Ran to meet me, his hands flying in front of him.

"Are you okay?" he asked as he ran, his face full of concern.

"Yes! I'm fine," I said aloud, hoping he could read my lips as we ran to each other. "I know! I know, Jeric! You and me—"

Behind him, on the periphery of my vision, Bethany's red head appeared in the same doorway Jeric had come from, along with the rest of her body, which was barely covered in cut-off shorts not much bigger than a bikini bottom and a halter top. Another young woman with darker hair and clad as skimpily appeared next to Bethany, both of them staring at Jeric. My gaze focused on him, my mind taking in what it hadn't seen at first, blinded by the thrill of him actually being there when I thought I'd lost him.

I stopped dead in my tracks.

Now I really saw him.

Saw his disheveled hair, as if he'd just woken up at 3:30 in the afternoon. The shoes in his hand. His bare chest, sunlight glinting off the nipple rings. His undone belt buckle, the ends hanging loosely on each side of his unbuttoned fly, the hunter green fabric of his boxers or briefs or whatever he wore showing.

I stood there dumbfounded, blinking against the image in front of me, against the bright sun, against the sting in my eyes. Trying to blink it all away, but it was still there, the truth in plain view. A half-naked Jeric—my Twin Flame, my forever love—stumbling out of the home of a girl dressed like a Playboy model.

So much for him remembering what I had. So much for his not wanting any girl anymore but me. So much for him being patient.

I'd had it all wrong. How unbelievably stupid I was!

He'd bolted last night because of me. Because I'd pushed him away. And he'd run to the first girl who'd open her legs for him, which, of course, was the first girl he'd come across. Jacey had been right about men, and I'd known it all along, the reason I was a virgin. I was just glad I was *still* a virgin today.

People had come out of their campers at all the ruckus I'd created, and I felt the burn of their stares now. They probably waited in anticipation for some white trash, trailer park drama to erupt, but I refused to be their source of entertainment.

"We're them," both my mouth and hands said, finishing my thought on their own. Then I spun on my heel and strode down the dirt road for my Airstream.

CHAPTER 28

Jeric
2012

Leni's panicked emotional state had ripped me out of deep unconsciousness. I had no idea where I was—on a couch, wood paneled walls, an old woman sitting in a rocking chair with a shotgun over her lap—but only cared about getting to Leni. I stumbled through the door, squinting against the brightest fucking day in the history of time. I couldn't see shit, but I could feel her. I turned in her direction, my own panic matching hers, and ran, barely noticing the gravel digging into my bare feet as I asked if she was okay.

She stopped mid-stride and stared at me with a pained expression that tore at my heart, ripped me in half, making me think I was going to die right there.

Her lips moved and so did her hands. "We're them."

Then she spun and strode to the camper, and I simply stood there like a damn idiot. She didn't run, but only walked, her shoulders squared back and her head held high. I followed after her, but when I reached the camper's door, she shut it in my face. The camper didn't shake—she hadn't slammed it. But I could feel her anger. Real anger. And her quiet fury was much more terrifying than a violent storm.

I tried the knob, but she'd locked the door. I pounded on it, more to let her know I was here, wasn't going anywhere, than expecting her to actually open it. If I'd really wanted in, the flimsy door wouldn't have stopped me. I decided to wait it out knowing she'd quickly get over her anger as she always did, and then I'd have to face what had ripped through my core last night. I sat on my old friend the picnic table and dropped my pounding head in my hands.

I couldn't blame her for being mad at me. She'd obviously remembered what I had last night. A truth beyond anything either of us could have ever expected. And I'd reacted like a damn moron. Stormed off and drank myself to oblivion. Like that helped anything.

Yeah, she had a right to be angry.

She calmed down after a while—I could sense it. Not the quiet but frightening aura she'd had a few moments ago, but a real sense of calm. I stepped off the picnic table and strode to the camper door. I stood on the single metal step, but instead of trying the knob or knocking again, I leaned my forehead against the smooth surface of the door, ashamed of myself. The door opened, and I fell through it.

I scrambled to stand, relief washing over me as I threw my arms around Leni and pulled her to me. She stood completely still, her arms stiffly at her sides, not returning my hug. She was still mad. Reluctantly, I let go of her and stepped back.

"I'm sorry," I signed hurriedly. "I'm sorry for being a fuck-up. I'm sorry for rushing out on you and taking off. It was all too much. You . . . me . . . I . . ." Shit. My fingers fumbled as I tried to form the words.

She grabbed my hands to stop me. "Enough. I get it. You are who you are, Jeric. I can't change that."

I shook my head. "No! You can. You *have* changed me. But it all crashed down on me, and I couldn't handle it. I needed a drink or two to take the edge off, and then more memories came and one thing led to another and—"

Her whole body stiffened. Her expression turned to stone, her green eyes like jade. "Wait. You *know*? You remembered?"

"I'm sorry for how I reacted. Please believe me. I promise to never hurt you like that again. I'll spend the rest of my days making it up to you. Please let me?"

She stared at me with wide eyes that looked on the verge of tears, then her gaze rolled to the ceiling. Her chest lifted with a deep breath. Then she lifted her arms away from her thighs and dropped them again. I would have preferred more commitment, but I'd take what I could get right now.

"So we're good?" I asked. "We'll get out of here when your truck's done and take off, right? We can go wherever you want—back to Georgia, maybe, and start over."

Her brows pushed together. "We still have to go to Tampa."

"No way," I signed, shaking my head. "I'm not doing what Micah did to Jacey . . . what *I* did to *you*. That place is a death trap."

"There's nowhere else to go!" Her temper suddenly—finally—flared. Her calmness before had been a temporary hold on the fire building inside her, a fire she could no longer control. Maybe she'd given up trying. With a shaking hand, she pulled a paper towel out of her back pocket and waved it in my face. My handwriting showed on parts of it. "You tell me to go home, but I don't have a home to go to! I have no one, but you, Jeric! And I don't even have you."

The tears filling the rims of her eyes poured over now, breaking me once again.

"Of course you have me," I signed as I stepped closer to her. "I'm right here."

I moved to pull her into my arms, but her face filled with disgust, and she shoved me away.

"They're still all over you!" she yelled aloud, so loudly my chest felt the vibrations. I stared at her stupidly, thinking I misread her lips. She pressed the paper-towel-note against my face and scrubbed my mouth and cheek so hard she might have taken a layer of skin off, then showed me the pink smear of what could only be lipstick.

Ah, fuck. I was the biggest cocksucker in the world.

"I can't believe you!" she screamed, her face bright red and the veins in her neck showing. "Even knowing what you did about us! And you say you're *here* for me? Bullshit!"

The hate in her eyes hurt worse than any physical blow I'd ever received. The knife in my heart an injury I'd never recover from.

How could I do this to her when she meant so much to me? How could I screw up this badly? Worst of all, I couldn't recall doing anything with anyone. And I *should* remember—I should have to live with the scathing memory forever, just as the image of the lipstick on my face would be forever etched in her mind. But the last thing I remembered was sitting on the picnic table and gazing at the stars.

I'd considered taking off, had packed up my stuff and left Leni a note and everything, but I couldn't bring myself to do it. My whole body had wracked with pain at the thought of leaving her, vulnerable and alone. So I'd sat outside, staying close in case the Shadowmen made an appearance. But some protector I was, considering I remembered nothing else until I woke up on that couch an hour ago with Leni freaking the hell out.

She shoved me again, toward the door. "Get out. Get the hell out!"

CHAPTER 29

Leni
2012

I'd been the biggest fool to ever exist on this earth.

I'd fallen for Jeric's charms, naively believing he'd changed for me. Grasping at the ridiculous idea I'd captured the heart of this man-whore because our souls were connected. We may have been lovers before. We may have even been the same soul. But this was a different life with different circumstances. Our history together didn't guarantee a future. But for some reason I'd believed in a happily ever after. With Jeric!

I'd set myself up for this heartbreak. It wasn't his fault. He was only being Jeric. How could I be mad at him for being himself when I could never be myself? Sure, he'd lied to me, although he probably thought he was simply feeding me lines. Everything he'd ever told me was part of his usual game. I knew what he was like that moment in the dark parking lot at the motel, when he'd come running out of his room, another girl following behind him. I knew this when I asked him to come to the lake with me.

Somewhere along the way, I'd become the girl who thought she could change the bad boy, rescue him from his past and make him want to settle down. I'd told myself going in to avoid such hopes and expectations, because they rarely came true. Bad boys were bad boys for a reason. Jeric was Jeric for a reason. It wasn't fair to blame him for my own idiocy.

This had been my reasoning when I'd opened the door for him, thinking he hadn't remembered what I had after all. He hadn't known we'd been together for eons. But now I knew. He *had* remembered.

"You say you aren't a runner," I said as I continued shoving him out the door, "but when the truth hit you, you ran last night, you coward. If you're not in this with me, you may as well go back to your bimbos."

He tripped over the threshold, barely catching himself before face-planting on the ground.

"Um . . . pardon may?" said a female voice with a heavy Southern drawl, and my head snapped up. Speak of the devil. The other bimbo, not Bethany, but the dark-haired one who could have been her sister based on their shared facial features, stood in the sun beyond the shade of the camper's awning. Jeric's belongings sat at her feet. "Ah'm sorry, but thought ya'll might want his thangs."

No, I didn't. She could have him and his *thangs*.

I slammed the door so hard, the camper shook and dishes rattled in the cabinet. And it felt good. Jeric had been right about the feeling of release. I screamed at the top of my lungs, my fists balled at my sides and the veins and muscles of my neck straining. That felt good, too. I dropped to my knees and punched the pillows and the futon. More adrenaline pumped me up further. I stomped through the camper, grabbed random items and hurdled them at the walls. Air rushed through my lungs. Blood flowed to my fists. I slammed my hand into the bathroom door, punching a hole through it and leaving a delightful pain on my knuckles.

Tears streamed down my cheeks as my hands gripped the edges of the bathroom sink and I stared into the mirror. A tiny part of me wanted to crumple to the floor, sobbing and cradling my broken heart. To cry away the hurt and the anger behind closed doors. But no. I didn't want to cry. Not this time. I *wanted* to be angry. I wanted to feel the rage roiling inside me and let it all out for once.

"I *HATE* YOU!" I shrieked at my reflection with so much force and volume, the words were indecipherable.

No matter. The person I meant them for was far, far away. Not Jeric. My bitch of a mother. Imagining her reaction to my words and my tantrum came easily—the sugary smile on her face accompanied by a warning I knew too well in her eyes. I saw her face now as I stared in the mirror. How could I ever doubt she was my mother? We had the same green eyes. But I wasn't her. I never was.

"I'm ME!" I yelled at the mirror. "Do you hear me, Mama? I. Am. *Me*."

And it was time to be myself. I'd let Jeric off the hook for being himself. Why did he get to have all the fun? Why did everyone else get to do what they wanted but I could never allow myself the same privilege? It was my turn. I was done trying to be someone I wasn't.

I stormed into the bedroom, dug through my suitcase and threw my clothes over my head until I found my favorite, tight-fitting jeans with the rip up the thigh and a snug, white tank top. I yanked my clothes off and changed, surprised I didn't rip anything in the process with the force I put into every move. My faded red cowboy boots made the outfit better than heels ever would.

Returning to the bathroom, I dampened my hair with my hands, trying to control the mane of curls as best as I could. A few strokes of eyeliner and mascara and a brush of blush accomplished what I wanted. I wasn't going for my stage look—no patience for that. I just didn't want to look like I'd woken up two minutes ago. I grabbed my fake I.D. and cash out of my bag, stuffed them into my back pocket and stomped for the door.

Jeric and his *thangs* were still out there, but the girl was gone. Surprise crossed his face as soon as he drank me in with his eyes, but then he crossed his arms over his chest and stepped into my path. He shook his head. I glared at him.

"Where are you going looking like that?" he asked.

I answered by shoving past him and heading on my way. He caught up with me and stopped me with a hand on my shoulder, spinning me around. I looked up at him with a raised brow.

"Where are you going?" he asked again.

"To blow off some steam," I said aloud. "Isn't that what you want?"

"Like *that*?" His gaze traveled up and down my body.

"I'm hoping to have some fun, too. You're not the only one who gets to do that."

His jaw clenched. "Don't do this, Leni."

I glared at him harder. "You wanted to see the real me? You wanted her to come out? Well, here she is, Jeric. The real Leni in all her glory."

I spun and strode off again, kicking up clouds of dust. He ran into my path once more.

"Please, Leni, don't." His eyes, his whole expression pleaded my mercy. "You're killing me, babe."

My eyes narrowed, and I spit my words at him, hoping he understood because my hands were too busy being fists at the moment. "You lost your right to call me *babe*. And if you think I care one tiny turd of shit about how you feel, you're sadly mistaken."

The corners of his lips jumped and his hands hung in the air with no words to say. When I stomped off this time, he didn't follow.

Horns blared at me and some guy yelled a catcall out his window as he passed by while I waited for the traffic to clear so I could cross the road. Finally, I jogged across, through the parking lot and to the bar. Several heads turned my way when I came through the door, letting the early evening sun into the lounge.

Inside wasn't nearly as dark as it had been earlier, with all of the neon signs lit on the wood-paneled walls, advertising beer and liquor. Being Happy Hour, the place wasn't nearly as empty either. Both truckers and locals crowded around the large, rectangular bar with two bartenders in the middle pouring drinks and chatting with their patrons. More people sat in booths and at four-tops scattered throughout the lounge, some with food on their tables, others with only drinks. An old-fashioned jukebox played country music, blasting over the conversation and laughter. The cacophony was shocking at first after nearly a week of living in near silence with Jeric, but then I relished it. Let the vibes fill me. I glanced at the mechanical bull, still lifeless in its corner, waiting for an operator. *Later*, I promised myself.

First, I needed a drink. Or three.

The bartender eyed my I.D. and my face for a moment, but then shrugged and made my drink. Jaeger and Red Bull. First the pungently sweet smell and then the taste took me back to my nights at the club. Where I'd dared to let the real Leni out. Three drinks had always been my limit—a good buzz, but not falling-down, blacking-out drunk. Just enough to loosen myself up and slip away from Mama's relentless hold. Enough to not care about the eyes all over me filled with either judgment or lust.

By the time I finished my first drink, I became chatty with the bartenders and anyone else around who joined in our conversation. I asked about the bull and they said the operator would be in shortly. After my second drink, I was feeling especially good. Too good. Probably because I hadn't eaten all day. The female bartender placed a plate of fries in front of me.

"On the house," she said, then she leaned forward over the bar and lowered her voice. "You need to be careful, hon. Some of these truckers—and even a coupla the locals—are sick fucks slobberin' for a girl like you, if ya know what I mean."

I nodded and ate the fries, then ordered another drink. By the time I finished that one, a few people had made it to the dance floor, and I joined them, loosening up and preparing to enter the zone. The bull operator had arrived and the first guy had already been dumped. The bar was growing crowded and I'd lost my seat. I ordered a beer, then sauntered over to the bull pit, where a small group gathered. Tough guy after tough guy gave their five dollars for a short ride and a throw to the mats. Only one lasted more than eight seconds. A nice-looking guy, if you like cocky cowboys. He kept harassing the others gathering around, daring them to beat his time. A larger crowd began to form.

I stepped over to the jukebox and was glad to find a few dance songs among all the country tunes. A little outdated and none my favorites, but these would work. I selected several to give myself enough time, then sauntered over to the operator. He started to argue with me when I told him what I wanted.

"Trust me," I said, "when I'm done, everyone will be wanting to ride. That's a lot of five-dollar bills."

He finally gave in with a shrug as my first song ended.

"Try to stay to the music, but not too fast, okay?"

He nodded as he dumped the cowboy. I drew in a deep breath and shook out my shoulders, then headed for the bull and waited for my next song to start. The guys gathered around started whistling and heckling.

"Whatcha doin' up there, pretty momma? Think you're gonna ride that thang?"

"You wanna ride something big, I got it right here."

"Bet she won't last two seconds." Cocky cowboy, of course.

My song started and the guys balked at it, but quieted when I mounted the mechanical bull with flair, then grasped it with my thighs and held on. It'd been a few months since I'd ridden and I wasn't used to this operator, so it took a couple of rounds to ground myself, and the heckles returned, growing louder. But riding the bull was like riding a bike. The operator did as I'd instructed, lifting and turning it slowly to 50 Cents' Candy Shop. And I danced.

Some girls did the pole. I did the bull.

I rode it like no one here had ever ridden it before, losing myself to the music and the moves. The bull rocked and turned, and I moved with it, falling into my zone. Into the freedom of being me, of doing something for no other reason than because I enjoyed it. Because it felt good.

I sprawled out on the top of the bull, lifted to my knees and then to my feet, came down again and straddled it like I would a man, arching my back until my head nearly touched the end behind me. Then I eased up again, all the way to my feet, hands down, butt in the air. When the bull slowly turned so both my eyes and my ass faced the crowd, several women had joined the guys, who all stared with mouths hanging open.

Including Jeric.

He stood back, closer to the bar, arms crossed over his chest and eyes smoldering. I came upright and down to straddle the machine over the bull's "shoulders," facing its rear, and the song ended. But I didn't dismount, and my next song began. Nobody argued about it being their turn. I tore my eyes from Jeric's, scanned the female faces and found the most likely one. I wiggled my fingers at her, then patted the bull where you normally sit. She came over and climbed on facing me. We'd dance the bull together.

She tightened her short-clad thighs against the bull and our bodies rocked and writhed back and forth to the rhythm. We were fully clothed and more than a foot apart, but I knew the effect we had when the guys went crazy, whooping and whistling and overall growing rowdy. Jeric had moved closer by now, almost to the front of the crowd. He'd cleaned up, at least, wearing a tight Affliction t-shirt and jeans. I winked at him when the song ended, then motioned for the cowboy next to him. Jeric became a statue. Obviously happy to be picked, the cowboy sauntered over the way cowboys do, hitched his belt, then climbed on across from me. The music and the bull started up once again.

But we didn't last eight seconds.

CHAPTER 30

Leni had me in her trance like she did every other guy and half the women in the bar, working the mechanical bull like a professionally trained dancer works a pole. I'd never seen anything so fucking sexy. She rode the thing like she was making love to it, and I became suddenly jealous of a machine, wanting it to be me under her, bucking her around like that. And when the other girl joined her . . . Shit. Every guy in the house, and probably the women, too, had to have grown wood.

So this was what she meant when she said she wasn't so pure. You didn't learn to dance on a mechanical bull in a ballet studio. Especially not those kinds of moves. She had to have learned it in a strip club. And the thought of Leni—*my* Leni—stripping for other men made me see red with anger.

Then she had to go and pull the stunt with the cowboy.

She did it to rub my face into the shit I'd taken at her feet. I couldn't blame her. I deserved it and honest to God, I tried to let it go. Tried to let her have her fun, since apparently I'd had mine, although I still couldn't remember it. I didn't *feel* like I'd had sex, my balls still blue from wanting Leni and Leni only.

But when the little douchebag reached over and put his hands on her thighs and leaned closer until only inches separated their faces, it was all over.

I barely noticed the flicker of fear that crossed Leni's face, not needing to. I was already moving. One punch to the cheek sent the asshole off the bull. The machine stopped moving, and Leni stared at me with disbelief. I picked her up, threw her over my shoulder and strode for the door before the cowboy or his friends retaliated. At least she didn't start kicking my thighs and punching me until we were out the door, so no one tried to stop me. Not that I couldn't handle them; I didn't want Leni to get hurt.

Once we were outside, her fists beat against my lower back and her feet kicked wildly as I made our way through the packed parking lot. I shifted her over and grasped her tighter before her boot nailed me in the balls, but I wasn't about to let go. Her yells vibrated through my shoulder and back, and I could only imagine what names she called me.

We'd almost cleared the parking lot without any problems, but someone must have heard Leni screaming because something big and hard crashed into my side. We slammed into the sidewall of a pick-up, and Leni's body immediately fell limp. I set her down, and she slid to her butt and slumped over. Shit. She might have hit her head. I didn't have time to check on her, though, because someone came out of the shadows again. Two forms, dressed in black pants and hoodies, their faces barely visible. Not cowboys or truckers. Shadowmen.

One lunged for me and the other for Leni. She still didn't move, didn't defend herself, so I had to take them both. I clocked one in the temple with my fist and threw another punch into his gut. He hunched over, and my knee connected with his nose, sending him sprawling. With two hands, I grabbed the other guy's black hoodie and yanked him off of Leni. His elbow jabbed out and slammed into my cheek. Stars shot across my vision with the impact, and I stumbled backwards.

I dragged him with me, and we went tumbling to the pavement. He lay on top of me, so I wrapped my legs around his in a tight hold while crossing my arm over his throat. I squeezed against his Adam's apple while punching him in the head at the same time. His hands clawed at my arm, and he thrashed and twisted, but I wasn't letting loose. I hadn't planned on his legs and the rest of his body disintegrating into smoke. Normal opponents didn't do that.

My mind had barely accepted the freaky escape maneuver when a shadow flew down at me and slammed my head into the pavement. If I'd seen shooting stars before, now I saw a whole galaxy exploding. A fist landed on my lip and the salty iron taste of blood filled my mouth. Shit. I hated it when the other guy drew blood.

I jumped to my feet to find both assholes standing, one again headed for Leni. A roundhouse kick knocked him off his feet. I pounced on him, tackled him to the ground and delivered blow after blow to his face without stopping, his head my own personal punching bag. With one final punch to his throat, his whole body broke apart and the pieces flew into the air. Shit. These Shadowmen were weird.

I spun to the other guy. He was gone. And so was Leni.

My feet moved without a thought, and I darted out of the row of cars. A glance up and down the aisle showed no one. I looked across the next row. There—a man's form carrying a woman toward the highway. I sprinted for them. The Shadowman didn't stop to check for traffic, but sauntered onto the road with Leni over his shoulder. She didn't kick and scream now. She still remained limp. Unconscious. He made it across the westbound lanes, but headlights shone on the eastbound side, headed right for them. My heart blasted into a gallop.

"Leni!" I tried to yell, not knowing what it actually sounded like. I ran for them, noticing the headlights belonged to a semi. They weren't going to make it. Maybe that was the Shadowman's plan. After all, he probably couldn't die. He didn't have much of a soul left anyway, so what did he care if he did?

I pumped my legs harder across the westbound lanes and into the first eastbound one. Intense vibrations shook through me—

the oncoming semi. I plowed into the Shadowman but his form exploded, just like the other one. Leni's body flipped over in the air. The truck barreled down on us. I lunged, reaching my arms out to catch her. We hit the ground and rolled right as the semi passed.

My heart pounded against my ribs as we lay in the ditch in the dark, and I tried to suck in a deep breath. With a grunt, I pushed up on my hands and knees and looked around. The Shadowmen had disappeared. Fuckers.

I hovered over Leni and assessed her body, glad to find she didn't have any obvious cuts or broken bones. When my gaze reached her face, her eyes fluttered open. The headlights of another passing car shone into them, showing full alertness, but she cringed and passed out again. I didn't know if she had any serious injuries, but no way were we hanging out on the side of a highway. I personally knew the danger all too well. Hoping her spine and neck were okay, I slid my arms under her and lifted as I rose to my feet to carry her home.

About ten steps in, she lifted her arms and wrapped them around my neck and nuzzled her face against my chest.

Thank God. She was okay.

I carried her to the camper, inside and to the back room, where I laid her on the bed and pulled off her boots. I considered removing her jeans, too, but didn't want her thinking I'd tried anything, so they stayed on. After locking everything up and wrapping some ice in a paper towel, I came back and lay down with her. My fingers gently pushed through her thick curls, searching for any bumps, but didn't find any, so I pressed the ice against my lip while I watched her sleep. I had to find a way to make up to her for what I'd done. I could only hope she'd forgive me in the morning.

I woke up to her pushing me off the bed with fire in her eyes.

"Your girlfriend's banging on the door," she signed angrily.

"My girlfriend?" I asked, bewildered. "But you're—"

She shoved me again. "Go take care of her and tell her to shut the hell up."

With that, she rolled over, putting her back to me.

I stumbled groggily to the door and pulled it open, blinking at the morning sun as Bethany and another chick stood in the doorway.

"We need to talk to your girl," the other chick's lips said, and her eyes flitted to something behind me.

With a glance over my shoulder, I knew this probably wasn't a good idea. Leni stood right behind me, fuming, and the next thing I knew, she was shoving me out the door again and throwing my bags and shoes at me. Her mouth moved as she did, and when I looked at the other two girls, their mouths moved, too, but all of them too fast for me to catch the words. By facial expressions and body language, I could only assume the girls were pleading with Leni for mercy and she was slewing a series of profanities in answer.

Dude. I'd known when she finally blew, it would be bad, but this? I half-expected her to grow fangs dripping with venom, and when she shook her finger in my direction as she yelled at the girls, I cringed as though she pointed a sharpened claw at me. I'd created a monster—one with me as her target. I wasn't so sure she'd ever calm down to her usual self.

But then her arms fell limply to her sides, and her reddened face blanched as her eyes grew wide. She lifted a hand to cover her mouth as her gaze flitted to me and back to the girls. What the hell had they said?

CHAPTER 31

 The anger from last night returned in full force when banging on my door and hollers from outside woke me up. Jeric lying in bed with me, cuddled against my body, didn't help matters at all. Had I not been clear enough last night? What had happened anyway? I vaguely recalled him carrying me out of the bar, some kind of fight and a blaring horn. If it had been the cowboy chasing after us, I hoped Jeric knocked him out. That one move of his on the bull brought back bad memories. But I also hoped he'd landed a few on Jeric. Just because. Not very nice, I knew, but hell, here he was with me, and his playmates were at the door.

"We need to talk to your girl," one of them said as soon as Jeric opened the door.

I bolted to the front.

"I have nothing to say to you," I said as I pushed Jeric out the door. "Take him. Do what you want. I don't care. Just get him out of my sight!"

I threw his bags, which he'd apparently brought in while I was gone last night, out the door after him.

"Ma sista needs to tell ya somethin', though," the dark-haired girl said, throwing her hand out toward Bethany who stood behind her, as if cowering.

"Really. I don't care," I said. "I don't need any damn details or excuses. If you don't want him, show him to the bus stop."

"Please don't do this," Bethany's sister pleaded. "I think he really loves you."

"Ha!" I barked. "If that's how he loves someone, I don't want it. The douche needs to go."

"Just listen for a sec! Beth, you gotta tell her."

"I said I don't want to hear it!" I yelled, blood pulsing into my head, making my brain feel on the verge of imploding. My hands balled into fists at my sides. If they didn't shut up and get out of here—and take Jeric with them—I was going to punch someone.

"Nothin' happened!" Bethany finally piped up.

I narrowed my eyes. "You seriously expect me to believe that? He smelled like a damn whorehouse. Your lipstick was smeared on his face. But it doesn't matter. He's not even my boyfriend."

"Please listen!" Bethany's sister yelled. "Yeah, she tried to kiss him, and I'm really sorry bout that, but that's how she is." She glanced at Bethany with annoyance, and when she went on, her voice came out lower. "She's always lookin' for love in all the wrong places, says my grams' favorite song. Bless her heart. But nothin' happened 'tween them."

"So it was you?" I accused.

"No! Bethany, explain!"

Bethany's eyes widened for a moment, but then she cleared her throat. "I, um . . . I found him layin' out here on the picnic table late the other night and your door was locked. All his thangs was out here, so I thought ya had a fight or somethin'. That ya kicked him out. So I brought him home, and I, uh . . ." Her eyes flitted nervously about as she wrung her hands. "I did try to kiss him, but he wanted nothin' to do with may. He wanted nothin' to do with either of us."

I opened my mouth to argue. Were they talking about the same guy I knew?

"I swear to ya!" she said before I could say anything. "He pushed me off and passed out on the couch, and Grams sat out there with him all night, a shotgun in her lap. You know, in case he changed his mind bout us and tried somethin'. But he never did. He didn't even move 'til you came hollerin' down the road. I don' even know how he knew, since he can't hear and all, but he did. Like he's tuned inta ya or somethin'."

I brought my hand to my mouth, too shocked to speak. My eyes darted to Jeric, confusion filling his face, and back at the girls whose expressions couldn't have been more sincere.

"I swear to God and sweet babay Jesus, nothin' happened," Bethany said again. "Ya can even ask Grams, if ya don' believe may."

You know that horrible moment when you're in a heated argument, on the verge of exploding and wishing you could spew lava all over the other person to return the pain they caused you—only to realize you're the one who's wrong? Yeah, never happened to me before either. But now it did.

I stared at the two girls, my mouth still hanging open. My whole body sagged. When I didn't say anything—*couldn't* say anything—they offered me warm smiles I didn't deserve.

"I'm, um . . . I'm sorry," I mumbled.

"We just thought ya should know," Bethany's sister said.

"And I think he really does love ya," Bethany added. "He, uh, kinda moaned your name while he slept."

With that, the two girls turned and sauntered toward the front of the RV park.

I stared after them, then looked at Jeric to see if he watched them, too. The way they swung their hips was bound to capture any hot-blooded guy's attention. At least, if he was heterosexual, which Jeric most definitely was. But he only looked at me, a mix of bewilderment, pleading and expectation written all over his face. Did he understand everything she'd said? Were their lips clear enough?

I went inside, and he followed.

"They say nothing happened," I signed once the door was closed. "With you and them, I mean."

His lips jumped as though he tried to control a smile. Relief washed over his face.

"Why didn't you say anything?" I demanded, trying to hang onto the anger because I hated the bile of guilt rising in the back of my throat.

"Would you have believed me?" he asked.

"Probably not."

He grimaced. "To be honest, I didn't really remember."

I rolled my eyes. The guilt lowered a notch.

"I really didn't think I had, thought I would know if . . . you know," he said, as if suddenly too shy to talk about sex. "But when you showed me the lipstick and I saw that look on your face . . ."

I didn't know it was possible to stammer while signing, but Jeric was certainly flustered now. I pressed my lips together and let him sweat as he continued to fumble along.

"The whole thing with Jacey . . .," he started again. "Her getting sick and then dying triggered a memory, and then the rest of everything started coming to me. What happened to her—I almost let it happen again. To *you*. I couldn't handle it. The shock . . . I couldn't take anymore. I was done with all the crazy shit."

"So you ran?"

He gave me a sheepish look. "Not far. I just needed a drink or two. I didn't mean to drink the whole damn bottle."

"And your note?" I asked.

His face softened, and his eyes gazed at me like no man had ever looked at me before. Not in this lifetime anyway. "I couldn't leave you, Leni. It's not physically possible for me to be apart from you." He took a step to close the gap between us, and when I didn't push him away, he took another, close enough to lift his hand to my face. To stroke his fingertips across my cheekbone. To grab my chin and run his thumb over my bottom lip. "I love you. Always have. Always will."

I didn't respond, afraid of what I might say or do with my heart palpitating from his closeness.

He reached into his back pocket and pulled out his phone. With a couple of taps on the screen, he showed me the text message app, with my question, "Did you really leave me?" And although I hadn't received his answer, he'd replied: "Never."

Tears formed in my eyes and my heart throbbed in my throat. I looked into his eyes—fell into them, actually—for a long moment, but forced myself out.

"I'm sorry," we both signed at the same time.

Jeric shook his head. "You have no reason to be."

"But you didn't do anything wrong."

"I did. I bailed on you. You thought I'd abandoned you. And I went and got drunk, which led to this whole mess."

"And I went ape-shit."

He glanced around the camper, which was still a disaster, and grinned, dimples showing. "You finally got mad."

A small smile tugged at my lips while heat rose in my face at the same time. "That's an understatement."

"It felt good, didn't it?"

My smile grew, but I shrugged. "Maybe."

He cocked his head. "And it took me—the thought of me being with some other girl—to do it?"

I narrowed my eyes. "You only sent me over the edge."

That was as much as I would give him. Yeah, the thought of him being with someone else had affected me like nothing ever had, but my feelings for my mother and all the crap she'd done to me had also reached the boiling point.

"There's more to my story than you, Jeric Winters," I said.

He stepped closer to me. "I know other ways to make you feel good, too." When my breath caught and my face flushed hotter, he grinned and flicked a curl with his finger before adding, "But I'm very interested in this story of yours."

I stepped back and steadied myself. "Over breakfast? I'm starving."

I needed a shower and my camper needed to be cleaned, but my growling stomach needed food more—all I'd eaten yesterday was the plate of fries—so I changed my shirt, delaying the rest for later. We crossed the road to the truck stop once again, through the store and into the diner.

"So are you going to tell me how you learned to do what you did last night?" Jeric asked after we ordered plates of pancakes, eggs and bacon, and biscuits and sausage gravy.

I grimaced. "You know how you asked if New York had been my dream or my mama's?"

He nodded.

"Well, you were right. Kind of." I paused as I gathered myself. "See, my mama was the product of a secret relationship her white birth father ended as soon as he found out my granny was pregnant. Sleeping with black girls was iffy back then, and marrying them was pretty much out of the question, especially in the South. So my mama was raised by a single mother. Her dream had been to be a ballerina. She had the talent and the drive, pushing on even when her life made things tough. Unlike me, Mama's tall and thin, like a reed waving in the wind. She had it all—talent, form, grace, everything. Then she met this guy, my daddy, and they had a fling. She got pregnant, and she wasn't about to have the same life as Granny who'd died single, so when Daddy asked her to marry him, she gave up her dream."

Jeric leaned back in his booth. "So she blames you."

I shrugged. "I don't know. She miscarried that baby. She had a couple of miscarriages, actually, until she was finally able to have me. By then she'd wanted children so badly, and Mama was especially happy to have a girl. I can't believe she denied I even existed." I paused, blinking against the sting in my eyes. "Her new dream had become for her daughter to be the internationally renowned ballerina she never was. She became more determined for it to happen than I think she'd been for herself. She pushed me hard, signing me up for class after class, show after show. Dancing filled every waking hour."

"But you enjoy it. Right?"

I smiled. "Yeah, I love it. But not really ballet so much. I mean, taking all those classes gave me a strong foundation, but the classes I really loved were the jazz, tap, and modern dance. When I got older, Mama compromised, letting me take the other classes as long as I stayed in ballet. She made sure I was in the best schools with the best teachers. That I had every opportunity to perform. She put the worst stage moms to shame. But there was one thing she had no control over—that I'd inherited my daddy's family's measly height with her mama's side's hourglass shape. She *tried* to control it, always putting me on diets until I . . ."

My hands dropped, and I cleared my throat, although I hadn't been speaking aloud. Jeric leaned forward, concern in his eyes. I swallowed and went on.

"I fought bulimia for a while," I admitted, staring at the table as I signed. "I wasn't really fat. Just round in certain places. But Mama tried to starve me, even with all the dance workouts I did. So I ate behind her back, thinking I was showing her, but as soon as I'd see her, I'd feel guilty, so I purged it."

I peered up at Jeric through my lashes, wondering what went through his mind. What he thought about me now. His expression was unreadable.

"Yeah, I was quite the head case," I said with a sigh. "It had been my attempt to control something in my life, but how screwed up is that?" I shook my head. "She always told me I couldn't be trusted to make decisions for myself, and I'd proven her right. So she kept control all the way from Alaska and pushed for the audition for New York. When I didn't get in, she finally gave up, after telling me—with a smile on her face, of course—that I was useless and worthless." I paused to swipe at a tickle on my cheeks, surprised to find them wet.

Jeric's eyes had grown wide. "Your *mother* told you that?"

I nodded. "Along with what a huge disappointment I was and she hoped I didn't pursue the idea of opening my own studio 'because no girl deserved to be taught by such inadequacy.'

Somewhere in there she called me talentless and lazier than a dog on a summer day." I shrugged. "Her usual rant when I screwed up."

"What a bitch!" Jeric said. "How could you let her bully you like that? How could you say she's taken care of you when she abused you?"

My hackles raised. "She didn't abuse me."

Jeric lifted a brow. "Like hell she didn't! Don't tell me you're not emotionally scarred after living with that. I know better."

I chuckled. "*You?* How would you know anything? How do you even know the term 'emotionally scarred'?"

He leaned forward and looked me in the eye. "Lots of therapy. And I *know* you. The way you hide yourself and the pain. I can feel it as if it were my own. Right here." He thumped his fist over his heart in the same way as the sign for "love." "And the bulimia? Don't tell me she didn't mess with your head and your heart. That's bullshit. She abused you, and you give her credit for taking care of you. Where was your dad throughout all this?"

"Working," I said. "Always working. And Mama did take care of me. She took care of everything I needed."

He gave me a look of wide-eyed bewilderment. "Why are you defending her?"

"She's my mama." My hands trembled as I signed the words, then they fell in my lap as I stared at the table with more tears in my eyes. "Or . . . she was. Maybe she did disown me, after all. Maybe New York was too much of a disappointment for her to handle, and now that she can't live vicariously through me, she tossed me out like a sack of garbage."

The revelation rocked through me, and I wasn't sure how I even felt about it. I missed Uncle Theo and really wanted to find him, and I was used to not seeing my daddy very often. But I really didn't miss my mama so much. I'd been so hurt at first, when she first denied knowing me, but I'd also felt so liberated over the past few days, especially after yesterday. Jeric had been right—I'd really needed that release to purge myself of everything I felt for her. To free myself.

But . . . she was still my mama. And he was my daddy. As dysfunctional as they were, I still loved them. And now they didn't even know me.

The waitress arrived with our food and started sliding plates onto our table.

"What about you?" Jeric asked after she left. "Did you really want to go to New York?"

Starving—and needing a few moments to center my mind—I took several bites of biscuits and gravy before answering.

"Only because I thought by being in New York, I could achieve my real dream. But I did feel bad about leaving Uncle Theo, so I was torn. He'd let me stay with him when my parents left for Alaska, saying he needed some help and I should be able to finish my senior year at my school. But really, I think he was trying to get me out from underneath Mama's thumb. Little did he know distance didn't matter to her."

Jeric shoveled in a few bites of his own, then asked, "So what was your real dream?"

I gave him a half-smile. "Promise not to laugh?"

"No," he answered honestly with a gleam in his eye.

"I wanted to be a back-up dancer. Like for Beyoncé or Christina Aguilera." I watched him for a reaction, but he didn't respond. "I'm kind of good at that kind of dance."

Now he nodded. "Damn right you are."

"But Mama would never hear of it, and Uncle Theo needed me, and I didn't make it to New York anyway." I sighed. "I resigned myself to caring for Uncle Theo and going to a normal college and leading a boring, normal life. He used to send me to the lake almost every weekend to give us both a break."

"So he's a bully, too."

I frowned. "No . . ."

"He made you leave your own home?" Although Jeric didn't speak, I could practically hear the accusation.

"It was *his* home; I just stayed there, rent-free. And we both needed the time away," I said, defending Uncle Theo, whether I believed it or not. I'd never considered the situation from Jeric's perspective, but I couldn't think of Uncle Theo as anything like my mother. "Anyway, one weekend I found out about this bar about halfway between Uncle Theo's and the lake. You know that movie 'Coyote Ugly'? It was like that. All female bartenders and servers dressed in barely nothing and doing dance routines on the bar throughout the night. It was connected to a strip club the same guy owned, but there were weird Bible Belt laws about liquor and strippers and whatever, so both places drew a crowd. Anyway, I wasn't old enough to serve, but he liked how I danced. He had this mechanical bull that had come with the place, but hadn't really used it. Someone had mentioned seeing dancers do the bull in Texas, so I agreed to give it a try."

Jeric stopped chewing and looked up at me. "So you never stripped?"

He looked especially happy about this. I picked up my fork to stall, but pushed my eggs around the plate, suddenly not hungry anymore. I put the fork back down.

CHAPTER 32

Please say no.

Leni didn't answer me, and the thought of her taking her clothes off so publicly turned my stomach into a rock. I'd been to enough clubs myself to know what that meant—sick fucks man-handling her, douche-canoes trying to stick their dollar bills where they had no right to touch. Not on Leni. Not on *my* Leni. I had a sudden desire to punch one of them now.

Neither of us was hungry anymore, so Leni hailed the waitress for the check, but I grabbed it before she could pay. She strode outside, across the highway and all the way to the camper, still without answering my question. Which meant . . .

"No," she said. We'd just entered the Airstream, and she turned to face me as I closed the door. "I didn't strip."

I hadn't realized I'd been so tensed up until my whole body deflated with relief.

"I was supposed to," she continued. "The show had been such a hit on the one side, the owner had the bull moved to the other side—the naked side. I'd practiced my routine like crazy, built myself up for it, but when it came time . . . I couldn't do it."

She gave me an apologetic smile. I didn't know what she

would be apologizing for. Next to forgiving me, this was the best thing she'd told me all day.

"I was up there, doing my thing, stripped down to a bikini. But when I was supposed to pull the string to the top, I . . . I froze. Total stage fright came over me for the first time in my life. And I realized I didn't want to do it. The show had always been so sexy, especially when I pulled others on with me. It made me feel *good*. Hot. Wanted. But taking my top off in front of all those slobbering men, some of them old enough to be my daddy?" She shook her head and made a face. "That didn't make me feel good. Some girls can get over it, but I couldn't. The guys began heckling me. Then one jumped on the stage, saying he'd take it off if I didn't, and grabbed at the string. My top fell and I threw my arms across my chest. Customers got angry. Bouncers jumped up on the stage. Somehow, I got pushed off the bull and hit my chin on the way down before I ran for the dressing room. I guess things got worse from there. Bad enough for Uncle Theo to hear about it."

"You have no idea how happy that makes me," I told her.

She gave me a look. "You're not disappointed? In me, I mean?"

"Hell no. Why would I be?"

"Everybody else was. I am in myself. I really can't be trusted to make decisions for myself."

"Bullshit. You trusted yourself with me. Think if you hadn't. If you'd taken off and never found my car going up in smoke. If you hadn't taken me to the lake."

"If I hadn't agreed to let you buy me coffee in Italy," she added.

I chuckled. "So this is the real reason you were there? Why your uncle sent you?"

She nodded. "He was so disappointed. I felt horrible. But then he gave me the trip. He said, 'I know what you really want to do, and that club was not it. I have no one in New York, but maybe this will help.' He told me to follow my heart, my instinct, to find the real me."

"And you found me." I dared to take a step closer to her. I'd been wanting to close the space between us I'd created the other night, what had felt like a wide chasm only hours ago, but now seemed crossable. I just didn't want to push her too soon.

She reached out with a finger and barely touched the cut on my lip. "What happened? The cowboy? I hope you slaughtered him. He reminded me of that night, and I almost freaked."

I cocked my head. "You don't remember?"

She shrugged. "I'd barely eaten anything since the day before, went through some really intense emotions, had been drinking, and dancing the bull is a workout. I was a little low on blood sugar, I think."

"But you're okay? No headache?"

She shook her head. "Did something happen to me?"

"The Shadowmen." I told her about the attack and her near death by semi.

"You saved my life," she said, her head tilting to the side. "Thank you."

"It's what I do," I said. "I can't lose you, Leni. I know I don't deserve you. God, do I know it. But I *need* you. You're the Coke to my Jack."

A smile played on her lips, and her head pulled back. "What?"

"For eight years, life's been one bitter bottle of whiskey after another. One burning shot after shot. But then you come along. Life's still harsh, but you make it sweeter. Easier to swallow."

She grinned, then fisted her hand in my shirt and pulled me to her. I wanted her to tug me down, to lean up on her toes and give me a taste. A long, deep taste of that sweetness. My mouth watered for her. But she didn't. Instead, she traced her finger up my arm and around the tattoos, and pushed my sleeve up, revealing the script on the curve of my shoulder: "No hero in this story."

"Each of these mean something, don't they?" she asked. I nodded. She hopped up to sit on the counter. "Your turn to tell me a story, then. And why there's no hero."

I fingered my brow ring, not wanting to go there yet. But after what she'd spilled to me, how could I not? She deserved my full story.

She trailed her finger over the next tat—a smatter of musical notes. "That's for your music." She moved to the next one of three blue flowers. "Forget-me-nots?"

I nodded slowly.

"For your parents and . . . ?" She looked up at me.

The memories slaughtered me, as they always did. I stared down at my hands for a few beats before signing, "My sister."

She touched her throat, and her lips parted. "You never said anything about a sister."

"The only other girl I loved. She died in the accident, too."

"What happened? You never told me."

No, I hadn't. I'd always tried to keep the past in the past. Both anger and sadness welled, and I hated the feelings. Hated how they always pushed me to the verge of losing control.

I pressed on. "She was beautiful. Sweet. The band's biggest fan. She could have had any guy she wanted, but she chose the biggest asshole in the school. I knew something was wrong from the beginning. She started to change. Became quieter. Always smiling still, but her smile wasn't real anymore. She stopped coming to our shows, and then bruises started showing up on her arms."

"How old was she?"

"My age. We weren't far apart. My mom was several months pregnant with her before my adoption was final."

"And her boyfriend?"

"A couple of years older. A senior. Star football player."

"Wow. He abused her?"

I nodded. "Yeah. A-1 asshole. She came home one night covered in bruises and crying. My parents were out for the night, but I was livid when I saw her. I didn't know what to do, and she begged me to take her away. She was so scared. Scared he would come to the house. I was a wimpy musician and couldn't do anything if he did.

"We were only fourteen, and I didn't have a driver's license yet, but I stole my mom's car and took off. I would have done anything for her. We were on the highway near home still and the tire blew out. Just so happened my parents were on their way home and saw us. They came around to help, angrier than hell, of course, but glad we were okay. Then a drunk driver came swerving down the highway. Plowed her SUV into my parents' car and all of us. The three of them had been smashed between my dad's car and my mom's. I was thrown into the grass. I woke up three weeks later with no hearing and no family."

Stupid tears filled my eyes and Leni's, too. God, I didn't want to cry in front of her, but I couldn't help it when I spoke of that night.

"You don't blame yourself, do you?" she asked.

I shrugged. "My grandfather blamed me, but the drunk bitch was who killed them. Still, I can't help but feel guilty about running in the first place. About being too much of a coward to stay home and face that dickhead. Maybe they'd still be here today, or maybe not. I don't know."

Her eyes squinted as she studied my face for a moment. Then her gaze dropped down to my arm again, and her finger moved to the tattoo below the flowers. An angel on her knees, doubled over, her hands covering her face.

"This is for your sister?"

I swiped at my eyes and nodded. "She was an angel. He'd broken her."

Not wanting her to see my pain and weakness, I turned my back to her and drew in a few breaths. Her hands clamped on my shoulders and pulled me backwards to the counter she sat on, then slid down my arms. Her finger traced the next tattoo—a broken shackle around my wrist—and she must have known what it meant. She ignored the last one and moved to the other arm, but they were all self-explanatory, too—a sunrise with "No Guarantees" written underneath it, a cross with a quote from 23 Psalm written across it, and the flame that matched her own. She returned to the last one on the inner part of my other forearm. A puzzle piece showing a heart with a lock clasped over it.

I turned and smiled. "I have the piece that fits into it stashed away, in case I ever did meet the right someone."

She lifted a brow. "What's the other piece show?"

I went over to my bags and squatted down to dig for my journal. I pulled it out and flipped to the page where I'd sketched the other half of the tattoo—another puzzle piece shaped to fit into mine, showing the key.

I didn't outright ask her if she'd get the tattoo. She did hold the key to my heart, and I didn't want it to remain locked forever. I just didn't know how to tell her.

So I moved closer to her again, to show her the best way I knew how—physically. As I leaned in for a kiss, though, she pushed me away.

"I need a shower," she said.

"I kind of like you dirty," I replied.

She smiled and shook her head. "I'm gross. Seriously. So are you."

Well, if that wasn't a blow to the ego. I could tell by the gleam in her eye, though, it was only an excuse. In fact, I was pretty sure she was trying hard not to cry. So I wrapped my arms around her and held her to my chest, relieved when her arms encircled my waist. That was progress. Short-lived, though, when she pushed away and headed to the back of the camper for her shower.

CHAPTER 33

 All of the talk about family, especially of Uncle Theo, made my heart ache. I truly did miss him, and I was scared to know what his long absence meant. The desire to go to Tampa still remained as a slight pull in the pit of my stomach, but I felt a stronger instinct to remain still for a bit longer. Something needed to be done before we moved on, and I had a feeling what that "something" was. Jeric and I needed to re-Bond.

But I was stalling. Putting off the inevitable. Knowing what I wanted to do, what Jeric wanted—not only our bodies, but what our souls needed—part of me still refused to give in yet. We'd only known each other for a week, at least in these bodies, in this life cycle. Our past lives, our existence as one soul, were only vague memories, although the connection felt very real and present. But before I could give him my gift, as Jacey called it, I felt the need to know I loved him for him *right now*, not because of something we had together before, as other people.

When the tears flowed for him while I showered, though, I felt it. His sorrow and grief and pain and anger at everything he'd been through had become mine, too. My heart pulled it in, sharing his burden, hurting on his behalf. He'd felt my heartache, pain, and disappointment, too, and he'd already told me he loved me.

In fact, he'd known long before learning our history together. Several days ago he'd said something about "the only other girl I loved." His sister was one. He knew then I was the other.

I finished my shower and threw on a tank and skimpy shorts. I didn't have lingerie, but it's not like I knew how to go about this anyway. I couldn't imagine throwing myself at him, although I knew he'd gladly catch me. When I came out of the bedroom and saw him sitting on the futon petting Ghost—everything I'd thrown around yesterday picked up and put away—I became a ball of nerves. He eyed me before getting up and, without a word, walked past to take a shower, too. By the time he came out, wearing only jeans, I'd nearly talked myself out of it. My body trembled with a mix of desire and fear.

His expression flickered, and he must have known everything going through my mind. He smiled.

"I can still be patient," he signed.

I nodded, although I didn't want him to be patient. I wanted to be with him. But adrenaline raced through my veins, making me edgy. Jumpy. I couldn't imagine letting him touch me in this state.

I needed to dance. To shut my stupid brain down and let my body do its thing.

"We forgot to check on my truck this morning," I said.

He nodded then pulled his shirt over his head. "I'll go."

As soon as he was gone, I could finally breathe again. I connected my iPod to the docking station and turned up the volume, not caring that unlike at the lake, there were people around here. I was done caring about what they thought. In fact, the louder I cranked the music, the better. My body did what it loved to do, twisting and turning, swinging and gyrating to the beat, and my mind did what I loved it to do—lose itself.

I swung around to once again find Jeric standing in the doorway. His eyes smoldered, and his tongue swiped across his lips. Like last time, I froze. He shook his head and held his cell phone against his chest, the screen facing me with a text message already typed out: "Don't stop. Ever."

Right. Remembering how he'd reacted last time, I began moving again. He sauntered toward me as his fingers moved over his phone's screen. He held it out for me to read again:

"If I could hear one more time for only a minute, it would be right now, to hear the music that makes your body move in that way."

Heat exploded within me. A small smile played on my lips as I moved my body to the music and pointed at the iPod's screen: Closer by Nine Inch Nails.

"Do you remember it?" I asked.

He closed his eyes and fell to his knees at my feet.

"You're fucking killing me," he signed before clasping my waist with his hands, pressing his forehead against my midriff and feeling the music through me as I danced for him.

He must have known when the song changed by my movements, because he reached up and pressed the back button to replay Closer. The ten seconds his hand had left my body were ten seconds too long. A thrill ran through every nerve when it returned to my hip and pushed my tank top up just enough to rest on my bare skin. He pushed the other side up, too, exposing a strip between my belly button and the waistband of my shorts. A small moan escaped my throat when his lips touched me there, and I was glad he couldn't hear, because I would have died of embarrassment. But then I felt his tongue, and if he hadn't had such a tight grip on my waist, I would have melted into the floor.

He pulled back and looked up at me, and I realized I'd stopped dancing. *Keep going*, his eyes pled. I'd always thought this song to be one of the sexiest tunes ever, but sexy took on a new meaning when I danced with Jeric's hands and lips and tongue on me. He slid his hands up, pushing my top with them, his mouth following slowly behind until his fingers reached my bra. He held my top there, exposing less than a bikini would, and he continued kissing every inch of my stomach and ribs, moving with me as I barely writhed against him, no longer able to dance. Barely able to keep myself vertical.

By the time the song finished its second run, I could no longer feel the cool air from the air conditioning unit on top of the camper, too hot and flushed and thinking, *too many clothes. I have too many clothes on.* I reached for the hem of my top, and pulled it over my head, but the fire burning within me only grew hotter as Jeric continued to kiss me. His hands slid up my bare back as he rose to his feet, his eyes locked on mine, drowning me once again.

He grabbed my waist once more and lifted me to the counter to put us at eye level, then he placed a hand on the counter at each side of my hips and leaned his head to mine. His lips pressed lightly against my forehead, and then to each temple, and then down my nose. Light kisses landed on my cheeks, on the corners of my mouth, up along my jawline. His breath in my ear as he gently sucked my lobe lit my whole body. My thighs clenched, and my legs locked around his waist. He moaned against my neck as his lips and tongue trailed soft but passionate kisses from one side to the other. I suddenly needed his mouth on mine.

I placed my hands on each side of his face and brought him up so he was only inches from my mouth. I looked into his eyes, now my turn to plead. His gaze fell on my lips.

"Kiss me," I mouthed, and I licked my lips slowly.

His eyes heated even more as something inside him seemed to break. He grasped my face, and we held onto each other tightly as his mouth covered mine. I immediately parted my lips for him, inhaling his breath, trying to drink him in, to pull his soul into mine. His tongue darted in, brushed against mine, lightly at first and then more forcefully. My tongue met his every movement as we explored each other's mouths for what might have been hours. Then his lips grasped my bottom one and he sucked, sending a spark to every nerve ending in my body until I thought I would explode. I returned the favor, and he moaned aloud.

I'd somehow ended up nearly on my elbows on the hard counter, which made me practically out of reach even as he pressed against me. I pulled myself up as best as I could, wrapped my arms around his neck and tightened my legs at his waist. He took the hint and lifted me, his hands on my butt and our mouths never separating as he carried me into the bedroom. We crashed together on the mattress, and his body pressed against me and, oh my God, there was way too much fabric between us. I reached to his back and tugged at his shirt, pulling it up to his shoulders, hating that his mouth had to leave mine so he could pull the shirt over his head, and grateful when it returned.

He held himself up on his forearms, which was too far away from me. I slid my hands under his arms and over his shoulders and pulled him down. His body welded to mine, and I felt every bit of him, including his erection through his jeans. He moved his hips, pressing it harder against me, and my head rolled back as I let out a gasp. Unable to reach my mouth now, his lips moved to my chin, my jawline, down to my neck as he once again explored every inch of it. Then he kissed along my collarbone, his nose brushing along the top of it, his breath hot as he panted against me.

When he reached my bra strap, he pushed it down to my bicep with a finger, his mouth never leaving my skin. He shifted his body to the side, only half on top of me now, but never allowing any space between us. His hand came to my stomach and slid to my side. His fingers pressed deeper as his mouth moved to the rise of my breast and kissed along the top of my bra. I arched against him, wanting him to continue, but he didn't. He looked up at me, asking for permission. As if I hadn't just tried to give it.

"I want you . . . to," I said with my mouth, hoping he understood. "I want you to . . . do everything."

He sat up on his knees, straddling me, and his gaze traveled from my eyes to my lips to my breasts and lower. A storm broke out in his eyes as if he were waging some inner battle.

"I want to do right by you," he signed. "I just don't know if I can."

"You can," I replied. "I trust you. This is right. It's meant to be. We're meant to be together, as one."

He closed his eyes and inhaled deeply. As rough as he looked, he possessed a dangerous beauty, like that of a majestic lion or a sleek jaguar. I lifted my hands to his perfectly sculpted abs and reached up as far as I could to his chest, then slid them slowly back down and curled my fingers under the waistband of his jeans. His eyes finally opened, and if possible, they were full of even more desire than before.

"I'll take it slow," he promised me.

"You don't have to." Slow sounded good, but I didn't think I had the patience.

"I want to." His eyes caressed my body again, and they may as well have been his lips or tongue the way my body reacted. My heart, already pounding, flew into a gallop. "I want to know every bit of you on the outside before I feel you on the inside."

Oh, God. I imagined his sexy voice saying the words as he signed them, and was surprised my panties didn't singe right off of me. I leaned up on my elbows and reached behind me to undo the bra clasp. When he saw the bra loosen, he slid his hands under the straps and pulled it off.

"*Oh, fuck, Leni,*" his lips mouthed before he fell against me and his mouth was all over me.

On my shoulder, my collarbone, my chest, my breast. He wrapped his lips around as much of my breast as he could and sucked my nipple inside, his tongue caressing it until chills swept over me. My pelvis jerked, and I felt his hardness, so I ground myself against him. He moaned over my breast, and finally let it go. But he kept me enraptured, wanting more.

He didn't falter on his promise. Although we moved sometimes painfully slow as he got to know every bit of me and I of him, it wasn't without passion. Our eyes and fingers and mouths explored, tasting and sucking, making each other writhe and ache for more. He kissed me all the way to my shorts and slowly slid them off, but left my panties on as he moved farther down, all the way to my toes on one foot, then back up the other leg. Another wave overcame me as he sucked on the inside of my thigh and my pelvis bucked again.

Before I let him in my panties, though, I returned the favor of being tortured. I clasped his face in my hands and sat up, bringing him up with me. Then I traced his face, his jaw, his neck, his shoulders with my lips. I pushed him to his back as I made my way over his chest, to the piercings that so infatuated me. I hesitated, studying one as I wondered what on earth they did for him, why he would do such a thing. Because it looked sexy as hell? Or was there more? I lowered my mouth and tasted one with my tongue. Jeric moaned quietly. I caressed it harder, and he moaned louder. I pulled the ring and his nipple along with it into my mouth, and he bucked against me, his hands clamping hard on my ass. Ah. That's why.

I drove him into a wild frenzy, exactly as he'd done to me, spending lots of time with those piercings, but also moving down. First my eyes and then my mouth appreciated every hill and valley of his muscular landscape, down to his hips until they disappeared behind his jeans. When my fingers clasped his button and my lips pressed against the skin right above it, his erection jumped against my chest, straining against the denim. Before I could free him, though, he sat up and pulled me into his arms.

I sat in his lap, straddling him and grinding against him as our mouths met again. We spent the entire afternoon kissing and exploring, our bodies heating and aching even more. We moved and shifted, teased and taunted. He ended up behind me, pushing the curls away so he could kiss my neck and shoulders. One hand kneaded my breast, and the other palmed my stomach, his fingers barely under my panties, slowly moving side to side. He pulled me to the edge of the bed, and I sat on my knees as he stood behind me. His hands left my body, and I missed them already, but I could hear him taking his jeans off.

I turned and lay on my back, waiting for him. Watching as he rose to his full height—all of him. My belly and thighs quivered at the thought of that inside me.

"You're still okay?" he asked me, and I nodded.

With a sharp exhale, he moved himself over me, then leaned back on his knees as his fingers glided under my panties. With hooded eyes, he gazed at my body as he slid the last piece of fabric either of us wore down, over my knees, off of my ankles. He teased me some more with his lips on my face, my neck, my chest, setting me on fire. Time passed. The room darkened with the sunset before he finally reached for his wallet and pulled out a condom. Something deep within my belly clenched with anticipation. He moved between my legs and hovered over me, his eyes asking me once again. My hands grabbed his ass, and I lifted my hips in answer.

I cried out when he first entered, although I expected the pain. He carefully moved inside of me, every one of my muscles clenched around him, then slowly stroked back and forth until I eventually relaxed and the pain turned to pleasure. We fell into a rhythm, rocking against each other, our moves becoming faster until we almost reached the brink. Then he'd shift us, turn us, put us into a new position, and start slow again, building up, up, up. He moved on top of me again and my legs braced against his shoulders and he pushed into me and I might have screamed as a wave of pure and unadulterated bliss washed over me. I shuddered even as I rocked against him. He drove into me again, harder and deeper. My world shattered. My body disintegrated.

I fell apart beneath him, but at the same time, I exploded outward, as if escaping the confines of my body. Jeric shouted as he exploded, too. Our souls soared, collided, combined, melded into each other. We hovered over the bed, still feeling the sensation of our bodies physically connected below us, but . . .

Oh.

My.

God.

The physical sensation didn't compare. Nothing on earth could possibly compare. Euphoria like no other as our souls united, *re*united, became one again.

I never knew how much I missed him, that a part of me, a *huge* part, was even gone until now.

CHAPTER 34

 *Holy. Fucking. Shit.*

The sensation of our joined bodies felt distant, on the far edge of any consciousness I still held onto. Our energies tangled together in the air as we hovered above the physical world below. That's what I felt more than anything—Leni's soul woven into mine. And nothing could have felt more right.

"Is this normal?"

I felt the question more than heard it, the words reverberating through us, so I didn't know if I heard Leni's real voice or not, but I could listen to its angelic quality forever. Damn. I could *hear* her. Feel her. Whatever.

"Hell no," I answered, and her energy within me sparked brightly at the sound of my "voice." Or the feel of it. Again, whatever. "This is all about me and you. Us."

"I could stay like this forever," she said with a sigh of pleasure that coursed through us.

I tried to move us, willing our energy to the right, to snag a better look at our bodies. They appeared to be frozen in place. A slight tug came from my physical body, as though if I tried to go too far, it would yank my soul back into it.

"Wow. Look at us," Leni said.

I chuckled. "We look sexy as hell. Especially you. That look on your face . . ."

The feeling of embarrassment ran through us. "Well, you are screwing me out of my mind. Literally."

"No, Leni. I'm making love to you."

Her energy heated around and through me. "This is the most amazing feeling. Ever. Will it always be like this between us?"

"I fucking hope so."

We studied ourselves for a moment longer.

"Should we go back?" Leni asked. "I really don't want to."

"Mmm . . . it's not nice to leave us like that. We're in the middle of the best part."

Her smile ran through me. "Exactly. I don't want it to end."

"Nothing's ending, babe. This is only the beginning."

I imagined wrapping my arms around her and pulling her into me, and our energies shifted, as if feeling my hug. Reluctantly, we disentangled our souls and slid into our bodies.

"*Oh, Jeric, yes!*" Leni's voice, like her soul's but more real, screamed in my head. She clenched my cock inside her, making me come harder than I'd ever done before.

Then we both collapsed.

✳ ✳ ✳

Leni lay on her stomach, her face turned toward me, looking unbelievably sexy as she slept. Maybe because I knew she was naked under the sheet. The morning sun had woken me about an hour ago, but with only a break long enough to take a piss, I'd lain here watching her sleep the whole time. Whatever had happened last night had totally wiped us out. We'd slept for over twelve hours. And my body ached with the need to do it again.

Please wake up soon, I thought, *so I can make you come like that again.*

Her eyelids immediately popped open, her eyes wider than

I'd ever seen. "Did you just say something?"

I bolted upright, my own eyes widening. Because I'd heard her voice. Like last night, right when she came—not with my ears, but in my head.

"I heard you," I thought, and her face exploded with emotion as she sprang to her knees.

"Me, too!" She signed and thought the words at the same time. "In my head! Oh, my God, Jeric!"

My heart swelled with excitement as did my dick, because the sheet had fallen to the bed around her legs, and her tits were bouncing beautifully. Her expression flickered, and she grabbed the sheet to wrap around herself. Oh, shit. This could be a problem.

"Can you hear my thoughts?" I asked her with my mind and my hands. "*All* of them?"

Her face turned a deep shade of red. "Can you hear *mine?*"

If she was thinking anything at all, which she had to have been with that heavy flush, I didn't hear her thoughts, only her direct question. But I couldn't help myself.

The corners of my mouth twitched with a grin. "You're thinking you want to play with my piercings again. Flick them with your tongue. Feel my muscles under your hands. Wrap your mouth around my—"

"Stop!" she shrieked in my mind as she curled over her legs and tugged the sheet over her head. Hiding from me. "I was *not* thinking that. Not all of it."

I laughed and tried to pull the sheet off of her, but she held it tightly.

"Not all of it?" I teased. "So you were thinking *some* of it?"

After a long moment, she lifted her head and peeked out of the sheet, her eyes narrowed. "Wait. You didn't hear my thoughts at all, did you?"

I teased her for a bit longer by not replying, but I eventually shook my head.

"Then how did you know I—" She didn't finish her sentence. Her face reddened again.

I stroked her cheek with my thumb, enjoying how I could touch her and communicate at the same time. "I was just hoping, because that's what I was thinking about you. And when you pulled the sheet up to cover those gorgeous tits of yours, I thought you'd heard my thoughts."

She sat all the way up, keeping the sheet around her as much as possible. "Are you thinking anything right now?"

I gave her a sly grin. "If you can't hear my thoughts, I'm sure you can guess what they are."

She looked down to my lap, the sheet now a tent over me, and returned my grin. Unable to contain myself a moment longer, I yanked the sheet out of her hands and attacked her.

Her perfect mouth met mine and opened for me, and I couldn't get enough of her—enough of her soft skin, the taste of her, the feel of her. Of her voice in my head, moaning my name and asking for more. The desire to do what we did last night built into an agonizing ache that hardened me like a rock.

"I need to feel you," I finally thought to her, our eyes locked. "*All* of you."

She kept her eyes on mine and nodded.

I couldn't rip through the Trojan wrapper or get the condom on fast enough, but finally, *finally* I was inside her. We fell into a rhythm and although I didn't want to rush it, we built up quickly. I couldn't help it. She felt so fucking *good*. Our souls exploded out of our bodies and came together once again.

The feeling was as amazing as the first time, but not quite as shocking. After a few minutes of enjoying the sensation, we agreed to see what we could do like this, with our souls out of our bodies. We moved around the room, and even out of it to the front of the camper, taking in this small corner of the world from such a different perspective. We both felt the tug to the physical world, and we returned, sliding back in as our bodies shattered together.

We collapsed to the bed and lay next to each other, hand in hand. I couldn't keep my eyes open and drifted off to sleep, awaking with a panic. To *Leni's* panic coursing through my body. I could feel it as if it were my own. I sat up, glad to see the sun hadn't moved too far in the sky—we'd only slept an hour or so, better than twelve.

Leni lay next to me and stared at the ceiling with her arms crossed over her chest, her fingers tapping a rhythm on her bicep.

"What's the matter, babe?" I asked her as I pushed up on my elbow.

"We need to go," she said. "The feeling's back. Is my truck done? Did you ever find out? We need to get out of here."

She suddenly sat up and bolted out of the bed. She grabbed clothes and pulled on a pair of white cut-off shorts and a loose-fitting, gauzy top that slid off one shoulder. She looked so sexy, I wanted to rip them off of her.

"Leni, what's the rush?"

She threw my jeans and t-shirt at me. "I feel it. We have to get out of here. They're coming again."

Her panic got to me, and I began to dress as hurriedly as she did. "Who?"

"The Shadowmen. They're coming to kill us. That's what they do."

I stood up and buttoned my fly. "How do you know this?"

"I don't know." She glanced around the camper as if it held answers. "I just do. I feel it. We have to get to the mansion, like right *now*."

My own heart flew into a panic now, and I stopped mid-motion, my shirt in my hands. "No fucking way. We're not going there."

She spun on me, her face filled with disbelief. "We have to!"

"No. Absolutely not."

"Why?"

My stomach dropped as the memories flooded over me again. My throat tightened. "I'm not doing that to you again, Leni. Please understand."

Her expression morphed from anger to understanding. "You blame yourself," her voice said softly in my head. "You think you killed Jacey . . . you killed me."

"How could I not?" I demanded. "It was my fault. I should have never taken you there. I won't make the same mistake twice."

"But Jeric, it wasn't—"

"Forget it, Leni!" I silently yelled. "You don't exactly have the best instincts, remember?"

Her face fell, and guilt stabbed my heart with the low blow, especially because I felt the pull, too, stronger than it had been for days. But I also remembered what had happened last time, when she'd been too out of it to know.

"We're not going," I said. "End of discussion."

I charged out of the camper door, turned in a circle under the awning and pushed my hands through my hair, not knowing what to do, where to go. Leni's fear about the Shadowmen felt very real, but so was my fear of going to the mansion. I wasn't taking her into that fiasco again.

Too many people had died because of me in that last life, including Jacey. Although I'd hurt a lot of people in this one—physically and emotionally—my body count was zero, despite what my grandfather chose to believe about my parents and my sister. Leni was absolutely not about to become the first.

✳ THEN ✳
1989

CHAPTER 35

Micah *1989* I sat in a chair in the darkened room, my elbows on my knees as I stared out the window, my head pounding as I tried to figure out what to do. Jacey lay in the bed, coming in and out of consciousness, her body weakening by the hour. But it was the look in her eyes that would forever haunt me. The gleam of life behind them slipping away. She kept insisting we continue on, but I had no way of following the pull. Not when it came from the middle of the water. And not with all those Shadowmen out there.

Several large, dark shadows flew wide circles in the sky, buzzards waiting for us to come out. I had no idea how many more lurked on the ground in the shadows of the building and trees around us, but the scene felt way too familiar. I was not leading her to her death as I'd done to my brothers.

I closed my eyes, unable to fight the memories.

A special ops mission in the Middle East only those with the highest of clearances knew about. My team of six men who were like brothers to me crouching in an abandoned building on the outskirts of the city. Across the street was a secured compound where a covert meeting of known terrorists was taking place. We were to go in, make the kill, and get out. But the target had way too many bodyguards surrounding the compound. One bad move on our part, by any one of us, and we'd blow the whole mission.

My men wanted to move in. I wanted to analyze the situation further, knowing there had to be another way. But we were running out of time. Fast.

"Let's do it, sir," Jeeves whispered from his crouched position next to me. "We got this. Let's kill these camel-fuckers and get the hell out."

He was just a kid. We all were really. At twenty-two, I was one of the oldest on the team. And the one in charge.

I knew there were too many guns out there. I should have never done what I did.

But still, I gave the order.

We charged out of our hole, everyone firing as we went. Gunfire filled the quiet night, and the bodyguards immediately shot back. We took down two. Three. A fourth. Then we lost control of the situation. *I* lost control. Smoke and the smell of gunpowder filled the air as my men began dropping in front of me. One after another. Until they were all down.

My men.

My brothers.

The only family I'd ever felt was real.

Gone.

All of them.

The details of what happened next were unclear. A backup team had arrived right as we'd moved in, but I hadn't known. Otherwise, I would have waited for them to get into position. And my men, my brothers, would still be alive. Instead, only I survived. The backup team completed our mission. Every accolade I was given for my efforts and sacrifice felt like a punch in the nuts, a reminder of those who had made the true sacrifice. I couldn't wait for the day of my discharge. It should have been dishonorable.

I opened my eyes and rubbed my hand over my face, not surprised to find it moist with tears. I wasn't about to take Jacey into that same situation. I'd thought we'd found backup when the people had pulled us into this abandoned hotel on the water's edge, thinking we'd found others like us, trying to help. But they'd led us into this room and left, not to be seen again. Besides, there were only two of them and two of us. We didn't even have Sammy anymore. He'd taken off, deeper into the building when we'd come in, and I hadn't seen him since. And there were a dozen or two Shadowmen out there, not counting the ones I couldn't see.

No, I wasn't doing it again.

I'd survived the death of my brothers. Of having to face their wives and parents because I'd felt I needed to. I owed that much to them. Each visit was harder than the previous one, creating another crack in my heart.

But losing Jacey would break it completely. Kill me. Literally.

"Micah," Jacey whispered from the bed.

I went over to it and crawled in beside her. I slipped one arm under her pillow and the other over her waist and pulled her back against my chest. She was already sleeping again. The pain in my head grew, spreading to my entire body. I fell unconscious beside her. *It's just the flu*, I told myself, and later Jacey, as we both floated in and out of consciousness.

I awoke one time to voices outside the door. I couldn't make out the words, but the anxious tones worried me. At some point, without realizing what I was actually doing but knowing I needed to get Jacey out of there—away from these people, away from the Shadowmen, far, far away, or shit, I was going to lose her—I forced myself out of the bed and lifted her into my arms. She felt like she'd gained fifty pounds in the hours since I'd first brought her in, but it wasn't her. I'd grown too weak. I stumbled. We both fell. The door flew open.

I didn't understand this couple who were no older than us. They acted like they wanted to help, but they did nothing. Made no sense when they spoke, something about re-Bonding and dying. When they left, Jacey rolled to face me.

"Who are they?" she asked.

I used what little energy I had left to turn to her. "I don't know. They said they could help us, but they haven't done anything but—"

Her face contorted and distress filled her dull eyes. She grasped my hand and squeezed it tightly.

"Micah," she gasped.

"I'm here, babe."

"It burns." Her lungs wheezed. "Micah . . . finish the journal for me . . . okay?"

"What?"

"Just . . . promise. Write this . . . all down. Okay?"

"I promise."

"I . . . love—"

Pain ripped through my chest. I was losing her.

"No, Jacey. Don't do this. Stay with me."

"I . . . love you."

"Help!" I yelled. "Hurry!"

"Always have . . . always . . . will."

"I love you, too, Jacey. But don't . . . Hang on, babe. Don't do this." I screamed as loudly as I could muster. "Get in here! She needs help!"

The door finally flew open and the overhead light came on, but the young couple hadn't returned. Instead, an older, familiar looking man came rushing in. He looked exactly like the portrait Jacey had drawn of her Pops in her sketchbook. But how? Wasn't he dead? Behind him stood a woman with chin-length, dirty-blond hair—shorter than the last time I'd seen her. My foster mother, Angie.

"I'm sorry, son, but we have to do this," Jacey's Pops said as he moved to her side of the bed. "You didn't get there this time. If we wait, we could lose you both for good."

Panic rose within me but I was too weak to fight. Angie stepped over to my side and grasped my hand between both of hers. I tried to yank free, to throw myself over Jacey's still body, knowing I needed to protect her from whatever this man—this man who was supposed to love her, who had taken care of her for half her life—whatever it was he was about to do. Because I knew it wasn't good.

"Shh," Angie whispered beside me, holding my hand more tightly than should have been possible for her size. "It's the only way, Jeremicah." She nodded at the older man whose palms hovered close to Jacey's chest. "Go ahead. It has to be done."

His hands lowered. Jacey's body jerked, and searing pain ripped through my chest. I fought against Angie's hold, but now she was practically on top of me, holding me down. I writhed against the torture in my body, in my heart, in my soul. A string of profanities and unintelligible sounds erupted as Jacey's soul was ripped from mine.

The old man's hands came away from Jacey's chest, cupped together as if he held something within them.

"We'll give you some time," Angie said, "but we have to return for you. It's the only way."

I ignored the meaning of her words, pushed them far out of my mind as they both seemed to simply disappear from the room. Perhaps they'd gone through the door, but I didn't know. I was too focused on Jacey next to me.

I pulled her into my arms, but my mind and soul already knew what my heart refused to admit.

She was gone. Only a body here in my arms, nothing in it anymore. Nothing entwined with me, my soul.

I'd lost Jacey. I'd brought her here when I shouldn't have. I'd kept us here too long. And I'd lost her, the only person I'd ever loved.

I'd failed her completely.

✳ **NOW** ✳

2012

CHAPTER 36

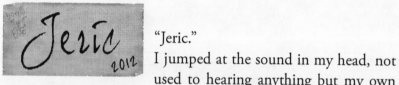 "Jeric."

I jumped at the sound in my head, not used to hearing anything but my own thoughts. I sat on the picnic table, my elbows on my knees and my head in my hands. Leni squatted in front of me with her hands on either side of my head. She forced me to look up at her.

"What's wrong?" she asked, apparently seeing Micah's pain in my eyes. My pain.

I gulped against the thickness in my throat.

"How can you even stand to look at me? How do you not hate me? Or at least blame me?"

Obviously, she wouldn't be here now if Jacey had lived. Neither of us would be. We'd be in our forties, probably even married, little Micahs and Jaceys running around. I'd taken all of that from her. Just as I'd taken it from my brothers in that past life.

"What do you mean? I could never hate you. And the only thing I blame you for is being too obstinate to listen to me."

"I killed you, Leni. I led you right to your death."

Her brows pushed together as she stared at me for a long moment, then understanding seemed to wash over her.

"You mean Jacey?"

I blew out a heavy sigh. "Yes, Jacey. And almost killed you, too, by going to the mansion, leading you right into the pit of the Shadowmen. Again."

She shook her head, and her perfect lips lifted in a small smile. "You didn't do anything, Jeric. Micah . . . you . . . it wasn't your fault."

"Of course it is. I couldn't protect you."

She pressed her finger to my mouth, although I didn't speak aloud. "While you've been sitting out here feeling all remorseful, I realized why I feel such a sense of urgency to go. I remembered something. It wasn't you or Micah or anything you did that caused Jacey's death. The two of us—our disbelief, our inability to remember everything, our *delay*—caused it. Caused both of us to leave that life."

Now my turn to look confused.

CHAPTER 37

 My hands clasped over Jeric's, and I tugged, trying to pull him to his feet. He reluctantly obeyed and followed me into the camper. Good, because we needed intimacy, and I wasn't about to try this outside. I pushed him onto the futon, and then straddled his lap. My hands braced his head as I leaned in and pressed my forehead to his, our noses barely touching, our lips only centimeters apart.

"I thought you were in a hurry," Jeric said in my head. Relief filled his tone, glad I wasn't forcing the issue of going to the mansion. I knew, or at least hoped, that before long, I wouldn't be forcing him. He'd know it was the right thing to do.

"What we do when we . . . um . . ." I blushed, embarrassment combining with the heat of the memory flustering me. "You know, when we leave our bodies?"

"When we come?" he said with a teasing smile.

My skin flushed hotter. "Yeah. That. But what we do that you said has never happened to you before? The leaving our body thing? I once read this book called *Intrinsical* and the characters left their bodies, too. It's called astral projection. I think that's what we did, and I want to do it again."

"Any time," he said with a grin as his hands slid down my back to my butt.

"But without the sex," I added.

His grin fell into a frown. "What fun is that?"

"I think this is something we're supposed to be able to do as dyads," I said. "And I also think we're supposed to be able to do it when we want, not just because we've exploded from our bodies in a heightened physical state. We need to practice. I feel like it's really important."

He eyed me. "This is what you remembered? Much better than my own memory."

"Actually, this is what I feel we need to do. I think if we can do this, if we can do the Bonding thing, you'll remember what I did. And you'll stop blaming yourself."

He narrowed his eyes, catching on to my scheme to change his mind about going.

"Please, Jeric," I nearly begged before he protested. "Trust me on this."

"Fine. I'm game. How?"

This part I didn't know. Based on Jacey's journal, she and Micah had never done it but the one time on accident, but I felt like we—Jacquelena and Jeremicah—had projected many times before. I just couldn't grasp any memories of it.

"Maybe if we imagine the feeling, try to recreate it without, you know, the action part of it."

He looked at me skeptically. With our foreheads still pressed together, it was difficult to look into his eyes without going cross-eyed, so I closed mine, and I tried to imagine the sensation of the physical orgasm and the release of my soul.

"Leni?" Jeric whispered in my mind.

"Hmm?" I asked, still trying to concentrate, though it didn't seem to be working.

"Can I at least kiss you? Because you keep licking those perfect lips of yours and you're grinding yourself against me and I can't . . ."

My eyes flew open, and I pulled back. I hadn't realized I'd been doing either one of those things.

He groaned. "Don't stop!"

He pulled my face closer to him, his gaze on my mouth the entire time until he brought it to his. I closed my eyes again as I lost myself in the kiss. Passion rushed through my body, but it was exactly what I needed, so I deepened the kiss, hoping he felt it, too.

"Try to leave your body," I whispered as I felt my soul beginning to rise.

"But it feels so good. *You* feel so good."

I couldn't argue with that, but we really didn't have time to let our physical selves rule. We needed to be able to do this.

"Jeric, please. Come with me."

I didn't know exactly how he took my meaning, but he moaned into my mouth and the next thing I knew, we both hovered over our bodies. Our energies automatically came together and rejoined our souls into one. The rest of Jacey's and Micah's story—of *our* story—danced on the edge of our memory, slowly coming into reach until it consumed us, and we were again in the Space Between with the Keeper.

"At least the two of you found each other, and you left your mark," the Keeper was saying.

"Our mark?" I—Jacey—thought of the tattoos on our wrists.

"The journal," he said. "The Book of Phoenix. You have helped the next souls who find it, giving them enough guidance so hopefully they will move to the Gate faster. You see, once your souls find each other, the Lakari can detect you. They will try to stop you from re-Bonding and from reaching the Gate. If they can, they will kill you and take your souls to Enyxa. The faster you re-Bond and the faster you get to the Gate, the more likely your survival in that life so you can serve your missions. We try to leave clues for future souls, to help them move to the Gate sooner rather than later. You left The Book of Phoenix."

"Well, it would have been nice if someone had left clues for us," I said.

"The Phoenix probably thought they had, bringing you together at a former portal to the Gate."

"A portal? Wait, in the apartment building? That's why I felt so disoriented in the hidden space?"

"Yes, child. The portal has been closed for safety reasons, but the Phoenix had hoped you would make the connection. And the Book itself offers clues on its cover. There's more to the Book than you know, the reason the Lakari desire it."

His instructions we couldn't remember previously also returned to our memory.

"Jeremicah," he'd said, "you must let go of the guilt and blame. It is not your fault you are here, either of you. And you must remember to follow instinct. Not only yours, but Jacquelena's, too. She is your torch, lighting your way." He focused on me now. "Jacquelena, you must believe in yourself. Believe in your instinct, especially if and when you find each other and begin to remember. And most especially after you re-Bond—the new energy will be strong and will draw the Lakari to you. You must get to the Gate as quickly as possible or risk becoming Dark. Whatever happens, however unbelievable anything seems, you must *believe*. And you MUST NOT DELAY!"

CHAPTER 38

Jeric
2012

We slammed into our bodies, and Leni bolted from my lap and into the bedroom. "You see? The only reason Jacey and then Micah died is because they waited too long," she said in my head as she rushed back to the front of the camper and sat down to pull her cowboy boots on. As if the flossy top and short cut-offs with loose strings hanging from the edges weren't sexy enough, the boots looked ridiculous but hot. "What? They're easier to run in than sandals. Now what about my truck? We gotta go."

As much as I loved "hearing" her voice, I didn't like the word "run" or "go." I hadn't told her about her truck earlier, hoping to convince her to drop the idea of the mansion first. She moved about, stuffing a backpack with some clothes and necessities, including the journal.

"They were waiting on a part that was supposed to come in this morning," I said. My eyes followed hers as she glanced at the clock on the mini-stove. How the hell was it nearly three o'clock in the afternoon already? We'd been out of our bodies for . . . four *hours*?

"It should be done by now?" she asked.

I let out a sigh. I couldn't lie to her. "Yeah. Probably."

"Then what are we waiting for? We're losing daylight!"

She slung the bag over her shoulder and ran out of the camper, and I sprinted after her toward the truck stop. Damn. I didn't know the girl could run so fast.

"We'll leave the camper," she mind-spoke as we ran. "We can't let it slow us down. If we leave now, we can be to Tampa/St. Pete before dark, right?"

"Leni, wait!"

She stopped, but probably only because she had to since we'd reached the highway separating the RV park from the truck stop. Already. I'd never cleared that much distance so fast, even when I ran sprints. Leni's legs were much shorter than mine. And neither of us were winded.

Several cars came from both directions, preventing us from crossing, so she turned to me.

"What?" she asked, her mental voice filled with impatience. "You got it all, right? You remember everything? We have to hurry up and get to the Gate."

"We need to think this through. How do you know the mansion is the Gate?"

"It has to be. Why else would we be pulled to it?"

"Maybe the Dark side has their own way of getting to us. Maybe it's their trap. It worked against Jacey and Micah."

Her eyes darted around as she seemed to consider this, but then returned to me and she shook her head. "It *has* to be the Gate. Everything—your dreams, the drawings, the postcard—they've all been pointing us there. I feel it in my gut." She looked up at me, locking her eyes on mine. "You know you do, too."

I held her gaze like a vice. "I also still feel what they did to Jacey, and then to Micah. Quite clearly."

Something flickered in her eyes, but she remained stoic. "They died because they took too long. No other reason. And we've Bonded more than they ever had, which means we're stronger than them. The Shadowmen will know it, and they'll be all over us any time now." She turned back toward the highway and the last car about to pass us. "We're supposed to follow our instinct, especially mine. We have to go, Jeric. We have to get there before dark. They seem to only attack at night."

She sprinted across the highway.

"So let's wait until morning, when we have plenty of daylight," I said as I followed her. "In the meantime, we can try to remember more. Make sure we're going in the right direction."

She came to a stop again, now in the middle of the truck stop's parking lot not far from where we'd been attacked the other night, turned to me, and placed her fists on her hips. I wished I *could* hear her thoughts right now, because I wasn't sure if I was reaching her at all. Even after remembering all we had, the idea of going to Tampa and the mansion felt too dangerous. We didn't know exactly how to get there, and it would certainly be swarming with Shadowmen once again. And those people, people Jacey and Micah had once trusted . . . Leni didn't have to watch them kill her Twin Flame right in front of her eyes.

"We're not sick," I said. "Not like Jacey was. How much difference can one night make?"

She pressed her lips together, then pulled her bottom lip between her teeth. I thought I might have had her convinced.

Then a dark shadow fell over us. Dark as a storm cloud moving in front of the sun. The back of my neck prickled as we both looked up, but the sun blazed in a clear blue sky. We looked at each other again.

"A huge difference," Leni said. She took off for the mechanic's bay.

Her truck still sat on the lift. She talked with the mechanic, her hands moving animatedly, but I stayed outside, not wanting to rush him at all. I turned my back to the bay, staring across the highway, but not really seeing. *Just one more night.* That's all I wanted. One more night to try to remember what the Keeper hadn't had time to explain to us. Like how we'd run here in record time.

The dust hadn't even settled to the ground by Leni's camper yet, over two hundred yards away, and we'd even had to wait to cross the highway. And how could I possibly see all the way to Leni's camper in the first place? How could we *mind-talk* to each other?

"He said it'll be another hour or two," Leni said when she returned to where I stood, outside the building. "Will we be able to get there before dark?"

I shrugged. I wasn't as familiar with the West Coast of Florida as I was the East.

"We need to get to Tampa before nightfall." Leni's mouth moved, her gaze on someone behind me, probably the mechanic. After a pause, she nodded and began to pace. I didn't know what that meant, but I was perfectly fine waiting here until it became too late. I leaned against the brick wall, lifted a foot against it to brace myself, and crossed my arms over my chest, enjoying the view of both sides of Leni as she continued pacing.

"He doesn't know if he can get the truck done on time," she finally said after a few minutes of this.

"We can always go in the morning," I suggested once again, but with perfect timing, the sun disappeared for another brief moment. Asshole Shadowmen.

An old, beat-up blue Mazda stopped in front of us, and Bethany's red head stuck out the window.

"I was going into the gas station when I heard you say you need to get to Tampa," her lips said. "I was about to take off for Orlando and can give you a ride. It's not that far out of the way."

Leni and I exchanged a glance, and I was relieved to see her answer in her eyes.

She gave Bethany a look as though disgusted by the girl, even after her admission, and waved her off.

I lifted my eyebrows. "Thought I proved you have no reason to be jealous."

She rolled her eyes at me. "It's not always about you, Jeric. If the Shadowmen are watching us like I feel they are, and they get the slightest indication the girl means anything to us, they'll go after her whether she's physically with us or not. Just like they did Bex. I'd rather keep them focused on us."

She returned to her pacing. The sun continued to beat down on us. I hated northern Florida weather. As humid as anywhere on the East Coast, hotter than Hell, literally, and no breeze off the sea because there wasn't one close enough. Sweat rolled down my back.

Leni's head snapped toward the mechanic's bay, and she stopped pacing. After a moment, her face slackened, and I thought she was going to burst into tears. But just as quickly, determination turned her expression to stone, and she stalked off for the convenience store part of the truck stop.

"We *will* get there," she said.

I followed her around the corner, but stopped at the glass front, keeping an eye on her as she went inside. She spoke to one of the cashiers and then another. I followed along the front as she went farther on to the diner, and then talked to a guy who was rising from his booth.

He looked like a stereotypical over-the-road truck driver—big and burly, dark hair with a receding hairline, mustache and beard. He wore the standard sleeveless flannel shirt exposing some ink and baggy Wranglers with black work boots. At least when he eyed Leni, he didn't look like he wanted to eat her like the other men in the restaurant did. All of their heads had turned when she walked in, causing me to scowl. But even as Leni led the guy outside, he wasn't watching her ass.

"Let's go," she said in my head. "He's going to Tampa to pick up a trailer and said he'll take us."

"Are you nuts?" I kept their pace as we walked toward the doors, them inside and me still out. "You really do want to get us killed, don't you?"

"Look at the book in his hand," she said, her eyes flickering toward me.

I noticed the black book as they pushed through the doors, and I silently chuckled. "The Bible? And you think that makes him trustworthy? You think that means we can just jump in his truck and hit the highway with him behind the wheel and in total control, and not have to worry at all?"

"No, but it helps. We have to go, Jeric. Besides, if something happens, I'm sure you can take him on." She slipped me a small smile as she grabbed my hand. I dragged my feet as we followed the guy to his truck.

Unlike the last dude, he didn't have a problem at all when I climbed in before Leni to sit in the middle, keeping my body between his and hers in the cab that had no trailer attached to it. As we merged onto I-75, I pulled Leni's hand in between both of mine. All I could think was, *This is nuts. Fucking. Nuts.*

"His name is T.J., he's married, second wife, two kids with one on the way," Leni told me after an hour or so. They must have been talking, but I hadn't noticed, too focused on the passing pine trees and mentally prepping myself for what we were headed into. "He'd been in an accident a few years ago and nearly died. Had his moment with Jesus and was born again."

"Leni," I said, and although we were mind-talking, it sounded like it came through gritted teeth as I clenched my jaw, "do you really think I give a shit?"

She frowned. "Sorry. It was distracting me from the nerves."

She turned away from me and toward the window, but didn't pull her hand out of mine, so I gave it a squeeze in apology, and she returned it. A shadow crossed over the highway, and several miles down the road, another. Leni gnawed on her lip, her eyes constantly on the sky as were mine. As the sun began lowering to our right, her leg started bouncing up and down.

Finally came the signs for the Tampa and St. Petersburg exits.

"He said he can take us wherever we need to go," Leni said once we pulled off the highway. "I'm having him take us as close as possible. The less we're out in the open, the better."

I nodded.

She placed a hand on my leg. "And stop fidgeting. He's getting concerned by our nervousness."

I hadn't realized my leg had been bouncing along with hers. Or that I'd been chewing on my fingernails. I dropped my hand into my lap and clasped hers again. Our wrists pressed together and now when the flame marks met, they were obviously wings. The marks had grown sometime since yesterday—since our re-Bonding?—showing what looked like would become a phoenix. We both marveled at the image, then Leni gave my hand another squeeze.

She must have been giving him directions as we went because we always turned as soon as the pull in my gut changed. We crossed to Saint Petersburg, then headed south. The tug grew stronger, and if I had my geography right, we'd be crossing water soon. Signs for the Sunshine Skyway Bridge started popping up, but before we reached the turn for it, Leni had the driver pull off. We turned onto a road lined with condos, water on the other side of them, in an area that felt uncomfortably familiar. The setting sun cast long shadows across the road from the taller buildings that blocked the waning daylight. My neck prickled with the feeling of being watched from the darker shadows. I wondered again if there were any way to convince Leni this was absolutely the worst possible thing we could be doing.

She stiffened next to me and screamed. In my head and apparently out loud as her mouth dropped open and she stared out the windshield. Her face drained of all color. Barely in time, I looked out the window to see what had her so terrified. A figure stood in the middle of the road with dark clothes on but a face white as chalk glowing in the darkness and eyes black as ink.

Our bodies flew forward against the seatbelts when T.J. stood on the brake, and my stomach launched into my throat. We jerked backward against the seats at the same time we hit the guy. Except . . . we didn't really hit him. He wasn't really a guy. A thousand or two tiny birds flew up into the sky.

The driver slammed the gears into park and climbed out his side, and Leni and I climbed out ours. T.J. rushed toward the front of the cab, but Leni and I both looked up. Shadows streaked against the darkening sky.

"We have to leave him," Leni said. "We gotta go."

As much as I'd rather stay in the truck until it left Tampa again, I agreed. We couldn't bring T.J. into this. He had a wife and kids. A baby on the way.

We took off running down the dark street, both of us pulled in the same direction. Whether it was to a place of refuge or to our deaths, I still wasn't sure. I glanced over my shoulder once to find T.J. staring after us, his arms in the air with exasperation.

We ran through a condo parking lot, across a green space, and into another parking lot. Shadows hovered on the other side, so Leni cut through a small area between two condo buildings. Three men—Shadowmen—stood in our path, one slightly in front of the others as if they were in formation. With nowhere to go, we picked up our speed and ran for them. At the last second, Leni veered off to the left but didn't slow as she approached the stucco building. Instead, she ran several steps up the side of it, flipped in an arch over the heads of the Shadowmen and landed against the side of the opposite building and slightly past the obstacles. She dropped gracefully to the ground and waited on me as if she'd done this a million times.

I plowed right into them like a bowling ball into pins and launched into a fight. Knowing Leni was safely beyond them, I focused on my punches and kicks. A fist to the Adam's apple. Another through a couple of ribs. A foot to a temple and another into a groin. In no time, they'd all fallen and then disappeared.

We continued our run, zigzagging through parking lots and access streets, following our guts as everything around us darkened more. We entered the parking lot of a closed, rundown hotel at the edge of the water, and I felt them on the back of my neck before they ambushed us.

Several dropped from the sky, surrounding us. Eight. Now ten. Now a dozen. We both fought, and I couldn't have been prouder of Leni as she swung and kicked and flipped over their heads. She was stronger and faster than I'd ever imagined. So was I. We knocked out some, but as soon as they disappeared, more came to replace them.

I should have known.

I *did* know. And I'd let her charge forward anyway. Just as I always did, in every life we'd ever shared together. She was the fire, the light for our paths. I was her protector, meant to lead alongside her but never in front of her, or I'd lose my way. But damn if she didn't get us into some really fucked-up situations.

"We'll never fight our way through this," she said in my mind as she dropped to a crouch and swung her leg out, knocking a Shadowman to the ground. "There has to be another way."

I inhaled a deep breath and pushed out as I slammed the butt of my hand into a nose. "I'll keep them occupied if you want to jump ahead and scope the area."

I knew she could do it. She'd done so hundreds of times before. She could spring over their heads and be running down the street beyond them before they even noticed she was gone. The know-how was there, if she could get her current body to cooperate. The way she'd been performing tonight so far, I was sure this wouldn't be a problem.

She nodded up toward the top of the mid-rise hotel building as a hand reached for her throat. She karate-chopped it away and bent her knees, ready to jump.

But more bodies fell into our circle.

And not Shadowmen.

"Looks like you can use some help," a male voice thundered through my head. The shock distracted me long enough to receive a punch to the jaw. The dark-haired guy who'd dropped in retaliated with a blow to the Shadowman's throat, knocking him unconscious. He disappeared before hitting the ground.

I didn't trust this guy, or the girl who had come with him, despite what he'd just done. I didn't like how I could hear him or her. I didn't like how they were better fighters than both Leni and me—I was a former champion so this said a lot. Like, "They could easily kill us." He stood about my height and size, but she was a bit of nothing, maybe five-three and a hundred pounds, and although Leni and I still fought, these two took out all but three Shadowmen in a matter of a few seconds. I swung at one remaining in front of me, and it disintegrated into black powder.

"Why do they do that?" I growled with frustration.

"They're the Lakari," the guy said. "Enyxa's death spirits. They can only take so much damage before they can't hold their physical forms anymore."

"Let's go before they come back," the girl said, already sprinting down the street, only her short blond hair visible above the dark clothes she wore. "You're almost there."

The guy followed her and so did Leni. I wanted to stop her, but she was already way ahead. I ran after her and by the time I caught up, they darted into the service alley where a sliver of yellow light shone through a partially open door next to a receiving dock. At least Leni hesitated there, waiting for me.

I grabbed her wrist. "I don't trust them."

She glanced up at the sky. More Shadowmen swooped overhead. "We don't have much of a choice."

My gaze darted around the alley, surrounded by the hotel's walls. I looked back the way we came. The Shadowmen had landed. Another eight or so, headed our way.

"Come on!" the girl yelled, and we were both yanked inside.

They slammed the door shut as soon as we were in and pushed several bars across it, bracing it closed. Either locking the Shadowmen out . . . or us in.

Leni and I turned to face the room together. We reached out for each other's hand and squeezed. But the room wasn't a room. Only a dark and dingy hallway, and the couple was already halfway down it, looking over their shoulders at us.

"Come on," the girl said. "You have to get to the Gate."

We still stood there, staring. They fought like us, but better. They knew about the Gate. This was either really good or really bad.

"We're Guardians, like you. Members of the Phoenix," the guy said. When they spoke, their mouths moved at the same time as the words in my head. "If you can't trust us, who can you?"

Leni and I exchanged a look, then stepped forward to follow them.

"I'm Asia," the girl said as we continued down the hall. "Well, Anastasia, but I go by Asia this time around. This is Brock, but his soul's name is Broderick. You obviously don't remember us, but you will soon."

We passed the massive but empty and dark kitchen, turned a couple of times then entered a stairwell and climbed several flights.

"You'll need to project to get to the Gate," Brock said. He looked over his shoulder and lifted a brow as a grin tugged at his lips. "Do you need a private room to do it? I mean, that's my favorite way—"

Asia punched him in the arm. "Don't be an ass. It's none of your business. We'll take them to the guides, then to a private room. They can do it however they want."

Leni grabbed my hand again as we went through the eighth-floor doorway and down another long, dark hall. We passed guest room doors on either side, though it was obvious this hotel hadn't seen tourists in decades. We finally came to a stop at the last door on the left. Brock knocked, paused, then opened the door.

We walked into a large open room, what may have been a suite at one time. Floor to ceiling windows lined the far wall, providing a nice view of city lights and lots of water. The all-too-familiar pull jerked in my gut. The mansion was out there on an island in that water.

Or maybe it was the Gate out there. Maybe they *were* one and the same. Asia and Brock seemed to be anxious for Leni and me to get there. Maybe we were safe after all.

Leni's grip on my hand tightened.

"Uncle *Theo*?" she shrieked, both aloud and in my head. "*Mira*?"

I turned toward the point she stared at with her mouth hanging open. Two people had come through a doorway from an adjacent room. Older people, the plump, gray-haired woman my so-called grandmother. Apparently the other Leni's uncle.

Except I now recognized both of them as someone else.

The people who had killed Jacey.

CHAPTER 39

Jeric jumped in front of me and pushed me away. "Run, Leni! Run! Through the windows. You'll make it!"

My heart ran off at breakneck speed as the rest of my body stood frozen in shock. I wasn't sure if seeing Uncle Theo or Jeric's reaction surprised me more. And I wasn't sure if it was my own fear or Jeric's making my heart race.

"We shouldn't have come," Jeric ranted in my head. "I knew this was fucked up. I should have followed my own gut. I'm sorry, Leni. I'm so sorry! But I'll get us out of this. I'll get *you* out of this, alive this time, I swear."

"Jeremiah, calm down." Uncle Theo held his hand out, palm up, his voice calm and comforting. His brown eyes warm and his wrinkled face open and inviting. He took a step toward us.

Jeric backed into me, pushing me toward the windows. "Stay away from her!"

Apparently everyone could hear his thoughts, because they all reacted. Uncle Theo and Mira moved closer together, and Asia and Brock flanked Mira's shoulder. Another couple—a blond-haired guy not much taller than me and a slender brunette woman, both probably in their thirties—came barging into the room and took the other flank, behind Uncle Theo.

"Jeremicah . . . Jeric, dear," Mira said, her gray brows lifted over her glasses, "we're here to help, not hurt. We've always been helping."

With that kind of offensive formation?

Jeric's hands balled into fists. He held them out, away from his sides, still in a protective stance as he continued backing me to the windows.

"Don't lie to me! You killed her before. But not this time!"

Mira frowned. "We did what we had to do. She was already dying. If we'd let her soul weaken any more, so close to that many Lakari, they could have taken it."

"We helped her last time, son," Uncle Theo added. "We helped you. Protected both of your souls until you could get to the Space Between."

Jeric's body shook, anger still pouring off of him in waves. I wanted to believe Uncle Theo, even Mira, but Jeric's soul was in mine and mine in his. I felt his hatred for them, his distrust. I couldn't remember what they had done to me last time, but I didn't have to. Jeric's soul remembered enough for us both.

And I did know what they'd done this time. Abandoned me. Both of us. They'd disappeared off the face of the Earth without the smallest of traces they were even alive. No phone calls. No texts. No emails. Not a single response they were okay, which they obviously were. Much better than Jeric and me, who'd been fighting off Shadowmen when Uncle Theo and Mira had people here, flanking their sides.

Jeric had backed us up as far as we could go. I glanced over my shoulder as my butt and calves pressed against the window. Night had nearly fallen, but I could still make out an area below with a wide sidewalk, more like a patio, and grass dotted with palms and oaks. Beyond was the water, tiny lights shining on the far side.

Eight stories was a long way down, but I could do it. The fighter in me that had come out only an hour or so ago had been scaling and jumping buildings, even mountains, for hundreds of life cycles. Jeric and I could both do this. I pressed the palms of my hands flat against the window at my sides. I knew I could cause it to break if I willed it.

Only thing was, we'd be jumping right back into the swarm of Shadowmen.

"Don't do it," Uncle Theo warned, and I frowned while peering at him out of the corner of my eye. "Yes, we know what you're capable of. Much more than you yourselves know. We've been Phoenix Guides for decades. We were *your* Guides in your last life and this one."

I turned my head to look at him straight on. "You're trying to tell me you were Jacey's Pops? Reincarnated as my uncle? What a lie! You're too old."

"We haven't reincarnated," Mira spoke up. They were still several yards away from us, but it felt like the whole group was closing in. Cornering us. "We've only taken different roles in your lives."

"He was dead!" I said, my chin quivering. "I remember seeing Pops' dead body."

"Did you?" Uncle Theo asked, and now that I did remember seeing Pops through Jacey's eyes, I noticed the resemblance. Only more gray hair and wrinkles made Uncle Theo look different. "Or did you see a corpse that looked more like a wax figure?"

I couldn't answer him. I couldn't remember clearly enough.

"The universe works in mysterious ways," he said. "Especially to help the Guardians. Mira and I were Guardians, too, in past lives. We chose a different path for this life cycle, allowing us to live to old age for once. Our identities changed to help you, and when you didn't need us in that capacity anymore, they went away."

"Yeah, you disappeared and left us to the mercy of the Shadowmen," I accused. "Some Guides you've been."

"Who the hell cares?" Jeric growled. "What do you want from us, if not our souls?"

"We only want to help," Uncle Theo said, holding his hands out palm-up. "Help you get to the Gate so you can be Forged. You have special strengths and abilities from the re-Bonding, but they're only temporary until you're Forged. We're on your side, Jeremicah."

Uncle Theo took another step, and so did Mira.

"No closer or I'll do it," I warned, although I wasn't sure if I actually would. If our new strength, speed, and other abilities were only temporary—if he told the truth—we wouldn't make it far.

Mira and Uncle Theo both frowned. The others behind them remained silent and tense, as if waiting for me to try. I'd seen them fight, at least Asia and Brock. I wouldn't stand a chance with them, and I didn't think Jeric would either.

"Please believe we're only here to help," Mira said.

"Why do you think I sent you to Italy?" Uncle Theo asked me. "Why do you think I made you learn sign language? All to lead you to each other."

"So which lies am I supposed to believe?" I seethed. "Because you either lied to me before or you are now."

"I only did what you needed, little bird. We knew Jeremicah was in Italy at the same time, traveling in the same area. I knew you needed to know how to communicate with him. And why do you think I left you the journal, both times?"

"Perhaps to lead us right to here, to your trap," Jeric snarled. "I'm sure abandoning me at the deaf school was all part of the plan, too?"

Mira's narrow lips pressed together. "In a roundabout way, yes. I had to get you away from that man. His soul was going Dark."

"But you loved him anyway?" Sarcasm dripped in Jeric's thoughts. "And now you want us to trust you?"

She shook her head. "I was never even married to him. You were too young to remember, but I came into his life only once you were in it. To protect you from him. After the accident . . . I had to get you away."

The muscles in Jeric's forearm twitched. "I don't believe you. She's lying, Leni. They both are. Don't fall for it."

"No, we're telling the truth. You—them. . ." Mira swept her hand backwards to indicate the other four. "All Guardians . . . you can't have family ties. You can't have a past to be able to do your missions. This is why your history must be erased—"

"Wait—you *wiped* away my parents' memories?" I asked with disbelief.

"Not us. It just happens. Once Twin Flames find each other, the universe responds. You must take on your new roles. Your new lives."

And they wanted us to trust them? They had to be kidding. As angry as I'd been with my mama, I was even angrier now. She and Daddy had no memories of me—nothing about me as a baby, as a toddler learning to dance, losing my first tooth, my first recital, holidays and family vacations . . . nothing. All wiped out. For what?

"You ruined our lives so you could lead us here!" I growled.

"We did lead you here," Uncle Theo said, disregarding the first part of my accusation. "We led you to each other and then to here—to the Gate. Surely you remember the importance of the Gate?"

"I also remember how you stopped us last time," Jeric said. "Why bring us to this run-down building if it's so important we get to the Gate with no delay? Why the detour?"

Jeric made an excellent point.

"This place offers safe passage to the Gate," Mira said.

Something within me turned with that statement. Regardless of how much I disliked everything they had to say, *that* felt right. In my gut. Instinct told me this place provided our way to the Gate. I didn't know how, but I couldn't deny the strong feeling.

"I think they're telling the truth," I mind-whispered to Jeric. "I *feel* it."

"Don't trust them," he replied. "They're trying to manipulate us. *Bully* us. They haven't helped this whole damn time, so why now? It doesn't make sense."

Another good point. I suddenly didn't know what to believe. Or whom. Did I trust my instinct—the fire I supposedly was and let it light our way? It hadn't always led me to the best decisions.

Jeric's instinct, however, *had* been more reliable, and it screamed distrust. So was he right? Were they trying to control us, make us do what they wanted, only to steal our souls again? Was I once again putting too much trust in my elders? People who had already failed me before?

Mira and Uncle Theo took another step closer, and the others followed suit. Why? Why didn't they all stay back and talk their way through everything if they really did have good explanations? Why were they moving toward us so slowly as if we didn't notice . . . as if they were trying to catch us off guard and capture us?

"I said not another step," I snapped. Without my intending it, the glass cracked under my hands, crooked lines spreading out and away, up and down, across the floor-to-ceiling pane.

The Gate pulled at me through the window, a throbbing in my gut, and my instinct centered on it. We *had* to get there. Soon. Nothing else mattered.

"You feel the Gate out there, but the only way to get to it is through here." Uncle Theo thumped his fist to his chest, as though we were supposed to understand. Then he held his hands out toward us, and we both pressed harder against the window. "Please. Don't do anything stupid. You'll *die* out there."

"Not only your bodies, but possibly your souls," Mira said, her voice calm and measured. "Come away from the window. Please, before something happens."

But something happened. The window cracks began to give under my and Jeric's pressure. Uncle Theo lunged forward, as did Mira. Her hands reached out to Jeric's chest, and Uncle Theo's for me. Were they trying to save us or push us or grab us? Panic stopped my heart as we teetered on the edge.

"Let's go!" Jeric silently yelled, and we sprang backwards.

Out of their hands. Through the window. Into the air.

Our bodies plummeted toward the ground. My stomach flipped and flopped, not used to the feeling of falling so far. Fifty yards out and we could have at least landed in the water, but without a running start, I didn't see us making it. Instead, I mentally prepared for the landing, as rough as it would be. I knew from past lives how to adjust my body for it. My arms went out to my sides. I concentrated on my breathing, on the perfect tautness of my back and leg muscles to absorb the hit, on the rush of air flowing past as it slowed down.

I expected to hit the ground on my feet with a hard jolt, which would have been normal, not only because of the way we'd jumped, but because it was my first time in this body. It always took a few tries for our bodies to catch up with our minds and souls. But I didn't feel a jolt.

Rather, something knocked into me, and I slammed sideways into the ground. Agony wracked through my head, side and back. Bones broke. I felt and heard the snaps. Jeric landed beside me on his back with a sickening thud, staring at the sky, his chest barely rising as he gasped for air. His lungs rattled and blood dribbled from his mouth. My heart sputtered and cracked, and I struggled to reach my hand out for his, but I couldn't move.

Several Shadowmen gathered into a circle over us, ugly smiles on their snow-white faces, exposing toothless mouths. Their inky black eyes didn't smile, though. They were blank. Utterly void of any emotion at all.

More shadows floated higher above. Their excitement crackled in the air around us.

"Why on Earth or any world would two Guardians jump from the only place they're physically safe?" one of the Shadowmen asked, his face coming into focus right above me. I remembered his spiky blond hair—Jacey's Billy Idol-wannabe. He tapped a long, bony finger with a pointy, blackened nail against his chin. "You leave your refuge as if you're trying to escape it."

"No trust in the Phoenix," another Shadowman said. His creepy grin widened. "Just the way we like it."

"Lucky us," blond Spike said. "My men blew it when they forgot I'd said your marks would be on your arms rather than your necks or backs. But here you are, weak again, giving us another chance."

A thrumming sound rattled through the other Shadowmen and they moved together into one being, leaving only Spike in a real physical form. The black mass of death spirits hovered over us. I tried to push myself up, biting back the pain, but my body refused to cooperate. Spike took a step backwards and raised his arms to his side, and the form shifted overhead—again, as one, big shadow—and then folded in on us.

With a grunt, Jeric rolled and managed to push himself on top of me. Guarding me.

"I have to get you out of here," he said, his voice faint and far away in my mind. "Can you move?"

"I don't think so. Everything hurts."

"I'm so sorry, babe. I should have listened—"

Spike grabbed the back of his neck and yanked him off of me, tossing him to the side like a ragdoll. The single entity above split into two, one over each of us.

And dove in.

I didn't know what they'd planned to do. Eat us like vampires, although they had no teeth? Do the Dementor thing and suck our souls out through our mouths? Push darkness through our pores and into our souls? From the pain screaming through my body, I guessed it was all of the above.

Sharp, pointy things like teeth or nails tore at my flesh, shredding it open. A searing pain poured into the open wounds and traveled through my veins like venom. And Spike's long-fingered hand, too large to be a man's, hovered over my chest, sending a thrum into my soul, which balked at the horrid feeling.

I screamed and lashed out with my good arm and tried to kick away the presence at my legs. Jeric groaned and yelled, his body bucking and thrashing in the corner of my eye, but they held him down, too.

"Project!" a man's voice yelled.

Asia and Brock and the other couple burst into the area of my vision. Brock pulled Spike off of me. The two large shadows broke into regular sized men again, becoming a large force ready to fight.

"Project!" Brock yelled again before punching a Shadowman in the head. "It's the only way we can save you."

"Hurry!" Asia called out as she ran for another.

Leave our bodies? *Here?* They had to be kidding. Or was this how they planned to kill us?

"You have to trust us," the older woman said as she came to my side and squatted between Jeric and me.

A Shadowman flew at her and knocked her across the sidewalk. Spike dove at me. His hand pressed into the raw wound of my arm, sending more venom into my system. My body weakened even more, and my vision began to dim.

"Jeric," I thought to him, but he didn't answer.

"Do it already!" Asia yelled.

With great effort, I slid my hand over to Jeric's that lay limply by his side. The tips of my fingers curled into his, but he didn't respond. I turned my head as much as I could. He lay perfectly still, his body a bloody mess.

"Jeric!" I screamed in my head, but no reply came, not even a flinch.

The older man came in our direction, swinging a long blade at several Shadowmen. Their bodies turned to smoke.

"They'll go away if you do it," he said.

"But what about our bodies?" I cried, staring at Jeric's gory form even while Spike continued to feed off me. "We can't just leave them!"

"We'll take care of you," the man said. "That's what we're here for. But you have to do it, or you'll both die!"

Panic swelled inside me. This didn't make sense. We'd leave ourselves vulnerable, easy kills for the Shadowmen or the others. But instinct told me to project.

"*That's your soul talking to you, little bird,*" Uncle Theo had once said. Could I trust him? Could I trust my instinct?

I didn't have a choice.

Finding the physical bliss that led to my soul exploding from my body wasn't possible under the circumstances, but somehow my soul managed to release itself.

"Jeric?" I said, not feeling his presence with me. "Jeric!"

I looked down on his body, and he stared up at the sky—not at me but through me—not moving except for a blink of his eyes. Spike left my body and leapt over to Jeric's. My soul whisked down and the blond Shadowman jumped back. I hovered right over Jeric.

"Project with me," I ordered, but he didn't respond.

Spike and other Shadows swarmed in on him.

"No!" I yelled. The energy of my soul, though weaker than usual, looped a circle around him, pushing the Shadows away. "You can't have him!"

I hung close to him, close to his heart, as close as I could get without entering his body.

"Jeric, please," I pleaded. "Come with me."

But I was afraid it was already too late. A bluish tint covered the skin that hadn't been shredded and bloodied. His lips were white. A sob wracked through my soul.

"Jeric! Come to me," I begged anyway. "Come with me, and we'll be okay."

The Shadowmen came closer again but I warned them off once more.

"Hurry!" Asia yelled again. Could she tell if I'd left my body? That Jeric hadn't?

"Come on, baby," I muttered, my soul weakening even more.

I didn't know what to do. My soul couldn't leave him. I couldn't go to the Gate without him. Maybe I could pull him with me, if I could only grasp his soul. I dared to push against Jeric and soak into his body, hoping I could mix with his soul and help him out. His energy felt heavy, dragged down by his dying body. And cold and dark.

Several Shadows bombarded us with my spirit halfway in Jeric's body. Spike's white face came within inches of my soul, his mouth opening wide over Jeric's chest.

We were both going to die.

CHAPTER 40

The solitude of silence filled my head once again. Brock's and his people's mouths moved as they fought nearby, but I could no longer hear their thoughts. It was kind of disturbing to have those voices in my head, but it'd been kind of nice, too, to hear something besides my own thoughts. Especially Leni's voice.

My body felt like it'd been through a meat grinder and then thrown into the ring for Cain Velasquez to use as a punching bag. And although I could feel every raw nerve-ending, I couldn't move. Even my eyes refused to roll to see how badly Leni was hurt. Her soul felt far away, our connection weak, but at least I knew she was still alive.

Something touched my fingers—Leni's curling into mine. I tried again to move, but my fingers wouldn't return the gesture. Her panic rose like a wave and crashed over me, and I hated knowing she was freaking out. Over me.

I didn't deserve her. She didn't deserve this. I'd really messed up this time.

I'd been so afraid of bringing her here, but I'd been the real danger. She'd been right, but I hadn't listened to her. I'd given in to my own fear and hatred of bullies, but instead of fighting or actually listening, I'd run. Jumped. And brought her to her death.

I'd been the one to kill her again after all.

My heart fell cold at the thought of losing her again. I could feel her pulling away from me—or me from her. Our souls being Separated once again. Mine as cold as my heart. My whole body frigid and numb.

A ghostly image floated over me. Leni? She'd died already? *No!* But the anger I should have felt rising never came. Only more numbness. I blinked, wishing I'd just die, too.

A trickle of warmth seeped into my body, into my soul, followed by a tugging sensation. Another ghostly face with ink-black eyes beckoned me. It was time to leave this broken and battered body. Time to leave this world once again. My soul slid out, but the tether to my body remained.

A dim light shone around me, and I felt Leni's presence.

"I'm sorry," I tried to say to her, but my energy felt sluggish, heavy and still cold. Darkness crept in around me.

"Don't do this." Leni's thoughts surrounded me, but from a distance. "Stay with me, Jeric."

"I can't, babe. Gotta go. It's better for you this way." I didn't know if she could even hear me. Feel me. Whatever. I could barely feel myself. Only long, icy fingers digging into my soul.

"No, Jeric. You won't take the blame for this."

"I should have listened to you. Let you light my way."

"I screwed up, too. But it's all about *right* now. You listen to me *now*, and follow my light."

I so badly wanted to. I wanted to rejoin her, to soak into her soul and let her warmth immerse into mine. But she needed to be free from me and the destruction I brought to everyone.

Darkness pulled at me with those cold fingers, testing the tether my body held to my soul, like the wind tugging on a balloon tied to a child's wrist.

"No, Jeric," Leni screamed around me. "Don't do this! You stay with me!"

But I couldn't help it. The tether loosened, almost free. Darkness blanketed my frigid soul, making it even colder.

"Jeric, please," Leni begged. "Don't give in. Nobody blames you. Only you, and you *have* to let it go. I can't lose you."

Her pain wracked at me, making me feel worse. The Dark began to descend. And then . . . *there*. Blackness. I was almost free. Free from the physicality of this world. Free from feeling. From self-hatred. From fear. I could give in and be done with it all. Never again have to think about my brothers or Jacey. About my parents or my sister. Or Leni—the only one I was really to blame for. Micah's Marine brothers, my parents and sister had been fucked-up situations, but not my fault. I knew this, but survivor's guilt runs deep. Especially time after time after time. But Leni . . .

"I jumped with you, Jeric. I didn't listen to myself. I didn't follow my instinct. I'm as much to blame for this, if not more. If you leave me, if you go Dark, I will have to live with that forever, and I'll *never* forgive myself."

That wasn't right. I wanted to yell at her, to tell her not to do that to herself, but the Dark continued to close in. But she must have felt something.

"See? It's stupid, isn't it? So let go of the guilt. Free yourself. Come back to me."

But it was too late. Her light dimmed more, faded into the distance as I drifted off to the Dark, my body barely holding on to the tether anymore.

"No," Leni cried, her voice on the other side of the world. "No, Jeric! Choose love. Follow my light. *Please*. You can't leave me. You promised me never!"

A pull from somewhere else other than my body. A light, far, far away, beckoning me. Tugging at my soul.

Leni.

I wasn't only tethered to my body, but also tied to her. And she refused to let go.

I *had* promised her never, and as much as I'd done to this girl—to this soul—I was not breaking this promise.

Her light grew brighter, closer, swirled around me . . . and into me. Her warmth heated my cold soul. Her love renewed my dying energy. Every fiber of her soul clung to mine, mixing and melding, and we became one again. And I don't care who you are, that was better than any prince-fucking-charming kiss.

The light around us bloomed brightly over our bodies. Together, we streaked toward the blond Shadowman who hovered over my chest, and we smashed into his physical form. A high-pitched siren wailed around us as we devoured his darkness with our light. More shrieking sounds tore through the night as the rest of the shadows of the Lakari scattered. Flying away as if we were the sun and would turn them to ash. They all disappeared, and the two Guardian couples blew out a collective breath below us, then gathered around our bodies.

"We'll take you to the Gate." Mira's voice came from around us before her image appeared—looking like her, sans glasses, though not quite there. Ephereal, I thought was the word. Leni's uncle appeared as well.

The pull of the Gate was stronger than ever, tugging us out toward the middle of the water. We didn't exactly need to be shown the way.

"Will you trust us now?" Theo asked, and I felt as though that was specifically aimed at me, although Leni and I were a swirling, hot mess of energy at the moment.

"Of course we do," Leni said, apology and regret filling her voice.

"Yes," I agreed, knowing I'd already screwed up bad enough for one night.

Mira and Theo's forms turned toward our bodies. Asia and Brock easily picked us up as though we were made of paper and carried us into the building. The other two seemed to be standing guard, their eyes to the sky, watching.

"We've never been this far away from our bodies," Leni said.

"You'll be fine," Mira said. "After you're Forged, you'll even be able to appear to each other, separate, yet still connected."

"Come now," Theo said, and he floated over the water where shadows still lingered.

"Like hell," I muttered.

"You're safe in this state," Theo said. "You are light; they fear light."

"Then why didn't we do this sooner?" I demanded. I'd learned my lesson to trust them, but that didn't mean I couldn't ask questions. Especially when they could have protected us better. "Hell, why didn't your guards down there project if it would drive them away?"

"Somebody has to care for the bodies," Mira said as she moved across the water as well. "And after that stupid jump you two made, you were in no shape for it. Now hurry! The sooner you're Forged, the faster you'll heal."

I didn't ask any more questions. Still joined as one, we moved slowly at first, feeling the tugs to our bodies as though our souls were elastic bands being stretched tight. As we pulled farther and never snapped back, though, we picked up speed. We followed Mira and Theo's rush farther out from shore until we reached the place in the water between the bay and the Gulf. There was no mansion, though. Only a tiny island barely big enough to hold a single, though huge, weeping willow tree.

"Is this even the right damn place?" I asked, suspicion rising again, then soaring when Theo and Mira suddenly dove into the water. "What the hell?"

Leni ignored my apprehension.

"It's the tree from the journal," she said excitedly. "We're here. It's . . ." Our souls felt out for the Gate. "It's under the water."

With confidence in her instinct, she dove our light down into the water. Pushed us down, down, down, deeper than this part of the harbor should have been, until we finally hit the sandy bottom. When we did, bright beams of light flamed from the sand in front of us.

A warm feeling swarmed around and through us.

"The Gate welcomes you," Mira said.

I moved us closer to it. Theo held his hand out, blocking us.

"Not yet," he said. "Before you can accept the powers of the Gate and be Forged, you must understand the Gate and the expectations of you. If all goes well, you'll be Forged. Made stronger, faster, less fragile. Given certain gifts that will allow you to fight the Lakari better. Then, you'll be ready for your first mission."

"How?" we asked.

"By the Gate's energy," Theo said.

"The Gate to all the worlds," Mira answered before we could ask. "Also, a shortcut to a special part of the Space Between. As Guardians, your primary job is to guard the Gate to keep souls from passing through it, in or out. The only souls you can allow to leave Earth through this Gate are the Broken ones so they can rejoin their other halves."

"You cannot allow *any* souls through the Gate and into Earth," Theo added more directly. "Enyxa is trying to open it for more of her Lakari to swarm through. You *can't* allow it."

"Understood." Thankfully, Leni felt the same need as I did to say this although we both had enough questions to interrogate them for hours. "If that's our primary job, what are our others?"

"You help the Broken and the Lost," Mira said. "After Separating their souls, Enyxa sets them on an endless loop to the same worlds, keeping them from finding each other. This is why Earth is becoming so populated. And so hopeless. You will help these souls before they grow Dark. This is the service you chose for this life cycle in the Space Between. Do you still accept it now?"

How could we not? I knew what it was like to be ripped apart from Leni's soul, when she was Jacey. Almost felt it tonight. Nobody should have to endure that. And nobody should have to live increasingly miserable lives searching for true love they'll never find.

"What if we don't?" Leni's energy created the question, and I understood when I felt her emotions running through us.

"We don't know," Mira admitted. "Nobody has ever denied, especially you, from what we understand."

"Will we go back to how we were?" Leni pressed. "Will my parents remember me?"

"Little bird, I understand—"

"Will they remember me?" she repeated.

"We really don't know," Mira said. "It's possible, but your physical bodies likely won't make it if you don't accept and Forge. So even if your parents do remember, they will be burying their daughter shortly."

Leni's emotions spiked within us. I tried to pull her in tighter, but we were already as close as can be.

"Leni," I murmured to her, "if we die, your parents will have to live with the grief, and we'll have to start over. We'll be separated for another twenty or so years."

"This is what you chose in the Space Between," Theo reminded us. "Your whole lives—and many other events—have been based on that choice."

Leni's energy shuddered through us as she recalled everything we'd been through, more me than her. And she decided. We wouldn't let it all happen for nothing.

"We accept," we finally answered.

"Very good," Mira said. "But before you may be Forged, now you must understand yourselves. Jeremicah, you finally released yourself from blame, the only reason you made it this far. But you must understand life on Earth is messy. Things happen. You can't control everything. You especially cannot control Jacquelena. You must forgive yourself when you are at fault. You must trust yourself and your Twin Flame. Remember, she is your light."

"Jacquelena," Theo said, "you must believe in yourself and trust your instinct. Know that your Twin Flame is there to catch you if you fall, but don't be afraid to take risks. You will have to take many in this life. You two must be able to trust yourselves and each other, as well as your guides and the other members of the Phoenix. Listen to your instinct. Trust each other. Work as a team. If you cannot do all of these, you will fail in your duties for the Phoenix. Do you understand?"

After everything we'd been through and barely survived, how could we not?

"We understand."

"You may enter the Gate," Theo said, stepping away from the lights shining upward from the sand.

After a few beats of hesitation, Leni and I knitted the energy of our souls as closely together as possible, and moved into the circle of light. The beams shot up higher around us and became a solid wall of light enclosing us in a cylinder and pulsing a rainbow of colors. For no more than a second, holes appeared in the round wall, and we barely caught glimpses of entrances to other worlds. The openings filled in with color before we could see anything beyond.

The water disappeared, as though drained through the sand below us, and bright light filled the cylinder, followed by intense heat. Our souls welded together as white-hot pain seared through us. A force pressed us harder into each other, compressing us, melting us, shaping us, broiling us. We silently screamed as we were pounded into each other, heated again, and molded more, repeating the process until I thought we'd become nothing more than embers and ashes. Then finally.

Cold water poured over us.

We strengthened.

We hardened.

We were Forged.

After some time, minutes or hours we didn't know, the light faded around us. As it did, Leni pulled away from me. Her soul did, but yet, it also remained in mine and mine in hers. By the time the lights dimmed into the sand, we were separate, yet still connected, and staring at each other. She looked like her normal and uninjured self, curls and all, though not *quite* there. Her soul gave the image of her physical body. I looked at myself doing the same, then I reached out for her hand, and my soul could feel hers clasping mine.

"I'm sorry," I said, no longer able to hold that in. "For almost getting us killed. Again. Most of all, for doubting you."

"Don't. You were only trying to protect me." She smiled. "And I love you for that."

I moved closer to her, wondering if she'd feel as good like this as she did in her body. Her breath heated my lips as I leaned in closer.

"I love you, too, babe," I said. "Always have. Always will."

The sound of a clearing throat came from behind me. The lights in the sand had almost completely dimmed, leaving just enough to show Mira and Theo still there—their souls, anyway—hovering in the water, waiting for us.

Shit. I owed them an apology, too.

"Sorry. About everything," I said.

"As are we," Theo said. "It would have saved you a lot of physical pain right now."

"We thought we'd lost you for a minute or two, Jeric," Mira said. "Thank God you found your light. Our healers are doing the best they can on your bodies. Your souls are very strong, so there's no danger, but your Bonding will help speed the healing process."

"When you're ready, concentrate and you can snap back to your bodies," Theo said, and then they were both gone as if they'd done just that.

My body had moved, but I could still feel its hold on my soul, which I supposed meant I was still alive. Which was a good thing. Leni gave a slight tug and could feel it, too, which was a really good thing. But before she could snap back to her physical self, I grabbed her soul's hand and shot us upward through the water, breaking the surface, and into the sky, which was beginning to lighten with dawn.

"Jeric, look," Leni said, her floating body facing toward the abandoned hotel that was apparently the Phoenix headquarters. Or something. We really didn't know much at all yet, but that was okay. There was plenty of time to find out.

I turned toward the building, not really wanting to return to our bodies yet, but that's not why she looked so intently at it. The first three floors of the hotel appeared to have been replaced by the mansion—the same mansion from Micah's and my dreams, from Jacey's drawing, from Leni's postcard—as though the hotel had been built around it.

"I don't really want to go back quite yet," Leni said. "Do you?"

I grinned at her and pulled her hand again. She floated into me, a quick bump, but the collision sent a wild arousal through me. Wanting to feel it again, I pulled her once more, closer, and the projections of our souls slid into each other, and we became one. I actually wondered if we ever had a reason to have normal sex again because this was so much better.

"If everybody could make love like this, the world would be a much happier place," Leni said. "Enyxa and her Lakari wouldn't even want to be here anymore."

True. But I was selfishly glad we had it to ourselves right now. Especially when everyone was oblivious to us, our souls intertwined in complete bliss as we flew through the early morning sky. Like a phoenix, risen from the ashes, we soared high over the water and the rooftops as the city awakened below us.

ABOUT THE AUTHOR

Photo by Michael Soule

Kristie Cook is a lifelong, award-winning writer in various genres, from marketing communications to fantasy fiction. She continues to write the Soul Savers Series, a New Adult paranormal romance/contemporary fantasy, with the first four books, *Promise, Purpose, Devotion* and *Power* available now and the next book coming in June 2013. She's also written a companion novella, *Genesis: A Soul Savers Novella*, currently available. Over 180,000 Soul Savers books have been sold, with *Promise* peaking at #54 on the Amazon Top 100 Paid list and at #1 in the Amazon Fantasy category.

The Space Between kicks off her second New Adult paranormal series, The Book of Phoenix.

Besides writing, Kristie enjoys reading, cooking, traveling and riding on the back of a motorcycle. She has lived in ten states, but currently calls Southwest Florida home with her husband, three teenage sons, a beagle and a puggle.

CONNECT WITH KRISTIE ONLINE

Email: kristie@kristiecook.com
Author's Website & Blog: http://www.KristieCook.com
UK Fan Site: http://www.kristiecookfansite.co.uk
Soul Savers Series Website: http://www.SoulSaversSeries.com
Facebook: http://www.facebook.com/AuthorKristieCook
Twitter: http://twitter.com/#!/kristiecookauth

Stay tuned to the author's site at www.KristieCook.com for updates on new releases, excerpts, special events, appearances and signings.

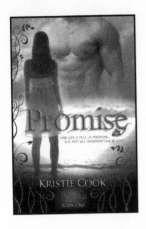

Read an excerpt from *Promise*, Book 1 in the Soul Savers Series

Chapter 1

9 Years Ago

The sensation of being watched clung to me like a spider web, invisible threads bristling the back of my neck and down my spine. I brushed my fingers across my shoulders, as if I could drag the feeling off and flick it away.

It was ridiculous, of course. Not just ridiculous to think I could pull it off so easily, as if it really was strands of a web, but it was even more absurd to feel it in the first place. Nobody ever held that much interest in me. Occasionally, people stared with curiosity when they picked me up on their "weird radars," but usually they just ignored me. No one ever watched so intensely.

Yet the hairs on the back of my neck stood on end at the feeling as I visited my favorite Washington, D.C., monument for likely the last time. I sat on the stone steps with the stately Thomas Jefferson behind me and gazed over the Potomac River tidal basin, enjoying the peace just before sunset. Well, trying to enjoy it anyway.

I blamed the ominous feeling on my unruly imagination, with it being twilight and the sky looking so foreboding. It was the perfect backdrop for one of my stories. The sun hung low— an eerie, orange ball glowing behind a shroud of haze, a column of steel-blue cloud rising around it, threatening to snuff it out.

I envisioned something not-quite-human watching it from the shadows, waiting to begin its hunt under the cover of darkness.

That's all it is, just my fascination with mythical creatures, I told myself. *Uh-huh. Right.*

Surrendering hope for a peaceful moment, I hurried to the closest Metro station. The feeling of being followed stuck with me on the train ride home, but at my stop in Arlington, I forgot the sinister sensation. Some kids from school stood near the top of the escalator as I stepped off. I'd witnessed before their favorite summer activity: dressing in all black and hassling people exiting the Metro station. So mature, but what can you expect? They were younger—they hadn't graduated with me over a month ago—and apparently, still stuck in the rebellious phase that I'd never been through myself.

I usually took the elevator to circumvent them, but had been too distracted tonight.

"Hey, there's the weird girl who heals," one of them said loudly to the others. "It's s'posed to be really freaky to watch."

"Hey, freak, got any tricks to show us?" another called.

I pretended not to hear and crossed the street to avoid them. My eyes stung, but no tears came. I wouldn't allow them. It was my own fault—I'd been a klutz with the Bunsen burner in Chemistry and my lab partner saw my skin heal the burn almost instantly. People harassed me about it every day the last two months of school. If I didn't let them get to me, they were usually just annoying. Usually.

Night had crept its way in during my ride home. I walked quickly through the bright commercial district and turned down the darker residential street for home, still four blocks away. Footsteps behind me echoed my own. I quickened my pace. *Two more days. That's all. Just two more days and we're out of here.*

"C'mon, dude, we just wanna know if it's true," a boy's voice said.

"Yeah, just show us. It doesn't hurt, right?"

I glanced over my shoulder. Three teens followed me and

I caught the glint of a blade in one of their hands. I realized their plan to satisfy their curiosity—slice me open and watch the wound heal. *What is* wrong *with people? Of course, it hurts!* Bungalow-style homes lined the street, each with an empty front porch. Not a single person sat outside on this summer's evening. No one to witness their fun and my agony. My heartbeat notched up with anxiety.

Pop! Crack! The streetlights along the entire block blacked out at the sounds. I inhaled sharply and halted mid-stride. The footsteps behind me ceased, too.

"What the *hell*?" Surprise and fear filled the boy's question.

A couple appeared from nowhere, three houses down, standing in the middle of the street. It was too dark to see their features and I could only tell their genders by their shapes. The woman's high-heeled shoes clicked on the pavement as they walked toward me. The man, big and burly, pulled his shirt over his head and handed it to the woman. Without breaking stride, he took off one shoe and then the other, leaving him with only pants. *What the . . . ?*

I considered my options. The woman and her half-naked companion blocked my way home, but I wouldn't just raise my chin and walk brusquely by them, pretending they meant no harm. Because I just knew they did. I stood trapped between the boys with the knife and the bizarre couple. Somehow, I knew the knife was less threatening.

"Boo!" The woman cackled as the boys took off running. As she and the man closed in on me, the alarms screamed in my head.

Evil! Bad! Run! Go!

My sixth sense had never been so frightened. I couldn't move, though. Fear paralyzed my body. My heart hammered painfully against my ribs.

The couple stopped several yards away. The woman studied me as if assessing a rare animal, while the man lifted his face to the sky, his whole body trembling. I followed his gaze to see the thin, gauzy clouds sliding across a full moon. The woman cackled again. Panic sucked the air from my lungs.

"Alexis, at last," the woman said, her voice raspy, like a long-time smoker's. "We'll get such a nice reward for you."

My eyes widened and my voice trembled. "D-do I know you?"

She grinned, a wicked glint in her eyes. "Not yet."

Or ever, if I can help it.

I turned and ran. My pulse throbbed in my head. Breaths tore through my chest. My mind couldn't focus, couldn't make sense of this absurd couple and what they wanted with me, but my body kept moving. The bright lights of the commercial area I'd just left beaconed me to their safety.

The woman abruptly appeared in front of me before I was half-way down the street. The shock sent me hurling to the ground and my head smacked hard against the pavement. Stars shot across my eyes. My hands burned from asphalt scrapes. Fighting the blackness trying to swallow my vision, I rolled onto my side, gasping for breath. A sticky wetness pooled under my temple.

My eyes rolled up to the woman, who now pointed what looked like a stick at me. Her lips moved silently as she waved a pattern in the air. I felt pinned to the ground, though nothing physically restrained me. Panic flailed uselessly below the surface of my paralyzed body, making my breaths quick and shallow. I was done for. They could do anything they wanted with me. There was no escape now.

My vision faltered. Now two women stood over me, two sticks pointed at me. Two moons wavered behind them. I didn't know if it was fear or the head injury that caused everything to slide apart and together again. I squeezed my eyes shut.

But I couldn't close my ears, couldn't block out the gnarl. My eyes popped open with terror, expecting to see a wild beast, but the feral sound came from the man. His eyes rolled back, showing only whites. His hands clenched into fists. His muscles strained, the veins protruding like ropes along the bulges. His body shook violently until the edges of his shape became a blur.

"I can't hold it," he growled.

"Then don't," the woman said. "Don't fight it. It's time!"

A ripping sound tore through the night as the man lurched forward, his skin shredding. A gelatinous liquid spurt out of him like an exploding jar of jelly. His pants tore into ribbons as his body lengthened and grew. The shape of his limbs transformed. His face elongated, his nose and mouth becoming a . . . *Holy crap! A snout?!* I gasped, a scream stuck in my throat. By the time his front . . . *legs* . . . hit the ground, fur covered his body. He was no longer man. He was— *A freakin' wolf?!*

The beast moved closer, a low growl in its throat. Its stench of decaying corpses and rotting leaves overwhelmed my sensitive nose, the disgustingly sweet odor gagging me and forcing me to breathe through my mouth.

Pop! Another woman appeared, again out of nowhere. Her pale skin glowed and her white hair shimmered in the moonlight.

"I smell blood," she said, her voice a flutter of wind chimes. "Mmm . . . delicious blood."

The scrapes on my hands had already healed, but not the cut on my head. It must have been deep enough for a normal person to need stitches. For me, it could take ten minutes to heal. So my blood was still fresh.

I could only smell the wolf's rancid odor as it hovered over me.

"Back off, *mutt*," the white-blonde snarled as she stepped closer. "This is too important for the likes of you."

"How dare you!" Stick-woman gasped. "We had her first!"

"Alexis is mine. Always *mine!*"

What the hell is happening?! What do *you want with* me? Whoever they were, they wanted to do more than just terrorize me. I could hear it in the way the blonde said I was *hers*. She wanted me to hurt . . . or worse. Cold fear slid down my spine and hot tears burned my eyes.

Pop! My heart jumped into my throat as another man materialized in the darkness and strode toward me. *Not more!* The wolf growled. Both women hissed. Goose bumps crawled along my skin.

The man stepped in front of me, placing himself between me and the others.

Good! Very good! Safe! My sense slightly calmed me.

"You're alone?" the blonde asked. "Ha! You haven't a chance."

The wolf lunged at my protector. He raised his hands and thrust them out toward the beast and it flew back as if blasted by something unseen. I heard a thud and a whimper as it hit the pavement. I blinked several times, disbelieving what I just saw.

The women hissed again. The first one raised her stick, pointing it at my protector. The blonde took a step toward me.

Pop! Another person appeared, between the two women and my human shield. The women responded immediately—their teeth gleamed in the moonlight as their lips spread into grins.

No way could my protector stand up against this second man. The new one was taller, wider in the shoulders, thicker in the torso and arms than my protector, who was now out-numbered and out-muscled. The second man took a single step toward us. I didn't dare look up at him, afraid of what I might see. But I felt his eyes rake over me. My trembling turned to quakes.

My sixth sense continued shouting conflicting alarms, everyone's intentions so strong. *Good* and *Evil* both screamed in my head and I couldn't tell which this new person was.

But then he turned to face the women and their expressions darkened. And I knew. He was on our side. I swatted down a leap of hope, though. The attackers still out-numbered my protectors.

The wolf, now back on all fours, stalked toward us. The fur on the back of its neck rose. Hunger shone in its eyes as its lips curled back in a snarl. Its pace quickened, my heart galloping with it. It lunged once more. I tried to scream. My constricted throat only allowed a whimper.

Then the wolf flew backwards again and fell to the ground a second time. The bigger man's hand hung in the air, palm straight out facing the wolf, as if he'd hit it, but I never saw the contact.

Both women eyed me with obvious greed. Then their eyes shifted back to my brawny protector and confusion and even fear flickered across their faces. He turned his hand toward them. Their eyes widened, looking as terrified as I felt.

They disappeared with two *pops*.

"I've got Alexis! Take care of that one!" The lankier man easily lifted me into his arms and sprinted toward my house. The beast's stench continued to fill my head, a persistent odor that wouldn't leave even as distance separated us.

A wolfish howl behind us diminished into a human cry of pain. I shuddered in the arms of the stranger.

Purchase *Promise* wherever books and ebooks are sold.

Made in the USA
Charleston, SC
04 April 2013